Finding Jack

Finding Jack

Sofia Due

The Book Guild Ltd

First published in Great Britain in 2023 by
The Book Guild Ltd
Unit E2 Airfield Business Park,
Harrison Road, Market Harborough,
Leicestershire. LE16 7UL
Tel: 0116 2792299
www.bookguild.co.uk
Email: info@bookguild.co.uk
Twitter: @bookguild

Typeset in 12pt Minion Pro

Printed and bound by CPI Group (UK) Ltd, Croydon, CR0 4YY

ISBN 978 1915853 172

British Library Cataloguing in Publication Data.
A catalogue record for this book is available from the British Library.

For Sasha and Joe

1

July 2018

The island of Livø, a place so small its inhabitants barely numbered tens, let alone hundreds, and accessible only by boat from the mainland. Gennie Beck sat between her daughter, Alice, and her mother, thin summer clothes offering no protection against the bare wooden boards digging into the backs of their thighs, as they rocked ever closer, propelled by the ferryman's smoky diesel engine. Gennie was in no hurry to get there; if she could go back, she would. Her father sat opposite, searching vainly for pleasant things to say about the view, challenging when all around was grey – grey water, grey sky, and a green and grey island in the distance. At least it wasn't raining.

Gennie held Alice's hand between her own and squeezed it, pressing comfort into her bones. So small and soft, if she gripped it any tighter, she risked crushing it. The child had absorbed so much in the last year, been brave for all of them. Could she endure any more? Gennie fixed her eyes on the

1

horizon. Wasn't that supposed to prevent seasickness? Her mother-in-law had stopped pretending and sat at the other end of the boat with a handkerchief pressed to her nose. No-one would sympathise. This was all her idea.

'C'est un cauchemar,' whispered Gennie's mother, reverting to her native French, as she did when saying something she thought she shouldn't. It was all a nightmare. 'No wonder Mikkel drank.'

'Did Daddy really like it here?' Alice whispered.

It was more Gennie's sort of place than her husband's. They'd spent a week of their honeymoon in Northern Jutland. Mikkel had taken her there, under sufferance, to please the relatives who couldn't travel. She'd loved the empty horizon and wide, windswept beaches; they reminded her of Cornwall and a childhood running along dunes and dipping in rock pools. Mikkel, meanwhile, had spent most of the time indoors. For him, the chilly breeze and solitude brought back memories of lonely school holidays at his grandmother's house in Aalborg. He'd vowed never to dip a toe in the North Sea again. And now they planned to return him there. Gennie turned her head so her mother-in-law couldn't hear.

'I wouldn't say it was his happy place. He may actually have hated it. He preferred Greece. Or the Caribbean. Anywhere with warm water and a bit of sunshine.'

Why was his mother insisting on this? Did she believe that bringing Mikkel's ashes to Denmark would restore him to her – and wrestle him from Gennie in the process? It wasn't as if the woman was even Danish; she'd lived her whole life in Berkshire. Despite what they'd told her, it couldn't have been Mikkel's wish. One whiff of seaweed and he'd have been off.

'We can't leave him here,' said Alice, becoming tearful.

2

'We're not. It's not really him, darling,' said Gennie, hugging her and kissing the top of her head, wishing she were somewhere else as well. 'He'll be lying on a beach somewhere. You wait, we'll sell the house and find ourselves a sunny spot and Daddy will find us there. He'll always be with us one way or another.'

They turned towards the harbour and the wind whipped Gennie's hair across her face, bringing a fresh taste of saltwater. She should have thought to bring a hat. She lifted the collar on her denim jacket, tucked her long hair down inside and knotted her scarf more tightly. As they neared the dock, her father-in-law lifted the black holdall containing the plastic cannister, the one they'd brought from England, and placed it on his lap. Gennie glanced towards the hill above the bay, the chosen resting place, and exhaled.

So, this is it, then.

2

October 2019

Gennie pulled into the gravel drive, stopped the engine and listened. Sheep. That was all she could hear. Sheep, and the gentle rustle of wind in the trees either side of the lane. Hope House was always quiet on a Sunday evening – or maybe it felt that way because once she'd taken Alice back to school, she'd be spending the evening on her own. Alone didn't have to mean lonely; she must remember that.

The farmhouse sat opposite, the glass-panelled front door with its fat brass doorknob and wide letter box like a well-proportioned face. Amiable, reliable. The house had a solidity to it, granite walls built to weather any storms, inside or out. Gennie walked around to the back, stones crunching under her trainers, to where the path opened onto the rippled concrete of the yard. It was hosed down and swept regularly but still a thin layer of mud clung stubbornly to the surface. The sweet tang of manure floated in on the evening air, not from their own fields but the ones beyond the sheds and brick barns which lined the perimeter, a further ring of protection – if any were needed. Hope Farm lay on the outskirts of St Illick, sufficiently far from the village to provide privacy and independence but not so isolated as to imprison its inhabitants. And there were usually plenty of those.

A narrow blue door marked the entrance to the cottage Gennie now shared with her daughter. She turned away and headed straight for the adjacent farm kitchen; there were still jobs to do before her working day was over. She dropped her jacket and bag on the corner armchair and filled the kettle at the sink, watching the darkening sky as she waited for the water to boil. The last of the daylight was just visible as a thin line at the top of the farm. This was what she loved about the south-west – the way the sun clung on as long as it could. She felt the same. Those extra few minutes of light were what had lured her back to Cornwall. It was so much easier pulling back curtains to open skies and distant fields, each day a new canvas, a chance to start again.

Large plastic laundry baskets overflowing with freshly dried bedlinen covered the battered wooden table, waiting to be sorted. The longer she took about it, the less time she'd have to spend next door. It was a roof over her head but not quite a home, not without Alice in it, but for the time being, it was the best she could do. It would have been worse to take her away from a school and friends that she loved. When every other aspect of her life had changed, the poor child needed some stability, some continuity.

Gennie lifted a pillowcase and pressed it to her face, seeking comfort in the thick white cotton. It still smelt deceitfully like summer, of warm fresh air. She replaced it hurriedly at the sound of footsteps in the flag-stoned hall.

Someone else was also still at work. It had to be Marion; the uneven tread gave her away. She must be on her way to her office.

'Hey, how's it going?'

A beaming face appeared in the kitchen doorway. Marion Hope smiled at everyone and everything, instinctively. It didn't necessarily mean she was delighted to see you, although it had that effect. It could be that she hadn't put her lenses in yet.

'All good,' said Gennie, and smiled too. This was what happened when you smiled at the world; it smiled back. She added a folded sheet to the growing piles on the table, ready for ironing. 'Tea?'

'Absolutely, but only if you're making some.'

'Sure, give me a sec.'

Gennie added a couple of ginger biscuits to the saucer before taking Marion's camomile tea through to the office. With all the metal filing cabinets and lever arch files crowding the shelves, the room had the feel of a school secretary's office. It was the mahogany desk which suggested the room belonged to the head of the organisation.

'Knee no better, then?' Gennie placed the teacup on the desk's leather top.

Marion sat peering at a computer screen. 'Ah, you know. Bloody nuisance.' She took a biscuit. 'Ooh, thank you. Now then, darling, what are we going to do about this?' She pointed at a spreadsheet. 'There's not an inch to spare anywhere. D'you think we can re-purpose one of the offices upstairs, move a sofa bed up there?'

'New arrival?' Gennie moved closer to look at the list. Keeping track of the young people's comings and goings kept

6

her on her toes. She'd installed a whiteboard in the kitchen to log all the room switches and dietary requirements, who needed packed lunches and who had dentist appointments. It seemed she'd need another row on her chart.

'It's Jack,' said Marion. 'He's back.'

Gennie recoiled as if she'd opened the biscuit cupboard and a spider had jumped out. 'And he's coming here?' she said, too quickly, but Marion's eyes were still fixed on her screen.

She was being ridiculous. Why shouldn't Marion provide a bed for her son? He might not be as difficult as she'd heard, although what she'd heard had been neither complimentary nor reassuring. People didn't get barred from their local or banned from driving for no reason. Even so, she shouldn't have been listening.

'I mean, that's good,' she said, remembering her smile. 'Sooner than I thought, but you must be pleased. And… is he okay?'

Marion swivelled to face her. 'I know what you mean, but yes, he's fine. Seems they finished the build early, which must be a first.'

Marion's attention was making her uncomfortable. Gennie held on to her smile, although her cheeks were feeling the strain. Her boss might not wear her glasses as often as she ought, but Gennie doubted she missed much. Even if she saw straight through her, it didn't matter. She'd been so generous in offering Gennie the housekeeping job and made her feel she was the one doing Marion the favour rather than the other way round. She owed her.

'Look,' Marion continued, 'we've got a bit of time to sort things out. Jack's staying in town for a few days with Max. Catching up with Millie.'

Gennie knew Max from her art classes. She'd also met Millie, Jack's daughter. She came by at weekends to see her granny and was a sweet little thing. Alice liked her, too; they sat and coloured pictures together. The thing was, Millie had her own bedroom in the house so Jack could easily have met up with her at the farm. Best not to speculate on his reasons for staying away.

Marion was still staring at her, but her expression was kind, concerned even. 'And before you ask, he's three months sober.'

'No, honestly, Marion,' she said hastily, 'it's none of my business.' Was she that transparent? A mention of alcohol and she'd head for the hills? In any case, where would she run to? Hiding in her cottage wouldn't take her very far.

'Look, darling, this is a village and the people of St Illick like to chat. I know what's been said.'

The heat rose in Gennie's cheeks. She knew what it was like to be gossiped about, and for people to cross the street rather than stop to chat and become involved in her latest domestic drama. She wouldn't be the person who believed all the stories, or have Marion think that of her.

Marion didn't seem perturbed. She was smiling again. 'I really think we're back on track.'

Back on track. So, Jack needed help to stay on the rails. How many times had he fallen off? Gennie didn't want to know. All the goodness of the past few months seemed to be slipping though her hands. Her fingers traced the edge of the bookcase, something solid to hang on to and stop the slide.

'Frankly, darling,' Marion continued, 'I could do with his help. He's the one who got the farm back up and running. We really do need another income stream and he's full of ideas.'

'So he'll be here for a while, then?'

'For the time being, at least. If he hasn't any other plans, he can get on with the building work at the back. May as well make himself useful. It's so hard to find a builder you can trust.'

Was Marion being ironic? It was hard to tell. She'd certainly never admit that part of the reason she wanted Jack around was to keep an eye on him. No doubt she was capable of discovering an urgent building need if it suited her. It was what mothers did.

3

Marion hadn't exaggerated about St Illick. Over the past two days, so many people had popped their heads around the kitchen door or stopped Gennie in the street to tell her the news about Jack, that if a minor royal or Elvis had turned up, they'd have been disappointed as no-one would have noticed and all the bunting would have been used up. It was a risk going down to the village, but without flour there'd be no treacle tart for dessert. Dessert featured large in the life of the farm; it was the only other thing anyone was interested in.

St Illick was lucky to have a shop. There used to be a petrol station too but that had gone and now only the convenience store remained. It was a good one, well stocked with fresh bread and baked goods, and it wasn't worth the drive into town if you could get what you needed in a ten-minute walk down the lane – other than to avoid Shirley because, as Gennie discovered during her first week at Hope House, you didn't want to get caught in the shop on a slow day. Escape could take a while.

The tarmacked forecourt next to the shop still bore the scars of the old petrol pumps. It was fronted by an old water trough, once a refreshment post for livestock being herded between farm and field, now used for leaning against when waiting for the bus to Wadebridge. Another place to hurry past for fear of getting buttonholed.

Gennie peeked through the shop door. Four people in the queue was a good sign. She could be in and out before Shirley got into her stride. She was second in line for the till when the young woman in front of her turned round.

'I hear Jack's back from Nigeria.'

Damn. She'd been so close to making it out of there. The woman looked familiar so she must be local, but Gennie still only knew a handful of people in St Illick by name.

'It was Rwanda, I think,' she said. Why was she getting involved? All she knew was what Marion had told her. She had no real idea where Jack had been. He could have been in rehab for all she knew.

Shirley rang up the woman's purchases. 'That's the thing with these soldiers,' she said. 'They don't know what to do with themselves when they come home. That's why they end up as mercenaries, you know, guns for hire.'

'I don't think...' said Gennie, and then checked herself. She wouldn't be drawn in.

'You've been watching too much telly, Shirley,' said a voice behind her. Gennie turned to see a middle-aged woman carrying a Jack Russell under her arm. 'He went out to build a school, didn't he?'

'Far as I know,' said Gennie.

'Marion must be pleased to have him back.' The older woman smiled.

'More than can be said of his wife,' said Shirley. 'Or ex-wife, rather. Poor girl.'

Gennie reached the till and placed her bags of flour on the counter along with a pile of coins.

Shirley put her hand on hers for a second. 'Gennie, love, if you're going back up the hill, will you walk Jan back to her cottage?' She nodded in the direction of the woman with the dog. 'Her arthritis is giving her trouble. It's on your way.'

'Yes, of course,' said Gennie, surprised by the abrupt change of direction. She moved to the end of the counter to wait.

'If I was Marion, I don't know that I'd want someone like Jack up at the farm with all those kiddies. Haven't they got enough problems? I know they deserve a second chance but how many chances has Jack had? Still, Marion loves a lost cause.' Shirley handed Jan her change, and, without pausing for breath, walked round to the front to pack the groceries into Jan's shopping trolley.

Gennie accepted the trolley from Shirley and followed Jan out of the shop. Taking a chance on people seemed to be Marion's thing. Was she also one of Marion's lost causes? It wasn't as if anyone was queuing up to employ homeless accountants. Hope House wasn't the only job offer she'd had, but it was the only one she'd seriously considered. Marion's manner was so gentle, even when her language was colourful and her Australian accent was more evident, that Gennie felt instantly calmer, and no longer the hopeless case having to explain how she'd lost her home and her husband in the space of twelve months. She would probably have dropped to her knees and begged for any job Marion offered, but this one was freely given and came with accommodation and use of a car. That was the beauty of it. Alice could stay at her school, and Gennie could pay for weekly boarding because she had no rent to cover.

Marion hadn't mentioned Jack when Gennie took the job, and he'd left the village before she arrived. It wouldn't have mattered to anyone else, but if she'd at least known, she could have weighed up the situation for herself. All she needed was time to catch her breath and find her feet again, ideally without daily reminders of how she'd got to this point. No discovering empty bottles hidden in the boots of cars or under the stairs; no piecing together torn-up letters to find court summonses or driving bans or unpaid credit-card bills or riding a roller-coaster of hope and dread each time someone was late or didn't turn up at all. No reminders of how it ended. No reminders like a resident alcoholic, even if he was her boss's son. Suppose she couldn't cope? She'd be on the move again and, worse still, so would Alice.

It would be a shame to leave so soon.

Jan was holding out her hand for the trolley. 'It's kind of you, but I can manage,' she said with a smile. 'I made the mistake of calling Shirley one day to see if someone could drop me off some milk and now, she's got everyone running around after me. She's very good-hearted but there's really no need.'

'She hasn't got much time for Jack,' said Gennie, pondering Shirley's good heart.

'Don't believe a word of it. Shirley adores Jack, you wait and see. He's got his demons, I'll grant you, but given what he went through, it's not surprising.'

That was the other thing. Everyone assumed she knew all about him. She wouldn't ask as it made no difference to her; she'd heard all the excuses.

'Well, this is me.' Jan stopped outside a cottage whose front door was set back from the street and down a couple of steps.

'Look,' said Gennie. 'I walk up and down here every day. If you'd like me to pick anything up for you, I'd be happy to help, and I won't tell Shirley.'

Jan laughed and looked at the little dog snuffling round her feet. 'What you could do – but only if you're passing and only if you've got time – is take Roxy for a ramble. She needs more exercise than I can give her at the moment.'

'You're on,' said Gennie, and bent to tickle the dog's head. 'She'll be my excuse to get out of the house.'

*

A boy, sixteen years old, a young person in the language of Marion's Restart Project, was waiting in the kitchen when Gennie got back.

'Hi there, are you on dinner duty?' She glanced at the whiteboard and her roster. All the teenagers in placement at the farm had to take their turn preparing menus, cooking meals and shopping. It was in the plans agreed for them with the county's social services department, part of their training for independent living. 'It's Hamid, isn't it?'

Amongst the group currently at Hope House were old hands who'd been there for six months or so and six new arrivals, including five girls from Devon and Cornwall, who, although they'd only been at the farm a couple of weeks, had already settled in and made their presence known. Hamid was the exception. He was polite and spoke when spoken to, but he gave little away. All Gennie knew about him was that he was from Afghanistan and was staying with them temporarily while his foster carer had medical treatment. Gennie wasn't usually briefed about the family and social problems that had led to placement at the farm. It was better that way, but when the residents told her their stories themselves, which they did without prompting, she'd realise with a jolt that she and Alice fitted in there very well. They could tick many of the same boxes.

'Shouldn't there be two of you?' Gennie asked. 'Is Leticia coming?'

'She swapped with someone.'

'And didn't tell them.' Gennie nodded. 'Oh well, never mind.'

It was easier, sometimes, with only one person to supervise. There'd be no giggling and whispering, no private jokes.

She took a laminated recipe card from her folder and placed it on the table. 'What about pizza? Happy with that?'

'No problem,' said Hamid.

Gennie helped him measure out flour and yeast, and stood back as he mixed and kneaded the dough. He worked swiftly and confidently, soon achieving a smooth round ball.

'You've done this before,' she said.

He smiled at last, dismissing his success with a shake of the head. 'It's easy, like bread.'

She waited, in case he was going to enlighten her about his bread-making experience, but he said no more so she put the bowls of dough to rise in the bottom of the kitchen range and passed him onions and peppers to slice.

'D'you like cooking?' Gennie asked as she wiped down the table.

'Sometimes. When I was in Iran I did cooking.'

'Iran?'

'Yes, at the factory.'

'Oh, I'm sorry, I thought you were from Afghanistan.'

'I went to Iran when my father was killed. To my uncle. Me and my brother,' he said.

'I see. I didn't know, I'm sorry,' she said again. 'For your loss.' She was straying into forbidden territory. Time to steer the conversation back onto safer ground. 'So, what do you cook?'

'Everything. But not pasta. I don't like making pasta.' He lapsed into silence and concentrated on slicing mushrooms.

'Well, you're welcome to come and join me if you want to practice your skills. Maybe you can teach me some new recipes? With no pasta.'

That was two commitments she'd made that day – cooking with a lonely teenager and walking an overweight dog – and just when she was contemplating leaving. Both, though, were more attractive prospects than keeping an eye out for an ex-soldier's lost soul.

4

It wouldn't do to be late. Tuesday evenings were life drawing class and they closed the door early. Gennie rammed her cycle helmet on her head and, high-visibility jacket flapping, set off on her bike at racing speed along the main road to Wadebridge. She preferred to take the winding lanes, brushing past the hedgerows, but that would double the journey time and she had fifteen minutes to cycle a route that on her best performance would take twenty. If she was late, she'd have to bang on the glass and wait for someone to let her in. If they even heard her. The local art community was tight-knit and while she'd made some acquaintances, she was still an outsider. They wouldn't notice her absence.

She skidded to a halt inside the gates of the college, locked her bike to the railings and took a moment to run her hands through her cropped blonde hair and stuff her jacket and helmet into her bag. Arriving dishevelled and out of breath was one thing, but she didn't want to look like she'd spent the day resurfacing the A30 – not that highway maintenance workers weren't entitled to their creative pursuits. She opened the door of the college and slipped down the corridor to the art studio, passing classrooms where flower-arranging, Spanish conversation and printmaking were already in full swing. To her relief, the art studio door was still propped open, the glass covered in several layers of newspaper to deter visitors and protect the privacy of the model.

There was a reason the class hadn't quite got going yet: the room was heaving. Gennie pulled up short in the doorway and watched as people shuffled round each other, manoeuvring easels into position, scraping the legs across the linoleum-tiled floor, and fixing canvas and drawing boards into place. Over the summer, the classes had been busy enough to keep them open and have other people to speak to but sufficiently empty to have room to work and the attention of the tutor. This class was so full the easels were overlapping, like a herd of oddly shaped animals crowded round a water hole. Gennie hovered, scanning the floor for an empty chair. She glanced towards the middle of the room. It was a new model, someone she'd not seen before, young and male. That shouldn't make a difference. Maybe it was the time of year, a beginning-of-term enthusiasm which would tail off in a few weeks.

Max, the tutor, slalomed towards her through the easels.

'Sorry,' she said. 'Bit late. Is there space?'

'Have no fear, we'll squeeze you in,' he said in a hoarse stage whisper. He tugged an easel from the corner of the room, expertly sliding it between two painters. 'Painting or drawing?'

'Drawing. Pastels, maybe. There isn't room to paint.'

There was barely enough room to draw.

Max conjured a place for her between two painters. From there, she'd see the back and side of the model. He was sitting on a red cloth-covered block with his chin in his right hand, mimicking 'The Thinker'. Not the most imaginative of poses, but from where she was, the angles should be interesting, and if it wasn't any good and she wanted a change, she'd swap places at the break. There was always movement then.

Gennie taped paper to her drawing board and sat down. She'd always painted, ever since school. It was the best way to lose herself, concentrating only on what she could see and putting it down on paper, emptying her mind of every other thought. She'd start slowly, getting the measure of her subject, closing one eye and comparing distances against an outstretched paintbrush, placing some markers and a few broad sweeps of colour on the page. Capturing the model's likeness was less important than getting the light right and finding her way into the shapes. She'd break down what she saw into blocks of colour – and hopefully an image would emerge.

Unfortunately, the man she was studying wouldn't dissolve so easily; he was already a mass of colour. In his early thirties, lean and sinewy, the sort who kept fit running and cycling rather than building a six-pack in the gym, but that wasn't what caught her attention. It was impossible, even in the muted light of the studio, to miss the heavy scarring which ran down his right leg from thigh to shin, livid in places, raw pink and puckered in others. It was painful to look at. What had happened to him? A car accident, maybe. Or a fire? There were paler scars on his back, like splatter marks, as if someone had thrown a handful of clay at him and it hadn't all washed off. These weren't so significant and Gennie hesitated, chalk poised, before marking them in, but she was working in vibrant colour and it felt dishonest not to show all his injuries. She wondered how he felt about it and whether he wanted to be painted damaged as he was. Was he testing them, to see who shied away from the task and smoothed it better with a lick of paint? If only things were that easy. She could see why Max wanted this model to sit for the class.

Max alternated male and female models in his classes. His regular male model was Clement, who was in his early sixties and ran an antiques shop in Bodmin. Clement never took any exercise and it showed. Gennie liked him a lot. He was good-humoured and a very good sitter, happy to be depicted in all his dimpled fleshiness, flicking his dreadlocks and grinning at his audience before settling into a pose. There'd been less than half this number of people the last time Clement had been in.

After an hour, Max called a break. The students moved around the room, pausing to admire each other's work, throwing compliments left and right. Max and the model, now wrapped in a hooded dressing gown, were deep in conversation. Several people, better-known local artists that Gennie had heard of but never spoken to, went to join them. She stretched her shoulders, picked up her purse and made her way across to Eleanor, her new friend in the class. Eleanor was on the phone and mouthed, 'Coffee, please,' at her when Gennie half asked, half signed whether she wanted anything from the canteen.

As Gennie worked her way back through the forest of easels, she felt in her jacket pocket for her cigarettes, reassured by the smooth cellophane of the unopened packet. It was ridiculous. She'd kept her promise to Alice to give up, but was she so weak the only way to stick to it was knowing there was comfort if she cracked? It was more than that. The need for a cigarette had been useful during all those times when she'd had to escape and grab a few moments to herself. That was the habit she couldn't give up. All she needed to say was 'fag break', and no-one questioned where she was going. As on so many other evenings, she went outside to join the smokers on the pavement to take the air and chat about the weather for a minute before heading back inside to join the tea queue.

By the time Gennie returned to the studio balancing styrofoam cups, another painter had squeezed in beside her easel. Her view of the model was now reduced to an ear and an elbow, challenging for the most imaginative of artists. Gennie grabbed her drawing board and a fresh sheet of paper and cast around for a spare chair, ignoring Max beckoning to her from the centre of the room.

'Gennie,' he whispered, but so loudly that most of the class turned to look. His gesturing now resembled semaphore signalling. What was wrong with him? Sometimes people could be allowed to hide at the back.

'Okay, okay,' she muttered, cheeks reddening, and went to sit where he wanted, facing the model's left knee.

It put her at the front of the class, which was fine if she wanted to draw detail but too close for perspective. It was also next to the heat lamps and uncomfortably warm, like being lightly toasted. They had to keep the temperature up in the room for the comfort of the model, but Gennie's fingers were sweating and sliding on her pastels. She turned her paper over and switched to sketching in ink, concentrating on drawing in the defined musculature of the subject's legs and arms. This was easier as he had no scarring along his left side. His face was turned away, half hidden in his hand, his skin quite pale, unusual in Cornwall in early October when everyone was still ruddy from the wind or sun. Only his forearms and the back of his neck were tanned. A white line showed where his dark hair had been recently trimmed. Unlike many models, he didn't close his eyes and doze but stared intently at the ground, as if genuinely lost in thought, removed from the heat and movement in the room.

The room was too crowded for Max to make his usual rounds, which was a relief. He was not a fan of pen and ink as it was difficult to make corrections and would not have been impressed with what she had created. It was fine for those of her classmates who could create a shape with just a few fluid lines. Her constant redrawing had a Gothic quality. She'd wanted to produce a sympathetic portrait of an athletic young man, but instead, he looked hungry and haunted.

Max called time at ten minutes to ten and the class began clearing away their materials with the familiar grumbles that they hadn't finished. He handed the model a dressing gown and took his place on the blocks in the centre of the room, waving his hands for quiet.

'Well, thank you all for coming,' he said, 'and if you haven't paid your enrolment fees yet, please do so or the director will have me in his sights. I don't care at all, of course. If you've told your other half you're doing cake-decorating or Mandarin as a cover for your unhealthy obsession with fine art, by all means enrol for that and come along to me instead. But enrol for something. And, if anyone wants to hang around for a drink, Jack and I are heading to the Pirate Queen for a quick one. Everyone welcome. In the meantime, will you join me in thanking Jack for once again stepping up to the plate? He's going to be around for a while, you'll be pleased to hear, so has promised to sit again later in the term.'

Gennie was half listening as she packed up her bag. She looked back at Max. Of course the stranger was Jack. The clues had been right in front of her; the friendship with Max, the crush in the studio, the almost insatiable curiosity about him. And the war wounds. She didn't need Shirley to tell her what had happened to Jack; it was visible to all. No wonder he had a few issues.

Jack, meanwhile, had jumped behind the modesty screen and reappeared in jeans and a T-shirt.

Max started up with his beckoning again. Gennie sighed and wandered over.

'Have you met Jack yet?'

'Er, no.' She held out an inky hand and was met with a puzzled frown. Her eyes refused to meet his, her gaze remaining fixed on the neck of his T-shirt. 'Hi, I'm Gennie.'

With her other hand, she held her rolled drawings behind her back and scrunched them in half. Max reached out to take them from her. Gennie pretended not to see and shoved the drawings in the top of her bag, hastily fastening the strap.

Max turned his smiling attention to Jack. 'This is Gennie, your mum's new cook-slash-housekeeper, and Gennie, this is my mate Jack, newly returned from foreign parts.'

'Hey, Gennie.'

Jack shot a furious look at Max, who shrugged.

'I, er...' Jack took a deep breath. 'I... er, hope you've settled in okay. I didn't expect anyone from the house to be here. Look, do you want to come for a drink with us? I'm... I'm not... I mean, you can have something soft. If you're driving.'

He looked up from his bare feet to stare at a spot over Gennie's left shoulder and she switched her gaze to the floor.

Eleanor was over at the door, waving and miming drinking at her. This is how it begins; Gennie had been here before. Every fresh start Mikkel made never really got out of the blocks because of the 'quick drink' to get to know people. Well, she wouldn't help it along. She lifted her head and stretched her mouth into a smile.

'Erm, thanks, but I'd better go. Early start,' she said, mirroring Jack's diffidence without knowing why, and edging towards the door. 'Well, you know, nice to meet you, and… that.' She was doing it again!

Once in the corridor, she ran for the exit. 'Oh God.' She cringed, covering her mouth with her hand to stifle the laughter that threatened.

'Are you sure you won't come?' said Eleanor when she stumbled outside.

Gennie shook her head and pressed her hand against her pocket and the rectangular-shaped box. This was not an emergency. A touch awkward, but not more than that. She put on her cycle helmet and clicked the chin strap into place. So, that was the famous Jack? Not quite the shaven-headed firebrand she'd been expecting. Stripped naked and battle-scarred, he was vulnerable, fragile even. Bloody Max, he could have warned her. Wait 'til she told Marion.

5

Marion limped into the kitchen at four o'clock, clutching a lever arch file bursting with paperwork, held together by a rubber band. She threw the file onto the table with a force which sent it skidding across the slippery wood, and then sank into the corner armchair.

'Tea?' Gennie said, taking a mug down. It was all she ever offered. She searched Marion's face for clues. There was a slight furrow between the eyebrows which was as put out as Gennie had seen her.

'If you've nothing stronger,' said Marion, and then waved a hand immediately to banish the thought.

'Trouble?' Gennie pressed a spoon against the teabag, watching the water in the cup turn a golden colour, and fought a rising sense of unease.

'Six-monthly budget-planning with the trustees,' Marion said. 'The problem, basically, is there is no bloody money. Anywhere. We can make ends meet, just, but there are no funds to develop anything new and we're bursting at the seams here. We need more accommodation, a classroom, key work rooms... I've got reserves and could use them to pay for a new building, but we can't do anything with it without more investment. So, where's the point? We can apply for grants but there are simply too many organisations competing for the same money.'

Gennie straightened her back, resisting the dread creeping up her spine. It was what they always said: if it looked too good to be true, it was. It had taken time to find a job, but once she had, she wanted to stay in it for a while – for Alice's sake especially. Nothing was reliable. Or certain. She passed Marion the jar of honey and returned to the sink and the pile of fruit resting in the colander, waiting to be transformed into crumble. She picked an apple from the top and peeled it vigorously, gripping the peeler so tightly her knuckles were almost white.

'It should get easier,' Marion continued, although Gennie wished she wouldn't. 'I built this place from nothing, and now we have the most amazing reputation. The only reason we became a charity was to make it easier to apply for funding to develop our work. Except it doesn't. Now I have to justify all my actions to the trustees, although in reality they control only a part of what we do here. However many budget forecasts I give them, they still want more information.' She sighed again, rubbing her forehead. 'We need some financial independence. Then we won't have to wait for them, and we can make our own bloody decisions. I really need the farm to start paying for itself.' She cradled the mug in her hands and stared through the kitchen window.

Gennie followed her gaze towards the back barns. It was unsettling to see Marion upset. Her plans were ambitious, but they always had been, and she'd been right so far. She deserved the same confidence she placed in other people. On the other hand, if the building plans were blocked, there'd be no work for Jack. Which reminded her.

'I had an odd experience yesterday,' Gennie said as she placed the apple peelings in the compost bin. 'I went to my art class and found that your Jack was the model.'

Marion looked up, caught Gennie's eye, and curiosity swept the worry from her face. 'Yes, he does sit for Max occasionally. It's been good for him, helps him feel whole again. How funny, I spoke to Max yesterday, and he didn't tell me Jack would be there.'

No, he'd kept that to himself, although if Jack was as flaky as his reputation, perhaps he wasn't sure he'd turn up and if Max had told her in advance, would she still have gone? It was a good question. Probably, was the answer.

'Marion, his leg… can I ask?'

'Roadside bomb. In Afghanistan. Everyone else in the vehicle was killed.' Marion was matter-of-fact, as Gennie had come to expect, but her voice was gentle, as if she knew the impact of each word. Put them together and the effect was devastating.

'Oh… that's horrible… I'm sorry.'

Marion nodded. 'Look, it's not been easy for him. He lost his best friend, and with that, he lost the reference points of his old life. That was hard, unbearably so, and then there was Claire… and things didn't work out there.' She sipped at her tea. 'It can be difficult to be the one who comes home.'

'But he was lucky,' said Gennie, rejecting the idea of Marion suffering loss. It would be too unfair; someone had to make it through. 'He did come home.'

'Yes.' Marion's nod was more emphatic, this time.

Gennie turned back to the kitchen counter and her dinner preparations. She'd been at school when the armies had gone into Afghanistan after 9/11 and at university when the war in Iraq had started. There'd been rallies and demonstrations against it. She remembered news footage of the coffins of soldiers who'd been killed in the conflicts being returned to the UK and carried in hearses from the airfield through the town of Wootton Basset, and couldn't imagine how Marion had felt when she received the call that Jack had been blown up. The thought of any harm coming to her own child stopped her heart. She hurriedly spooned the chopped and peeled apple into a dish, sprinkled it with crumble topping and brown sugar, and shoved it in the fridge for later.

'Yeah,' she said, changing the subject, 'I didn't know who he was until the end. I spent at least an hour drawing him in minute detail from a very interesting angle.'

'He won't have minded,' said Marion, 'although, I see, from your perspective, it could be awkward when he's back and you put in your farm order for mixed veg.' She burst out laughing.

Gennie stared at her. How was it funny? The strain of the morning had obviously been too much.

A door slammed somewhere along the corridor and Hamid's maths tutor appeared in the doorway, the outstretched arms and frowning face indicating his annoyance at the disturbance. He grinned when he saw Marion convulsed, gestured that it didn't matter and went back to his room. The more she tried to stop laughing, the more Gennie laughed too.

28

6

Pancakes for breakfast. Only possible if Gennie started early and could let the batter rest while she sipped a mug of tea and flicked through whichever reading material had been left on the table the night before. Today was a toss-up between *The Cornish Times* and *Psychology Today*.

Pancakes weren't the treat they seemed; they were for those mornings when she gave up on sleep and, rather than toss and turn any longer, went next door to the farm kitchen to begin her working day and pretend that had been the plan all along.

Sunday nights were the worst. Without Alice, Gennie's tiny cottage felt huge and uninviting, although it was neither. Astonishing how their weekday separation, initially so unthinkable, had become the only workable solution while they got back on their feet. Up to now, it was the only downside to life at the farm. Pancakes were her way of capitalising on any surfeit of lemons life provided. It was so much nicer to claim she was up early to make a special breakfast rather than share she'd been awake since 4am. Not that she couldn't share it; no-one would judge, they'd try to help. And that was worse.

'Hello again.'

Gennie leapt to her feet. Jack was standing at the end of the table. When had he crept in? He hadn't come from the yard or she'd have heard the kitchen door. She glanced at the clock. It was fine, only seven o'clock. It would have been ironic if she'd dozed off at the table. Seemingly the only place she couldn't sleep was her own bed.

'Hi,' she said. 'Can I get you something? I'm making pancakes for the gang, but do you want something else now?'

'No, don't worry, I'll help myself. Is there cereal?' He opened one of the cupboards and rifled through the packets. 'Ooh, Sugar Puffs. Haven't had these in a while.'

Of course he knew his way around the kitchen; it was his mum's house. Gennie crossed to the range and made a start on breakfast. Making pancakes was a thing she enjoyed. It wasn't to be rushed: ladling out the batter in strict measures, the hiss as it hit the pan, waiting for air bubbles to appear before flipping them over. She heated two pans and gave the batter a last stir, conscious that she had her back to Jack. It felt rude. She had a job to do, but after the strangeness of their first meeting, she didn't want him to think she was ignoring him, or worse, was embarrassed in some way, so once she'd set the first batch to cook, she turned towards him.

'Did you get here yesterday?' she said, settling for the obvious. It explained the unfamiliar green Land Rover in the yard.

He nodded, mouth full.

'Room okay?' The room she and Marion had hastily cleared of folders, filing cabinets and computer accessories to create a space for her son to sleep.

'Yes, thanks. S'fine.' He continued to eat.

Gennie twisted to flip the pancakes and then spun back to face him. As she did, Jack looked up from his bowl, spoon in mid-air, and smiled. She had the strangest feeling. Either she'd turned too fast or the lack of sleep was catching up with her. Jack really did look astonishingly like Marion.

The pancakes! She swivelled again and rescued them before they burnt. With shaky hands she wrapped them in greaseproof paper, put them in the oven and stood up to put more batter in the pans.

No, no, not Marion. Nothing to do with Marion. She knew that face. She knew this man.

'D'you need a hand?' Jack asked, from the other side of the room. He couldn't miss the smell of burning butter. He stood and opened the kitchen door. 'Smoke alarm's over-sensitive.'

'Right, yes, thanks,' she said. 'It's fine, all under control.' She didn't dare look at him as she shovelled more pancakes into the oven to keep warm. 'You must have loads to do. I think Marion has a huge list of jobs.'

'Undoubtedly. I'll see you later, I expect. Marion said you'd need potatoes and carrots.'

Gennie stared at him, horror creeping into her bones, until the smell of burning pulled her back to the frying pans. What a mess she was making! She should have stuck to cereal and toast.

Jack went out into the yard, closing the door after him. Gennie took a couple of deep breaths and forced her attention back to turning the misshapen splodges into something edible.

Jack Aspinall. There could be no doubt, even after… how long? Must be fifteen years. Almost half her life. There were many times when she'd have been delighted to see him, catch up on his news, but not now. And certainly not here. So strange that Marion's Jack should turn out to be Jack Aspinall, and she'd been dreading the man's arrival for entirely different reasons, and yet somehow not strange at all. It must be why she'd warmed so instantly to Marion. Something known, something sympathetic about her.

Without her teenage helper, who'd clearly slept in, Gennie laid the table, put out chocolate spread, syrup and sugar, and opened the door to the kitchen yard to await the arrival of the masses.

So sweet Jack Aspinall had turned into an angry, womanising drunk? How could that be? Not only was it difficult to reconcile with the pale and wounded individual she'd witnessed last week but it felt like a betrayal. Somewhere, subconsciously, she'd held Jack out as the antidote to Mikkel and his selfish excesses, yet here he was, infected by the same poison. She didn't want to see it.

And what had she turned into? Jack hadn't recognised her. Was that insulting or a relief? Thinking about their last meeting felt like a punch to the chest. The memory wasn't painful, far from it, but how to explain to her twenty-one-year-old self, that naïve and happy-go-lucky individual, how she'd found herself here? It was hard enough feeling comfortable in the present. Then there was Mikkel. Her head was flooded with images of him and how he'd been in those days – tall and tanned, carefully tousled hair, broad shoulders in show-off suits, all the swagger of a twenty-four-year-old making money in his first proper job – and her legs buckled.

She slid down to sit on the doorstep, leaning her head against the doorframe while she took a deep breath.

She hadn't looked at Jack properly when Max introduced them, too busy planning her escape, but she'd seen him full face now. He looked almost as he had then. Older obviously, and he was taller, broader, his build more angular, but he hadn't changed that much. She had, though, physically as well as emotionally. She was no longer the sylph-like figure with the glossy brown hair that curled halfway down her back and a faith that life would protect her.

Why would he remember her? Seven days at the end of December 2004 and then a couple of postcards. That was it.

7

Three in the morning and it felt like her breath was trapped in her chest and she had to force it in and out of her lungs, like trying to push a pillow through a straw. When she stopped concentrating, the air caught again like a lump in her throat, and she had to sit upright in bed to exhale. Was she actually having a heart attack? When she finally dozed off, Mikkel was there, holding out his hand, summoning her to go with him. She tried to speak, to tell him she couldn't, she had to look after Alice, but her mouth wouldn't form the words. He said it was because she didn't want to, and she shook her head, or tried to. It seemed she couldn't do that either. Because it was true, and she didn't want to go with him, and he knew that. That made her sad but he must know she couldn't do this anymore. If it was even him, because when she looked more closely, it wasn't his hand and it wasn't his face and she was glad she hadn't been fooled. She had to tell him that, but she couldn't see him anywhere. Where had he gone?

When she woke again, the room was still dark. It took her a moment to remember where she was. She sat up and looked around, smoothing the sheet beside her, preserving its cool emptiness.

It was a relief when her alarm went off.

8

Gennie tugged her jacket round herself and settled in the armchair facing the bay window in Stella's lilac-painted consultation room. The streets of Exeter were visible over her counsellor's shoulder. Living on the farm was getting easier, but back in an urban landscape of pavements, lampposts and autumn leaves clogging gutters, Gennie felt more confident. It reflected her life, she supposed; she'd been a child in the country, an adult in the city.

She dressed differently for town too, stepping out of her shorts and wellies and into clean jeans and heeled boots. It was another way to hide. Even on those days when she felt like an empty shell of a person, hollowed out by loss, all she need do was put on a fancy jacket, a bit of hair gel and some lipstick, and no-one would know. No-one need see what was going on inside because, and here was the point, no-one really wanted to. It wasn't that they didn't care, but they wanted to believe she was doing fine. Her friends and family had been sympathetic to her marital woes, but she understood when, at times, they avoided her, and news of the latest drama. It was just as tedious always being the person with the problem. That was where Stella came in. Gennie could provide cheery progress reports to friends and family while spending an hour each week privately working through her confusion.

Marion had been completely amenable to adjusting Gennie's working hours so she could continue with her therapy and switched her Friday-evening responsibilities to Saturday to accommodate it. Now she had no choice but to spend an hour each week with Stella before she got to see her daughter. She wouldn't have minded if Marion had refused, but it was in her contract now, part of her working day. It wouldn't surprise her if Marion had a clause for all staff that they had to have access to some kind of support.

'So, I had this weird thing this week,' Gennie said, understanding that it was usually helpful if she started the conversation. 'Something, well, someone, I haven't thought about for years, and now I can't get it out of my mind.'

'It? Or them?' asked Stella.

'It,' said Gennie, firmly. 'The whole situation. It was just, well, this person I met on holiday years ago, I mean, Mikkel was there and everything, and anyway, it seems he's Marion's son and now he's living at the farm.'

Stella raised an eyebrow. 'That is a coincidence.'

'Yes.' Gennie nodded. 'We used to go skiing every winter, and the first time we went, it was for New Year. Mikkel and his friends had booked this amazing chalet in Austria. It was slightly out of town and had these huge windows and a balcony all round, so in the morning, you'd open the curtains to nothing but mountains and snow and total quiet. There were other people there, another family, I think, and then Jack was there with his friend. I couldn't remember his name at first, but I'm pretty sure it was Andy. They were about to join the army and were determined to make the most of their time. Mikkel spent most of the night drinking with his friends so couldn't or wouldn't get up before ten, which meant I got up, and rather than having breakfast by myself, I joined the boys.' She paused. Stella wasn't a fan of the rambling tale. She considered it an evasion and, to be fair, she tended to be right. This time, however, Stella's brief nod was accompanied by a smile.

'So...' Gennie continued, in the same slow style. Each time she thought about it, another fact emerged from the fog of her memory – and she'd thought about little else for days. 'While Andy made totally lame attempts to flirt with the chalet girl, I chatted to Jack. He was very funny. They both were, Andy especially. He had blond curly hair and the kind of clear blue eyes that should have looked innocent, but you just knew he was up to no good. Jack and I spent our whole time laughing. I've got this memory of sitting opposite him at the table – eating, playing cards, joking around, you know...'

'And is there something that troubles you about it?' said Stella, finally. She sat with her hands folded across her stomach, perfectly still. When someone remained as still as that, it was impossible to avoid answering their questions.

'No, no,' said Gennie, untruthfully. 'Well, yes. It's just... I don't know... Looking back, that week was a turning point for me. For Mikkel, too. I didn't realise at the time. We came home and decided to get married and I put everything else behind me.'

Stella nodded but didn't respond. This was Stella's way. It was up to Gennie to decide how much she wanted to tell her.

'Okay, it's this,' said Gennie, leaning forward in her chair, looking down at her toes in their black suede ankle boots. Her knees were clamped together and she folded one hand over the other, pressing down against the trembling, which was bound to start once she gave voice to her thoughts. It was what generally happened. 'It's not good but I know that if I'd been single, I'd have got together with Jack that week. Hundred per cent. Obviously, it wouldn't have gone anywhere. He would have gone off to the army and I was three months into my post-grad accountancy training. We spent a fair bit of time together and we talked. He was different from the others – kind and funny and sort of playful. D'you know what I mean? Didn't try too hard. The whole holiday had a kind of "last fling" quality to it.'

'For you?'

'No, no, not really. For him, I mean. He was going to start his basic training when he went home.'

'So that's Marion's son?'

'Yes.'

'And does she know you knew him before?'

'No, no.' Gennie shook her head, beginning to wish she hadn't started this. 'I didn't know him, not really. I knew him a bit, a long time ago.'

'Okay. I'd like you to work through with me why you think this is a problem,' said Stella.

Gennie could understand why she'd assume that having a nice young man around, particularly one who was a blast from the past, would be a bit of a laugh.

'You see,' she said, grinding her palms together, 'maybe I looked at things the wrong way. I thought that because it didn't happen with Jack, it was a sign that I was meant to be

39

with Mikkel, but the fact I even thought about it... I mean, should I have left Mikkel? Given him more respect? But I didn't. I found I was pregnant and decided to marry him. So... so, I'm wondering, did I force him into it?'

'Did you?'

'I worried about it at the time but I'm sure he wanted to marry me. He would have married me anyway, baby or no baby.' She was being defensive, could hear it in her own voice. 'He didn't hesitate, Stella.'

'So, back to my first question, what is it that's worrying you?'

'It's the same thing. Over and over again. Was it all my fault? The drinking, the way we lived our lives. Now, though, I wonder whether it started much earlier and I could have stopped it much earlier. It's like that poem where the guy gets to a fork in the road and takes the path less travelled. Well, I got to the fork and I took the well-travelled path, the path of least resistance, the one that was expected.'

'And Mikkel took that path too.'

'Yes, I guess so.'

'Willingly?'

'Yes. I'm sure of that.'

'So does it really matter how you got to that point, if, when you did, you both made a decision you were happy with, you both took the same path?'

'I suppose not.' Gennie paused. 'You're not going to ask if I'd make the same choice again, are you?'

'No,' said Stella with a smile.

'Well, I would,' said Gennie emphatically, sure in that moment that it was true. 'Ten times over.'

'And how does that realisation feel for you?'

'It feels good,' said Gennie, leaning back in her chair and relaxing, finally. 'I couldn't bear to be without Alice – and I loved Mikkel. I really did. He was exciting to be around – well, most of the time. But, you know, I guess it's time to take the other path now.'

'If you insist. But don't make it too hard for yourself, not too much of an uphill climb,' said Stella. 'Take regular breathers and stop to admire the view.'

'Yeah, whatever,' said Gennie, smiling back.

'And should we talk about Jack?'

'There's nothing to say.' Gennie shrugged. 'He drinks and that's all I need to know.'

9

December 2004

The chalet in Austria is horribly expensive but Mikkel says it isn't overpriced because it's peak season. It also has a hot tub, which is great because often the good places only have a sauna. He likes to splash the cash. His friends are the same. There's Tom, who also has a job in the City, his girlfriend, Isobel, and two other guys from work. There are twelve guests in total. The others are a family of four – a woman, her two sons and her sister. Those boys are still at school and when they're not on the slopes, they lounge on the sofas, eating cake and glued to a Game Boy Advance. Jack and Andy, the last two, are slightly older at nineteen. Andy's dad, who was in the army himself, has paid for the trip as a last gasp of freedom. The boys couldn't have afforded it by themselves. They count out coins on the table each time they have to buy a drink.

The contrast with Gennie's party couldn't be greater. Mikkel and his group are in their mid-twenties, and a year or so into careers in banking and law but already feel like they've made it. They know where they want to be in ten years' time. They order expensive wines at dinner, followed by liqueurs, and talk finance and trophy toys until the early hours. No-one else gets a look-in with the hot tub.

Jack and his friend are kids by comparison. They play football with rolled-up socks and spend their evenings hanging out with the tour reps in the bars in town or playing cards and dominoes in the chalet. Mikkel talks to them minimally. He can be like that, ruthless at seeking out people who might be useful to him and ignoring those who aren't. It's something Gennie hated until she realised how insecure he is and how much he needs the approval of people he admires. Then she feels a bit sorry for him but also flattered that he thinks her worthy of his interest. He has this thing where he turns the spotlight on you and you bask in his attention, but when his interest is elsewhere, you have to work hard to be noticed. It's tough when you're back in the shade but he's charismatic enough that, usually, people do try hard, Gennie included. She's not proud of this. Jack and Andy aren't particularly bothered by Mikkel's rudeness. Tom is nicer to them and includes them in games of pool, table football and, of course, all the drinking.

As well as sharing breakfasts, Gennie joins the boys in their evening card games – noisy rounds of racing demon, cheat and blackjack. Isobel often joins them. She shares Gennie's reluctance to squeeze into the hot tub with four semi-naked drunk men, smoking cigars and bragging.

Three days in, Mikkel tells Gennie that he and Tom have hired a guide for the day and are going with their friends to the top of the resort to ski the black runs.

'Tom thinks it's better if you and Isobel don't come,' he says.

'Why not? What am I going to do instead?' she asks.

'It's not about your skiing. You're a great skier but you'd need to keep your speed up and it's more dangerous for everyone if I keep stopping for you. You'll have more fun on the runs round here.'

Gennie's about to protest that she can make her own decisions about what's fun and what's not, but then hears Tom asking Jack and his friend if they'd like to join them. She doesn't bother to hide her smile when they shake their heads.

'We were up there yesterday,' Andy says. 'It's horrible – icy, windy, mogully.'

'See?' says Mikkel. 'I don't want you to hurt yourself.' He drops a kiss on the top of Gennie's head, and she almost forgives him.

Jack says, 'We'll ski with you, if you like.'

'Yeah, we'll be your personal guides for the day,' says Andy. 'Won't that be fun?' He puts his fist to his mouth and chews his knuckles, eyes wide with mock terror. Jack cracks up.

'What d'you think?' Gennie asks Isobel.

'Sure. Why not?'

Gennie's grateful. She wants to be the person who tells her boyfriend to enjoy his day and heads off to the lifts confidently with her friend, but the truth is the piste map makes no sense to her, and whatever Isobel says, she's just as clueless. With no-one to direct them, they're likely to stay on the nursery slopes until they get bored and head into town for an early lunch and a spot of shopping. She puts on a good show but her cover is blown when, having exited the boot room all kitted out for the day, she props her skis against the chalet wall while they wait for Isobel and takes the piste map from her jacket pocket.

'Where shall we go, then?' she says, looking at the web of red and blue lines snaking their way across snow-capped peaks.

'Where've you been so far?' Jack asks.

Gennie looks up at the mountain and back at the map again and tries to relate it to the network of lifts and slopes radiating from the town centre which she'd successfully navigated for the past few days. 'Er, where exactly are we?'

'Never mind,' says Andy, as Isobel tumbles out of the boot room. He hoists Gennie's skies and his over his shoulder and tramps off in his ski boots along the well-trodden path to the ski lift. 'Follow us. D'you like surprises?'

Jack, laughing, grabs Isobel's skis from her and scampers off after his friend. 'Come on,' he orders.

'Oh God,' says Isobel, widening her eyes at Gennie before they set off after the boys, walking in that clumsy heel-toe fashion that ski boots necessitate.

A hierarchy establishes itself. Isobel, as partner of Tom, the unchallenged head of the chalet, commands the attention of Andy, the self-proclaimed leader of the day's expedition, while Jack concentrates on Gennie.

'Show me that map again,' Jack says as they squash into the first ski lift, a gondola which takes them up the mountain to the mid-station. He unfolds the printed rectangle of A4 and smooths it against the plexiglass of the lift's window. Gennie assumes he's checking the route he's planned.

'Look,' he says, pulling off his glove and planting a forefinger on the map, slightly to the left of centre. 'We're here. And we're taking this lift up to here.' He traces the black line up to where it joins a squiggle of coloured lines. 'And then we're taking this chairlift.' More tracing. 'And then we're going there, over the back. D'you see, over there? You can just see the lift.' He points towards a distant peak.

Gennie narrows her eyes and squints in the direction of his finger.

'And to get back, you pretty much do the same in reverse. There are lifts at the bottom of every piste.'

'Aren't you taking your job a bit too seriously?' she asks.

'Making sure you'll get home safe. In case I get called away unexpectedly.'

Who does he think he is? Special ops? Gennie raises her eyebrows dismissively, but Jack's expression is sincere.

'You never know,' says Jack. 'But don't you like the way it all links up? All the runs and the lifts? And you can go over to the next valley and then come back this way.' He moves his finger along a few more coloured snakes and black ladders. 'And even better, all piste maps – at least in Europe – are the same. You can go anywhere, pick up a map and know what's going on.'

'That's kind of my problem. They all look the same.'

Jack sighs. 'Oh well.' He refolds the map carefully, handing it back to her with two hands as if it's a precious object.

'But I appreciate the effort,' Gennie says, tucking the map into her pocket and smiling at him. Mikkel wouldn't have bothered. Or his friends. If they'd stopped to point out a mountain to her, it would only have been to tell her they had shares in it.

They stop for lunch at a mountain restaurant and Gennie offers to go to the counter while the others save the table. There's no way the boys have money for food and drink – not at mountain prices and not for four of them.

'Will you manage, G?' asks Isobel. 'D'you want some help?'

'She'll be fine,' says Jack. 'Just keep the Matterhorn to your left like I said,' he tells Gennie, with a wink and a thumbs-up. 'You can't go wrong.'

Gennie knocks his head with her gloves as she swishes past. When Jack spots her on her way back, trying to negotiate the tables with a huge tray loaded with frankfurters, fries and beer, he leaps to his feet.

'You made it,' he says, faking relief as he takes the food from her. 'What do I owe you?'

'My treat,' she says. She'd contemplated wobbling a little, not so hard in ski boots, and slopping the beer, but with that one gesture, he wins her over. He's young after all.

They detour through a snow park and after they all try the speed challenge and a small jump, Gennie and Isobel stop for a drink outside a mountain cafe while the boys entertain them with ill-fated attempts at ski tricks.

'I am the Racing Demon!' yells Andy as he skies backwards down the slope before hitting a bump and doing an excellent impression of Scooby-Doo, arms and legs flailing as he tries to keep his balance while skidding towards a padded barrier.

The queues for the chairlift home are huge, a heaving mass of slowly shuffling people.

'This is a pain,' says Jack. 'I'm dying for a smoke.'

It strikes Gennie that shuffling along in large groups and waiting patiently for something to happen is a thing Jack will have to get used to.

'Can I ask you something, Jack?' she says, as they edge forward in the queue. 'Why are you joining the army? You do know there's a war on.'

'I do,' he says, with a slow nod. 'And that's not why I'm going, believe me. I guess, I dunno, it's just something I always wanted to do.' He shrugs.

'But what about your family? Aren't they worried?'

Jack smiles now. 'Okay, so, have you heard of Greenham Common? The women's peace camp?'

'Vaguely.'

'It was this big protest about American cruise missiles being based in the UK. It went on for years. Well, my mum was there, doing the sit-ins, chaining herself to fences, all that stuff. Then after she had me, she'd take me there so she could meet her friends and join in the protests.'

'You went to anti-war protests?'

'Oh, yeah. I know all the songs.' He throws his head back. 'We are the women of Greenham...' he sings in a loud enough voice to alarm the man wedged shoulder to shoulder with him on the other side.

'Ssh,' says Gennie, giggling. 'So what changed?'

'Nothing. That's the thing. There were all these women in rainbow-coloured hand knits holding hands along the barrier, and then there was me, this mad little toddler, gazing at the airmen through wire fences. I'd be sent to collect sticks for firewood and I'd make them into guns and planes. The women would sit round the campfire, singing songs and making daisy-chain crowns for my head and I'd take their matchboxes and turn them into tanks with roll-ups for gun turrets. I was hooked. The more I saw of the place, the more I wanted to be part of it all.'

'Your poor mum,' Gennie says through her laughter. 'She must have despaired.'

'And her friends! They didn't know what to do with me.

Mum thought I'd turn into a peacenik but instead I became obsessed with Land Rovers. She's still waiting for me to grow out of it. She thought doing the Cadets at school would be enough, but...' He shakes his head. 'It's honestly the only thing I could have done to upset her.'

'Oh no. Is she okay with it now?'

He shrugs again. 'S'my mum,' he says. 'We compromised on the Royal Engineers.'

They reach the front of the line, wait for the lift to come round and settle themselves on the seats.

Jack pulls his cigarettes from his pocket. 'Want one?' he says, offering Gennie the packet as he lights up.

She takes a cigarette, lights it from his and then sits, quietly smoking as they're hoisted above the slopes. She contemplates the idea of a woman with long hair, bare feet and an embroidered kaftan – because that will surely be Jack's mum – sending her son off to war, and a lump forms in her throat.

The next day, Lottie, the chalet host lays on a special dinner for New Year's Eve, the wine supplemented by several bottles of fizz supplied by the guests. Everyone, even the youngsters, is at least tipsy by the time the entire group sets off on foot through the snow to the centre of town to watch the fireworks, and a couple are already verging on tired and emotional. They join the large crowd at the foot of the slopes, abuzz with alcohol and anticipation. Gennie holds Mikkel's hand as they wait for midnight. They cheer when the first rockets go off. He's already drunk but coordinated enough to wrap his arms round Gennie, lift her off her feet and offer her a New Year's kiss. Children and dogs run around, people cheer and sing as they drink from hip flasks and embrace perfect strangers to a background of bangs and flashes. In the chaos, Gennie spots Andy in a clinch with Lottie and looks around for Jack. She picks up a trampled bit of foliage and waves it at him.

'What's up?' He walks across to her.

'Austrian mistletoe,' she says, holding the twig above their heads.

'You don't need it. It's New Year. Everyone's at it.'

'Exactly. Come on.' She closes her eyes and puckers her lips in comedic fashion.

'Okay,' he says, leaning forward and kissing her on the cheek. 'Happy New Year.'

Gennie laughs and calls him out for cowardice. There's a hand on her shoulder.

'S'all done now,' says Mikkel. 'Shall we go back and carry on the party?'

'I might stay in town for a bit,' says Jack. 'But Happy New Year.' He holds out his hand to Mikkel.

Mikkel shakes Jack's hand with his right while clasping his shoulder with his left. 'Happy New Year,' he says, beaming. 'And good luck to you. It's a great thing you're doing.'

He slaps Jack on the back a couple of times. Gennie shouldn't be surprised. One thing about Mikkel is he's not a miserable drunk, and if you're ever short of someone to share a bottle or an evening with, he's your man.

New Year's Day dawns overcast and misty, the perfect excuse for the more hung-over to delay venturing out until the weather clears. Gennie's up early but Mikkel sleeps most of the morning and she feels obliged to wait for him to surface before taking to the slopes. It's their last day of holiday and she wants to spend it with him. Come tomorrow evening they'll be back in their separate beds and separate lives with work in the morning and only laundry to look forward to. Her resentment returns in the evening when the group go into town to eat and celebrate their last evening together. As Mikkel hadn't woken until eleven, he's still fresh twelve hours later while she's exhausted and grouchy. By midnight, he's settled in at the restaurant bar with a bottle of schnapps and his friends, and Gennie is forgotten – bored, excluded from the conversation and not enough of a drinker to want to try and insert herself into the group. These are the guys he spends his working days and half his working evenings with. Does he really need to go so heavy on it tonight?

Lottie has come into town with them and Andy seems finally to be making progress with her. When they suggest going back to the chalet, Gennie and Isobel decide to go home as well.

'I'll walk back with you,' offers Jack, putting his beer glass down on the counter.

'Will you? That would be great, Jack,' says Tom, patting the younger man on the shoulder, with alcohol-fuelled bonhomie.

Jack and Gennie exchange a glance. They both know they're being patronised, but Jack's slow smile says he doesn't care. He's as glad to get out of there as she is.

They tramp off along the snowy path towards the chalet and pretty soon, Lottie and the Racing Demon fall behind. Isobel grabs a handful of snow from a wall by a hotel and forms it into a messy snowball which falls apart as soon as it hits Jack. That's a mistake as he's better both at making snowballs and hitting his targets. The girls stumble here and there in their snow boots, trying to avoid him and shushing each other's shrieks. They reach the snow-covered field beside the chalet. Jack runs across, trips and falls flat on his back.

'You okay?' asks Gennie, panting as she looks down at him.

'I'm looking at the stars,' he says.

Gennie and Isobel flop down as well. The sky is cloudy, no stars in sight.

'You must have hit your head, Jack,' says Gennie. 'No stars up there.'

Isobel giggles and chucks more snow at them. The snow is soft and fresh, and Gennie starts moving her arms and legs, sweeping through the perfect powder, creating tidy arcs.

'Oh, I'll make one too,' says Isobel, sliding her arms and legs like a complicated variation of backstroke.

'What are you doing?' asks Jack.

'Snow angels,' says Gennie, struggling to her feet. She shows him the indent in the snow – the crescent-shaped wings, triangular skirt and small hollow where her head had been.

'Sweet,' he says. He staggers off to the hedge by the side of the road. At first, Gennie thinks he's taking a comfort break and is disappointed in him, especially as they're so close to the chalet, but after rummaging round on the ground for a bit, he returns with some pinecones and bits of fir tree. He places them unevenly around the edges of the wings in decoration.

'Put some here,' says Gennie, quickly jumping into the role of artistic director.

'I need the loo,' says Isobel, and weaves her way towards the chalet entrance.

Jack kneels and places a ring of pinecones above the angel's head. 'S'posed to be a halo,' he says, and sits back on his heels to admire his handiwork.

'I see that.' Gennie sinks to her knees as well. 'Very pretty. Your mum would be proud.'

'Nah,' he says. 'Religious imagery. She's not into that. My dad might like it, though – well, Mr Aspinall, that is. He always wanted me to go to art school.'

Gennie bursts out laughing, before noticing Jack's slight frown.

'You're serious?' She shuffles forwards on her knees.

'Yes. Why's it funny?'

'It's not.' She edges forward some more until their knees are touching and then kneels up, takes his face between her gloved hands and kisses him. He doesn't move. 'I owe you from yesterday.'

'Okay.' He nods slowly.

She kisses him again. 'And this one's for luck.' She really hopes he won't need it and will survive the war unscathed to make more angels at more snowy New Years.

This time he leans forward and kisses her.

'Now we're even,' he says, and gets to his feet. 'At least I think so, I don't know how it works. We better go inside.'

10

October 2019

Gennie leaned back in her car seat and let go of her breath. It was the same whenever she thought about the past, as if her heart stopped beating and time was suspended. The past was a place that hid behind the marker formed by Mikkel's death. Time didn't exist there. It wasn't a measured progression to the present but a jumble of events wedged up against a line – the point when everything changed.

Yes, she cringed when she remembered that holiday, but she laughed too. Without Jack there at the chalet providing entertainment and company, she would have been utterly bored and miserable. She'd liked him a lot. It wasn't about making a point to her boyfriend.

Away from the mountains and back in the real world, she couldn't believe she'd been tempted to cheat. She felt mortified. No-one must ever know. Mikkel had never given her reason to doubt his loyalty and, since the day they got together, treated her like she was there for the long haul. If they were going to break up, she'd be the one to do it. She couldn't; he'd have been devastated. When, a couple of weeks later, she found she was pregnant, she was sure marrying him was the right thing; she wanted to be with Mikkel. She'd told Stella that it had been the safe thing to do, but while life with Mikkel had been comfortable for the most part, it hadn't been safe. She'd known what he was like; he never knew when to stop. Perhaps hitching her life to his was the more reckless option after all.

The wheeze of tired hinges announced the arrival of Alice and the opening of the car boot. She slung several bags in before slamming the boot shut and moving round to the passenger door.

'Hi, Mum. Can we drop Emma off? I said we could.'

'Hello to you too,' said Gennie. 'But, yes, that's no problem. Where are we dropping you, Emma?'

'Bodmin, please.'

Gennie nodded. Bodmin was certainly on their route home but was miles from the school. How long had the girls been planning this and why she was always the last to know?

11

Hamid was as good as his word and joined Gennie in the kitchen almost every day. Perhaps it was because, whilst he got on with the other young people well enough, he remained slightly outside the main group. In any case, it was to his credit, in Gennie's view, showed an instinct to stay out of trouble. He avoided the petty squabbles that flared up from time to time and coming under the influence of some of the stronger personalities at the farm, the ones with the cheeky confidence, insolent lack of respect for authority or the more worrying ones, who isolated themselves. Not that Gennie didn't enjoy the kids' company and the daily challenge of removing the graffiti and obscene doodles they'd added to her whiteboard and spotting the random room and meal changes they'd made. If she wasn't in the kitchen when the young people came in from school and college, the cupboards would be ransacked for biscuits and snacks – if she hadn't got there first and hidden them. She'd learned to leave her cigarettes in the cottage rather than in her jacket hanging up by the kitchen door or they'd disappear too. It was all part of the fun.

She watched as Hamid chopped vegetables for a casserole. 'So, why don't you like pasta?' she asked. If it was anything to do with gluten, she'd have to change his menu.

'It's too difficult,' he said.

Gennie thought of the huge catering packs of fusilli in the larder. Surely all you had to do was chuck a few handfuls in some water.

'You mean the sauce?'

'No, the pasta. With the flour and the water.' He mimed sticky hands and trying to free himself of the mess.

Gennie laughed. 'Did you do that with your foster carer?'

'No. In Iran. If you were too small to work in the factory, you had to make the food, and if it wasn't good, they got angry.'

Gennie stopped slicing peppers. 'Who? Who got angry?'

'The bosses.'

Gennie froze. What was he going to say? She had to stop before she strayed into forbidden territory.

Hamid went to the sink to wipe down his chopping board and wash his hands. The water started to run over the cuffs of his sweatshirt.

'Roll up your sleeves,' said Gennie. 'You'll get soaked.'

He hesitated.

'And your sleeves will drip in the food.'

At the moment when she realised he might have cultural reasons for covering his arms, he shrugged and pushed up his sleeves. Gennie took one look and realised she'd got it wrong again. Hamid's forearms were marked with dark diagonal scars.

'Are they burns?' she asked before she could help herself.

'Yes,' he said. He picked a long ladle out of the rack alongside the sink and showed her the handle. 'Like this,' he said. 'And sometimes this,' he said, indicating the largest of the wooden spoons.

'My God,' she breathed. 'I'm so sorry.'

'It's okay,' he said. 'I have on my legs too.' Before she could stop him, he pulled his tracksuit leg up and showed a similar scar on his left calf.

Gennie tugged opened a kitchen drawer and tucked the ladle and wooden spoon inside. He didn't need reminders.

'Hamid, if you don't like cooking because of... what happened before, I'd understand. I can speak to Marion.'

'I like cooking.'

'Really?'

'Was better than working in the marble factory,' he said simply.

'Oh,' she said, suddenly very glad that the farm existed and a little ashamed at being so wrapped up in her own issues. She'd thought she and Alice had had a rough time, but compared to some children, Alice's life had been very secure. She did a quick calculation. From what she could work out, Hamid must have spent three or four years in that hellish place. He hadn't been alone; there'd been another boy there, too.

'Did your brother come here with you?'

'No. I leave him in Iran three years ago. My uncle sent me first and he told me he will send my brother after me but I think he had no money and my brother is still there.'

They should tell Marion. Maybe there was something she could do to find him. Before Gennie could pursue the idea further, Hamid lifted a box of vegetables onto the table. He often came straight to her from the farm, carrying the daily delivery from Jack. It was convenient for both of them.

'Jack says there are two sorts of potatoes,' Hamid said as he sorted through the box. 'Red and white.'

Gennie smiled. 'Like apples. There isn't just one variety of apple, there are loads of different ones.'

'This is nothing,' said Hamid, with a dismissive wave of his hand. 'We have a lot of fruits in Afghanistan. So many type of grapes. And we have all different type of oranges, not just this sweet ones. We have oranges which are bitter and lemons which are sweet.' He lifted his chin, proudly.

'I'd like to try those,' said Gennie.

'I'll grow some,' said Hamid. He narrowed his eyes as if assessing whether to confide in her. 'I'm going to have a farm and grow fruit. I'll grow watermelons. Like at home.'

'Here?' She pointed outside at the grey light and autumnal rain.

'You don't believe me?' Hamid was indignant. 'I can use the greenhouses. Jack said. And in the spring, I will grow watermelons.'

Jack had better not be giving the boy false expectations. Hamid was only at the farm temporarily; Marion had repeatedly reminded them of that. Hamid, too. It was sad as he seemed so at home. He also got on very well with Jack, which Gennie hadn't expected. She often saw them together, working in the greenhouses or sitting on the wall chatting while Jack smoked. She wondered whether they spoke about Afghanistan and if Hamid knew Jack had been a soldier.

12

December 2004

Gennie follows Jack to the steps of the chalet. He pauses at the bottom and gestures for her to go first. She waits at the top and holds the door open for him, playing for time. Once in the hallway, she hangs up her coat with its fur-trimmed hood and tries to kick off her snow boots. She's flailing around, although she hasn't drunk much. It's her tired muscles and the late hour which are making her clumsy. She leans back against the wall of coats and sighs before bending down to have another go.

'D'you need some help?'

Gennie lifts a foot and Jack tugs at her boot and drops it on the floor. Maybe it's his nearness or the touch of his hand under her knee, but within seconds they're kissing again. It's not casual anymore.

'Are you gonna leave him?'

It's something she wonders herself. Mikkel would be different when they got back to London. He's always different when they're by themselves, but is it enough?

'It doesn't matter,' Jack says, opening the door to his room, the first on the right. He cocks his head to one side, an invitation of sorts. Gennie follows, limping in her single boot.

The room's a horrible mess, with open travel bags, socks and empty biscuit packets strewn around the floor. It also smells a little like damp dog. Jack looks at his bed and quickly dumps the pile of clothes covering it on to the floor.

'It's mostly his stuff. He's a slob,' he says.

Gennie collapses on the bed and raises her leg in its remaining boot. 'Please?'

Jack obliges, chucks the boot on the floor and flops down beside her. They lie looking at the ceiling.

'Would you like me to write to you?' she asks.

'What? Why?'

'Isn't that what people do? Write to soldiers, try to keep their minds off things.'

'I dunno. Maybe. What would you write about?'

'Oh, you know, I could tell you what's going on, what I'm up to.'

'Your life as a trainee accountant?'

'Well, yes.'

'Would you be very offended if I asked you not to?'

She giggles. 'No, not at all.'

He turns towards her, leaning on his elbow. 'And what if I don't kiss you again? Will you be very offended, then?'

Gennie stops laughing. 'Actually, yes, Jack. I will be.'

She pulls his face to hers. Kissing someone else, someone other than Mikkel, should not be this comfortable. What does it mean?

Jack's less sure of himself. He asks before he slides his hands under her clothes and before a single button is undone, but it's not long before the rest of their clothes have joined the mess on the floor and they're in his bed under the duvet. Gennie can't help thinking that if he and the Racing Demon have a bet about who would score first, and it wouldn't surprise her at all to discover they do, then Jack's about to clean up.

'You still okay?' he asks as he hovers above her. 'I mean, I hope… but we can stop if you…'

'No, no, I mean, yeah, I—' Before she can go further, there's a yelling outside and thuds as someone kicks the door.

'Jack, where are you? Open the door. What the hell are you doing in there?' a voice shouts, accompanied by giggling.

'Oh shit,' Jack says, resting his forehead on Gennie's naked shoulder. 'He's back. Sorry.'

Gennie's paralysed with fear. She thought she wouldn't care if Mikkel saw her but now she's terrified. He'll find them and kill them both. What the hell is she doing?

'What are we going to do? I need to get out of here,' she whispers.

They stare wide-eyed at each other, now trying not to laugh. It's probably nerves.

'Jack, open the door!'

'Fuck off!' Jack shouts back.

'What are you doing in there?'

'I wanted some private time!' Jack yells before whispering to Gennie, 'Look, if you go through onto our balcony, you can walk round the corner and go in the balcony door to the next room. That one's yours, isn't it?'

'Yes, I think so. Suppose it's locked?'

'Then I'll have to find a reason to sneak into the room and open the balcony door. Is your room locked?'

'I don't remember. But the key's in my coat pocket. Where are my clothes?' She slides out of bed and rifles through the heap on the floor.

'Jackass!'

'I'm coming! Hang on!' Jack yells again, nearly deafening her.

Gennie finds her T-shirt and knickers and pulls them on. 'Where are my jeans and my jumper?' she hisses, running her hands through her long hair.

'Look, just take these and your boot and get dressed outside!' Jack mouths. He shoves an armful of clothes at her, opens the sliding balcony door and pushes her outside.

It's below freezing on the balcony and the wooden slats stick to Gennie's bare feet. She tiptoes round the corner, drops the pile of jumble on the floor and frantically rummages for her belongings. With chattering teeth and hopping from one foot to the other, she puts on what are not her jeans, and something that might once have been a nice jumper, and stuffs one foot in her single boot. There's another T-shirt and three socks but no sign of her bra.

Jack, meanwhile, has shut the door and pulled the curtains. Muffled shouts and laughing can be heard from inside the room.

The balcony circles the front half of the chalet. Gennie shuffles round the corner and tries the next balcony door only to find it locked from the inside. She rattles the handle again to prove the point. So now she'll die of exposure and be found in the morning frozen to the metal. After what seems like hours but is probably only a minute, the door slides open and Jack ushers her in.

'Quick,' he says under his breath. 'He's next door with

Lottie and mighty suspicious. The others are coming back now. I can hear them on the steps.'

There's just enough time for Gennie to shrug off her boot, throw the borrowed jumper and jeans at her co-conspirator, and leap into bed before the front door crashes open and there are male voices in the hallway.

'Jack?' Her teeth are still chattering. 'Can we keep this to ourselves?'

'Course.' He smiles. 'S'long as you don't tell Andy about the snow angel.'

She holds up her hand, crooking her little finger. 'Pinkie swear.'

He hooks her finger round his own. 'Or about the pinkie swear.'

He dives out of the room and she hears him explain that he'd been getting his hat back from Gennie as he'd lent it to her for the way home. How is he so relaxed?

In the morning, they leave the chalet at six for their airport transfers. It's still dark outside and everyone is too tired, hung-over or not sobered up enough to be coherent. They swap goodbye hugs. Gennie saves Jack for last.

'Look after yourself,' she says, unable to meet his eyes. She hopes he will.

Her next hope is that, if Jack has come across her missing underwear, he finds some rational explanation for it.

13

Gennie had a prime view of the yard while she sorted the unclaimed clothing from the laundry. The kitchen window, while it was at the back of the farm, was the best spot to keep an eye on all the comings and goings. No-one used the front door. Anyone coming to the front must be visiting in an official capacity.

'Flush the stash,' Marion would call whenever the doorbell rang.

She must have decided to go ahead with the new building project because there was Jack at the far end of the yard, demolishing the barns with the help of two labourers Gennie hadn't seen before. They created plenty of noise and dust with their power tools and bulldozer, but from Gennie's perfect lookout point, progress looked slow. Time wasn't on their side either now the days were getting shorter and the weather colder.

Occasionally Jack broke off to chat to the others or walk to the other side of the yard to fetch something. Gennie watched, the oh-so-casual observer, minding her business as she moved from sorting socks to peeling vegetables. She could see the difference in him now. Not in his appearance, that hadn't changed very much. He walked in the same way, upright and square-shouldered, and he moved as energetically as his younger self, but his energy had a restless quality now, fractured even. When he'd set off for a run the previous day, teeth gritted, fists clenched, his intensity was unnerving. He rarely stopped working, other than to lean against the wall to roll a cigarette and maybe share a joke with someone passing. He tried hard, she had to give him that. In fact, she'd probably never seen anyone try so hard. The only time she'd seen him sit still was when he modelled for Max's art class, but even then, he'd been tense, every muscle strained.

All those plans she'd made to avoid interacting with Jack, the jobs that needed urgent attention and last-minute trips to the village... She needn't have bothered. He spent very little time in the farmhouse, at least not when Gennie was there, seemingly coming in only to sleep and eat, and even then, he kept to himself. She was hypervigilant to his movements and yet, she had almost nothing to do with him. When, a couple of days after his return, Jack came into the kitchen and found himself surrounded by the youth of the house, back from college and pushing each other out of the way to grab a seat at the table and a piece of cake, he took one look and left. Another time, he left it half an hour before slipping in to make a cup of tea. By then, the youngsters had quietened down and were playing games as they munched their tea-time toast. They often dragged Gennie into a card game with them and, spotting Jack, demanded he joined them too. Gennie quietly left the table and went into the utility room, but when she came back to the kitchen, Jack had gone.

'No Jack?' she said, trying not to appear interested.

'Said he didn't have time,' said one of the boys, barely looking up from his game.

Jack smiled or waved when he glimpsed her at the kitchen window, but their contact was limited enough for her to wonder if he might be avoiding her too. He couldn't be spending that much time surfing and nor was he with his daughter. Millie only came by at weekends. Gennie wasn't disappointed exactly; she simply wanted to know if she could let her guard down and if it was safe to relax.

Jack appeared to be a model of good virtues. He worked hard and lived quietly. Could it be he didn't deserve his reputation for being difficult? Unless all the bad behaviour happened after dark – and that would not surprise her – but if something was going to happen, she'd prefer it was sooner rather than later, while she was still prepared.

In the meantime, if he was skipping mealtimes and bypassing the kitchen in general, there was a risk he'd starve. He couldn't rely on there being leftovers if he sneaked into the kitchen after hours; the kids had healthy appetites and all portable snacks were locked away if Gennie wasn't around. She started putting something by for him in a plastic tub in the fridge. He wasn't getting special treatment; she'd do the same for anyone who missed dinner. It was in her interest; she wouldn't want him rustling something up in the middle of the night, leaving a mess for her to clear up, or worse, using all the ingredients for meals she'd planned and carefully budgeted for.

He ate what she left for him. The empty containers were in the dishwasher in the morning and there was no evidence the contents had been binned. She'd checked.

14

It was a surprise when Jack turned up for dinner on Tuesday evening.

'Is there enough?' he said.

'Sure,' she said, and set another place at the table.

'Thought I might go to Max's class,' he said. 'D'you want a lift?'

That Jack would be at painting class was less of a shock. Gennie had spotted him sneaking into the back of the art room a couple of weeks before. She'd frozen, pencil hovering over her paper, fully expecting him to slip behind the screen, strip off and take the place of the model. What should she do? Carry on regardless, or make her excuses and leave? Could she claim this as her space or was it his? She watched as he helped himself to an easel while Max, barely interrupting his instruction to the class, taped paper to a board for him and handed him some sticks of charcoal. He must be a regular. At break time, she'd circled through the easels on her way to the canteen, taking a moment, as instructed by Max, to admire the others' work. She waited until Jack left the room and then took a peek at his easel. He drew fluidly with broad strokes – all shape and shade and no fussy detail. It was so much better than her effort, which was irritating, especially when he didn't seem to take it at all seriously. He didn't even keep his drawings but left them with Max at the end of the class.

'Are you modelling?' she asked warily.

'No, I'm drawing. I'll warn you if I'm sitting. Max did that on purpose. He's such a wanker.'

Gennie wasn't sure what exactly Max had done on purpose other than create a little amusement for himself, but she let it pass. 'D'you draw a lot then?'

'Not consistently.'

'But you've been going to Max's classes for a while?'

'Off and on. More off than on to be honest.'

She handed him a pile of plates and he obliged by placing them round the table.

'It's just,' she said, lifting dishes from the range and onto the table, 'you and Max seem very, you know, tight.'

'Oh right, I see. No, I know Max from school. We did art together and then, you know, Max went off to art school and I joined the army. With Andy.'

Andy, the racing demon. Where was he now? And why did Jack expect her to know who he was? She hadn't given herself away, had she?

'Did you grow up down here? I thought you lived in Canterbury,' she asked, nearly doing it that time – although Jack didn't seem to notice.

'I did. Marion bought the farm when I left school. I didn't move down 'til I left the army, although Andy and I came here on leave, obviously. Max moved here about ten years ago, after he finished teacher training. He doesn't teach at the school anymore so you don't need to worry about the children's well-being,' he added with mock concern. 'He seems to be making a decent living from all the college classes and his own work.'

'But he's done a few classes here,' she said. 'The kids all love him.'

'He does that for free as a favour to my mum. Don't tell him I told you, though. He wouldn't want anyone to think he's a soft touch.' Jack smiled. 'I sit for him in return. My mum used to model for him too, years ago. When we were still at school. One of his final exam pieces was an abstract of my mum.'

Jack laughed at Gennie's raised eyebrows.

'The trouble with having Marion for a mother is you're expected to be as open-minded as she is and it isn't always easy.'

'So you could've gone to art school?' she said, suddenly transported to a midnight conversation in a snowy field.

'Maybe,' he said, 'but I went in a different direction. As they say.'

'Sure,' Gennie said, backing away, as the door to the yard opened and the teenagers streamed in. 'Look, thanks, but I'll cycle in, I need the exercise. All those puddings.' She patted her stomach and immediately wondered why.

*

She accepted the offer of a lift back; cycling home on a damp November night had lost its appeal. She hadn't checked in with Jack during the class. This was her time, to do with what she wanted. All her tensions and anxiety went onto the page. The results weren't perfect, a little heavy-handed in her view, but by the end of the class, she felt differently – simultaneously drained and revived, better able to embrace her new reality.

Jack slung her bike in the back of his Land Rover while she settled herself in the passenger seat. He winced as he climbed back into the car.

'You okay?' she asked. Was this some kind of performative thing to point out that he was a war hero and she needed to pay proper deference?

'Ingrowing toenail. Spend too much time in boots.' He grimaced.

'Oh. Sorry, I thought… Does your leg still hurt?' She had to ask, might as well.

'Not really. Swells up sometimes. Aches a bit. But it's fine.'

He wasn't engaging, concentrating instead on his driving. Time to change the subject, think of something else to talk about.

'Have you seen Hamid's scars? On his arms and legs?' Why were these the only thoughts popping into her mind?

Jack flashed her a look. 'On his legs too?'

'Yeah. I know we're not supposed to discuss the kids but I thought he might have told you because, well…' Because you've got scars too, she didn't say.

'No, I only saw his arms by chance. I didn't say anything. Didn't know whether it was self-harm or inflicted by someone else.'

'He's been beaten and burnt. With metal spoons,' said Gennie slowly.

'Jesus.' Jack sighed. 'Kids have a crap time.'

He said nothing else until they reached home and he swerved violently into the drive. There was a crunch of gravel as he braked sharply behind the farmhouse. He took a deep breath.

'D'you know, my lot had left Afghanistan by the time his dad was killed. But it's good to know what a grand fucking job we made of improving people's lives.'

He slammed the door of the Land Rover as he got out and went to the back of the car. Gennie shrank as she went to take her bicycle from him. She'd been clumsy and now he was angry and she had no idea how to deal with it. It was pointless telling him it wasn't his fault or his responsibility, he'd just been doing his job and Hamid's life would be better now and so on. He had the same fierce look as when she'd spotted him charging out of the yard in his running shoes.

She settled for the inadequate, 'Thanks for the lift, Jack. Should I give you money for petrol?'

It made him laugh, not genuinely amused, but it broke the tension, nonetheless.

'No, of course not. But you can give me a fag for later.'

She offered him the packet, still in its cellophane.

'Ah no,' he said, waving the packet away.

'It's fine,' she said, peeling away the wrapper and pulling out the foil. 'I thought you only smoked roll-ups.'

'I'll smoke anything,' he admitted, taking the packet from her and helping himself. 'I'm smoking roll-ups to cut down.'

'I'm not sure it's working that well.'

She rarely saw him without a cigarette.

'It isn't working at all,' he said, wasting no time in flicking open an old petrol lighter, lighting up and inhaling. He smiled when she laughed, relieved the storm appeared to have passed.

She left him leaning on the back of the Land Rover and, rather than go straight into her dark and silent cottage, went into the main kitchen to make tea. Marion was there with Alex, lead social worker and second in command at the project, poring over the accounts. They looked up expectantly.

'I may have inadvertently upset Jack,' she told them, wrinkling her nose.

'Yes, well,' said Alex, smiling over his glasses. 'It's easily done. I wouldn't worry about it. Come and look at this instead.'

Gennie took her tea to the table and sat down heavily. Her eyelids were drooping too. 'What is it?'

'A proposal,' said Marion, pointing at the sheets of paper on the table. 'It's Jack's idea. Offering future entrepreneurs a two-year apprenticeship in farming and running a start-up. It will be practical, on-the-job training. We can also develop the same programme in building, carpentry and plastering because Jack has the necessary skills for that. It would be perfect for someone like Hamid, for example. He's been moved around so much, he's never going to catch up on the volume of education he's missed, but he could run a small business.'

That must be what Hamid had meant when he spoke about his fruit farm, and judging by Marion's expression – the lift of the eyebrows and the nod of the head – he wasn't the only one who was keen.

'Is that what the new building's for?' Gennie asked.

'Yes, semi-independent accommodation. We've still got a couple of planning issues but I'm sure that will resolve itself.'

She wrinkled her nose as she smiled. 'So, darling, what d'you think? Will you help me with all the numbers? First, we have to sell it to the trustees and then we need to apply for grants for the staffing, tuition and upkeep of the students. We could never charge students the true cost of the programme so we'll have to underwrite it in some way.'

'Of course,' said Gennie, pulling the pages towards her to get a better look but the figures were dancing about on the page. 'You know, you might be able to persuade industry to sponsor your building apprenticeship.'

Marion beamed at her.

'There,' said Alex. 'I knew she didn't hire you just for your cooking.'

Gennie would have asked what was wrong with her cooking but she was too tired, their smiles were kindly and it didn't matter.

15

It was the sort of day which barely grew light. By mid-morning, the sky was still a heavy grey and the rain lashed down. Gennie stared as fat drops of water splashed into the sand-coloured puddles that had formed in all the hollows of the yard and was glad she was indoors in the bright cosiness of the kitchen, radio on and apple pie in the range. Jack and the labourers were hanging around the barns sheltering from the wet. Their hunched shoulders and drooping heads said it all. The building work was already behind schedule and this would not help.

Jack crashed in through the kitchen door at lunchtime, headed for the fridge, grabbed his Tupperware box of leftovers and slammed it in the microwave to reheat.

Gennie stood at the ironing board pressing the bedlinen and surveyed him warily. The kitchen had been nicely warm until he'd arrived and propped the door open while he took off his boots. As soon as the microwave pinged, he took the plastic box and a fork and slumped in the corner armchair, still in his wet coat. He still hadn't spoken. Gennie decided against offering him a plate; he looked wired to explode. She waited until he'd finished eating.

'Tea?'

'Er, no, it's okay, thanks, I'll get my own,' he said haltingly, as if he was bumping up against every word. 'Actually yes, I would like some. If you're making some.'

Gennie moved towards the kettle as he threw the plastic tub on the table, making her jump.

'I'm sorry,' he said through gritted teeth. 'I'm so fucking angry. Those bloody idiots didn't cover the materials last night and everything is waterlogged and we can't use it. I've covered it all now but we'll have to wait until it is pretty much dried out before we can carry on. Because of that, I can't fucking do anything today, even if we put a tarpaulin over the site.'

He was rigid with tension, his breathing shallow and looking as if the prospect of inactivity terrified him. Gennie was glad the ironing board was still between them, though she suspected he was more of a danger to himself than to her. He was in that bad a state that if he'd been anyone else, she might have offered him a brandy, or suggested he call a friend so he wouldn't be alone. But Marion was out and Alex was doing key work. She was on her own.

'Well,' she said gently, prepared for the brush-off, hoping if nothing else to make him smile, 'if you're looking for something to do, you can help me if you like. I've got ten kilos of potatoes to peel and there are twenty sets of sheets to iron. Which do you want? You could take the ironing board in the sitting room and watch the telly. That's what I usually do – sneak a look at programmes I'd never admit to watching. No-one will ever know.'

Jack stared at her as if she'd gone mad. 'I'll do the ironing, but I'm not watching *Loose Women*.'

'I was thinking more *Selling Sunset*,' she said.

He scowled and got to his feet. 'Move over,' he said. He hung his coat by the door, rolled up his sleeves and hefted the plastic baskets of laundry onto the table. 'Nice lasagne, by the way.'

Gennie busied herself at the counter, making vegetable bake and chocolate sponge from her collection of comfortingly stodgy recipes, and watching Jack from the corner of her eye. He ironed ferociously, headphones jammed in his ears, unlit cigarette dangling from the corner of his mouth, but he'd clearly been taught to iron in a crease and he was doing a very good job. She knew he'd started to relax when the odd bursts of tuneless singing became more frequent.

When Marion came in for her camomile tea, she looked from one to the other, dressed almost identically in their flannel checked shirts and jeans, and asked Gennie if she'd had to clone herself.

'You will tell me if you have too much to do, won't you, darling?' she said.

By the evening, the rain was still too heavy for Gennie to cycle to Wadebridge, and when Jack offered her a lift to art class, she accepted. There was no reason to refuse. It would have been ridiculous to take two cars, especially when they'd spent the afternoon in each other's company.

The way he drove took more getting used to. He careered around the country roads like a person used to driving armoured vehicles over difficult terrain, paying no heed to dips or bumps in the road – which was what he was, she reminded herself.

Max offered the usual drink after the class and Gennie held her breath. Today would be a prime day to fall off the wagon.

'Not for me,' said Jack. He turned to Gennie. 'Unless you want to go?'

She shook her head emphatically, exhaling surreptitiously. However nice a gin and tonic would be after a day like this, she wouldn't be an enabler.

'Can you believe it's only four weeks to Christmas?' she asked as they raced round another hairpin bend, wondering whether she'd be lucky enough to survive until then.

Jack grunted noncommittally and then, as if remembering how to make small talk, said, 'Er, yes. D'you have plans?'

'Alice finishes school in two weeks,' Gennie said, talking rapidly to curb her anxiety. 'I'm not sure what we'll do. I'd like to go to France to see my parents and Marion has said I can take time off before Christmas if it's cheaper then. I haven't looked into it properly, I don't seem capable of making plans,' she admitted. 'D'you have to share your daughter with your ex-wife over Christmas?'

'What?' Jack looked confused. 'Oh, no, my ex-wife isn't Millie's mother. Claire is Millie's mother. We were never married.'

'Oh, I'm sorry. I haven't really got the hang of who's who yet.' Gennie shrank back in her seat, embarrassment hidden in the darkness of the car.

'I can't believe you haven't heard the story. This is a village after all. What've you been doing? Everyone knows everything here or at least thinks they do.'

Jack smiled but there was that touch of bitterness that characterised his speech nowadays.

'I don't want to pry,' Gennie said carefully, 'but can you fill me in a bit so I don't put my foot in it again?'

'You haven't put your foot in it,' he said, and this time the smile was genuine, more like the Jack she remembered. 'So, Claire was Andy's wife and Andy was my best mate. They met each other when we came down here on leave. She's from Bodmin and still lives there with Millie. My wife lived near the base in Kent. We got married just before we deployed to Afghanistan, you know, some kind of mad romantic crap,' he said. His smile faded. 'Andy had already been married about a year by then.'

At first Gennie thought that he was heading to a confession that he'd run off with his best friend's wife but then, with a searing flash of horror and pain, realised he was going to tell her Andy was dead. How could she have been so insensitive, and, yet again, failed to understand any of what had been put in front of her? It was obvious that Andy was the friend who'd been killed – and the reason Jack had unravelled. Andy. So young, so full of laugher and life. He could only have been in his early twenties. She covered her face with her hand to prevent any noise escaping.

Jack didn't seem to have noticed her reaction, too busy concentrating on the road. He continued his story as if on autopilot.

'Well, Andy's killed very soon after we're posted. And it's very hard for Claire because she'd wanted him to leave the army. We'd been thinking about submitting our notice but then there were new operations in Afghanistan and we decided to stay in for a bit. After all, we'd got through Iraq and it was the same guys going out again. It was all so random. He'd been on ordnance clearance for months, really dangerous stuff, and then one roadside bomb and it's all over.' He shook his head. 'So, I'm on leave and spend a lot of time with Claire. My wife doesn't like it, especially not when Claire falls pregnant.' He took a sharp breath. 'And then I transferred regiment to one in Germany before I deployed again. I was glad to be away… I couldn't stand to be here, to be honest. I was a bit out of control, drinking and so on. Probably shouldn't have been trusted with a gun in my hand.' He laughed humourlessly.

They arrived back at the farm and Jack parked and turned off the engine. Neither of them moved to leave the vehicle. He turned and she saw the blank look in his eyes.

'Why am I telling you all this?' He shook his head. 'Oh yes, I'll pick Millie up the day before Christmas Eve and have her until Christmas morning.'

Gennie couldn't think of anything sensible to say and had such a lump in her throat it hurt. She handed him her cigarette packet and then reached with her right hand to touch his arm.

'That's, erm, that's… Thank you for telling me…'

He looked in the packet and took a couple of cigarettes out. 'You haven't smoked any.'

'No, I'm, er… emergencies only,' she said, opening the car door. 'Thank you for the lift… and er, thanks for the ironing.'

'No problem, see you tomorrow,' he said bleakly.

Gennie stumbled out of the Land Rover and, avoiding her cottage, went into the farm kitchen where Alex was sitting at the table once more, completing reports. She poured a glass of water and sipped at it, keeping her back to him until she'd recovered herself sufficiently to speak.

'Are you okay? You look a bit… burdened.'

'Yeah,' she said flatly. 'I was talking to Jack. About Millie. And Andy and Claire. It all seems so sad and such a mess.'

Alex patted the table next to him and Gennie slumped into one of the kitchen chairs.

'It's less of a mess than it was,' he said matter-of-factly. 'Two years ago, Jack and Claire couldn't manage a civil conversation and she was applying for a court order to prevent him seeing Millie.'

'Oh God, that's awful. Where's his wife now, then? It can't have been much fun for her, either.'

Alex thought for a moment. He'd been indiscreet and was probably trying to decide if his duty of confidentiality extended to Jack.

'Erm, yeah, Emma. Nice girl. From what I understand, she divorced him when she found out about Claire. They were married for barely two years. It became quite bitter.' He winced, suggesting it was an understatement. 'I don't imagine they have any contact now, though I suppose Marion might keep in touch with her.'

'And did Claire and Jack get together then?' Gennie asked. She might as well find out as much as Alex was prepared to tell. She'd swear he shuddered.

'When Millie was tiny, Jack was based in Germany and back and forth from overseas postings and deployments, so Claire was often on her own. Even when he was around, Jack wasn't always easy. Marion helped as much as she could and I've even done a couple of all-nighters, walking Millie up and down the hall when she was teething.' He smiled over his glasses at her. 'When Jack got his release and came back here, he really tried to make it work with Claire – and not just for

Millie, who by then was about two years old. It was a disaster. They both thought they loved Andy more than they loved each other and were only there because of him. Personally, I don't think that's true but there was too much pain and they ripped each other apart. Jack was drinking, of course, and it got very nasty, especially after he was banned from driving.'

'They get on all right now?' Gennie said, looking for some positives.

'Let's just say Marion's had to do a fair amount of mediation. There's still conflict almost every time they meet. Thing is, Claire's now made the break and has a new partner. That was the main reason Jack went to Africa. He wanted to be out of the way while Nick moved in.' He paused again. 'On the plus side, though, he was working on projects for war and AIDS orphans while he was there and researched their small business and entrepreneurship models. He came back with a lot of good ideas.'

The tears were pricking the back of Gennie's eyes and by the time she made it into her cottage, she could no longer stem the flow. If there was a plus side to the story, she couldn't see it yet. Look at them all! They'd started out with such promise. So much loss, so many damaged people and disrupted lives. She curled on her sofa, hugging her knees and gulping, bent double by the ache beneath her ribs, a hurt dug in too deep for her to reach or soothe. This wasn't grief only for Andy and Mikkel but also for Jack and Claire, and the lost childhoods of Alice and Millie. She pulled a blanket around herself.

She woke in the early hours, freezing cold and with a stiff neck. She crawled upstairs and slid fully clothed into her bed. Reality had invaded her safe haven. Perhaps the protective bubble of Hope House was not a shield while she recovered and rebuilt her resources but more like a preserving jar for her sorrow, a trap, preventing her moving forward. She'd call her mother in the morning and arrange to take Alice to France the second she finished school.

16

The windows were covered in paper snowflakes and stars but also suns, moons and mosaic-decorated elephants. Marion had decreed that all Christmas celebrations must be specific but in a non-denominational way. No-one really understood. For Gennie, that meant turkey and nut roast and anything else anyone insisted was traditional and could make a case for. In the meantime, she kept knocking her head against the paper chains suspended between the kitchen lights.

She couldn't be the only one scared of Christmas, or perhaps not scared exactly, but she certainly didn't trust it. Not that it wouldn't live up to expectations, it was more that just as you thought you'd made it through, it would chuck something else at you. Last year had been the first without Mikkel, a low point but at least it was predictable. The few before sounded like bad episodes of *Friends*: the one where Mikkel fell and cracked his head on the kerb and spent Christmas in A&E getting glued back together; the one where he disappeared on Boxing Day; the one where he missed the plane; the one he spent wired up to a drip.

When she was young, she'd looked forward to Christmas with the same crazy excitement as the young group at Hope House, wishing it would go on forever rather than thanking God when it was all over. She wanted the same for Alice. Maybe they'd get that this year; it was looking good so far. They'd returned from France the day before, after a week of sleep and soul-warming meals cooked by Gennie's mother, sunshine food full of aubergines and peppers. Now she was back in the kitchen stuffing chickens with clumps of sage and onion in a break between Christmas baking workshops. The morning's sausage rolls – vegan and meat versions, as baked by Sam, Charley and Joseph – were cooling on trays on the table. She checked her whiteboard. It would be Kerry, Hamid and Chantelle making mince pies with her in the afternoon.

The phone was ringing in the main office. Hopefully it was nothing urgent as Gennie's hands were covered in sticky green crumbs and she'd struggle to reach it in time. The house was ready for last-minute referrals. They had room as some of the young people had gone to family for Christmas and, as Marion had pointed out and as if Gennie needed reminding, relationships tended to fracture at this time of year. She washed her hands as best she could and rushed to the doorway, slamming into Jack, who was coming in the other direction holding the telephone.

'It's for Genevieve Beck. Is that you? Are you Genevieve?' He studied her, eyes narrowed. 'I've only ever met one Genevieve before.'

Gennie nodded, gesturing that her hands were still wet and slightly sticky and that he should tuck the phone under her chin while she dried them on a tea towel. He carried on talking.

'Oh my God, it is you. You're G! I knew I'd seen you somewhere, but I was kind of scared to ask. I didn't track back far enough.'

While he ranted on, Gennie moved to the side to listen to the caller, who was telling her that they'd found the bag she'd lost on the flight back from Lyon and would send it on to her if she could post them her baggage claim stub.

'I thought it was Jenny, short for Jennifer, but of course it's Genevieve. I should've realised, what with the French mother and the growing up in Cornwall. Oh my word, G, we have unfinished business here!' He paced up and down in front of her.

Gennie disconnected the call. 'Can you stop inspecting me? I'm not on parade.'

He wagged his finger and tutted. 'You're different, though. It's not just the name. Your hair was long, wasn't it? I've remembered that right, yeah? And I'm sure it was dark, and now it's...' He gestured to her bleached-blonde crop. 'What happened? Rapunzel had enough of all the hangers-on?'

'Something like that, yes.' She laughed wryly. It was the hair event that started her family nagging about counselling. They'd had a point.

'And you're more... er...' He made round shapes with his hand.

'Fatter?'

'No, no, not fatter, more erm... More erm...?'

She raised her eyebrows.

'Well, maybe, but you look good with it... You sound the same, though. I can't believe I couldn't place you...'

He laughed and Gennie had the feeling it was for the same reasons the memory made her laugh. Everything that happened had been ridiculous, especially compared to what happened later.

'Oh yes, G, we definitely have unfinished business. Did you recognise me?'

She nodded slowly.

'Why didn't you say?'

'Oh, you know,' she said, with the slightest shrug. 'It wasn't that big a deal.' And she hadn't wanted to find out he'd forgotten her. 'And anyway,' she continued, 'isn't that the thing with traumatic memories? You shouldn't prompt them but let them come to the surface when they're ready.'

'Don't mock!' He looked at her again and shook his head, his expression some kind of wonderment. 'Fuck. That was so long ago. Well, you know, good to see you again.'

'You too.' Gennie smiled at him and received the full Jack Aspinall light-up-your-day version in return, the first real signs of the old Jack. Something to store for when she needed a reminder she'd once been young. She felt a bit dizzy.

'And anytime you want a bit of company, let me know,' he said, and just like that, she was over him again.

'Fuck off,' she mouthed.

Jack laughed and pointed to the sausage rolls on the table. She nodded, signalling for him to help himself. He took a couple and winked at her as he headed to the door.

'Jack.' She took a deep breath. 'I'm really sorry about Andy. I didn't know until you told me.'

Jack turned back and nodded. 'It's okay.' He paused. 'And... your husband? Did you marry that whatsit Mikkel?'

Gennie nodded. ''Fraid so.'

'Well, I'm sorry for your loss too. For your sake, and Alice's,' he said, sincerely. 'But you have to admit...'

'What? That he was clever and exciting and funny and generous?' Who was Jack to criticise Mikkel?

'Maybe, but the rest of the time he was an arsehole.' He shoved a whole sausage roll in his mouth and left the kitchen.

She laughed and then checked herself, but when she thought about it, it was fine because it was Jack she was laughing at. He might have been raised in a liberal and supportive environment, full of empathy and inclusion, but he was still too alpha to tolerate even the ghost of a similar beast in his vicinity.

17

When Hamid came back to the farm alone, Gennie didn't want to assume he and Jack had fallen out.

'How was the Christmas shopping?' she asked, brightly.

'Why Jack doesn't let me drive the Land Rover? Why I have to get the bus?'

Was that it? Was he sulking because Jack wouldn't let him drive back to the farm on his provisional licence?

'Is everything okay?'

Hamid shook his head, a refusal to speak rather than a denial.

Gennie left him at the kitchen table with a glass of water and went to get Alex. He sucked his teeth when he saw Hamid.

'Where's Jack?'

'In Bodmin. He wanted to go on his own.'

'Is Jack allowed to leave him like that?' Gennie whispered to Alex as he left the room to find Marion.

'There are actually more rules about taking him in the car than putting him on the bus,' said Alex over his shoulder.

'He'll be back in his own time,' said Marion, calmly, although the way she patted Alex's arm suggested otherwise.

Gennie went back to her Christmas catering plan and marked off the things that had arrived. The list didn't seem to be getting any shorter. Strictly speaking, she wasn't required to work on Christmas Day, but if she and Alice were spending the holiday at the house, it was obvious who'd be cooking. She was looking forward to it. It would be her first time in sole charge of the feast; usually she played commis chef to her mum, and had to present all vegetables, sauces and appetisers for inspection before they were passed fit for the table. She picked up her phone, intending to call the butcher about the turkey, but the handset rang before she could dial.

'Hello there, is that Gennie?' said a masculine voice.

'Yes. Who's that?'

'It's Dr Woodburn. It's...'

Not Jack, she thought, squeezing her eyes shut.

'It's about Mrs Perryn.'

'Mrs Perryn?' Gennie couldn't place her for a moment. 'Jan? Is everything okay?'

'I'm with her now. The ambulance is here too. I'm recommending she goes to hospital but she's, how shall I put this, reluctant to leave her dog. Is there any chance you could...?'

'Of course,' said Gennie, without thinking. She should have run it by Marion first. 'How long d'you think she'll be in for?'

'Difficult to say. How soon could you get here?'

'On my way,' she said, pulling on her wellingtons and lifting her coat from the hook by the door.

Gennie could see the flashing blue lights outside Jan's cottage as soon as she turned out of the lane. She picked up her pace. When she arrived at the cottage, Jan was already wrapped in a red blanket and strapped to a gurney. Paramedics in green uniforms were lifting her into the ambulance. She looked dreadful, her face colourless and drawn with pain and anxiety.

'I've told them I can't go,' she told Gennie. 'And I won't.'

'And I've told her she can and she should,' said a man standing by a car. The illuminated sign saying 'Doctor' gave away his identity.

'You absolutely can,' said Gennie, mustering what she hoped was a reassuring smile and giving Jan's hand a quick squeeze. 'Don't worry about Roxy, she'll be fine with me. You concentrate on getting better.'

'Will you lock up?' said Dr Woodburn, handing Gennie a set of keys. 'I've packed the dog's stuff for you.' He pointed at the two large plastic bags by the front door.

'Let me know if you need anything,' Gennie called, as the doors of the ambulance closed.

She turned to speak to the doctor but he was already in his car. No doubt someone would fill her in at some point. She waited for Jan to leave before walking Roxy slowly back up to the farm. Another refugee for Hope House.

18

Jack reappeared at eleven o'clock the following morning. He staggered through the back door of the kitchen, threw off one boot and fell into the armchair in the corner. Gennie had had too much to do since the previous evening to worry about whether or not he'd returned, but given the state he was in, she would certainly have noticed if this creature had turned up, resembling something that had risen from a swamp in a bad horror film. He was drunk, of course, as drunk as she'd ever seen anyone – and she'd lived her entire married life with an alcoholic. He couldn't focus, couldn't speak, and he had cuts on his cheek and above his eye. Worse still was the smell. His olive-green coat was covered in vomit stains.

'Oh, Jesus,' she said, briefly so shocked that she couldn't move, or even breathe. What had he done to himself? She couldn't bear to look; the sight and stench of him made her retch. But he wasn't her responsibility. It felt like a load had been lifted from her shoulders. All she had to do was get him out of the kitchen before anyone else saw him. If the residents reported this, they'd have social services ringing at the front door.

'Stay there,' she ordered, and ran up the stairs to find Marion.

Marion limped down as fast as she could and the two women stared at Jack, who raised his hand in greeting.

'Hi, Mum,' he managed, head rolling on his neck.

How did Marion stay so calm? All Gennie wanted was to fill a bucket with cold water and chuck it over the monster stinking out her kitchen and sweep him into the yard with the rest of the rubbish. How could he do this? And so close to Christmas. She'd started to hope he was something different, but she'd been naïve. It turned out he was exactly what everyone said he was.

'What d'you want to do with him?' she asked. 'Shall we try and clean him up or just put him to bed?'

'Put him to bed, I think,' said Marion. 'He can clean himself up. Fuck knows what's gone on here. Can you help me get him upstairs? And then I'll have to phone Claire. He can't go and get Millie like this. Maybe we can put it off until tomorrow.'

Millie would be waiting! Gennie forced her mind to stay in the present and not rebound to a past of hurts and disappointments. Alice would have been around the same age as Millie when Mikkel became seriously ill and his behaviour utterly erratic. Before then, he'd been only charmingly unreliable. Gennie lost count of the number of birthday parties, nativity plays, dance shows and parents' evenings Mikkel had missed because he was held up somewhere, but Gennie had always been there to cover the cracks, finding explanations for her husband, who she knew had gone out with clients or had to make up time at work because of a lengthy boozy lunch.

'I hate this, Marion,' she blurted. 'Poor Millie! Drunks are so selfish. I know he's your son but this is a shitty thing to do. I don't get it. He was really looking forward to it – and so was she.'

'Look, I think something must have happened,' Marion said as she persuaded Jack to his feet. 'He knew he was going to do this. That's why he made sure Hamid got home.'

It was no excuse, Gennie thought as they dragged and pushed Jack up the stairs between them, but she'd help Marion, if only for the children's sake. They got him into his room and had removed his coat and other shoe when he leaned over suddenly. Gennie reached instinctively for the waste bin and her fears were confirmed when he duly vomited into it. There was no time to react before he turned and was sick on the floor as well as his bed.

Oh, good God. Gennie surveyed the devastation. Jack, you are truly disgusting.

'Jack, darling,' said Marion, her tones still soothing. She looked at Gennie, hands on hips. 'What the fuck are we going to do now? We'll have to put him in my bed.'

'Yeah, okay,' said Gennie, 'but I don't want to touch him.'

He was covered in puke and the smell was making her retch again. Maybe if they just held him up by his arms?

'We'll have to take his clothes off here. You'll help me, won't you? At least you've seen it all before.'

They peeled off his clothes between them, each one propping him up as they took off another layer. Gennie left the trousers to his mother. While he swayed before them in his underwear, eyes closed, mumbling something about souls and souljas, Gennie fetched a damp towel and flannel from Marion's bathroom. They sponged him down before coaxing him along the corridor to Marion's room. The ease with which Marion manoeuvred Jack into the recovery position, arranging his limbs and propping pillows behind his back, confirmed it was something she'd done before. As they closed the door, Gennie caught sight of the photo on Marion's dresser, a black-and-white studio portrait of a smiling baby, unmistakeably Jack, wrapped in Marion's arms. Poor Marion, still cradling him, still protecting him.

Marion went downstairs to try and reach Claire, who wasn't answering her mobile, while Gennie got on with cleaning Jack's room. She'd throw out the rug – if she could find a way of hauling it down the stairs without covering herself and the landing in vomit and Jack, when he came to, would have to sleep on Millie's floor for the next night or two. His own room would not be usable by anyone with an active sense of smell.

'Are you going to get Millie?' asked Gennie when Marion reappeared.

'I'll need to speak to Claire first,' said Marion, phone in hand.

'Oh,' said Gennie, struck suddenly by the notion that this might not be entirely Jack's fault. 'D'you think they've said he can't have Millie for Christmas?'

Marion was tight-lipped but her expression suggested she was thinking the same.

'Is Jack back?'

The women jumped as Hamid appeared behind them on the landing. They ushered him away, insisting that Jack was very tired and needed to sleep, but he kept slipping past them.

'I need my things. The shopping's in the Land Rover. Can I have the keys?'

'Oh God, where's the Land Rover? He couldn't have driven it, could he?' Marion looked from one to the other.

The three of them raced back down to the yard, where there was no sign of the vehicle.

Marion turned to Hamid. 'Now then, do you remember the last time you saw the car? D'you know where Jack was going?'

Hamid looked scared. It wasn't the tone of Marion's voice, which was always pleasant, but the grip on his arm. He stared at her hand. 'Jack wasn't in the car. The car is at the pub.'

'Which one? Do you remember?' said Marion.

'Why did he take you to the pub?' Gennie interrupted.

'We parked in the car park and when we came back from the shopping, I was hungry. Jack said I can have chips but the shop was shut so we went in the pub and then there was some people Jack knew. And Jack said we had to leave and we went somewhere else and then Jack said I had to come home.'

'Can you find the place again?' Marion asked Hamid.

'It's near the bus stop,' said Hamid.

'I'll get the keys,' said Gennie, and ran back upstairs to go through Jack's coat. Neither his keys nor his wallet were there. Only a phone whose battery had died, leaving no clues at all as to how he'd got home.

'Look, don't worry,' said Marion, when Gennie trudged back down again. 'There are spares in the office. I'll get the bus back in with Hamid and go find the car. It'll take some time. Can you hold the fort?'

Gennie would rather have taken them to Bodmin in one of the other cars but Marion must have reasons for taking the slow route. First rule of conflict resolution: take the heat out of the situation. Or was she preparing Hamid for the possibility that the Land Rover, and its precious cargo, had been lost?

Alice, alerted by all the commotion, came out of the cottage and demanded to know what was going on. Gennie racked her brains for an explanation which would pass muster until she received orders from Marion and almost missed the ringing of the office telephone.

'Hang on,' she told her daughter, glad of a reason to escape.

'Is Marion there?' asked the man at the other end of the line.

'I'm sorry. She's just popped out for a couple of hours,' Gennie said hurriedly, rummaging in the desk drawer for a referral form. 'Can I take a message?'

'Is she on her way to get Millie?' the voice continued. 'It's Nick, I'm Claire's... partner. Only we thought someone would be here by now.'

Oh! Gennie shut the drawer and stood up straight. 'Ah yes, I'm sorry about that,' she said in her smoothest voice. 'We've had some issues with the Defender so everything's a bit delayed. D'you have any time pressures at your end? Have you got to be anywhere?'

'To be honest, we've got some issues here as well and I would really appreciate it if someone could come for Millie sooner rather than later.' Nick sounded strained. 'And don't take this the wrong way, but I would rather it was Marion than Jack.'

'I can't be sure how long Marion will be,' said Gennie, thinking fast. Evidently, Millie's visit was still on – for the moment at least. What was worse? Getting involved or watching it fall apart? 'Look,' she said, 'if it will help, I can come now. I'm the housekeeper and Millie knows me.'

'Ah, could you?' said Nick, relief obvious.

She wrote down the address and sent a quick text to Marion, who almost never had her phone with her, and Alex, who always did, scooped up Roxy and her car keys, and went next door to fetch Alice.

'Right then,' she said, cheerily, 'we've got to go to the butchers to pick up the meat for Christmas, so I thought we'd pick up Millie on the way.' She handed Alice the dog, confident that her daughter's grasp of geography was too patchy to spot there was no way that going south-east to Bodmin could be on the way to Wadebridge to the west.

Millie was waiting at the window when they pulled up outside Claire's house. She had her coat on and, if Gennie knew anything about children, had probably been packing her bag for days. Nick shook Gennie's hand at the door and was about to walk them to the car when Gennie looked up to see a woman rushing down the stairs towards them. She was around Gennie's age with blonde hair tied up on top of her head, but that was the tidiest thing about her. Her T-shirt and jeans were crumpled as if she'd slept in them and her face was puffy with crying. She pulled Gennie back into the house.

'Millie, love, go and sit in the car while I speak to Gennie.'

Nick sighed and raised his hands as if he'd had enough of the whole thing and disappeared into the front room.

'I won't be a minute,' Gennie told the girls, and stepped further into the house. She followed Claire through to the kitchen.

'Is Jack back? Is he all right?' Claire said as soon as she'd closed the door behind her.

'Yes.' Gennie nodded. Well, he was back.

'I'm so sorry about this,' Claire continued, standing with her back to the kitchen counter, arms wrapped around herself. 'I hate it when he's drinking, but this time, it's my fault.' The tears streamed down her face.

Gennie went instinctively to Claire's side, as she'd do with anyone who was crying. She touched her shoulder gently. 'Did something happen?' she said, regretting the words as soon as they left her mouth. This was not her business, except she'd already taken a liking to Claire. The way she'd taken her hand and tugged her back into the house said they had things in common.

'It's awful,' said Claire, starting to sob. 'Jack found out Nick and I are getting married, and he went mad because I hadn't told him. I was trying to find the right time. Nick only asked me a week ago. When I spoke to Jack yesterday morning, I told him that we needed to speak about something when he collected Millie. I asked Nick to stay out of the way 'cos I knew Jack would take it badly. We went to get an engagement ring yesterday, and then, afterwards, Nick went to the pub and he told everyone, and they were busy congratulating him when Jack came in with that kid from the project.'

'Oh, God,' said Gennie, imagining Jack's shock and Hamid's confusion. The poor boy had no clue about Jack's family issues.

'Exactly,' said Claire. 'Next thing, Jack's on the phone to me and yelling about why was he the last person to find out. I don't know why Nick couldn't have kept his mouth shut until after Christmas,' she said, between sobs. 'I knew Jack would go off on one. I spent all afternoon trying to find him and, when I did, we had the most massive fight in front of everyone in the pub.' She winced. 'I managed to get his keys and wallet off him so he couldn't drink anymore, or drive, and I left them behind the bar with the landlord. He knows me but he called this morning to say that Jack hadn't been in and the car was still there. And then, when I came home last night, Nick and I had a big row. He says we need to talk.' She rolled her eyes. 'He wants Millie to stay at the farm for a couple of days while we sort things out. That's why he called you. But how can I send her over there when Jack's like that?' Her voice rose, accompanied by a fresh round of sobbing.

Gennie exhaled. It all made sense now.

'Look, don't worry about Jack,' she said. 'He'll be a bit hung-over, that's all, and Millie will be perfectly fine at the house. We've got loads of stuff planned for the kids. There'll be lots of food and games, Millie's going to have a great time. Jack's been really looking forward to this so he's going to make it special for her – and Marion would be devastated if Millie didn't come.'

Gennie couldn't believe the words coming out of her mouth. The state Jack was in, he probably wouldn't have sobered up before Boxing Day, and there was no guarantee he'd make it special for Millie, but Marion would. She'd help too. All her experience rescuing ruined Christmases would come in handy. Apart from anything else, if Millie didn't come to the farm, she'd think her mother had stopped her seeing her dad and the cycle of blame would begin. She knew all about that. At least Jack would be there, unlike the last Christmas Mikkel had been well enough to enjoy, when

Gennie's family had agreed an alcohol ban and Mikkel had disappeared for two days.

She forced herself to concentrate on what Claire was saying.

'I know he's upset, but why can't I be happy? I've had ten years of crap to deal with and now I've found a man who's so predictable, you could set your watch by him. I love Jack, I always will, but I can't live with his moods, and I loved Andy, but he's not here and I have to move on. I can't mourn him for ever. Jack wants me to be preserved in stone like some memorial but I can't do it. I know I should speak to Marion, she's left messages for me, but I can't bear to. I've handled this so badly.' She was gulping back tears again.

'Marion will be understanding,' said Gennie. 'I can say that for sure. Meanwhile, do you want me to keep this to myself?'

'No need. Enough people heard us arguing,' Claire said bitterly. 'Everyone will know what's going on.'

While the two girls chatted on the way back, Gennie mused on what Claire had said. Would there really be a time when she'd stop feeling like a memorial to her dead husband, as if she was wearing a badge saying 'widow' which permitted the world to skirt round her? Thing was, whilst she'd been angry with Mikkel for the way he'd lived, she was even angrier with him for dying and leaving them. She missed him and lately, when she dreamed of him, he wasn't as he'd been in the months before he died, when he'd been so ill, but young, and that made her miss him more and the life they could have had. He'd loved her, despite everything else.

*

Gennie laid the table for twelve. Was that enough? She counted again: eight residents plus Alice, Millie, Marion and Alex. Lasagne – two types – in the oven, watched over by Sam and Charley. There was one more thing before she jumped in the car and set off for Truro and the hospital. With luck and good traffic, she should be able to get a good hour or so with Jan before visiting closed at eight. She grabbed a pint glass of water and the kitchen first aid kit and headed upstairs. Jack's room was still empty, windows open, bed stripped bare, so she continued along the corridor to Marion's room. Jack answered when she knocked. Awake, then. She opened the door slowly and ventured in. The room was dark, although the curtains were open. Jack hauled himself upright and sat with his arms resting on his knees, one hand rubbing his forehead.

'Here.' She handed him the water glass.

'Thanks.'

He looked unsure, disoriented rather than wary. It was almost appealing. Gennie dismissed the thought.

'Paracetamol or codeine?' she said briskly, unzipping the first aid bag and flicking through the medicine packets.

'Both,' he said, holding his hand out for the tablets.

Gennie hoped he'd sobered up enough to avoid causing any further damage, but right then, she wasn't sure she cared that much.

'So,' she said, not bothering to hide her disdain, 'you'll be pleased to hear that we've picked up the pieces for you. Your mum and Hamid have retrieved the Land Rover, all gift shopping still safely aboard, and your daughter's downstairs, watching a film with Alice.'

'Oh, I'd better...' Jack made as if to get out of bed.

'Hang on a sec.' She held up a hand. 'You may say I'm taking my own issues out on you, and to be fair, it's probably true, but honestly, Jack, how could you do that to Millie? What's happened to you? Who did you think was going to sort this out? Were you really going to lay all this on your mum?'

'No, no, I—'

She couldn't let him continue. The anger had taken hold. 'You were the one calling Mikkel an arsehole but you're just as bad. Maybe you're worse, because at least Mikkel knew I was there, so Alice was never forgotten.' She was shaking now. 'You've seen how horrible it is for Alice; she thinks her dad abandoned her. Is that what you want for Millie? A little girl looking forward to spending Christmas with her dad and you just leave her. I won't watch it happen. I can't. You have to sort yourself out!'

She turned and left, wondering whether her employer would take issue with her lecturing her son. Well, if she did, she did. Some things were too important.

19

Gennie woke early on Christmas Eve. She lay for a while, following the crack in the ceiling from the centre light to the window and pondering how much had changed. There were still things to be sad about; there always would be, it was a fact of life. But this year, she wouldn't have to try and make things right for everyone, pretend everything was fine and she couldn't be happier. Her job extended only to delivering the catering and no further, and while no-one could say they weren't a tough crowd, they wouldn't care if things weren't perfect or the seasoning not quite right. Their interests were simple: quantity of food and frequency of snacks.

It would be a while before Alice roused herself, so after showering and dressing, Gennie picked up Roxy and went next door to the farm kitchen. She might as well make a start.

The kitchen door banged open and Jack came in. He dumped down a sack of potatoes. 'Millie's getting the eggs,' he said.

The dog, curled in the corner armchair, had pricked up her ears at the approach of visitors, jumped down and headed for Gennie and reassurance. Gennie tickled her head. 'It's only Jack,' she said.

Jack looked to the window and then at a spot over Gennie's shoulder and finally made eye contact. 'I'm sorry about yesterday. I'm embarrassed you had to clean up after me.'

'I'm sorry about what I said.'

He frowned, clearly had no recollection of their conversation.

'But if it hadn't been for Millie and Marion, I would have left you there.' She indicated the chair in the corner with the point of her knife. She didn't say, 'Left you there to die,' but that was pretty much how she felt about it. 'How are you feeling, anyway? You don't look that rough.'

He didn't even look that hung-over. No clammy pallor or red-blotched skin, only tired and a bit hollow-eyed.

'Don't worry. I'm suffering.' He grimaced.

'Good,' Gennie replied, and Jack snorted.

'That's not what I mean,' she said, wagging the knife at him. 'You'll recover soon enough. I'd be much more worried about your long-term prospects if you'd got up this morning feeling fine and slipping brandy into your coffee to ease yourself into the day, topping yourself up at hourly intervals and winding down with a gin and tonic or two in the evening. Never sobering up, in other words. Believe it or not, I find it reassuring that you drink yourself to a standstill. But,' she said primly, and knowing she sounded so, 'it's Millie I worry about. I'm not watching you wrecking her life.'

'Millie was always safe at her mum's,' he said sulkily.

Gennie stared at him. 'That's not the point, though, is it?'

Was it possible that, despite his environment and his experiences, he simply didn't consider the possibility of emotional damage once he had eliminated physical danger? And yet, his own mental scars were as visible as the bodily ones. Risk of harm was more than just life or death. She shook her head and went back to her chopping and stirring.

'I didn't understand what people meant before because most of the time you are perfectly nice. But you really are horrible when you've been drinking.'

'So I've been told.'

'No wonder you drive everyone mad.'

'Yeah, okay. I know this stuff, all right,' he said wearily.

How far would he let her go? He could always leave if he'd had enough. He was right by the door, after all. She plunged in anyway.

'You also need to talk to Claire. I saw her yesterday and she looked like she'd been up all night. She didn't want you to find out that way and she was worried about you.' Jack shook his head but Gennie continued to speak. 'She knows she handled it badly but you need to hear her out. She wants to move on but she thinks she has to have your permission and forgiveness for even wanting that. That seems unfair to me. But she obviously loves you and if you still love her... well, you need to tell her.'

Jack closed his eyes at this tangle of advice. 'Too many words.'

'Okay – just call her,' Gennie said. 'And whichever way you go with it, make sure Millie gets her a really nice present. Claire will get the message.'

Jack nodded and opened the door. 'Noted. All fucking noted.' His tone was resigned. 'You done now?'

'Yes.'

'Good.'

Roxy had wandered over to the open door and was sniffing the air. Jack bent down to stroke her.

'Did you go see Jan? How is she?'

Now Gennie was the one scrunching her face and closing her eyes against the memory. Jan was the sad thing she didn't want to contemplate.

'She's really sick, Jack. Did you know she'd been having cancer treatment?'

'I didn't, no. Hope she's okay.'

'Yeah.'

She didn't tell him she'd driven home with tears running down her cheeks. Jan had pressed £50 into her hand to cover Roxy's food until they let her go home. She was sure she'd be out soon but Gennie knew intravenous morphine when she saw it and the way the staff had checked and adjusted the pump looked ominous. Gennie recognised the signs.

Jack was still in the doorway, as if he was about to do or say something sympathetic. She couldn't cope with that.

'Actually, Jack, there's something else I wanted to say.'

She leaned back against the sink and paused, choosing what she hoped were the right words. 'I'm probably not the first person to say this, but you need to stop living in Andy's shadow.'

The kindness vanished from his face. He closed his eyes and shook his head.

'Okay, you don't like this, but you're living like you're trying to preserve his dreams, his future. Set yourself free from that, live for yourself, make your own choices. You can't make things right for him.'

He was silent as he yanked the door wide open and went back out into the yard. Gennie had to respect the way he stood his ground, even when she was doing her best to punish him, probably – almost certainly – unfairly, for something only she would feel that keenly. Mikkel would never have done that. He would have walked away. He refused to listen to her.

*

Gennie missed Millie leaving on Christmas Day as she and Alice were out with Roxy. Once Christmas lunch had been eaten and cleared away, Jack went back to work on the farm. The crops could probably have coped for a day but Gennie didn't blame him for staying out of the way. With all the young people off school and hanging around on the farm, thumping up and down stairs, slamming doors, begging for snacks, arguing about video game controllers and taking each other's things, Gennie spent a lot of time breaking up fights. She was glad she only had one child; she really could not have coped with more.

Roxy offered escape. Whenever Gennie needed a break, she took the little dog for a walk. She was a perfect companion. They had a lot in common – still in their prime, making the best of lives that hadn't gone quite to plan. The only problem was Alice's cat, Sergio, who was used to sleeping on Gennie's bed at night. He was horribly jealous. Even if Alice took one of them into her room, the animals spent the night growling under the door at the other. Get a grip, Gennie told Sergio. It's only temporary. She crossed her fingers as she said it.

20

Jan died on the morning of New Year's Eve. Marion took the call in the office and came to the cottage to break the news to Gennie. She insisted they sat on Gennie's small sofa with a cup of tea. Marion did things the right way. It was the news Gennie had dreaded even if it wasn't entirely unexpected. The last time she'd visited, Jan had been dozing. She opened her eyes briefly, mumbled something and went back to sleep. Gennie sat by the bed, read the newspaper for ten minutes and then left, feeling useless. As she passed the ward desk on the way out, the nurse gave her that sympathetic half smile that told her everything she needed to know.

'What about Roxy? Can she stay here with me?' Gennie asked Marion, wiping away her tears.

'Yes, of course,' Marion assured her. 'Well, unless Jan's made other plans.'

'Has she got family?' Gennie said. She'd never asked. She'd stopped prying into other people's lives. If she didn't ask, they didn't either, and that suited her very well. No need to provide explanations.

'I know there was an ex-husband and I think she's got a sister somewhere, but beyond that... Shirley will know more.'

Undoubtedly. Gennie pulled Roxy onto her lap. She felt very protective of the orphaned dog. Did she know what had happened? Animals were supposed to have a sense of these things.

'You're going to stay in tonight, aren't you?' said Alice, when she heard the news. 'Because of Roxy. Does that mean I have to stay in as well?'

Gennie looked at her daughter's anxious face. It seemed like yesterday that she'd been dressing as a Disney princess for playdates, and now she was begging to go with Sam and Charley and the other children from the farm to a New Year's Eve party. It had made sense when Gennie thought she'd be spending the evening at Eleanor's and could collect Alice on the way home.

'How will you get back?'

Alice was so much younger than the other children and it made a difference at that age.

'Jack's taking the minibus. He'll drop us and collect us. Please, Mum. Literally everyone is going, and Marion says we have to stick to the rules and if there's any drinking, we'll have to come back early.'

That sounded like an empty threat as Jack was hardly likely to interrupt his evening at Max's to drag them home before midnight.

'Can I go then, Mum?' said Alice. 'As Jack will be there...'

'I suppose so,' Gennie said, unwilling to embarrass her

daughter by refusing, but fairly sure Alice wouldn't enjoy it. 'But if it's boring, call me and I'll come and get you.'

'I mean, I'll stay with you if you want me to,' said Alice, cuddling Roxy. 'I don't want you to be on your own but I think you'd prefer it that way.'

Gennie smiled then. It was true. She had ambivalent feelings about Christmas but she hated New Year. Visiting Jan and seeing her immobile in her hospital bed, wired up to drips and catheters and morphine, while the corridors and waiting areas drooped with mismatched Christmas decorations reminded her so powerfully of her last New Year with Mikkel, she'd had to dig her nails into her palms to stop herself making a mad run for the exit.

As far as she'd been aware, her husband had kept his promise and followed doctor's orders, spending Christmas totally sober, probably his first dry Christmas since he'd been a child. So how to explain why two days later she'd woken to find him yellow, puffy and vomiting blood into the bathroom sink? Frantically, she woke and dressed Alice and waited in a state of panic for the ambulance to arrive. Mikkel was rushed to hospital and, six anxious hours later, diagnosed with kidney and liver failure.

While Alice was scooped up by a friend, Gennie spent New Year's Eve by her husband's bed, inert with fear and shock, watching the monitors measure his organs' functions and listening to his promises that this New Year would be a turning point, that once his kidneys were stabilised and he could be considered for a liver transplant, all would be well. She'd wondered who he was kidding. He must have had the same conversation she'd had with the consultant. She'd seen in the New Year with the realisation that her husband was dying and the turning of the year was just bringing his death closer. She hadn't known before what it meant to wish for time to slow down – or, better still, reverse – so she could go back to the day before and the week before and the year before. She'd often wished it since.

Instead as each day ground unstoppably into the next, Mikkel became sicker, simultaneously wasted and bloated, as little by little, his body gradually gave up on him. Towards the end, in his more lucid moments, they spent peaceful times, dozing and chatting together. He saved his more ludicrous optimism for other visitors. Gennie hardly dared go home during his last week as almost every time she left the hospital, she was called back, so frail was he. The horror of watching him die was matched only by her terror that she wouldn't be there when he needed her. She got so used to the routine and the heat and smell of his hospital room that she felt utterly lost when Mikkel gave up the fight in mid-March. There was a void in her day which couldn't be filled.

21

It was still dark when Gennie woke the next morning, the forecast cloudy with a light drizzle. Maybe not the brightest start to a New Year but perfect to take Roxy out for a long ramble. She'd choose a route from the book of Cornish coastal walks Secret Santa had kindly gifted her. It had to be from Alex. Anyone younger would have got her a subscription to an app. She dressed and checked in with Alice, who had no intention of joining her before going next door to the farmhouse. Marion was in the kitchen making tea and toast.

'There you are, darling. Happy New Year.' Marion hugged her. 'Look, there's no point in doing breakfast for the kids yet. It'll be hours before they surface.'

'Midday brunch it is, then,' Gennie said, but laid out cereal and juice for any early risers and grabbed a slice of toast for herself. 'You okay if I go out for a bit?'

'Sure. Jack's going to Watergate Bay to surf. You could catch a lift with him if you fancy a change of scene.'

Gennie went outside into the lightening day. She wasn't sure she wanted to spend time with Jack, or he with her, but she was curious to know how he'd resolved things with Claire. Jack was in the yard strapping his surfboard to the roof of the Land Rover.

'Hey. Happy New Year,' she said.

He turned and smiled. 'You too.' He hesitated before pulling her towards him with one arm, very gingerly as if he risked electrocution, and touching his lips to her cheek. 'Coming surfing?'

'Ah no. Sadly, Roxy's got no wetsuit. We're going for a walk. Marion said you were going to Watergate. Can we get a lift?'

'Course. Hop in.'

'And thank you for last night. Alice said you were summoned to their rescue, repelling gate crashers and pacifying the neighbours. She reckons they're all in danger of being grounded if you spill the beans.'

He laughed. 'Don't believe a word. You know what this lot are like, they love a bit of drama. They were very well-behaved.'

She wouldn't ask how high he set the bar for bad behaviour. She still felt slightly cool towards him. He could go off the rails at any time. Then there was Claire. Their relationship still had some heat in it and she had no intention of being caught in the crossfire – or used in any way. Jack would enjoy reminding her about their past encounters. He could forget any ideas he might have in that direction. She'd be crazy to get involved with him.

'Are we friends again, then?' he said suddenly. He could have been reading her mind.

Gennie sighed. 'I'm not angry anymore, if that's what you

114

mean, and I'm sorry I was so nasty to you.' She paused before adding, mock-seriously, 'I'm not really sure I want to be your friend, though.'

He shot her a nervous glance. She didn't blame him. She wasn't sure what would come out of her mouth either.

'If being your friend means I have to clear up your vomit, cover for you, make excuses to your daughter and listen to drunken rambling justifications for your behaviour, I don't want to do it. I've been there before. I can't do it again. What's in it for me?' She raised a questioning eyebrow.

'Jesus!' He looked stunned. 'You said you weren't angry anymore. I said I was sorry. Friends just means friends – that we hang out a bit. Although if you want benefits, that can be arranged too.' He tried a smile. Gennie ignored it.

'I'm serious, though.' She hadn't been entirely sincere when she started this conversation, but the more she thought about it, the more strongly she felt. If she was going to take control of her life, this was how it had to be. Jack was taking the brunt of it, and that might not be fair, but he'd do what he had to do to look after himself. 'What do you think being friends means? Does it mean you trust each other not to do stupid things, that you help each other to get things done, that it's positive and supportive and cooperative?'

'Okay,' he said, taking up the gauntlet. 'No, I don't. I think it means you understand each other, you put up with each other, and when someone screws up, you cover their back, you don't hold it against them, you keep your team together. What you're describing isn't true friendship, it's more of a business relationship.'

Trust! That was it. Essentially, they both needed to trust – but for different reasons.

115

'Then, Jack, that's what I'd prefer. I'd rather be your co-worker than your friend. I like you and all that but I can't take on the responsibility of being your friend. I've spent too much of the past ten years covering for Mikkel, fudging situations, cleaning up messes, but I had a vested interest in it as I loved him, I was married to him, I was compelled to do it. I won't choose to do the same again. Don't be offended but I can't get involved. I need to protect myself.'

They drew up in the car park by the beach. Jack pulled the handbrake up, the ratchet grating like the atmosphere in the car, and sucked his teeth. Gennie didn't dare look at him.

'Fine.'

He must be regretting bringing her.

'Maybe you'll feel better after a walk.' He pointed towards a path. 'You can walk up the cliff there and back along the beach. Keep an eye on the tides, though. Shall I meet you at the beach café in a couple of hours?'

Gennie collected the dog and climbed out of the Land Rover, feeling a bit sheepish. Jack wasn't the only one shocked by the strength of her feelings. He was right: she needed to walk it off.

The wind was strong on top of the cliff and she was glad Roxy was in her tartan coat. She was regretting the fold-out map, though, as it was impossible to read while it flapped around and her eyes watered in the cold air.

She was on safer territory back down on the beach, where the horizon was vast and promising, the soft morning light refreshing. The tide was out and the sand, sparsely populated with early walkers and cheerful dogs, stretched as far as the eye could see. There were more people surfing but she couldn't pick Jack out with any certainty. All the black-clad figures looked alike.

When Gennie grew tired of throwing the ball and Roxy of chasing it, they went to sit on the deck of the beach café. Gennie placed Roxy on the chair beside her and ordered tea for them both and poached egg with chips on the side for herself. As she ate chips with her fingers, alternately dipping them in the egg and offering them to the dog, she scrolled through her phone, exchanging New Year greetings with family and friends and checking out the day's news and gossip. Some weird virus in China. More good news. She didn't notice Jack until he was in front of her, still in his wetsuit, wet hair dripping. She smiled back at his cheerful grin.

He pointed at the two teapots. 'Is one of those for me?'

'Erm, no, it's actually Roxy's,' Gennie admitted. 'She won't drink my Earl Grey. I'll get you some more.'

'No need.' He reached for the teapot. 'I'll share hers.'

'Are you hungry?' Gennie asked. 'I'd offer you a chip but I think Roxy must have eaten them all. The egg too. It can't have been me. Are dogs allowed to eat that?'

'The egg should be fine, the chips maybe not. Can you get me a burger of some sort?'

Gennie went inside. When she came out with an order number, Roxy was on Jack's lap, drinking tea from the saucer while he used the cup. They sat for a while in comfortable silence, watching the sea as they waited for Jack's food.

'Are you coming to Marion's party this evening?' said Jack, once his plate had arrived. 'It's a bit of a tradition. You should know a few people. Max will be there and Clement and people from the village. You'll be able to hear the delights of my mother's 1970s record collection and watch people dance who really shouldn't. I'll be there but you won't have to speak to me as it's outside business hours.' He smiled. He didn't seem at all perturbed by what she'd said.

'Yeah, I promised to make a cake. I also promised brunch so I'd better get back, if that's okay.'

They got to the car and Jack put the board back on the roof rack. The car park had filled up and there were plenty of families milling around. It had also got quite cold.

Jack sucked his teeth. 'Okay. Now, I have a colleague task for you to do. I need to take the wetsuit off. Normally I'd strip off in the showers, but they're shut. Would you hold this towel up for me? Don't want to scare the children.'

Gennie assumed this uncharacteristic modesty was a ruse to tease her some more, but she obliged and held the towel at chest height, passing him items of clothing as he requested them.

'You can peek if you want,' he said.

She smiled. 'Don't take this the wrong way, Jack, but I've seen what you have to offer, and that was when you hadn't spent a couple of hours in the Atlantic and weren't all pasty and shrivelled.'

'Pasty and shrivelled? Fucking hell, you really aren't my friend, are you?' He was amused rather than offended. Once in shorts and a T-shirt, he perched on the back of the Land Rover, reached into the car for a bottle of water and rinsed off his lower legs before carefully rubbing bio oil onto his scars, which were pale but still evident in this light. The comparative hairlessness of his damaged leg also drew the eye. 'You know,' he said, 'a kid once asked me if I'd been attacked by a shark.'

Gennie grimaced and moved the towel closer, hiding him from view until he was back in his jeans.

'Can I pinch a fag?' he asked as they got in the car. 'Or can you roll for me while I drive? I'm sure you used to smoke roll-ups.'

She handed him the packet and her lighter. 'I did. And you had earrings.' She pointed at the top of her ear.

He nodded, lit up and exhaled. 'So long ago.' He handed back the packet. 'Not smoking?'

'No, I, er… like I told you, I keep them for emergencies. If I haven't smoked, it means I haven't had an emergency.'

Jack stared at her and shook his head. 'You don't have to live like that. If we're exchanging life advice, here's mine. Make a New Year's resolution to stop counting.'

'I daren't,' Gennie admitted.

'You know,' he said, gesturing towards her with his cigarette. 'Everyone thinks I have a screw loose but yours are even looser. Fortunately, you don't stand out in a place like this – good camouflage, hidden in plain sight.' He drove out of the car park, crunched the gears and hared up the hill. 'So what are the boundaries of our co-worker agreement then?' He was smiling now.

This was her own fault but she couldn't give way now. What did she want?

'Okay,' she started formally, 'I will happily work with you on anything that is to do with Hope House or the general well-being of all the residents. I am quite happy to cook for you and do your washing, etcetera, although Marion pointed out to me a couple of days ago that actually I don't have to do that. But it's no bother, and I don't mind. I will cover your back during working hours on work issues. What I don't want is to be involved in your private life.' She continued more gently, 'But I'll always help with Millie if you need it. That's the exception to the co-worker limitation. Single parents have to help each other out and Millie's sweet.'

Jack nodded, spat on the palm of his right hand and offered it to her to shake. She looked at it and wrinkled her nose, but there was only one thing to do. She spat on her hand too before gripping his. He laughed, of course. He was humouring her for now but he'd probably speak to Marion when they got back and she'd take her aside and recommend she saw Stella more often.

22

Gennie's phone buzzed as she was in the kitchen, attempting to slide her chocolate cake onto a plate without making thumbprints in its neatly glazed sides. She used one clean finger to connect the call to loudspeaker.

'This is a colleague announcement,' said Jack. 'Would you like to come and join us as we're about to toast the New Year?'

He hung up before she could tell him where to go. Okay, so perhaps she wasn't going about things the right way, but even Jack ought to appreciate that she had good reason to steer clear of him. She dusted the flour off her work shirt and went next door to change, flicking without interest through her wardrobe and settling on a cleaner pair of jeans and a black satin shirt. With some make-up and a bright red lipstick, it would do.

Alice was downstairs watching films with some of her new friends from the farm. Gennie popped her head round the sitting-room door on her way out.

'You coming?' she asked.

Alice widened her eyes with that 'Go away, Mum' face that Gennie must have used on her own parents at least once, and almost certainly more often than that, in her life.

'Yeah,' said the others, with a look that said they didn't want to comply but didn't want to disappoint either. 'We're just watching this thing...'

Gennie went back next door and found that, even on her own, without the back-up of family members, it was fine. She knew more people than she thought, and they knew her, too. Shirley grabbed her arm and, after introducing her to her husband, pulled her to one side.

'Such a shock, Gennie, about Jan. You will come, though, won't you, to the funeral?'

'Yes, of course! And if, there's anything I can do...'

'Well, we were wondering whether, and only if you had time, you understand, whether you could do some sandwiches? And maybe a cake?'

Jack leaned across. 'Should we prepare for a couple more fatalities, then?'

'Oh, Jack!' said Shirley, with an indulgent smile.

Even allowing for Jack's bleak sense of humour, it wasn't funny. Poor Jan. Gennie stalked off to find Clement. He was always good for an anecdote or two. She was having a very pleasant discussion about her mother's method of preserving fruit in alcohol, when Max and Eleanor came over, trailing a wary-looking Jack. Max's dark eyes were more hooded than usual, probably still suffering the effects of the night before.

'So, who's made any New Year's resolutions?' asked Clement.

'I don't know about anyone else,' said Jack, throwing a glance Gennie's way, 'but I'm going to get a spray tan. I can't sit for you again, Max, 'til I've done that. Gennie refused to look at my naked body today on the grounds that I was pasty and shrivelled.'

Three pairs of eyes turned to Gennie.

'Oh, for the love of God,' she said.

'I'll take a quick look if you need a second opinion,' offered Clement.

'But would she have peeked if you were all buff and bronzed?' said Eleanor.

Gennie fought the instinct to cover her eyes and ears. Eleanor was flirting with Jack. Was she expected to do the same? She looked at Jack and shook her head.

'I can't do this.'

Jack raised his hands in defeat. 'Oh, Gennie, for fuck's sake, it doesn't mean anything!' The others fell silent and stared down at their feet and into their glasses. Clement and Eleanor drifted off to join a livelier group and Jack swiftly followed. Max stayed and linked his arm through Gennie's.

'Gennie, love, let me make you a proposal. You seem a bit low. I think your self-esteem needs a boost. You know what the best medicine is for that? Come, sit for me and I will paint you.'

'I'm not sitting for your class!' she spluttered, disentangling her arm from his.

'No, no, not for them,' he said, soothingly, pulling her back. 'For me. And if you like the portrait, you'll buy it from me. Let me tell you.' He lowered his voice. 'I perform a major service for this county. People come to me because they feel ugly and unappreciated. I paint them beautiful, and their other halves pay me a fortune for the work so that I don't exhibit their naked loved one in the county show.'

'I haven't got an "other half" to buy it, though.' Far from helping, she now felt even sorrier for herself.

'We'll do a special price. Trust me, it works. Jack sat for me a lot when he first came back and it helped him and everyone else to come to terms with how he was now. A little changed, a little damaged but essentially the same. It made him feel wanted and whole again.'

'Okay, I'll think about it,' she said, making a resolution to do nothing of the kind. 'Now I'd better...' Gennie pointed towards the kitchen and made her escape, collecting a few empty plates on the way.

Jack came in while she was re-stacking the dishwasher. He stopped when he saw her. 'Sorry,' he said.

Sorry for intruding? Or sorry for embarrassing her?

She shook her head. 'Don't worry. I'm just in a funny mood today. You know, Jan and Roxy. Reminds me of things I don't want to think about.'

'Don't say the T-word,' he said, feigning alarm.

She smiled. 'I won't.'

He came towards her.

'And don't be nice.' If he was nice, there was a real risk she'd cry, and that was another thing she had no intention of doing. She concentrated her attention on the tea towel she was wringing between her hands.

'Me? Nice is not my go-to. You know that.' He stood alongside her and gave her his familiar one-armed hug. 'Look, this is a new year. I'm sure things'll get better. At least, I'm pretty sure they won't get worse! Nice cake, by the way.'

He smiled, and she relented enough to put an arm round

his back, returning the hug, suddenly reminded of an earlier New Year. Maybe he felt it too, because he squeezed her shoulder and kissed the side of her head.

'Hey, Jack,' she said, before her thoughts got too sentimental, 'you'll never believe what Max suggested. He wants me to sit for him!'

He didn't laugh but instead nodded his approval. 'Good idea.' He leaned against the kitchen counter.

'What? No way!'

'Why not? Apart from anything else, he's an amazing painter, and if you're going to have a portrait done, why not when you're still young and pretty?'

This was a surprise. She felt old and worn, and it must show.

'And also,' Jack added, 'I'll help with Roxy. She can come out on the farm with me. You can add a dog clause after the children clause in your agreement.'

'Thanks.' She smiled, and her mood improved with the effort. 'Anyway, didn't you promise me glam rock?'

'I did indeed,' said Jack, and held out his hand. 'Come on.'

'At last!' said Clement when Gennie re-joined the party. 'Someone who'll dance with me.'

'Here you go,' said Jack. He grinned as he joined Gennie's hand to Clement's and the opening chords of 'Ride a White Swan' filled the room.

Dancing was something she could do, the thing she'd always done while Mikkel hung out with the men, telling loud jokes and working his way down a bottle. When Alice and her gang came in from the cottage, they stood in the doorway, horrified, as Clement led Max and Eleanor in a mad Charleston, jazz hands flapping, to 'Tiger Feet' while Gennie taught Jack to jive, ducking and diving to avoid Clement's flailing arms.

23

It was two weeks into January before Gennie plucked up courage to talk to Max about the painting. She went to his studio on the outskirts of Bodmin, one cold Saturday morning, accompanied by Alice, whose support had not yet been negotiated, and Roxy, who couldn't be left alone.

Max's cottage had been converted, and where others would have opened up the space for a large kitchen/diner with a sunroom overlooking the Camel River, the ground floor of Max's cottage was devoted to his craft. A small sitting room with low sofas and a wood burner led to a traditional kitchen with wooden worktops and cream cupboards before double doors folded back to reveal Max's workroom. Alice poked her nose in, sniffed and then retreated to sit at the kitchen table.

'Right then,' Max said.

He made tea in a glass infuser pot, arranged biscuits on a plate and joined Alice at the table. He propped up an iPad and showed Gennie the gallery of his work. Alice sat glaring while she sucked the chocolate off a digestive.

Max opened another file of pictures – full-face portraits against simple pastel-coloured backgrounds. 'And these,' he said, addressing his words to Gennie, 'are some of the children I've painted. They work very well, nice and small, about the size of an iPad screen, and because I can do them from photographs, no-one gets bored. They make excellent Christmas gifts.'

Gennie watched fascinated as he slowly turned Alice, gradually edging the screen around until it was facing her.

'Would you like one like that?' he asked her, the first comment he'd addressed to her directly.

'Maybe,' said Alice, shrugging.

'Well, how about we paint you first, and then, if everyone's happy with the result, we do your mum?'

'I thought you disapproved of painting from photographs?' asked Gennie.

'Generally, yes, but you know, kids and cats. It would be impossible otherwise. A man's got to eat.'

Alice posed for Max's camera and together they chose a three-quarter profile of her face from the images he uploaded on to his iPad. This was something about the Insta generation. They'd never known a time when you didn't film or photograph everything. They had a familiarity with examining images of themselves. Task accomplished, he shovelled Alice out of the front door with instructions to take the dog for a short walk while he spoke to her mother. As soon as she was gone, he turned the iPad face down on the table and beckoned Gennie into the studio.

'Now then, what are we going to do?' he said, stressing the 'we'. He pulled a screen from the side of the room and threw

127

some fabric over it. He paused, finger to cheek, and looked around before leaping out of the room and returning with a red velvet chair with carved feet and a buttoned back.

'I think we'll go classical,' he said. 'Sit, please.'

When he had arranged her limbs in the way he wanted, he adjusted the lights and got his camera out again.

'Saturday any good for you?'

'Yes, sure,' said Gennie. 'I'll come over after I've done breakfast.'

'Good,' said Max, still concentrating on his camera screen and taking an extra couple of shots. 'I'll probably block in the background in advance. Let's aim for three sittings and then I can always get you back in if I need. So, now, let's talk money.' He put down the camera and beamed at her. 'I admit that for me, pricing is a flexible concept, taking all factors into consideration like the sitter's shoes, the husband's guilt, you know the sort of thing.'

Gennie looked at her feet in their threadbare socks, her muddy boots having been left outside the front door, and her anxiety grew. 'How low can you go?'

'Well, usually I charge between £1,500 and £5,000 per painting, but given that this is something of an emergency, I'll do both for £800. Unframed, though. And you can pay in instalments.'

He was being overdramatic, but Gennie accepted the offer. 'So, do you go scouting for lonely widows to paint?'

'In a sense. I advertise selectively. I've got a bit of a following in the Home Counties, particularly among people in their forties who think their partners might be straying, or about to. You see, the realisation that, under my expert care, their other halves have rediscovered their belief in their own beauty and sensuality and are spending so much time with me in what we'll call a vulnerable situation, tends to revive their interest in them. Some of the husbands have grown so jealous, if it were the nineteenth century, I'd have spent my life fending off duels. They don't seem to realise I'm doing them a favour.'

Gennie wasn't sure how much of this to believe although she was quite taken with the idea of Max, in the guise of louche and handsome artist, creating waves in Surrey drawing rooms.

'And occasionally,' he confided as he went back to the hall to open the front door to Alice, 'the portraits are bought by someone entirely different, someone other than the husband, and for a higher price. I tend not to ask too many details about that. But honestly, Gennie, they should prescribe me on the National Health. I make people feel beautiful! And I don't flatter them particularly, either. It's the process, the journey, if you like. You'll see.'

*

They started work the following Saturday. Gennie set out from the farm on the dank and chilly late January morning wrapped in her down-filled anorak, fleece hat and heavy boots, and could not imagine anything she wanted to do less than peel off her clothes and sit in a cold, brightly lit room for two hours, but ducking out now, when she'd made such an issue about it, was not an option. Imagining Stella's gentle enquiries, exploring why she'd agreed and then changed her mind, was enough to propel her towards her car. Jack would be easier to deal with. He'd tease her, she'd say she couldn't afford art when Alice needed a school uniform, and he'd leave it at that.

Even if she'd lost her nerve by the time she reached Max's cottage, she could already see the benefits of Max's 'process'. Having forced herself to take a good look at her body in the bathroom mirror, there was no way she could remove so much as a sock without a programme of rigorous waxing, exfoliating and moisturising. And then there was her stomach. One baby and that's what you got! Alice wasn't to blame. It was a doughnut ring, although it wasn't doughnuts she'd been scoffing but the scones she made for the kids' afternoon tea. That had to stop, and exercise, the sort that developed a strong core, had to start. Consequently, she was already in better shape physically than she'd been for some time. Mentally, it was a different story. She'd still have preferred to hide in the cottage drawing pictures of the dog.

Max, on the other hand, was brimming with enthusiasm. He opened the front door and looked both ways before pulling Gennie inside and hugging her.

'No Alice?'

'No, Jack's on children and dogs this morning.'

She folded her arms and followed him into the studio. Far from being cold, it was very warm and lit only by the white winter light filtering through the high windows at the back. It was too hot to keep her outer layers on so she dropped her coat and jumper on a chair in the corner. Max handed her a dressing gown and it felt natural to pop behind the screen and leave the rest of her clothes on the chair as well. She'd thought it would be like entering a doctor's consulting room, awkwardly removing as few garments as possible – troubling a busy person to examine something which would probably turn out to be nothing – but it wasn't like that at all. She didn't feel like a nuisance; she felt like the most important person in the room.

Max described the image he had in mind – half profile, one leg outstretched – and she sat on the red chair while he started draping fabric around her. He was worried that Gennie's punky blonde crop would not be conducive to the romantic image that he had in mind so he conjured up a tangle of long silk scarves in shades of dark red and green from a chest in the corner of the studio, wrapping one round her head and draping it over her shoulder so just the front of her hair showed bright against it. Another scarf snaked round to fall over one knee.

'All right, then,' said Max, tearing off strips of masking tape to mark all her edges against the floor, the chair, the screen at the back. He hid behind his easel to sort out paint before reappearing alongside his canvas and starting to sketch. While he worked, he entertained her with outrageous stories about artists he knew, commissions he'd taken and gossip about people she knew in the village. He expounded his views on life, love, art and the universe, throwing out the occasional compliment about the colour of her skin or the curve of her back. Max had a slow, husky way of talking that compelled you to listen and it was this rather than his painting which Gennie decided should be prescribed on the National Health. It was soothing to sit so still and so quietly while being spoken to in soft and intimate tones, with no expectation of response. It didn't matter that the content was often irreverent and occasionally obscene.

'So, Jack's babysitting, eh?' Max said when she settled down again after a break. 'Very cosy.'

Gennie almost flinched. What was he getting at? 'Yeah, well, you know. We trade the odd favour. I mind Millie if he goes surfing.'

'You're always together.'

'That's because you only see me on Tuesdays. It saves petrol if I come with Jack.'

'That's it?' Max pulled a face.

'That's it.'

'Not tempted at all? As romantic heroes go, surely he has the full deck – handsome, troubled, scarred, needy?'

Gennie hoped the reason she felt a little hot was because of the lights and that there was no blush spreading across her chest and up her throat to her face.

'You lost me at "troubled",' she said. Not to mention, needy. 'And if we're talking handsome, Max…' She shot a smile at him over her left shoulder. For her money, it was Max who was the most appealing, with his black hair, dark eyes and breathy voice. How the ladies must swoon when the bohemian and, with luck, slightly dangerous, portrait painter turned up.

'Ah, the healing power of art,' said Max the following Saturday, when without prompting, Gennie went straight into the studio and behind the screen. She didn't exactly throw off her clothes but she definitely felt easier about it.

In the break, Max beckoned her over to one of the drawing tables. He opened a couple of the shallow drawers and pulled out sheafs of drawings and sketches.

'Look at these,' he said. 'Seriously, Gennie, I should do a project for the war museum or something.'

Gennie wrapped herself in the silk dressing gown and stretched her limbs, stiff from sitting still. Max handed her a pile of pictures – ink, charcoal and painted studies of Jack, mostly clothed.

'After Andy died,' said Max, 'Jack tried to come home a couple of times, but he couldn't settle. It's hard to describe how disturbed he was. He was seriously injured when his vehicle blew up but the other two died. As it was it nearly blew his balls off.'

He chose one of the drawings from the pile, a rough sketch, the sort you'd do in fifteen minutes because it was all the time you'd been given, of Jack hunched and gloomy, cheek resting on his fist.

'I don't think the timing helped. He came home when the troops were being pulled out of Iraq so everyone thought it was all over. No-one wanted to talk about Afghanistan and he couldn't deal with the idea his friends would be forgotten. He was brittle as an empty shell. I did what I knew how to do. I sat with him, drawing, not talking, just keeping him with me, staying in the moment. Take a look.'

Max opened up another drawer and selected one of several plastic portfolios. He handed Gennie a charcoal drawing of a landscape and then a life study. She wouldn't have recognised them as Jack's work. There was none of his usual fluidity, the technique she envied. Instead, the drawings looked fussy and overworked, simultaneously scruffy and over-detailed. He handed her another and another and Gennie could see the progression. Little by little, the drawings became looser, with fewer lines on the page, less shading yet more shape.

Max turned one of the pages over. 'I've written the date on the backs of all of them. It's interesting, isn't it?'

'It's fascinating. He totally lost his way for a while. Have you kept all of them?' Gennie asked, amazed at the sheer numbers of drawings, filed away in plastic portfolios.

'He doesn't want them.' Max shrugged. 'I'm the repository of our efforts. Maybe I'll write a book one day.'

'You've known him a long time,' said Gennie, when she was back in pose. No need to explain who she was talking about. Max seemed to assume they'd be talking about Jack.

'Twenty years. At school, we were the only two, apart from the girls, of course, who took art class seriously. Everyone else threw paint at each other. It was the only thing Jack and Andy did differently. They'd been friends their entire lives, real brothers from another mother, and if you were friends with one, you had to be friends with the other. They pulled me into their gang, even got me to join the cadets, which I hated, obviously. Well, apart from the uniform, which had its appeal. And then, when it came to leaving school and what we did next, Jack went with Andy.'

This was new. Was Max trying to suggest there'd been conflict in Jack's decision?

'I thought he'd always been a bit obsessed with the military.' She wasn't going to tell Max how or when she'd heard this – or that the stories of Marion's friends' shocked bewilderment had Gennie laughing so hard she'd dropped her poles off a ski lift and she and Jack had had to clamber down a slope to retrieve them.

'Maybe, but I doubt he'd have gone on his own,' said Max. 'He had options. Could have gone to art school. Or university. Jack was the most academic of all of us. But Andy was his brother and he followed his lead. He wouldn't have stayed on if Andy hadn't wanted to.'

Max was unemotional, eyes flicking between his model and his canvas. Maybe he needed to believe that Andy had been the architect of his fortune to make it easier to bear.

Everyone concentrated on managing the impact on Jack and Claire, and no-one thought about how Max had felt.

'Did you think they would leave then?'

'I was sure of it. Jack'd met this girl,' Max paused and shrugged, 'and Andy and Claire were married. I'd followed the crowd and got a job down here, teaching. I thought we were all set. Jack and Andy had done their three years and were about to give their notice, and then suddenly, they decided to stay. I suppose because things looked like they would get exciting. I never understood it. Claire wasn't happy about it, or Jack's wife. And then Andy was killed.'

'You lost your friend, too,' Gennie said, wishing she were close enough to hug him or squeeze his hand.

'I nearly lost both of them,' said Max. 'They were in different regiments, but on that day, they were travelling together.'

24

Millie and Alice were at the kitchen table playing cards with Hamid when Gennie arrived home.

'Hi,' she said, washing her hands before heading straight for the fridge. Soup? Would that do for lunch? They could have sandwiches too. 'Have you eaten? Where's Jack?'

'He popped out,' said Alice, collecting the cards to deal again. 'I'm teaching Millie Racing Demon. Do you want to play, Mum?'

'Oh, go on, one hand,' she said, and took a seat at the table.

Alice was a ruthless player but she reduced her speed considerably so Millie could keep up and helped her choose which card to play next. Hamid ignored Alice's cheating, which was sweet, unless he was too shocked to mention it. By the time the game had finished, and the piles of hearts, diamonds, spades and clubs were heaped in the middle of the table, half the cards were on the floor and Alex had popped his head out of the office, alarmed by the racket.

'I thought there was a fight going on.'

'Only if Alice doesn't win,' said Gennie, laughing.

The door to the yard opened and Jack came in. 'Still at it?'

Gennie leapt up. She had the strongest urge to hug him. He'd been in the car when Andy was killed. How did he bear it?

'D'you want to play?' she said instead.

'Are you?'

She nodded.

'Daddy can't play, he doesn't know the rules,' said Millie.

'He does,' said Gennie. She'd taught him. Jack and Andy, Andy who'd been the biggest cheat of them all.

Jack considered for a moment. 'Fuck it, I'll play. I'll share with Millie. I'm a bit rusty.' He gestured to Gennie to sit back down and moved Millie so she was sitting on his left knee. 'You hold the cards,' he told his daughter, 'and I'll put them down.'

This round was fast and furious. Alice played at full speed but was well matched by Gennie and Jack, who cheated as much as she did.

'Did you play this with your dad?' Jack asked Alice, as he dealt out the cards again.

'Not much. He didn't like Racing Demon because JP always beat him,' she replied, not lifting her eyes from her cards.

'My brother,' explained Gennie. 'You know that Racing Demon's a tradition in our family. JP and Alice fight it out.'

'But Dad always beat JP at poker,' Alice added.

'Figures,' said Jack, signalling the start of play.

Jack's hand shook as he turned the cards. Gennie caught his eye, and the expression on his face was heart-breaking. A picture of despair. She put her left wrist to her eye as her eyes pricked. Her vision was becoming blurred, and she couldn't tell her clubs from her spades. When she looked up again, Jack's eyes were wet too. Her nose started to run. She wiped it on the back of her hand and carried on playing. By the time Alice's last card went down to win the game, Jack's face was wet and Gennie had tears running down her face. Jack threw his cards down, gently moved Millie off his lap and went outside.

Millie was staring horrified at Gennie.

'Don't worry,' said Alice casually. 'She cries all the time. She's an emotional wreck. And she hates losing. Let's play something else.'

Hamid, reassured, grabbed the cards and started separating the decks to play cheat while Alice looked questioningly at Gennie.

'It's okay, Ali. I'm fine,' she said. 'Tired and hungry, that's all. Give me two seconds and then I'll get lunch on the go.'

She went to join Jack on the doorstep.

'I'm sorry,' she said, declining his offered cigarette. It wasn't an emergency yet. 'That was a bad idea.'

'Not your fault. I can't cope with the adrenaline anymore. And I swore I'd never play Racing Demon again. Andy and I spent years playing that.'

'Well, I feel like I've paid my respects to him at last,' Gennie said, struggling to master her voice. 'You didn't tell me you were there when… I can't believe I didn't know.'

'It was in the papers. Maybe you didn't recognise the name. You might not have recognised the photo.'

'What happened?' She finally felt brave enough to ask.

'He wasn't supposed to be there,' Jack said, bleakly. 'I was in Helmand, not in combat, we were just there to build a bridge.

He was in ordnance somewhere else. Can you imagine how many bombs he'd defused? Anyway, they needed someone to come out to our control post. We hadn't seen each other for a while so he came to see me, basically. We went out to check on something and the convoy was attacked. I was blown out of the vehicle and the next time I properly came to I was in hospital.'

'That's so awful,' she said, inadequately.

'I couldn't believe he was dead, couldn't make sense of it. I was a bit nuts for a while. I had that thing where I kept seeing him everywhere, which wasn't helped because everyone in uniform looks the bloody same.'

His voice thickened and he wiped his nose on his hand. 'Everyone's scared they'll die but I always thought it would be me, not him. He had more life in him than anyone I ever knew.'

'You're not to blame,' she said, knowing she must be the latest in a long line of people to say it, and knowing it would make no difference.

'Can I ask you something?' he said suddenly. 'D'you dream about Mikkel? About saving him?'

'I used to,' Gennie said. 'I'd dream they made a mistake and they'd be giving me bad news and I'd say, "Oh, no, that's not my husband, my husband's in the room next door," or that I'd arrive just in time to stop them turning off the machines and then they'd say, "He's fine, now. Good to go home." Now he just appears from time to time.'

'And how is that?'

'It's different every time. Sometimes I know he's not here anymore and I talk to him about it in the dream. Other times, I have to remind myself when I wake up. Do you dream about

Andy, then?' She dreaded asking the question, unsure what kind of Pandora's box she was opening, but he wouldn't have broached the subject if he didn't want to tell her.

'Yes. I don't have flashbacks anymore. I've had all the treatments, Marion saw to that but I still have the dreams. It's because I don't know anything, only what I was told. They say it's good I was out of it because the others were blown to pieces, and I would not have wanted to see it. But I do see it. I see it when I sleep. I wake up beside a burning vehicle and everything is chaos and I run around trying to find him, looking in all the gulleys and under the trucks.'

'And you can't find him?'

'It's worse when I do. The worst ones are when he suddenly pops up from behind a rock and I'm so relieved and I tell him to hurry, we have to get out of there. I try and grab his hand to pull him along with me but I can't move and neither can he. And then I wake up and he's dead again.'

He ran a hand across his eyes again. Why did he still feel so guilty? Gennie put her hands to her face to wipe her tears and stem the flow of more, inhaling deeply to stop the sobs choking her. She wanted to offer comfort, to put her arms around him and hug him tight, but then the tears wouldn't stop. She picked up Jack's hand and squeezed it. It was better than weeping all over him. He didn't need that.

'Do you dream about him often?'

'If I've thought about him during the day, I know I'll dream.' He turned to her and smiled, a sad smile which almost reached his damp eyes. 'But if I drink, I don't dream. If I drink enough, that is.'

'Oh God, Jack,' she said, shaking her head and closing her eyes for a second. Knowing he had good reasons didn't make it easier to accept the outcome. She knew how it felt to be scared to sleep but she wasn't scared to dream of Mikkel. It was good to see him, to know he was still somewhere in her head.

They turned to go back inside as Alex walked out through the doorway. He stared at their red eyes. 'Oh no! What happened? Did Alice lose?'

'We're fine,' said Gennie, brightly. She and Jack exchanged a look. 'I was chopping onions.'

'I was helping,' said Jack.

25

Gennie climbed into the Land Rover. Quite where accepting lifts back from art class fitted into her agreement with Jack, she wasn't sure, but as it was so much easier to transport wet oils in the back of the Defender than in a hatchback or on her bike, she'd started painting again.

She had something to tell him and she couldn't work out why she felt so awkward about it. He wouldn't care.

'I've got a date!' she blurted, still feeling a bit stunned.

'Have you? Who with?' Jack looked just as surprised.

'Jim.'

Jack frowned, as if trying to place a name to a face. Gennie wasn't fooled.

'You know him. Divorced, two kids, one of the smokers.'

The smokers formed a subgroup among the regular painters and they'd braved many a winter evening in the schoolyard in frost, snow and rain to get their fix during the tea break. Gennie often joined them and took turns with Jack and Eleanor to get the coffees in. This evening, Jack had nipped back in to have a word with Max while Eleanor had gone to join the canteen queue, leaving Gennie and Jim alone outside for a minute.

'Got anything nice planned for the weekend?' Jim asked.

Gennie laughed. Apart from her last sitting with Max, she had nothing planned, nice or otherwise. 'Not much,' she said. 'Have you?'

'Not yet, but there's still time. The kids are at their mum's so I've got a free pass. You don't fancy dinner, do you? Saturday night?'

Gennie was about to decline politely; she had Alice to look after. Then she remembered that Alice was staying in Exeter for a friend's party and her easy excuse was gone.

'Oh. Yes, okay, why not? Thank you.'

She was further taken aback when he asked, 'You're not seeing anyone at the moment, are you, Gennie?'

'No,' she agreed, 'but...' and she had no time to say anything more as Eleanor was back.

'Isn't he a bit old for you?' said Jack.

Gennie shrugged. Jim was probably ten years older than she was but she didn't know many single men of her age, of any age, in fact.

'Well, I hope you're ready for this. Time to put Max's self-esteem improvement strategy to the test.'

Gennie shrugged again. She was definitely feeling better about the world, but whether that was due to Max's beautification therapy, or because there were daffodils appearing along the lanes, was difficult to say. Life was being renewed after the cold and muddy winter.

'I didn't know you were interested in him,' Jack continued. 'Or that you knew him that well.'

'I don't and I'm not, not really, but you know, it's only dinner.'

She could admit it to herself, she was scared to go out with Jim but also scared not to. Suppose no-one ever showed any interest in her again. Yes, she was the only single woman under the age of fifty in the class, apart from Eleanor, and for all Gennie knew, Jim might already have tried Eleanor and been knocked back.

'Also,' she said, 'I'll tell you this, even if you think it's bats. It might be easier to go out with someone I don't know that well. Lower expectations.'

'If you say so,' said Jack.

26

However Gennie tried to steer the conversation, she and Max always drifted back to Jack.

'Did you always plan to live down here?' Gennie asked, as she resumed her position in the red velvet chair. She knew when she'd found the right angle as her limbs groaned with familiarity.

'I'd half planned to go back to London at some point but I could never have afforded a studio like this, and after Jack came back, I couldn't leave Marion. We felt terrible, you know, for being grateful that Jack was alive. It didn't mean we didn't hurt for Andy but I don't know if that came through. All they saw was that I tried to protect Jack. Claire hasn't really forgiven me. Or Jack's wife. You know, half the time I was lying to both of them while he was passed out on my sofa. Can you imagine? Me? I was scared he'd get himself killed as some kind of crazy compensation. I don't know how Claire coped. Marion and I kind of propped each other up.'

'I can see how that would bring you closer,' said Gennie.

'If we hadn't been close already, it would've driven a wedge between us,' said Max. 'Marion and Jack were always important to me. It's difficult to explain. They knew I was gay before I did. The friends they had, and how they lived, made it acceptable for me to come out, and because they knew so many people who worked in the art world, they made painting seem like a viable career choice. My parents weren't keen on it at all and wanted me to do something with "prospects". He made quotation marks, paintbrush in one hand, dirty rag in the other. 'But Marion gave me the confidence to go for it and not make it an issue with my family.'

He worked in silence for a while before changing the subject and telling Gennie about Jack's attempts to help Max launch his career by getting his father to introduce him to agents and galleries.

'I thought his dad had some sort of property business. In Australia.'

'That's his stepfather. Jack's real dad is an artist. John Aspinall. That's how he and Marion met. She modelled for him. She arrived in London in the seventies when everyone was in a band or at art school or both. You should get Marion to show you the wedding pictures. It's like a who's who of the King's Road.'

'I see,' said Gennie, as realisation dawned. 'So that's why he's Jack Aspinall – and Jackass for short. What happened to his dad then?'

'Marion took Jack and left when he was a baby. Times had changed and Jack's dad hadn't. She got together with his stepfather a couple of years later. He's a really decent guy. When he went back to Australia, he helped Marion buy the farm. Jack's still close to him. His father, on the other hand, is a real piece of work. He drinks, by the way. That's one of Jack's fears – that he's like his father.'

During the break, Gennie went upstairs to the bathroom, and admired the painting hanging on the wall outside.

'That's Jack, isn't it?' she asked, looking at the image of a young man sitting on the edge of a bed with his back to the artist, respecting the privacy of anyone about to use the facilities.

'Yes.' Max nodded. 'Here are the others.' He opened the door to the spare bedroom with a flourish. Gennie gazed awestruck at two large oils in gilt frames, facing each other from opposite walls of the room. Jack standing, a classical ideal of a battle-scarred warrior, elegant and poised. The two portraits were swiftly and lightly painted, with care and tenderness.

'Oh my,' she breathed. 'These are wonderful. Are there any others?' She looked round the room.

'Not here. Marion has the only other oil I've done of him.'

Gennie touched his arm. 'Who is ever going to love him like you do?'

'Who indeed?' Max raised his eyebrows. 'You can't blame him. We are what we are. Clement's nagging me to take the pictures down. He says it's like a museum and Jack won't sleep in here when he stays. He makes me switch rooms with him.'

Gennie laughed. 'So, who paints you then?'

'Only the students if the model doesn't show up for the class!'

'Well, that's no good,' she said. 'After we finish today, I'll make us some lunch and then I'll draw you, standing at your easel, in full painter pose.'

27

Gennie stood on the toilet seat, leaned across the tiled window ledge to open the window and crawled halfway out. What sort of godforsaken place was this that you had to climb out through the Ladies to get a phone signal? This was the third time she'd tried to call the farmhouse and there was still no answer. Why had she agreed to do this?

She'd been nervous all afternoon, ever since she came back from Max's and her attempt at immortalising him in charcoal.

'Actually, that's not bad at all,' he'd said when he inspected her handiwork. 'See how much you've improved?'

With nothing to occupy her, she'd made dinner for everyone else before going back to her cottage to change into the only thing she thought suitable for a winter Saturday-night dinner with someone she didn't know very well. When she reappeared in the kitchen in her purple and black dress, black suede boots and heavily made-up eyes, all heads swivelled in her direction. She picked up her apron and tied it round her waist. She might as well keep busy until Jim arrived.

'You look really nice, Gennie,' said one of the girls. 'I like your boots.'

'Are you going out?' asked Millie, before Jack, who was sitting beside her, could distract her. 'Where are you going?'

'Yep,' she answered. 'I'm going to eat food cooked by someone else for a change.'

She waited for Jack to comment that they'd all like to do that but he said nothing. The sound of a horn tooting in the yard made her jump.

'Go,' said Marion. 'And have a lovely time. We'll clear up.'

Gennie untied her apron again, all fingers and thumbs, and then grabbed her coat and bag.

'Have fun,' said Jack, mildly, and gave her a wink which she knew he knew would irritate her.

*

Where were they all? There was nothing else for it. She'd have to try Jack's mobile.

'Gennie?' He answered in a whisper. 'What's up?'

'Jack, it's me.'

'I know,' he said. 'How can I help?'

'I'm having a nightmare,' she wailed, wriggling a little to adjust her ribs on the window ledge. 'I can't do this. I've got to get outta here. Can you give me a number for a taxi, or better still call a taxi to come and get me? And then can you text me to say there's some kind of emergency and I have to come home?'

'Where are you? Are you okay? You don't sound like you. You're not drunk, are you?' he said, curiosity turning to amazement.

'Totally trashed. I'm hanging halfway out the toilet window of the restaurant as the only place with a phone signal is the car park. I can pay for a cab, I've got money, but I don't have any numbers and I've got no Wi-Fi, and why isn't anyone answering the phone?' Her voice rose plaintively. 'I keep making excuses to go to the loo. He's gonna think there's something wrong with me.'

'No kidding. It's movie night, G. Did you forget in all the excitement? They're all at the cinema. There's only me and Millie here. Maybe they can pick you up in the minibus on the way home?'

'No-oo,' she wailed.

'All right, I'll sort you a cab. Where are you, though? I'll need the address.'

'Port Isaac. It's a Chinese restaurant on the corner just before you turn left into the town. It's a new place, you can't miss it. Something dragon, I think. If I don't get out of here soon, things are going to get nasty.'

'Okay! Don't panic. Leave it with me.' He sounded like he was laughing.

Gennie inched her way back into the cubicle and stood on the toilet seat as she brushed the windowsill dust off her dress. As she did so, she swept her phone from her hand and into the pan. Why hadn't she shut the lid before she clambered up onto the seat?

She stepped down to the floor and fell back against the door with a thump that rattled the lock. There was no way to escape without first going back into restaurant and facing

Jim and the fact that although she'd still had nothing to eat, he'd ordered a second bottle of wine. She peered into the toilet. It didn't look too disgusting. She wrapped her hand in toilet paper nonetheless before plunging it into the watery depths to retrieve her phone. It wasn't the most successful operation as now there were clumps of soggy tissue stuck to her hands and the phone. She flushed the loo and staggered out of the cubicle to wash her hands. She rinsed her phone under the tap to get rid of the remaining bits of tissue and tried not to cry. No matter how carefully she dried it on paper towels, it would never work now, and so she'd never get a text with a minicab number and would be stuck forever in this hell.

She picked her way back to the table in the darkened restaurant and managed to make it to her chair with barely a stumble.

'Everything okay?' asked Jim.

'Oh, er,' said Gennie, forcing a rueful smile to her face so she'd be convincing in her lie, in case Jack came through with a taxi. 'There seems to be some issue at the house. I had a text to phone them but the signal is really poor and my phone's stopped working so I'm not sure what's going on.' She waved the dead phone as evidence. 'I should really go back.'

'You're joking. Surely they can manage for one evening. Give them a ring when we're on the way home and you can check that all's well.'

Gennie didn't miss the implications, and when Jim refilled her wine glass, she took another gulp to take her mind off the situation. Perhaps if she passed out, it would all be over when she came to.

A waiter appeared with a tray of food.

'At last!' Jim said. 'Better late than never.'

Gennie wasn't so sure. She'd now drunk too much to manage her chopsticks and, after dropping most of her noodles on the tablecloth, settled for moving her food aimlessly around her plate.

'So have you been divorced long, then?' she asked, although she was finding it difficult to string a sentence together and the words might not have come out in that order, probably just as well as it was hardly the most tactful way to start a conversation.

Jim didn't seem to mind. 'About six years. I—'

He had no time to say more as the restaurant doorway was filled with a blinding light. The diners turned instinctively towards the source and immediately shielded their eyes. The beam swept the room and homed in on Gennie. From what Gennie could make out, there was a smaller light above it but she was now flash-blinded.

'There you are,' said a child's voice she recognised. 'You have to come home now. There's an emergency.'

'Oh, hi, Millie.' Gennie grimaced. 'Could you put the torch down, though? It's getting in everyone's eyes.'

Millie lowered the torch. Gennie could still see the imprint of the beam on her retinas but could make out that the little girl was wearing pyjamas, a camouflage jacket, a balaclava and a head torch. If her wellies hadn't been pink, she could have passed for a marine. If his daughter was here, it could only mean that Jack was outside. This could not get any more embarrassing.

'What sort of emergency?' asked Jim. Everyone in the restaurant was staring at them.

'A really bad one. Gennie needs to come now. The car's

outside.' Millie sounded so fierce that Gennie doubted anyone would argue with her.

Gennie stood up unsteadily. 'I'd better go. I'm sorry about this, Jim. Let me pay for the meal.'

'No, no, don't be silly. Maybe I should come with you? Give you a lift?'

'It's fine,' said Millie with authority. 'I have it covered.'

'Well, bye then, and thank you,' said Gennie, and grabbed Millie's hand.

'You don't need to hold my hand,' said Millie, losing her military composure and reverting to small girl. 'I know where I'm going.'

'Yes, okay, but I need you to hold mine. I'm still blind from your damn torch,' muttered Gennie. She staggered out into the street to find the Land Rover waiting by the 'No parking' sign on the forecourt of the shop next door. Jack sat at the wheel, smoking, his arm hanging nonchalantly out of the Defender's window.

'I've recovered her, Daddy,' Millie sang out. 'But she's really messy.' She gave her father a high five.

'I'm not. I just can't see properly.' Gennie climbed into the back of the Land Rover and flopped onto her stomach, finding herself nose to nose with Roxy. 'Sorry about this,' she said to Jack. 'I might be sick. Could you go slowly?'

Jack threw his cigarette out of the window, strapped Millie in, revved the engine and screeched up the hill and round the corner. Gennie cringed with shame. She wrapped her coat round herself, pulled Roxy onto her lap and curled against the window.

'You didn't have to come and get me,' she whimpered. 'You could have sent a taxi. And what is that poor child wearing?'

'It would take too long to get a taxi to you, even if we could get hold of one. And anyway, when Millie heard it was "Search and Rescue" she insisted that we came. Rescuing someone from behind enemy lines. She's been wanting to wear her head torch and balaclava since Christmas. You got off lightly. She wanted a smoke grenade to create a diversion.' Jack smiled at her through the rear-view mirror.

'What sort of father gets his eight-year-old daughter a balaclava for Christmas? And how many watts was that torch? You could probably have guided planes in with it.' She felt obliged to offer up some sort of defence and attack was still the best means.

'I think that's its primary purpose,' he said matter-of-factly. He started to laugh. 'Please, will you tell me what happened?'

'Oh God, it was so awful.' Gennie had her head in her hands, which wasn't a great idea as she felt dizzy already, and Jack's Rally Cross driving style wasn't helping. 'First of all, he got lost going to Port Isaac and we ended up going the long way round. It took ages to get there. He lives the other side of Wadebridge but Port Isaac isn't far from us. We could have walked it quicker. It was so awkward and I tried to be so charming and make out it didn't matter at all, but every time I said anything, he patted my knee and I just wanted to open the door and run. By the time we got to the place, they'd given away our table so we had to sit at the bar and wait for another table to come up. He ordered a bottle of wine and then said he'd only have half a glass as he was driving so I basically drank the rest before we made it to a table. But he obviously had completely the wrong idea about me because he kept touching my leg.' Gennie groaned. 'He'd heard about Max's painting and must have thought I was kind of advertising myself. And then when he asked about Alice and I said she was in Exeter for the weekend, he assumed he was on to a sure thing. That's when I knew I had to get out. I got to the stage where if he laid a finger on me again I'd have to defend myself, stab him with my chopsticks or something. The food didn't come until after I'd phoned you and by that time I'd already started on the second bottle of wine because I dropped my phone down the loo.'

Jack burst out laughing.

Gennie ignored him. 'That bloody painting! Sorry, Millie, shouldn't swear. I don't see how he knew about it.'

'I don't think Max would have told him,' said Jack. 'Who else knew?'

'Only you, Alice, Max, Clement, Marion and Eleanor. And Stella, obviously,' Gennie said. 'So no-one really.'

'Well, between Clement and Eleanor, that should cover half of Cornwall.' Jack laughed again. 'Where would you have stabbed him?'

'In the eye,' said Gennie.

'Good choice.'

'She wouldn't really have stabbed him,' Millie said. 'She's just drunk.'

'Quite right, Mills,' said Jack. 'Remember you never strike first. I'm not sure what sort of example Gennie is setting – getting blind drunk and stabbing perfectly nice men who kindly offer to buy her dinner. But, of course, when you behave like this, the only person you're letting down is yourself.' He looked in the rear-view mirror and smiled sweetly at her. 'But seriously, G, if you want some close combat training, you only have to ask.'

'If we were actually friends, I would cancel you right now.

This is awful,' she wailed. 'I'll never be able to go back to life class again. Everyone will know what happened.'

'Never mind. We can go to Max's Thursday class instead and paint some nice landscapes. I wish I'd seen you climbing out of the toilet window, though.' He started laughing again.

'I expect someone will have filmed it and it will be posted online tomorrow for Alice to see. Oh my God, I feel sick now.' She leaned her head against the window of the jolting vehicle and hoped she'd make it home before she embarrassed herself some more.

The minibus was outside the back door when they rattled into the farmyard.

'Get yourself some water,' he told Gennie, 'while I put this one to bed.'

He hoisted Millie over his shoulder and carried her up the stairs, reappearing a couple of minutes later with Roxy. 'Come on. Put your boots back on. Marion's going to keep an eye on Millie while we take the dog out. You need to sober up a bit before you go to bed.'

He filled a water bottle and handed it to Gennie. She followed him back outside and down into the lane. The dark and cold was reassuring, a place to hide her shame. She walked for a while, concentrating on putting one foot in front of the other as she weaved along beside him.

'Honestly, Jack, why would he assume I wanted to go home with him?' Gennie said, when coherent speech felt possible again. 'I don't know anything about him. Should I want to get involved with the first man who asks me out? If that's what it's going to be like, I don't want to do this. I can't.'

Jack said nothing but steered her away from the hedgerow and the ditch at the side of the road.

'What do you think? Is that how men see it? That if a woman's on her own, she must be available? Or is this what people do and I'm really out of touch? Is it my fault?' she asked. 'Do you think I gave him the wrong idea?'

Jack didn't reply.

Gennie nudged his arm. 'What d'you think?'

'What?' he asked. He lifted the hood of his sweatshirt and pulled out an AirPod. 'What is it?'

'Haven't you been listening?' she asked.

'No, sorry. I usually listen to music when I walk Roxy. Was it important?'

She stared at him. He was certainly telling the truth. 'No,' she said wearily. 'Just pouring my heart out to you. Complete waste of time, obviously.'

'Are you sure it wasn't drunken rambling justifications? Because that's outside the boundaries of our agreement,' he said straight-faced before laughing and tugging at her wrist. 'Come on, let's go home. Now what was it you were saying?'

'I'm never speaking to you again,' she said, sticking her nose in the air, her attempt to maintain her poise futile when she couldn't walk straight.

'What if I promise to listen?'

'Nope. Actually, Jack,' she said as he dropped her back at her cottage, 'if it's okay with you, can we never speak of this again?'

28

Jack crept into the kitchen on Saturday morning and sat down opposite Gennie, his hands folded on the table in front of him. She waited for him to speak, but when he said nothing, she carried on with her menu plans for the week. Eventually, she gave in and looked up. He smiled, not the full-wattage version she received when he was teasing her, but something softer.

'I need a favour.'

Gennie cringed. 'If this is payback for last Saturday—'

'Don't know what you mean,' he interrupted, signing that his lips were sealed. 'A promise is a promise. This is something else, but you won't want to do it, so I need to invoke the Millie clause.'

'Go on.' He'd piqued her interest.

'Claire's getting married next Saturday.'

'I'd heard.' Millie had talked about nothing else for weeks.

'Yes, and she's blackmailing me. She won't let me have Millie while she's on her honeymoon unless I go to the wedding reception,' he said with a wry twist of the mouth. 'She says it's too difficult to bring her here afterwards and so I have to go there to get her. I don't want to go. I wish her all the best and so on, but you can imagine what will happen if I get drunk. And I will get drunk.'

Gennie refrained from pointing out he'd get drunk whether he was there or not and that Claire probably wanted to keep an eye on him.

'She wants me to make it clear to everyone, especially Millie, that I support her.'

Gennie nodded. She admired Claire's skill, manoeuvring Jack to where she wanted him. 'Okay,' she said. 'What d'you want me to do? Go shopping with you? Help you choose shoes or a present or something?'

'No! Come to the fucking wedding with me! Do it for Millie's sake. Otherwise, I'll be there with my mother, looking like some real sadass.' Jack paused. 'And there's more chance I'll see the thing through if you're there, doing your best impression of the ghost of Christmases and birthdays future.'

Gennie laughed, although it was a cruel comparison. She stood to look in the mirror above the armchair and practised pulling disapproving faces. 'Doesn't seem to have worked so far,' she said.

'And think about the benefits. You'll be able to tell Shirley all about it. She'll bump you to the front of the queue and give you extra pasties.'

'She only does that for you,' said Gennie. 'Are you sure you want me to come? What about that girl you're seeing? Elizabeth, the key worker.'

He narrowed his eyes. 'Look, I'm not exactly seeing her. She kind of seeks me out when she wants company. I thought about asking her but she'd read the wrong things into it. How d'you know about that, anyway?'

'The kids told me.' Shirley didn't have the monopoly on gossip. 'Do I have to pretend I'm your date? As you know, I don't have a great track record.'

'No, not at all. You can tell people whatever you like. Say you're my probation officer for all I care. They won't believe you anyway. Max says most people think we've hooked up.'

'What! Why?'

'Because we're single and live under the same roof. This is a small village next to a small town. What did you expect?'

'I wonder how you and Max filled your time before I arrived and you could amuse yourselves at my expense,' she said drily, unsure whether to believe this latest assault on her reputation.

'You're so touchy,' he complained. 'But will you do it?'

'Yeah, okay.' Jack was right. If she didn't go, she wouldn't know what happened; the village shop wouldn't satisfy her curiosity. It made a change to agree on something. She also didn't see why Jack needed to be at the wedding to prove that Claire's past relationships were laid to rest. Marion might be confident that Jack had accepted Nick but Gennie wasn't so sure. It would be kinder to let him stay away.

29

Gennie and Marion sat silently in the Land Rover, staring out of opposite windows. Jack drove, unlit cigarette hanging from the corner of his mouth, having given way to the women's pleas to shut his window against the wind and the rain. Apart from the scowl, he looked the perfect wedding guest in his sharp navy suit and highly polished shoes. For her part, Gennie had enlisted Alice's help the previous afternoon, trawling the sale rails in Exeter for something suitable for a winter wedding and which she might find a use for somewhere down the line. She'd settled on a pink fitted dress with a scooped neckline and heels in roughly the same shade, affordable because no-one else was interested in shoes that colour in February.

It was a shame about the weather. All the photos would have to be indoors or everyone's hair would be ruined. For the first time in months, Gennie had made an effort with hers. Her razor crop was growing out and she'd spent almost an hour trying to curl her hair back off her face, aiming for 1950s movie star in place of '70s punk.

Jack swung off the A30 towards Lanhydrock. Gennie could see the stately home in the distance so the hotel couldn't be far now.

'It will be fun,' said Marion, firmly, as they turned into the car park. 'Weddings usually are.'

Jack scoffed. 'We're only here to show our faces. We'll get Millie and get out as soon as possible.'

There was a joke to be made about balaclavas and rescue missions but Gennie caught sight of Jack's expression and thought better of it.

They walked up the path to the hotel, heads bent against the wind, umbrellas blown inside out and a beaming Millie ran out to meet them, not at all bothered by the weather. She grabbed Jack's hand and, chattering away, tugged him towards the entrance. Gennie pulled up short at the sight of Nick and Claire in a reception line just inside the door but Jack didn't falter. He smiled, shook hands with all the men, kissed all the women and exchanged a few whispered words with Claire. Gennie felt a strange tightening in her chest. Could it be she was proud of him? It didn't last long. The second they reached the end of the line, Jack took her elbow and dragged her off to find a table at the back of the room. It was just as well there was no formal seating plan as Jack had no intention of socialising. Marion would have to do the job for all of them.

Gennie glanced round the room. A band was setting up in the corner and there were young people in white shirts and black trousers, circulating with trays of something sparkling in champagne flutes. Gennie waved them away before they reached their table and opened one of the bottles of water which flanked the floral table decoration. If Jack was staying sober, she would too. She poured a glass for them both and sipped at it while Jack rolled a cigarette. She knew, by now, that this was what he did when he had nothing else to do, stocking up for later.

'D'you think things would have been different if you and Claire were married?' she asked, unable to think of anything more tactful to say.

'I've wondered the same thing. But at the time when we might have got married – you know, when she was pregnant or Millie was born – I wasn't divorced yet, and then I was deployed again and the moment passed. It seemed more important to sort out the finances. I'm not sure she would have married me anyway!' He licked the cigarette paper. 'D'you think it makes any difference?'

'I don't know. To me it did. I wouldn't have supported Mikkel in half of what he did if we hadn't been married. We were a team, I thought we had to stick together. My parents wouldn't have encouraged me to stay with him if we hadn't been married. They assumed he felt enough responsibility towards me and Alice to make sure we'd be all right.'

'And he didn't feel that?'

'He did but it had the wrong effect. He put huge pressure on himself. He should have shared the burden a bit more.'

'Did you have a big wedding?'

'What d'you think?'

Jack smiled. 'I'm guessing massive stag do, followed by tiny wedding. They probably went to New York or something.'

'Las Vegas! And we had our reception in France at my parents' restaurant, with tables outside, fairy lights, garlands of flowers everywhere. This is making me sentimental. What was your wedding like?'

'Very small. Just our families and a few friends and then we went for lunch. We got married on a Tuesday. It was the only way they could fit us in. And then we went to Paris.'

'Very romantic.' Gennie smiled at him.

'Well, you know, I did my best.' He sniffed and straightened his tie. 'It was freezing cold. I don't remember doing much sightseeing.'

Gennie laughed and choked on her sparkling water. When she recovered she said, 'Don't you think that we were all too young?'

Jack nodded. 'You know I was best man when she married Andy? I did the speech and all that.'

'Ah.' Gennie grimaced. Jack was right. Weddings were fun for some, but for them, they were reminders of all the things that could no longer be.

'She's promised me there won't be any big speeches today. That's the trade-off.' He waved the cigarette at her. 'You okay if I…?'

'Yes, sure.' It would give her a chance to check out the company. As they stood, several other guests approached the table and exchanged brief pleasantries with Jack, including an older man, who introduced himself to Gennie as Graham, Claire's father.

'Nice to put a face to a name. I've heard about you from Millie,' he said, shaking her hand.

Gennie wondered what he'd heard and hoped it didn't involve chopsticks. She left them to chat and went to the bar. Jack found her there on his way back in. He looked amused.

'Know what that was about? He was checking I'm going to keep up the financial support. Funnily enough I always got on really well with Graham. Claire's mother thinks I'm a nightmare but Graham liked me and you know why? Because I always made sure the money was there. He wants Claire to have some independence.'

Gennie smiled wryly. How cynical life had made them. She'd been the same. Once Alice was at school and she'd requalified as an accountant, she'd started keeping her earnings separately from Mikkel's. That way she always had money to pay the bills. He'd been furious when he found out but it was the only way they survived after he lost his job.

When the band started playing, Millie dived over to their table and demanded that Jack dance with her. Gennie shooed him off, insisting that it was compulsory for dads to dance badly at weddings, and wandered over to join Marion, who was chatting to Claire and her mother.

'Lovely wedding, Claire,' she said. 'You look gorgeous.'

Claire also looked happy, an entirely different person from the one Gennie had met two months ago. In her long satin dress, tiny flowers amongst the curls of her updo, Claire was the perfect bride, glowing, blissful future ahead of her. Gennie hoped it all came true. Claire deserved it. Was that how it worked, though? The more you endured, the happier the ending? If only. And that pang she was feeling, was that envy? Envy and regret. She wanted to feel that hopeful again.

Jack returned after a couple of songs with Millie hanging on his arm and jumping up and down.

'Hi, Claire. All okay? Can we take Millie back in a minute? Is all her stuff upstairs?'

'Good idea. I'll go get her bags,' said Nick, who had just

165

joined the group. 'You all go and dance.' He downed his glass before leaving the room. To Gennie's practised eye, he was still on the merry side of drunk, but things could change fast.

Millie grinned and Jack cursed as she dragged him off again. Marion introduced Gennie to Claire's aunt, who gave Gennie a tight-lipped smile.

'How's Jack coping, Marion? It's a shame he's on his own because I think Claire would be much happier leaving Millie with him if he was properly settled. Wouldn't you, Claire?'

Claire didn't respond. Gennie looked across at Marion, who was standing straighter, weight evenly balanced, rather than leaning on her good leg.

'Look, Jack's doing very well,' said Marion in her most pleasant tones, the ones she used to mediate between the farm residents. 'Working hard, several building projects in the pipeline—'

'He hasn't really got over Claire, though, has he?' Claire's aunt interrupted. 'Will he leave them in peace now or cause a scene whenever he can? He needs to make a new life for himself.'

Gennie's jaw dropped open. This was hugely unjust. Jack hadn't said a single word in criticism of either Claire or Nick. She couldn't imagine him setting out to cause trouble for them.

Claire's mother whispered something and Marion patted her arm reassuringly. Claire wasn't as restrained. 'You should stay out of this. You don't know anything about it,' she told her aunt.

Gennie left to find Jack and Millie on the dance floor before the argument escalated. She was soon joined by Marion.

'You two dance,' she said, addressing Gennie and Jack. 'Show off your New Year jive and I'll dance with Millie.'

Gennie was surprised, but if this was about making a point to Claire's family, she was up for it.

'They're not playing our song,' muttered Jack as he shuffled without great enthusiasm towards Gennie.

'What song? We haven't got a song,' said Gennie, taking his hands. 'Oh my God, d'you mean "Tiger Feet"? Is that our song?'

He smiled, and for a change, Gennie didn't mind being the butt of the joke. She hoped they had an audience and the worst they'd be able to say about Jack was that he spent the evening laughing and dancing like he didn't have a care in the world.

As the music finished, Claire came to join them. 'Sorry about that. That woman's totally poisonous.'

Millie was delighted her mother had come to dance and hugged her tightly. 'Now you have to dance with Daddy,' she ordered.

'No, no, no,' said Jack and Claire in unison.

'Pleeease.'

'Oh God, come on then,' said Claire, pulling Jack towards her. 'Just smile and get it over with.'

Gennie and Marion swayed alongside, laughing as they twirled Millie around between them. From the corner of her eye, Gennie saw Nick return to the room with two holdalls. He stood with Claire's mother and aunt, exchanged a few words and surveyed the dancing couples, before suddenly dropping the bags and storming across the floor towards them. Before Gennie could say anything, Nick reached Jack and grabbed his arm, pulling him away from Claire.

'What the hell do you think you are doing?' he snarled.

'Woah, it's okay, mate,' said Jack, stepping back, hands raised in surrender.

Claire grabbed hold of Nick's other arm. 'What's wrong with you?' she hissed. 'Millie wanted us to dance. She's going in a minute. Just calm down, for God's sake!'

Nick continued to push Jack away from Claire. 'You need to go. Right now. What is it with you?'

This was evidently too much for Jack. The man was pushing him around in front of his daughter. He squared up to him. Gennie didn't know what to do. This was not her fight, not her business, but nor could she stand by and watch it happen. Claire's beautiful day was being ruined.

Graham rushed over and grabbed Marion's arm. 'Can't you do something?' he yelled.

The dancing had stopped as the other couples watched the developing action. Gennie looked at Marion, who was trying to calm Graham and release her arm from his grip.

'We need a diversion,' said Gennie. 'I'll ask the band to play something else, something like "Shake It Off", to get the whole room dancing.'

She took Millie's hand and forced her away from the scene, while Graham tried to separate Jack and Nick.

After a minute's negotiation with the band, they struck up a clumsy version of the conga, and Gennie turned back towards the room to see Nick take a wild swing at Jack. Jack leaned back to avoid the punch. Without a slow-motion replay it was impossible to determine whose fist or elbow was to blame as two or three other besuited individuals had launched themselves into the fray to hold Nick back. Jack remained alone outside the mêlée but as the group separated, Gennie saw something make contact with Graham's nose which immediately spurted blood. Gennie gasped, her hand to her mouth. Marion put herself between Millie and the group, shielding her granddaughter from the knot of people arguing in the middle of the floor. The two of them tried to distract the other guests by pulling them into their conga snake and dancing around the room.

Gennie made her second circuit, teeth bared in a forced grin, while Claire's mum tended to her husband's nose, mopping the blood with table napkins, and Nick and Claire had a heated argument in the middle of the floor. Marion was behind her explaining to Millie that Grandpa had bumped into someone but would be fine. If Marion was losing her composure, it was definitely time to go home. She beckoned a bemused-looking Jack towards her as she passed.

'What the fuck is going on? Why are we doing the fucking conga?' yelled Jack.

'Because the band didn't know the fucking "Macarena",' Gennie yelled back at him.

He stared at her and she glared back, unable any longer to muster her smile. As they passed the side of the room nearest the door, she added, 'Can't we just fucking go?'

'Thought you'd never ask,' Jack said, guiding Marion off the dance floor and scooping up Millie as she passed by.

Gennie collected Millie's bags and their coats while Marion said a few goodbyes. Jack re-joined them, looking considerably more cheerful, and they made their way to the exit.

'You're developing a real potty mouth nowadays, Gennie. I'm not sure you're fit to be around my family.' He grinned as he put his hands over Millie's ears.

'It's being around your family for six months that's done this to me!' she retorted.

Millie fell asleep in the car on the way home. Marion

tried to lighten the atmosphere by passing on all the local news about people Gennie had barely heard of to Jack, who'd managed to avoid talking to all but a few and wasn't interested in the others.

When they reached home, Jack switched off the engine and turned to Gennie, who was sitting in the back, Millie asleep on her shoulder.

'I need a walk. I'll take Roxy with me. Could Millie stay with you tonight, G?'

'Yes, sure. She can sleep with Alice,' she said, disarmed whenever he used her nickname. A thought struck her. 'Where are you going?'

He didn't reply but helped carry Millie into the cottage and up to bed in Alice's room before going into the farmhouse to fetch his waxed coat and the dog. He didn't bother to change his shoes. Gennie stood in the doorway of the cottage while Alice hovered behind her.

'Where are you going?' Gennie repeated, now anxious. Jack didn't need a babysitter while he walked the dog; Marion was in the house. Why wouldn't she be able to cope with Millie? Or did he want Millie out of the way? She spotted the neck of a bottle peeking out of one of the poacher's pockets of his coat and her blood froze. 'Where did you get that bottle?'

'Bought it from the bar,' he replied, expressionless.

So that was why he'd suddenly perked up when they left the hotel. Not because they'd successfully negotiated the wedding and collected Millie but because he'd bought in his supplies. She hadn't helped him avoid his demons; she'd enabled their embrace. She felt utterly betrayed.

'Why are you doing this? This isn't fair!'

'I'll see you later,' he said bluntly, and started walking.

170

'Jack! Don't do this!' She tugged on his sleeve. 'I won't help you do this. You can't leave me with Millie. I'm not covering your back and I'm not cleaning up after you. I swear, Jack,' she hissed, 'if she wakes up and asks where you are I will tell her you abandoned her.'

He'd know this was an empty threat; she'd never hurt Millie. He ignored her and carried on walking.

Marion was in the kitchen of the farmhouse. Gennie pushed her way in, hands up, imploring Marion to do something.

'Let him go,' Marion told her, placing her hands gently on Gennie's shoulders. 'As long as he's not a danger to anyone else, we have to let him get on with it. Save your energy for the fights you can win and don't let it get to you. Don't take it personally.'

'Okay,' Gennie said, clenching her fists and forcing herself not to scream. She stomped next door to the cottage and kicked the door shut. He had used her and now he wasn't the only one needing a drink. She rifled through her kitchen cupboards in vain, before settling for herbal tea, which she drank sitting on her doorstep, passing her cigarette packet from hand to hand, pressing the sharp corners of the box between her finger and thumb. She would not give in. He would not do this to her. She had let herself get too close and she was the one left smarting. It would not happen again.

30

Marion had shut the door to her office but Gennie could still hear her sweet tones drifting across the hall, interrupted by Jack swearing and Sean, the other senior key worker, attempting both to pacify Jack and get a word in for himself. Gennie busied herself unloading the dishwasher and tried to make sense of the snatches of conversation that reached her. It was something to do with Hamid as he'd been sitting listlessly at the kitchen table since lunchtime.

The office door clicked open and Jack stormed into the kitchen.

'I'm sorry.' He put a hand on Hamid's shoulder. 'There's nothing Marion can do. You have to go back and finish school.'

Marion and Sean followed. Sean must have been the same age as Jack but they wore their years differently. Where Sean sometimes appeared unsure of himself and looked to Marion and Alex for guidance, Jack behaved as if he'd already learned everything he needed to know but took none of it for granted. Nothing could be relied on; it all needed testing.

'Hamid, you know if it was up to me, you'd stay,' said Marion with a rare failure to smile. 'But now your foster carer's well again, social services are insisting you go back to her and I have no power at all to argue with their decisions. I've got them to agree that if we get the apprenticeship scheme up and running, they'll put you forward for it, but until then you have to go home and work for your exams.'

'It's fucking ridiculous.' Jack continued to rant from the kitchen doorstep. 'This is only about the money. It's cheaper for them to place him with a family. It doesn't matter at all that he'll lose everything he's done here.'

'Jack,' said Marion, with both a smile and a warning note to her voice. She turned back to Hamid. 'The time hasn't been wasted. We'll use all the work you've done on the greenhouses and the farm planning to show how you'd benefit from learning about farm management.'

'What about the watermelons? And the other fruit? My grapes?'

The other three turned to Marion. Jack's eyes burned with an unspoken challenge to his mother. Go on, offer the boy something concrete. Marion stared back at him for a moment.

It was like watching a tennis match. Gennie's head snapped from one to another, astonishment growing with each exchange. In the six months she'd spent at the farm, no-one had ever had a row in public.

'Okay look,' said Marion, finally, 'I'll try and get you back for the holidays, but if it can't be done, we'll start the planting for you. When you're out of school, you'll be free to make your own choices, which include coming back here to find a job.' Marion's raised hand stopped Jack from commenting further.

'Surely there's another way to keep him at the farm,' said Sean. 'Can't the trustees—'

'Not unless social services pay for his accommodation,' said Marion. 'If his place isn't funded, we can only keep him short-term. As soon as another child with funding needs a place, the trustees will insist we take them instead and Hamid will have to go. It's not even a question of keeping him as a hardship case because Hamid does have funding, but not to stay here.' She appeared genuinely frustrated.

To Gennie, it looked a bit shortsighted. She'd been listening to the news and the mystery virus was creeping closer. China and Italy were both still locked down and she'd had an email from Alice's school that day talking about school closures. If Hamid's college closed, what would happen then? He might as well stay at the farm. Gennie made a note to double her orders of dry goods. If the kids were home all day, they'd get through a lot of food.

'I will come back,' said Hamid, eyes filled with tears and as angry as Jack. 'I don't care what they say. When I am eighteen, I will come back.'

'Good lad,' said Sean.

Marion led Hamid away to the office while Gennie escaped to the utility room to sort out the laundry. She was still side-stepping conversations with Jack and wasn't hanging around to listen to more moaning about the arbitrariness of council decision-making. She sympathised with him over this. No-one had considered the effect on anyone else at the farm – the other children, the key workers and Jack. It was his first attempt at designing an apprenticeship programme and his prime candidate had been stolen away. It wasn't fair; they'd worked so hard. Jack would take it very personally. Fortunately, he wasn't her problem. She could do something about Hamid, though. A private invitation to stay with her and Alice in their cottage in the school holidays. No-one could object to that and he'd get a chance to do all the planting he'd planned.

When she came back into the kitchen, Jack was still there, leaning against the counter as he rolled a cigarette.

'You wait until next year,' he said to Sean, nodding as he spoke. 'By then, the farm will be making a real profit, at least I hope it will, so we can subsidise placements ourselves and tell everyone else to fuck off.'

Jack picked up Roxy from where she was curled in the armchair and went outside to work off his rage. Gennie had lost Roxy too. She still took her for rambles through the countryside, but the rest of the time, the little dog hung around the farm with Jack. She even shared his breakfast tea. She was probably happier that way. At least she didn't have to compete for attention with Alice's cat.

31

Gennie zipped up her reflective jacket. She was going to art class. She'd weighed up the pros and cons. Jack would be modelling, but if he was occupied, he wouldn't be able to talk to her; Jim would be there and it would be only the second time she'd braved the class since the 'dinner date debacle', but it was as much her space as his so why shouldn't she go; and the government had now said everyone should limit social contact to stop the virus spreading. Well, she had no intention of hugging anyone or shaking their hands, and if they were all going to be ordered to stay at home, she might not get many more opportunities.

She rode her bike into Wadebridge, found a space in the studio facing Jack's side and settled down to draw. Whatever else she thought of him, he was a good model. He sat quietly and didn't sink too much into his pose. Then there was Jim. She was still too embarrassed to speak to him, but she could avoid him if she didn't go outside and hung around in the art room instead. He showed no sign of wanting to speak to her either. Six months after moving back to Cornwall, her social circle was narrowing rather than growing, but perhaps in the current circumstances, it was just as well.

Jack came over at the end of the class and helped her pack up her materials, resisting her attempts to brush him off.

'Come on,' he said. 'I'll give you a lift home. I'll even let you smoke in the car. You must be desperate for a fag.'

'That's you, not me. I'm not smoking,' she said, but she accepted the lift. 'And anyway, it's not exactly a concession. You smoke in the car whether someone else is there or not.'

'Don't you want to know the gossip?' asked Jack, once they were on the road.

'If you insist on telling me,' she said with a fake yawn, which turned into a genuine one mid-way.

'Nick apologised. When he picked up Millie. Proper hanging head in shame, handshake, no hard feelings job. Claire's aunt said some stuff to him and the red mist came down. Can you believe it? He blamed it on the drink and said he didn't know what came over him.' Jack laughed. 'It was hard to keep a straight face.'

'But you did?'

'Yes, of course. I said don't worry about it and these things happen. We may even have bonded over it. He said Claire's now worried it's something about her that sends her men reaching for the bottle.'

Gennie smiled. 'I know just how she feels,' she said, although it wasn't the need for alcohol itself that made her feel so inadequate but rather her apparent inability to offer any alternative.

'So, how did you enjoy being mum for a week – doing

your packed lunches and ballet runs?' she asked, changing the subject.

'Piece of cake. I don't know what all the fuss is about. I couldn't do it all the time, though. I'd never get anything done. She doesn't seem to be in school for more than five minutes.'

'Ah, but that's when you get together with the other mums and lift share,' she said.

'Yeah, some of the mothers offered to help with Millie. I said I wanted her to myself for the week but several women gave me their numbers in case I needed a hand in the future.'

Gennie burst out laughing. 'I bet they did! I expect you were a bit of a hit in the playground. Helpless single dad. You could do quite well there. Not much competition.'

'You sound like Max. He said I should help him tout for business among the playground mums. Refer the married ones to him and follow up the unmarried ones myself,' said Jack.

'Would you get commission?'

'He didn't say. I wondered if they were going to report back to Claire on how I did. It was like I was on probation.'

Gennie was still laughing. 'I can see it now. Did you lean against the gate of the playground with the dog, looking a bit lost? Or were you doing the chain-smoking moody thing? I bet the mums were falling over themselves to help you. They'll be bringing you casseroles next.'

'Funny you should say that. I got invited to dinner. But I made an excuse.' He pulled a face.

'Why?'

'Because I don't want to do that. I can't do that – turn up for dinner, be interesting, stay sober. I'm an even worse date than you.'

'Surely not!'

'I can't deal with people's expectations. And then they get pissed off with me.' It almost sounded like an apology.

'Aren't you being a bit dramatic?' Gennie said dismissively, before remembering with a twinge how she'd complained to Jack about Jim's expectations. Fortunately, he hadn't been listening.

'Maybe,' Jack continued, 'but look how pissed off you get. Refusing to speak to me. I don't want to get involved in all that.'

Gennie was shocked. 'I didn't think it made any difference what I thought – or anyone else, for that matter.' She paused. Just because she didn't want to get involved with him didn't mean he should avoid other people. She touched his arm. 'You shouldn't feel like that, Jack. I have problems with your drinking, but that's all. If other people can deal with it, then it isn't an issue, either for you or them. I can't bear it because I watched my husband die from liver failure before he reached the age of forty – after years of constant, daily drinking. There was always an excuse. We're "out with friends",' she said, making quotation marks with her fingers, 'it was "a work thing", it's been a "bad day". And if I watched him die, that means that Alice did too, and I wouldn't wish that on Millie. Neither would you.'

'No,' Jack replied shortly.

'The way you drink scares me. It's reckless and self-destructive,' she added.

Jack looked surprised.

'But apart from that, you're okay,' she continued, in a more positive tone. 'You're tidy and useful around the place. And you're easy enough on the eye. There were just as many people putting pen to paper in there as sitting back drinking tea and staring.'

He grimaced now.

'I also assumed it suited you not to have any commitments and that you enjoyed the freedom.'

'I do like the freedom,' he admitted. 'But also, look, I've fucked up enough. I'm in no hurry to do that again and there's other stuff I need to do, like find somewhere to live. Maybe do up a house.'

Gennie paused again. 'You think I've been harsh on you?'

'Very. You'll have to think of a way to make amends,' he said, pulling into the farmyard and turning off the engine.

And he was back to himself. How did he do that? Bounce back so quickly from disillusion and despondency. While she marvelled at Jack's powers of recovery, she caught sight of Marion in the yard, hands waving wildly, trying to attract their attention.

'I've had a call from Hamid's foster carer,' she said, when Gennie reached her. 'He's missing. Look, has he been in touch with either of you?'

'Oh,' said Gennie. 'Well...'

'You too?' said Jack, looking across at her.

32

'What happened?' asked Gennie, following Marion into the kitchen, where Alex and Sean sat next to each other, as if they'd been kept in after school.

'He didn't go home last night,' Marion said, motioning for Gennie and Jack to sit down, 'but the family didn't call the police until today. He didn't leave a note or tell anyone where he was going. He was supposed to be at taekwondo yesterday evening so they didn't realise he was missing until late evening. It seems he left college before lunch.'

'Did something trigger this? Do they know why he went?' said Jack.

'Not so far, but do you two mind telling me about the contact you've had with Hamid, bearing in mind all the rules we have in place here about safeguarding children?'

Marion must really be angry to have told them off in public. Her usual practice was to take people into her office for a quiet word.

Gennie looked at her hands. They were still covered in charcoal and her nails were filthy, the hands of someone who'd failed to wash away the evidence of their dirty work.

'I'm sorry,' she said. 'I only had a couple of messages saying he'd try to come down at Easter, but that's three weeks away.'

'I also had a message like that,' admitted Jack, 'and one complaining that his social worker wouldn't help him trace his brother.'

Sean cleared his throat. 'Erm, I had a message too.' He paused. 'But I didn't reply.'

'Caught in possession but he didn't inhale,' said Jack, smiling and patting Sean's shoulder.

'He couldn't have been taken by anyone, could he?' asked Gennie, looking from face to face as if the answers were hidden there.

'The police could track his phone,' Jack said.

'Perhaps,' said Marion. 'If we knew why he'd gone, we could guess where. But look, there has to be a strong chance that he'll try to come back here and we need to be ready for that. If I'm honest, I'm worried that because he's young and a refugee, no-one will put much effort into looking for him.'

Sean cleared his throat.

'So,' Alex started. 'Sean and I were considering how to manage this, given the professional boundaries and so on, and we think it's acceptable for us to try to contact Hamid through the formal channels open to us—'

'Which are?' interrupted Jack.

'Well, through the police and social services. And obviously, we can make it known that, provided he wishes to, he can be brought back here initially as a place of safety.'

'That's it?'

182

'Well, yes.' Sean shrugged, apologetically.

'Fucking hopeless,' Jack told Marion, and went outside to smoke.

*

Marion called a meeting on Wednesday evening. Gennie missed it as she was at the cash-and-carry stocking up on flour, cleaning products and paper goods. The local council had warned Marion to be prepared for school closures. Word had obviously got round as the scenes at the warehouse were apocalyptic; shelves were stripped bare and customers were racing trolleys between the aisles to beat other shoppers to kitchen roll and shower gel. Gennie returned to the farm with a car packed to the gunnels to find the place in a state of hysteria. Teenage girls were crying in the yard as the key workers tried to calm them and usher them back indoors.

'What's going on?' Gennie asked Sean, her heart pounding. It looked horribly like they might have had bad news.

'The police put out an announcement about Hamid on TV and the kids didn't take it well.'

'Oh,' Gennie said, exhaling, relief fighting it out with anxiety in her chest. She pointed at the car. 'Is there anyone who can help me unload this stuff?'

'I will,' said Jack, moving from his spot by the kitchen door.

'I'm surprised you haven't worn holes in the doorstep, the amount of time you spend there,' she said. He rubbed her arm in response.

She opened the boot and handed him a twelve-bottle pack of bleach. 'Aren't you tempted to go looking for him?'

'I am,' said Jack. 'I'm very tempted. And I would if I knew where to start. The only thing is, I think he can look after himself better than most. He made it from Iran to the UK in the backs of lorries, don't forget.'

She might have believed him if his shoulders weren't hunched or he'd made eye contact. Stranger still, he joined the entire household in the sitting room to watch television, which in the time Gennie had lived at the farm had only happened once before – on Christmas Eve. It wasn't something she did often either, but it was curious how they all felt the need to come together, instinctively. One of their number was missing and the rest of them would look after each other.

Gennie went to bed when she could keep her eyes open no longer. Her mind, though, had other ideas. The last few weeks had been hard going, even without this, and as soon as she pushed one uncomfortable thought aside, another one intruded. By three in the morning, the muscles in her back and legs had stiffened up and her throat was so tight she could hardly breathe. There was as much chance of her sleeping as climbing Kilimanjaro. She pulled her clothes back on, stuffed her feet into her boots and went next door to the farmhouse for a proper torch, nearly jumping out of her skin at the sight of the person in the armchair. The burning cigarette gave away his identity.

'Don't tell Marion I'm smoking in the kitchen,' said Jack, still in his coat, Roxy asleep at his feet.

'My God, you scared the life out of me,' she gasped, taking in the open window, which must be why he hadn't triggered the alarm. She sniffed suspiciously. 'You haven't been drinking, have you?'

'No, I fucking haven't! I haven't even been doing your ironing. You didn't leave any.'

'Oh, was it you? I thought it was the piskies,' she said, innocently. She knew when Jack had had a particularly bad night by the piles of freshly pressed laundry which greeted her in the morning.

'Funny. What are you up to anyway?' he asked as she rootled in the cupboard under the sink.

'I can't sleep,' she answered. 'Thought I'd go for a walk. Can I take Roxy?'

'On your own? Is that a good idea? We could end up scouring the hedgerows for you as well as Hamid… I'll come with you. All this waiting is doing my head in.'

As they set off down the lane accompanied by the sleepy dog, Jack asked, 'How far do you want to walk? I have a couple of nocturnal ramble routes.'

It started to drizzle and Gennie pulled the hood of her sweatshirt over her head. Jack held the torch in his right hand and after a while, Gennie put her arm through his left so that she didn't slide in the dark. It felt so natural, she barely registered she was doing it, and Jack didn't object.

The dog was tired after a mile or so and Jack tucked her under his right arm and gave the torch to Gennie. The lanes were quiet and black as pitch without the torch light. Occasionally there was a rustling from the hedges and trees, and once or twice, some small creature ran away from them or across their path, making Gennie jump.

Jack broke the silence. 'So why can't you sleep then?'

'Oh, the usual. The world's a sad, scary place, I'm a miserable, sad person, and Hamid's missing,' Gennie said.

'Is that all?' he said, and Gennie wasn't sure whether to

185

laugh. 'I'll admit I thought Hamid would have turned up by now, but I'm sure he'll make contact sooner or later. And the pandemic? Yeah… that's not looking too good. But you…? You seem to be doing okay to me. I mean, no-one's starved yet and everyone has clean underwear.'

'Is that it? My life goals? Oh, Jesus.' It was worse than she thought.

Jack started to laugh.

'It's not funny,' she protested. 'I feel trapped. The walls are closing in. I can't move forward and there is no back for me to go to. I didn't want to recreate what I had before and, like you, I was in no hurry to get into something new, but I'm so tired of taking my life one day at a time and now there's all this. Have we missed our chances?' A thought suddenly occurred to her. 'Are you listening?'

'I'm listening. Look, you are where you are. You can't change it,' he said matter-of-factly.

'D'you believe in fate, though?' she asked. 'D'you think this is where we were destined to get to? That when we first met all those years ago, the paths of our lives were laid out?'

'No, I think life is just luck and coincidence,' he answered, reaching in his inside pocket for a packet of cigarettes, 'and the paths we take are random. If you'd told me then that there was some grand plan, that I had to live through all that pain and destruction to get to some predetermined place, I would have said the price was too high.'

Gennie had no answer to this. She hugged his arm tighter. 'Can I have a cigarette?' she asked. Acknowledging she was having a crisis was not a defeat. Some schools of thought would call it progress. 'Or maybe just a drag of yours?'

'Certainly not,' said Jack. 'You've given up, remember?

I'll say one thing, though. You need to be braver. You will be miserable if you sit in your cottage drawing pictures of the dog. You need to go with the flow, trust in life to take care of you, as Marion would say. You need to have some fun. Come surfing. It always works for me.'

This didn't seem like the answer. 'I haven't been surfing since I was about seventeen,' she said.

'Why not? Surely it's in your bones.'

'Probably because I was working and then, none of the boys I liked were into surfing.'

'Well, there you are. That's the root of your problems. Hanging around with the wrong boys,' Jack said smugly.

'Almost certainly.' Gennie nodded. 'But I'm not sure the right boys were surfing either.' He wouldn't see her smile in the darkness.

'I see.' Jack took the hit. 'Can I ask you something, though? Were you happy with Mikkel? Did he treat you okay? I s'pose what I'm asking is whether you strayed, I mean, when you were married and the cracks started to show.'

She reflected that he was the only person to have asked that – and the only person to assume that alcoholism would break a relationship, rather than brushing it away as not a big deal and completely manageable. It was easier to be accepted, and accept yourself, as a grieving widow if you could depict your marriage as happy and your loss as overwhelming rather than face the fact that you had problems. It was much harder to tell people that you were furious with your husband by the point he was terminally ill and harder still for them to accept that the death of your alcoholic, unemployed husband was just as devastating as if your marriage had been perfect.

Gennie sighed. 'Apart from that one episode, with which you're familiar and which we'll gloss over, I was always faithful to him and we were happy in the beginning. Really. It only got difficult after a few years. And then things became impossible when he was told to stop drinking and didn't. And just when I thought I'd had enough, he became really sick. I wouldn't have left him then. I can't think about this,' she said, cross to hear her voice crack, 'I'll get upset. Whatever else, it was such a waste. The thing I struggle with is that he had a choice. He chose to carry on drinking when he knew it would kill him. It's as if he chose to leave us, chose to throw it all away and nothing I said or did made any difference.' She took a deep breath. 'You need to make better choices, Jack.'

'Yes.' He took a breath. 'I also need to move the dog as my hand's going to sleep.' He moved Roxy to his left arm and Gennie moved round to his right with the torch. He put his arm round her shoulder and hugged her.

'I'm not apologising for him,' Jack said slowly, 'but maybe he didn't really have a choice. It's a disease. It was there when you married him but you didn't see it. Or maybe you did and it made no difference. You think people will change.'

'And they don't?'

'No. People's circumstances might change but they don't, at least not fundamentally. Traumatic brain injuries aside, obviously. You are what you are and you just have to get on with it,' he said, rather bleakly. 'You can certainly be knocked off course by the things that happen, like the way light or sound change direction when they hit something, or a wave refracts and changes direction but it doesn't really change. There's no transformation. And I don't think people really change. It's how you react that makes the difference.'

'Are those surfing metaphors for me?' she asked.

'Yeah, if you like.' He laughed. 'The way you react is determined by who you are. Marion has a lot of crystals and prisms. Well, she would do.' He shrugged. 'I spent hours when I was a kid, watching the light pass through them, trying to make rainbows. I think it's the same thing with people. You hit an obstacle and change course or you break into your constituent parts.'

Gennie nodded and they walked in silence for a moment. The philosophy of Jack Aspinall. She'd certainly been knocked sideways by the events of the last couple of years and from what she'd seen, Jack had fragmented. They were both trying to get used to their new direction.

'D'you know what else is hard?' Once she'd started, she needed to tell him everything. 'His parents blamed me. I don't have anything to do with them now. They assumed he drank because I was such a witch. I became a witch because of it.' She moved the torch to her left hand and quickly wiped the tears from her face with her right. 'I suppose the hair thing didn't help.'

'What hair thing?'

'Oh God,' she said, glad of the dark as she started her story. 'You remember I had long hair? Well, when Mikkel died, he was cremated as per his wishes, but he hadn't left instructions about his ashes. Alice and I weren't sure what to do. We had a vague plan to take him somewhere hot as he loved the sun but his parents wanted us to scatter his ashes on this tiny island in Denmark, because that's where his dad's family is from. So off we went – his parents, my parents, Alice and me, with the ashes in a grey plastic flask. It was so awful. We had to get a boat to the place and, although it was summer, it was freezing, you know, low grey skies and gale-force winds, everyone seasick, no-one speaking to each other.' She started to shiver at the memory.

'We got to the island, and when we'd recovered, we tramped up a hill to a spot where there was a good view of the sea. His dad said a few words, but they were in Danish, so we didn't understand them, and then he took the canister from me and unscrewed the lid. And that's when all hell broke loose. Are you sure I can't have a cigarette?'

'Positive. Tell me about the hell.'

'Well, it was really windy at the top of the hill so he didn't need to do much to release the ashes but he kind of threw them up in the air and a gust of wind caught them and threw them straight back at us. I got most of it, along with Alice. The ashes were in my mouth, my eyes, my hair, all over my clothes.'

'I don't think that's unusual,' said Jack.

'So I've heard, and that's what my dad tried to say. Alice was brilliant about it. She took it as a sign that Mikkel wanted to stay with us.'

Gennie remembered the taste and feel of the ash in her mouth and how she'd stood, flapping her hands, as her mum took a tissue to her face and whispered exhortations not to swallow, while Mikkel's dad looked on, horrified, apologising endlessly.

'The problem was his mum. She was shrieking that she'd lost her son and kept pulling at my jacket and my hair. I kind of overreacted. I marched down the hill and into the village – well, it was more like a road with five houses – and I knocked on all the doors until someone agreed to give me a pair of scissors.'

'Go on,' said Jack, amused.

'And then I stood in the street and cut all my hair off and stuffed it in the plastic canister to give it to her.'

'What did his mother do?' asked Jack.

'Well, of course, when I started chopping at my hair, she got scared. She thought I'd gone completely mad and scuttled off with her husband to get the ferry back to the mainland. But the boats only run every hour and they were still waiting on the jetty when we arrived and I presented them with the hair. And then we all had to get the ferry back together. In stony silence.' She paused. 'Then when we got back to the hotel, I went to the hairdressers' and got my handiwork tidied up. And they asked me whether I wanted colour and I chose blonde. So there you are. And we haven't spoken since.'

'I'm not surprised. I bet they wouldn't know where to begin. I have to say that I thought I'd done some crazy things, but that – that's beautiful. Respect, G!' And he took his arm from her and tried to high five her free hand.

'It may sound mad,' said Gennie, 'but the other options weren't great. Alice was upset by the idea that if I washed my hair, her father would go down the drain.'

'What did Alice do while you were making a spectacle of yourself?'

'My dad took her off for an ice cream, of course, while my mum stayed with me, saying, "Oh my God," every thirty seconds and trying to stop a crowd forming.' She paused to take a deep breath and change the subject. 'So what mad things have you done?'

'Nothing that would compare. Picking fights with people who would have killed me, drink, drugs, getting a tattoo, usual dull stuff. But,' he added, 'I like your hair blonde. It reminds me of my first real crush.'

'Go on then,' said Gennie, hearing the smile in his voice and knowing the comparison wasn't going to flatter her.

'I was about eleven years old and she was a lesbian, feminist, performance artist and poet. She had bleached, spiky hair and so many piercings it took about ten minutes to get all the jewellery in. She stayed at our house. I used to come in from school and watch her doing her hair. Vanna, she was called. I thought she was amazing.'

'Was she any good?' asked Gennie.

'As a poet?' he asked. 'Difficult to tell. Her English was terrible.'

Gennie burst out laughing and nudged him in the ribs with the torch. 'You've just made that up.'

'Really not. Ask Marion to find a photo of her.'

'So, tell me, did you cheat on Claire?' she asked.

'Oh, no, you don't want to go there.' He half laughed. 'Technically, I only cheated with my wife – until Claire threw me out. Well, for the second time.'

'How many times did she throw you out?' Now Gennie was curious.

'Three, I think?' he said, with a question in his voice.

Gennie laughed. 'I'm sorry,' she said. 'It isn't funny at all. Maybe you should be stamped with a government health warning.'

'Isn't that your job, though? Resident government health warning.' He had his arm around her again which softened the effect of his words. 'But don't believe everything Shirley tells you.' After a pause, he asked, 'Are you okay financially?'

'Yes. Well, obviously I had to sell the house. Mikkel was fairly careless. When we had money, we'd go on fantastic holidays or he'd buy me amazing presents. And then I'd find there was no money to pay the gas bill. I still have all the jewellery Mikkel bought me – mainly when he'd behaved badly. So I'm wearing diamond earrings with my wellies. Only two piercings, though.' She pointed to her ears with their elegant studs.

'And diamonds are a girl's best friend?' Jack asked.

'Yes, and they are forever. Maybe you don't need love when you have diamonds.' She tried to laugh but it felt hollow. She was lucky, though. She had Alice, and that was enough love to be going on with.

'And are you cleaning out my chickens in diamond earrings?' asked Jack, whose thoughts were obviously following a different track.

'Yes – and rings under my gloves.'

'I like it that you wear your best for my girls. I've been told it's important to accessorise, though. Maybe you could add a tiara? Millie has one.' He laughed when she pushed him away from her.

They had now circled back to the farm. There was a hint of a rosy dawn in the sky but the buildings were still dark.

'Oh God, I have to get up in an hour to start on the kids' breakfast.' Gennie sighed and rubbed her face.

'Take a sickie this morning. I'll tell Marion. She won't mind looking after the kids. If the schools close next week, things could get a bit interesting here. Take the time while you can,' said Jack.

'Are you sure?'

'Absolutely. Go to bed. Take a sleeping pill. You must have some. Or you can have one of mine.' He nudged her towards her cottage. 'Night, night. Dream about big waves.'

33

Gennie woke with a start. Jack was leaning over her. She put her arm over her face, hiding her mascara-clogged eyes.

'Oh, God, what time is it?'

'It's after twelve. I tried knocking on the door but you didn't answer so I got worried. You should lock your door. Anyone could walk in.'

Gennie yawned and closed her eyes again. 'I suppose I better get up and start putting dinner together.'

'I've got good news on that. You've got the day off. In lieu of next week. We're locking down, it seems, so let's go to the beach and do some surfing. Could be our last chance.' He chewed his knuckles in mock terror. Andy's habit.

Her eyes were open now, her stomach tense. It wasn't only the lockdown making her anxious. 'I thought you were joking about surfing! Anyway, I don't remember how.'

'I'll show you. Come on, get up and get something to eat and we'll head out to Polzeath. It's a lovely day.'

He left while she got washed and dressed, pulling her swimming costume on under her T-shirt and fleece and filling a bag with her towel and underwear. Still yawning, she went next door to the farmhouse, where Jack handed her a fried egg sandwich, barely giving her time to eat it before hustling her out of the door. Roxy jumped and barked around their heels as they made their way to the Land Rover.

Gennie picked her up. 'Yes, you're coming too,' she said, settling into the front seat with the dog on her lap. She stroked the dog's ears between her fingers, a useful distraction while she chose the right words.

'You know, Jack, I've been thinking. I may have been a bit oversensitive about things and I might have taken it out on you. You've always been a decent friend to me – I mean, rescuing me from Jim and so on.'

'Well, I'd never leave a man behind.' He grinned. The bright smile was a reflexive response, like his mother, and it took your attention away from how tired his eyes were. The more used Gennie became to the smile, the more she noticed the eyes.

'Okay, so say that was a duty call. But I do appreciate the things you've done for me – like giving me lifts and that time you fetched Alice from school when I was ill. So I was thinking I would like to be your friend now. Will you upgrade me?' she asked, stroking the dozing dog.

'Yeah, okay.' Jack was still concentrating on the road.

'So you don't mind the things I said?'

'I wouldn't say that. I thought you were a bit nuts is all. I was always your friend but you didn't want to be mine and that's fine. Marion said you needed to put boundaries in place so you felt like you were in control.'

'I knew you'd tell Marion!' Gennie had also told Marion, whose response had been the same, although she'd added that it was good for her to seek out healthy rather than unhealthy relationships and most people would have concerns about the widow of an alcoholic befriending a recovering drinker whose previous relationship had been with the widow of his best friend. She wondered sometimes if Marion had hired her as a living, breathing victim impact assessment, a cautionary tale for Jack.

'I told Max too,' Jack added.

'And what did he say?'

'He said it proved you were interested in me.' He looked across at her and smiled.

'I see,' she said carefully, 'and what did you say to that?'

'I told him he was way off the pace.'

'And did you tell him why?' she asked, equally slowly.

'No, we'd never hear the end of it if we gave him that little nugget but I don't think it's ever been about not being attracted to each other.' He smiled again.

'No,' she admitted. Before she could say more, her phone rang. When she saw the caller's name, she touched Jack's arm to get him to slow down. 'It's Marion.'

'Gennie? Is Jack with you? Look, darling, the police have traced Hamid's phone to Birmingham. They've contacted West Midlands Police and they'll take it from here. I thought you should both know. You mustn't try to contact him.'

'Oh, right! We'll come back, then,' said Gennie.

'Absolutely not,' said Marion. 'What are you going to do here? We have to let the police get on with their work.'

Jack had been trying to get a word in. Finally he swung into a passing place. Gennie handed him the phone and listened to his side of a conversation, consisting of 'Yeah, but…', 'I know, but…', 'Okay, but…'. After a minute, he handed the phone back and pulled back onto the road.

'She doesn't want us there,' he said shortly.

Gennie looked away to hide her smile. Marion must have the same mental image as she did of Jack, pacing the yard and waving his cigarette about. He was better off surfing.

They arrived at the beach and stopped in the small car park on the sand. Jack was right: it was a beautiful day – bright, sunny and slightly breezy. He took Gennie in to one of the hire shops, whose owner he seemed to know well, and kitted her out with a rash vest, wetsuit, shoes, gloves and a huge soft board, and made her carry it all to the beach while he went to get his own board down from the roof of the Land Rover. It was a little chilly to strip off, but Gennie did as she was told, and by the time Jack returned, she had wriggled out of her street clothes and into the vest and wetsuit. It was rather snug and she was having difficulty pulling up the zip.

'Here,' said Jack, and turned her round, yanking the shoulders of the suit higher on her shoulders and the sides of the zip tight together, sealing her firmly inside, treating her much as he would an overstuffed suitcase.

Gennie lifted her board and looked at the sea, glistening at the end of the funnel-shaped beach, gentle cliffs on either side. It seemed awfully distant.

'Start walking, while I put your stuff away,' ordered Jack, and ran back to the Land Rover.

She hadn't made much progress by the time he caught up with her. Her arm was already aching and the board kept slipping out of her grasp, narrowly missing Roxy, trotting along by her side. He sighed and took her board and told her to run to the water's edge and back instead.

'You need to warm up,' he insisted.

When she returned, he made her do star jumps before suggesting that she lay on the sand and did star jumps to stretch her arms. She was already on her back before she realised what she was doing. She picked up a handful of sand and threw it in Jack's direction.

'This is a sand angel,' she said. 'You're not funny, you know.'

Eventually after some basic training, Gennie fastened her surfboard cuff round her ankle and stepped into the sea. Surfing on water was a different kettle of fish to play-surfing on sand. Even paddling out was a challenge. Each time she climbed on the board, she slid off the other side, and within minutes, she had eyes full of salt.

'I'm going to do this,' she told herself, as she made it from her stomach to four-point kneeling before a wave tipped her off again.

It didn't help that the first time she got to her feet, Jack slid by calling encouragement. Where had he come from?

'Go away,' she yelled as she fell head-first into the surf.

'Okay?' he asked as she resurfaced.

'I was 'til you showed up.' She sprawled across her board, legs flailing as she tried to get some purchase. No sooner was she back on than Jack reached out a hand and tipped her off again.

However hard she tried, she couldn't dislodge him. He remained sitting smugly and securely astride his board. She needed a change of tactics. She cradled her arm and rubbed her elbow, pursing her lips in pain, before turning and heading for the beach, pushing her board before her. Jack followed, lying prone as he paddled towards her. When she reached the shallows, she undid the velcro ankle cuff and shoved her board onto the sand. As she waded back into the water, still cradling her arm, Jack leaned up on his board, brow furrowed. When she drew near enough, she bent her head to him. He raised his chin and she kissed him. His eyes widened in surprise and she took her chance, using all her might to force him off the board and into the water. It wasn't deep, mid-thigh at most, but it was the victory that counted. She clapped her hands in delight but changed her mind when he righted himself with a roar. Running away was impossible. He pounced before she'd taken a step, grabbed her round the waist and pushed her back down and under the water. She was concentrating so hard on holding her breath against the incursion of seawater, it took her a second to realise he was kissing her.

'Enough,' he said, climbing back onto his board. 'I'm going further in. Will you be all right for a while?'

'Yes, fine.' She smiled brightly. If he thought she'd gone too far, why had he kissed her back? She'd only done it because it was the last thing he'd have expected. Still, it was hardly going to ruin a relationship which veered between fractious and semi-frozen.

While Jack chased better waves, Gennie tried a few more times to get on the board and then gave up and switched her attention to Roxy, who was livid with the tide for swallowing up her beach and barked her fury at each approaching line of foam. Gennie found some shells and between burying them in the sand for the dog to dig up, she watched Jack. He was different on the water. He didn't race for every wave, fighting it out with the current in some war of attrition, but took his time, choosing his moments carefully, dropping back gracefully into the water at the end of each ride. By five, the light was starting to fade and Gennie was cold and tired of squinting at the horizon. She signalled to Jack and he paddled in.

'Had enough? Okay, we'll get changed and then go and get some tea or something.'

The surf shop was now shut so they propped Gennie's board by the back door. Gennie struggled out of her wetsuit and went to drape it over the board. Jack took it off her and started walking to the car.

'Don't we have to give it back?' asked Gennie, shivering in her wet swimsuit and rash vest.

'No, it's yours. No need to thank me. It's second-hand. No diamonds from me, I'm afraid. Just rubber.' He raised his eyebrows.

'It's not even rubber,' said Gennie, pulling a face despite her chattering teeth. 'I remember now why we weren't friends.'

As they reached the car, she asked, 'Have you got a dry robe?'

Jack's expression was scathing. 'I'll hold the towel for you, though.' He kept his eyes averted as she dragged off her wet clothes, too cold to care who saw her. Once in her T-shirt and knickers, she climbed into the back of the Land Rover and rubbed her frozen legs before trying to cram them into her jeans. After a few minutes, Jack opened the door and, checking she was decent, climbed into the back of the Land Rover, bare-chested and already in his jeans.

He pulled a T-shirt and socks on, and squinted at Gennie, who was still shivering.

'Why aren't you wearing a shirt? You always wear one. Here, take mine.' He gave her his flannel shirt and then his fleece to put on over the top of her own, insisting he'd be fine in his T-shirt and jacket. She wouldn't have taken them but she was so cold she feared she might develop hypothermia.

Jack rubbed her arms and shoulders. 'We'll get some tea and you'll warm up soon enough.'

They made their way to the café facing the beach. Gennie and Roxy took up residence on the banquette, backs to the steamed-up windows while Jack fetched tea and chips from the counter.

'Earl Grey,' said Jack, plonking a mug in front of her.

She was surprised he'd remembered, but he'd also remembered to get a saucer for Roxy.

Gennie sipped at the tea and felt warmth returning to her extremities, including her nose and ears, which must have been glowing pink in the fug of the café. She combed her fingers through her damp hair to coax it into some sort of order and tried to ignore the pressure of Jack's thigh against hers. They were sitting shoulder to shoulder and the physical warmth of him was unsettling her. There were times when his vulnerability induced such tenderness in her, she could imagine her arms around him, holding him, rocking away the pain, but at other times, she had nothing for him and the well was dry. Right now, he was the hot guy at the beach, showing off his surfing and lending her his fleece. She needed to impose some space. After all, he was the one who'd distanced himself in the sea. She edged away but noticed after a minute or so that her thigh was again brushing his. She pulled Roxy onto her lap and moved nearer to the end of the banquette.

'Why do you keep moving away from me?' he asked suddenly. 'Every time I move nearer to you, you move away.'

How could she explain this? 'It's because I'd like to move closer, but… I know that doesn't make much sense.'

'I've come to expect that,' he answered. 'But if you want to move closer, move closer. You're about to fall off the end of the bench.'

She inched nearer. 'I wasn't sure it was what you wanted.'

He leaned against the back of the bench, stretched out his legs and exhaled. 'Oh, Gennie! Shall we go home?'

When they were in the car and Jack had started the engine and turned the lights on, he turned to her. 'I'd like to point out that it was you who kissed me first. As usual, I might add.'

Gennie grimaced and held up her hands to acknowledge her guilt.

'And you've always had terrible timing,' he added.

She nodded. 'Yes.'

He didn't speak again until they reached the farm. There were lights on in the kitchen and upstairs in the farmhouse. 'Will you help me put the stuff away?'

Jack lifted the surfboard from the roof of the Land Rover and handed her the wetsuits and boots. She rinsed them under the outside tap and carried them into the shed. When, if ever, would she be wearing the suit again? Neither of them spoke while he was stowing all the equipment, which he appeared to be doing as slowly as he could. He stopped her as she turned to leave and turned her back to face him, resting his forearms on her shoulders.

'Look, I think it would be a mistake, don't you?' he said, avoiding eye contact.

202

Gennie smiled. 'Yes,' she said, knowing then with absolute certainty where their evening was headed and finding that, she was quite in favour of the plan. Perhaps it was the promise of human warmth that swayed her, although it was typical of Jack to think he could evade responsibility for any dire consequences if he had warned her of them in advance.

'We don't need any of this last-fling-before-the-shutters-come-down vibe,' he said.

'We don't.' She shook her head.

'We'd probably regret it,' he continued, managing to look at her this time.

'I'm sure we would,' she said, sure of this too. She pulled him gently towards her by his T-shirt until their noses were an inch apart. He held her gaze, unsmiling for a change, but he didn't need to: he had nothing to disguise; the tension that lay at the back of his eyes had gone, and his expression was soft and open.

'Shall we go?' she said softly.

They walked slowly back into the darkened yard via the Land Rover, where Jack briefly rummaged in the glove compartment, and towards the adjacent doors of the farm kitchen and Gennie's cottage. Jack opened the farm kitchen door and tucked Roxy inside.

'I'll come in for a minute, then. Get my clothes back.'

Gennie unlocked the cottage and Jack followed her in. They were kissing before she'd even shut the door, smiles colliding, followed by tongues and hips, rocking slowly from foot to foot. She moved her hand from his cheek to the back of his neck, stroking skin still grainy with salt and sand.

'Upstairs,' she said, needing a moment to catch some air.

'Hang on.' He bent to unlace their boots, pulling hers off her feet before throwing his on the floor.

She wanted to reach her bedroom before he did, but apart from the dirty mug on the side and the books on the floor, it wasn't in too bad a state. She flicked off the ceiling light in favour of the side lamp and just had time to shove the cat off the bed as Jack arrived, intent on helping her out of her two layers of fleece, dropping them in a tangle on the floor. He pulled her towards him and set about freeing her from her shirt.

'Why did I make you wear so many clothes?' he complained. 'And why are there so many buttons?'

'Jack?' she said as he stripped off his T-shirt and reached for hers. It had been a while since anyone had touched her or since she'd wanted someone to. Someone meant someone new. It would need an adjustment.

'No?' he said, hands pausing halfway up her ribs, thumbs nudging the underside of her breasts.

'No, it's yes, but…' If she was going to break her fast with someone, it was right it should be this one, hands she trusted, in a place she felt safe.

'I know,' he said, and kissed her, gently. 'We'll go slow.'

He lifted the quilt on her bed with exaggerated courtesy and guided her in, still in her jeans and T-shirt, before dropping his own clothes and hopping in beside her.

'D'you need a hand?'

'Nope,' she said, untangling his fingers from the button of her jeans, and sliding the denim down her thighs an inch at a time.

'Hurry up,' he said, and turned his attention to her collarbone.

The look of him was familiar, and his voice, the things he said, but the feel of him was new and the taste of his breath. Was that mint? The drinker's giveaway.

The cat had crept back onto the bed by the time, a little later, that Jack sank, breathless, onto Gennie's shoulder. He kissed her neck and she hugged him, instinctively. They'd shared a glimpse into the past and closed the door on it.

After a moment Jack lifted his head. 'Worth waiting,' he said, a statement rather than a question. 'And better waiting 'til we were married, don't you think?'

She couldn't help laughing. 'You mean to other people?'

Before he could respond, Gennie's attention was caught by a knocking at the cottage door. Was she hallucinating? 'Can you hear that too?'

'How do you do it?' he asked, looking down at her with respect. 'D'you summon the spirits to come to your aid?'

'I'll see who it is.' Gennie climbed out of bed and pulled on her jeans and Jack's shirt, indistinguishable from one of her own, and ran down the stairs. She was surprised to find Marion at her door, Roxy under one arm.

'Sorry to disturb you, Gennie. D'you know where Jack is? The dog's going mad and I need to speak to him. The police have contacted social services about Hamid and they've been on to me. They want details about the apprenticeship and completion dates.'

'Have they found him, then?' said Gennie, fighting the urge to follow Marion back into the farmhouse and hear the latest news, but she'd have to sort out the man in her bed first. She hoped his boots weren't visible behind her in the hallway. 'I'm not sure where Jack is, though. He might be in the shed. We've only just got back so he won't be far away.

Shall I keep the dog 'til he shows up?'

She took charge of Roxy and went back up to where Jack was already dressing.

'I'd better see what she needs, but I'll be back. Don't move.' He tickled the top of the dog's head and bounded down the stairs.

34

Gennie shut Sergio in the kitchen and Roxy in the hall, each with a bowl of water and some treats, and strict orders to behave. They immediately took up positions either side of the kitchen door and resumed their habitual growling match, Roxy jumping and scratching at the floor.

'Be reasonable, guys,' Gennie said. 'I need a moment, maybe two.'

Maybe ten. Her bed was full of sand, and her attempts to brush it up only spread it further. She untucked the sheet and bundled it up, lifted the sash window and shook the sheet outside, only remembering as she pulled the sheet back in to check there'd been no-one underneath the window. It was just as well her room faced the side of the farm and not the yard, where there were passers-by, not to mention witnesses. Her hair was also full of sand and stiff with salt, and her scalp had started to itch. She climbed into the bath and turned on the overhead shower. Jack wouldn't be back; and actually, that was fine. There were worse ways to while away an afternoon waiting for the apocalypse.

Gennie lifted her face to the rush of hot water and willed it to cleanse her of emotion along with the seawater. Her day had been filled with physical sensations and her body felt pleasantly used, stretched and purposeful, released temporarily from the tangle of confusion which nested at her core.

There were sounds outside the bathroom door. She shut off the water to listen.

'Gennie?' His voice was quiet, not much more than a whisper.

'In here,' she said. 'I'm nearly done. You can come in.' She turned the taps back on. She wouldn't think too deeply about what she was doing. Going with the flow, wasn't that it?

Jack came into the tiny bathroom, half filling the space between the basin at one end and toilet at the other, staring directly at her through the shower screen.

'Get in if you like.'

'Is there room?' he asked.

'Room to wash,' she answered. She averted her eyes as he peeled off his clothes again and climbed in with her.

'Here,' she said, pressing a bottle of shower gel to his chest as he pulled her wet body towards him. She squeezed shampoo into her hand and started to wash his hair while, his hand on her hip, he turned her this way and that.

'Where's your tattoo?' he asked. 'Max said you had a tattoo.'

'And you believed him? I haven't got a tattoo.' She was struggling to keep her balance in the cramped space. 'Is that why you came back then? To check out my tattoo.'

'No. Well, maybe,' he said, shaking his head obligingly as she lifted down the shower head to rinse his hair.

'Show me yours, then,' she said, and he obediently swivelled to show her the design on his right shoulder blade, which until now she'd seen only as a blur from the safe distance of the life class but which she deciphered as a homage to his regiment and Andy.

'You see,' she said as she gently rinsed the soap off his back and watched goosebumps appear, 'I know the lines of your back so well I reckon I could draw you from memory. You've got more flesh on you than you had six months ago. You were a bit lean then. You're softer now.'

'It's your lasagne. And because I'm eating regularly.'

It wasn't what Gennie would have called regular, munching leftovers at odd hours of the day and night, but perhaps his habits had been more erratic before.

'What did your mum say? Is there any news of Hamid?' she asked, as he faced her again. She washed the foam from his chest, ignoring her own skin tingling as he caressed her back.

'Okay,' he said, replacing the shower head in its bracket and pushing Gennie's wet hair off her face to kiss her. 'Briefly,' he said, passing his hands over her body as Gennie held her breath. She wouldn't twitch or gasp. 'Either Marion doesn't know what's going on or she's not telling. The police must have found him but she doesn't know if they'll bring him back. Problem is that he turns eighteen next week so if social services don't take him back by then, he's on his own. They won't support him if he's not in education or training. That's why they want to know about the apprenticeship.' He paused. 'Why are we talking about this now? I can't concentrate.'

Gennie hadn't absorbed much of what he'd said. She eased herself out of the bath, wrapped a towel around herself and held out a towel for Jack. He sat on the side of the bath and pulled her to him, drying her slowly with her towel while she dried first his hair and then her own. His hands slid lower as he kissed her stomach. She gave up on her hair and leant against him. They'd moved on. This wasn't about the past anymore and what might have been. This was what they could give each other now. She closed her eyes.

35

There seemed to be an awful lot of mess – wet towels amid the pools of sand and water on the floor.

'Give me a cloth and I'll mop,' said Jack.

'No, you sort out the animals while I mop,' said Gennie. She could check out her appearance while she restored the bathroom to order. She smoothed moisturiser onto her face and neck and scrunched mousse into her still damp hair. No make-up; he'd notice. Except mascara and lip balm; that was compulsory, surely.

Jack reappeared, still wrapped in his towel and with Roxy under his arm. 'I've left the mad cat in the kitchen with food. He doesn't like me much. Can Roxy stay up here for a minute? Can we sleep over?'

'If you like,' she said, casually, heart rate rising again. She fetched fresh sheets from the cupboard on the landing. 'Are you hungry?'

'I already looked in your kitchen and there's nothing there

except cat food and oatcakes. Doesn't look like you entertain a lot.'

I don't entertain at all, she thought. You're my first guest.

'There's other stuff as well,' she said. 'Give me a minute.'

She pulled Jack's shirt on again, went down to the kitchen and threw together a plate of cheese, apple and grapes with a pile of oatcakes in the centre. What would he drink? He didn't look like an elderflower cordial sort of person, but what did she know? She filled a jug, added a bar of chocolate to the tray and climbed back up the stairs with her haul.

Jack was still in his towel and leaning out of the window, smoking.

'Someone might see you,' she said.

'D'you mind?' He closed the window, helped himself to an oatcake and shoved it whole into his mouth.

She covered her hesitation in an elaborate performance of clearing space on the dresser for the tray.

'Don't worry, if anyone's out now, they're breaking curfew,' he said, through a mouthful of cracker. 'No-one goes round that side of the house anyway.'

Gennie lifted the plate from the tray and went to sit cross-legged on her bed. She was suddenly ravenous. She smeared brie onto a couple of crackers, bit into one and handed the other to Jack. He'd made the bed and now she was about to fill it with crumbs.

'Is that Max's painting?' said Jack, pointing to a bubble-wrapped package in the corner. 'Can I see it?'

'Sure.'

He unwrapped the picture and carried it over to where she was sitting. He held the painting up to the lamplight and studied it. 'I told you he was good,' he said, voice full of awe, or was it envy? 'The girl in the diamond earrings. The colour's beautiful, really luminous. Do that pose for me. Take the shirt off and sit like in the picture.'

Gennie frowned but put down her second oatcake, licked her fingers and unbuttoned the shirt. Jack angled himself so that he could compare Gennie and her painted image, wrapping the shirt round her so that the fabric draped as it did in the picture. Now he was studying her, examining each curve and how it had translated onto canvas. He ran his finger down the side of her waist, tracing the same line as in the painting. She closed her eyes. She was too exposed.

'Yeah, just as lovely,' he said, putting the painting carefully back in its packaging. He propped it on the floor again before joining her in her bed.

'I wish I could paint like he does,' Jack sighed. 'Why haven't you hung this? You can't spend your life in bubble wrap. Hang it in here. I'll do it.'

Gennie was still holding her breath. She reminded herself to exhale as she extricated herself from the tangle of shirt and wrapped it round her shoulders.

'So are you going to model again? Did you enjoy it?' He ran a finger down her back.

'Not enough to want to sit for anyone else.'

'Even me?' He was teasing her now, nudging up against her to kiss the top of her shoulder.

'Especially not you.' She looked at him. He waited, head to one side. 'It's really difficult to be scrutinised like this,' she said plaintively. 'And be found wanting.'

'Wanting what, G?' He pulled her towards him, rescuing the plate of cheese before it tipped onto the floor and balancing it precariously on a chair. He returned to his excruciatingly slow tracing of the lines and planes of her body. 'Tell me.' His eyes were closed, his forehead just touching hers.

Wanting you, Jack Aspinall, to make me feel like this, like every piece of me matters, every cell is alive. And wanting, like you, to lose myself for a while.

*

Gennie woke to the sound of snoring. Jack was already out of bed and dressed and carrying two mugs.

'Tell me that horrible noise is the dog and not you.' She closed her eyes again. 'What time is it? And is it a school day?' She'd completely lost track.

'It's 6.30 and yes, still Friday.' He sat down, propping himself against the pillows next to her. 'I made you tea.'

She pushed herself up and took the offered mug. 'Thanks,' she said. She'd have rather popped to the bathroom first but he was in the way. His 'good morning' smile reminded her of something.

'You know when we were skiing?' she said. 'Did you and Andy have a bet on? Did you lose and end up with me rather than Lottie, you know, the chalet girl?'

'No! Of course not.' He flinched, kissing his teeth as he did so. 'We were nice boys back then. There was no bet. But it's funny you should ask because there is one now.'

'What?' she squealed. 'What d'you mean, there's a bet? Who with? Oh, let me guess! Max!'

'I'd forgotten about that. Perhaps I shouldn't tell you.' He looked at her horrified face. 'Okay, okay. When I came back from Rwanda, I stayed with Max. He filled me in on everything and said that Marion had hired a new housekeeper. There was all that stuff going on with Nick and Claire and he was trying to cheer me up so he bet me £100 I couldn't pull the new girl.'

'And you took the bet?' What sort of people were they? 'How could you?'

'Course I didn't. Don't be offended, it's not personal, it's just Max.'

'That's worse!'

'Look, he didn't know you then. He'll kill me if I mess you about now,' he said, somewhere between defensive and sheepish. 'But anyway, I wasn't interested, especially when this mystery blonde appeared, turning up late for class and knocking everything over. I thought, "Ooh, who's that?"' He smiled at her.

'I didn't knock anything over.' She didn't buy his narrative. Not one bit.

'But you turned out to be one and the same person, which was a shame as it put you off-limits.' He took a cigarette from the packet on the side. 'Basically Max set up our first meeting to embarrass us both.'

'Explains why you looked so cross. I suppose it's funny, in a way.'

'He thought so. Don't worry. I won't collect on it.' He paused and then nudged her conspiratorially. 'Although, I could, and we could split it fifty-fifty.' He ruffled the front of her hair. 'You could get your roots done. Or maybe a tattoo? And I could get a spray tan.'

'Hmm.' She still wasn't convinced.

'Listen, G.' He got to his feet. 'I've got to go, but are you okay with this? Do we need to talk?'

'What about?' She was suddenly irritated. He didn't have to bump her down to earth so rapidly. 'What do you want to say? Do you want a chit saying all debts are paid and all bets are off?'

'No!' He had the gall to look hurt. 'I mean, we don't know what's going to happen and there could be a lot of stuff going on and...'

'And we might all be dead by Easter.'

'Now you're catastrophising.'

She sighed. 'Don't worry, Jack. We're cool. Everyone needs company now and again.' She could be cool. If she tried.

His relief was even more hurtful. She looked away as he kissed the top of her head. He shrugged on his fleece and felt in the pockets.

'What's this?' he said, pulling out her bra like a magician with a string of coloured handkerchiefs.

'Oh, sorry. My hands were too cold so I stuffed it in the pocket.' She held out her hand.

'Maybe I'll add it to my collection,' he mused, putting it back in his pocket. But when he reached the door he hung it on the handle. 'See you later.' He lit his cigarette and whistled to Roxy. The dog jumped up and then they were gone.

36

The first of the teenagers drifted into the kitchen for breakfast and Gennie greeted them with her warmest smile. The night before was history. This was her life, keeping up with the noisy, hungry rabble.

'Where's Jack?' the two girls asked.

'Jack?' Gennie said warily. 'Outside, I guess.' What did they know?

'Is he doing breakfast?'

'No, of course not. Why would you think that?' Why had she been worried? They weren't interested in her.

'He made breakfast yesterday. We thought it was a new thing.'

'I thought it was Marion.'

'No,' said one. 'It was Jack. It was really fun. He made us all line up in height order.'

'We all had to help,' said the other. 'I did the toasts.'

'And he wouldn't let anyone leave until it was all tidied up and he'd inspected it. He marked us out of ten.'

'I see.' Jack hadn't mentioned any of this. 'Do you want to do it like that again?'

'No,' they said. 'It wouldn't be the same.'

Of course. The world was filled with people whose life was more fun when Jack was around. There was no escaping him.

Her phone was beeping so she handed the girls the box of eggs to start their breakfast preparations and read the incoming messages. Her stomach clenched.

When the breakfast rush was over, she stuffed a bap with leftover omelette, and went out to the farm to find Jack. He was standing by the greenhouses, chatting to one of the labourers.

'Breakfast,' she said, handing him the parcel.

Jack squinted at her, avoiding the early morning sun.

'Thank you for sorting the kids out yesterday,' she continued, diffidently. There were other eyes on her. 'They've asked me to stay in bed every day as they prefer the way you run the kitchen.'

'That's okay, I don't mind helping out. Man down and all that. It's part of our deal, isn't it?' He smiled but his tone was detached, standoffish even.

'Look, I'm going to get Alice in a bit. Her school's closing. Seems we're locking down next week.'

'Yeah, I heard,' he said, still expressionless.

'Right, I'll see you later then. Maybe.' She walked quickly back to the farm buildings. What was his problem? He had nothing to worry about. Hadn't she made it clear from the start she wanted nothing to do with him? This was a small aberration and it would be back to Plan A. It wouldn't be so hard.

Meanwhile, she needed to get her hands on some toilet paper.

*

Stella parked Alice in her kitchen and showed Gennie through to her consulting room. It was a relief to see Stella; everything else was closing down.

'I've done what I said I wouldn't,' Gennie said, once she was settled in Stella's armchair, 'and had an encounter with Jack.'

'I see,' said Stella.

'And okay, he's not completely avoiding me, but… he might be embarrassed.'

'Why would he be embarrassed? Did he take advantage of the situation in some way?'

'Oh no,' Gennie assured her. 'In fact, I may have started it.'

'Could that be why he's embarrassed?'

'What? He thinks I used him?'

'Did you?'

Did she? More likely that he was worried she was going to make something of it, pin him down in some way.

'D'you think it was a mistake?'

'I couldn't say,' answered Stella, smiling. 'Do you?'

'I don't know. It felt right at the time but now… It won't happen again. I was curious and I think he was too, but I'm not curious anymore.'

*

Marion and the key workers were sitting round the kitchen table, sharing a pot of tea, when Gennie returned. It took her a moment to realise it was the weekly team meeting. She'd never been back in time before. She sent Alice next door to the cottage and hung around to eavesdrop.

Alex, who was taking notes, beckoned Gennie to join them. 'We're talking apprenticeships again.'

'If we're to launch in September, we need everything in place by the end of June,' said Marion. 'That will give us time to advertise.'

'We'll promote it to local councils so we get some take-up to underpin the scheme,' Alex explained to Gennie, 'but, and this is the main thing, we won't restrict it to them and we can't be tied to their decisions on who they'll support.'

He didn't need to explain the thinking behind that decision.

'We're going to need some grants, at least to start with. That way we have some independence and can extend the programme to other young people who have fallen out of the care system.'

'While you're here,' said Marion, sliding some sheets of paper across the table, 'we've been meaning to talk to you about this.'

Gennie sensed she was being inducted into their gang. Sean and Alex shuffled closer as Marion talked through her plans.

'Now, look, we're applying for charitable funding to pay for tuition, college attendance and salaries for the tutors for three years. It's a lot of money. We need financial forecasts and sample business plans for the students' small enterprises and I'd welcome your input. You know how to make the numbers stack up.'

'I'll help with whatever you need,' said Gennie.

This was how they'd get Hamid back. If they could offer him a place on a scheme like this, no-one could object.

'That's great, darling, because the other thing is we'll

need to include taught modules in accounts and business skills. It would be so much easier if we could provide that in-house.'

Marion smiled at her over her glasses and Gennie wanted to laugh. Alex had been right about his employer's intentions. Little by little she was being drawn further in.

'Do we have a progress report from Jack?' said Alex. 'The grant assessors will be visiting in May so the building needs to be completed by then. Where is he anyway?'

'Builders' merchants, I hope,' said Marion. 'He needs to pull his finger out. Alex, can you minute that?'

While Alex made a note, Gennie thought of the time Jack had wasted the previous day doing her jobs and messing about on the beach and felt even worse. This was their best chance.

'Is there news of Hamid?' Gennie asked over the sound of scraping chairs as the others got up to leave.

'It's a little odd,' said Marion. 'He's in Birmingham, sharing a house with some friends from Afghanistan. The police went to see him, and he told them he wants to leave school and earn some money. Apparently, these guys have found him a job in a factory and he's renting a room in the house.'

'Are they bringing him back?' asked Gennie.

'They couldn't find a reason to. He said he went of his own accord. He isn't officially in care and if he walks out of his foster carer's and says he doesn't need any help, social services aren't going to interfere. Even if they agreed to do a risk assessment, it wouldn't happen for months. If he's eighteen, he's no longer a child and no-one can do anything.'

It made no sense. 'But he was desperate to come back here. What about his apprenticeship?'

'His social worker wouldn't put him forward for something that only exists on paper. The choices the police put to him were coming back and going to school or staying where he is. He wants to stay there.'

Gennie thought fast.

'Do we know where he is in Birmingham? Mikkel and I lived there for a while and I've still got friends in Edgbaston.' She and Alice could easily invite themselves to see their old neighbours. 'I was thinking of asking for a couple of days off to go and see them. Maybe I could pop in on Hamid too?'

Marion's smile wasn't quite a nod and a wink but it wasn't far off. 'I expect we can get the address from social services,' she said. 'If they're happy there's no risk to Hamid, there should be no reason why they wouldn't tell us.'

*

'Shall we go and see Carrie and Lee?' Gennie asked Alice, picking up the bags and shoes her daughter had dropped in the hall of the cottage and tucking them into the tiny cupboard under the stairs. 'You could catch up with Lucy and we could also check in with Hamid while we're there?'

'I don't mind going to see Lucy but I think you're making a big fuss about Hamid. He just didn't like being at his foster carer's,' said Alice as she went to lie on the sofa with her laptop.

Why would Hamid choose to work in a factory? And why were she and Marion the only ones to think it was strange?

37

The stocks of paper goods were now worryingly low. By Gennie's calculation, they had less than a week's supply of toilet roll. One young person with a stomach upset or heavy cold could wipe them out. Before she left for Birmingham, she'd have to try Shirley again and beg for a heads-up on when the deliveries were due.

Jack was in the yard. Gennie called out to him, 'You off to get Millie? Could you give me a lift to the village? I've lost the keys to my bike lock. I might need to borrow your bolt cutters later.'

'Yeah, sure,' he said, but the customary smile was still absent. 'Why d'you lock your bike up anyway? Who would nick it? Especially from here.'

His suspicion was insulting. He really had nothing to worry about.

'The kids ride my bike down to the village. They dump it at the bus stop and I find it later in the hedge,' she said. Now her bike was chained securely and uselessly in the shed with the keys nowhere to be found. 'If it's inconvenient, it's no problem, I'll drive myself. Alice will have to load her stuff up later.'

'It's fine,' he said, brusquely. 'Hop in.'

'I wanted to talk to you, anyway,' she said. He tensed. 'For God's sake, Jack. About Hamid! Don't you think it's weird that he took off like that?'

'Not really,' he said. 'People behave differently in their own community and maybe he's decided he's happier doing his own thing. There's nothing we can do about it.'

'But d'you think, though, that when he contacted us, it was really a cry for help? Is it our fault he went?'

'No. He knew we'd be breaking the rules by even replying. He only had to wait a couple of weeks and he could have come back. Well, I mean, he won't be able to now.' He frowned.

'Maybe he thinks we let him down, though. I'm going to Birmingham to check that it's really what he wants and he isn't just having a teenage episode.'

Jack exhaled heavily, as if this idea was intruding on something much more important and he was a busy man. 'Look, he told the police it was what he wanted. If he changes his mind, he only has to call someone or come back. It's up to him. You can't go chasing all over the country after him. Aren't you making this a bit too personal?'

'What d'you mean?'

'You can't save him. Not if he doesn't want to be saved.' He glanced across at her.

It stung. Even if it was true and she was reflecting her own needs onto the situation, Jack was doing the same. It wasn't so surprising if he saw Hamid's behaviour as a personal rejection of his project.

'So, you won't come with me, then?' she asked, only half joking.

'You aren't serious, are you? I don't think it would go down very well if I was to go around knocking on the doors of Afghan households. "*Asalamu Alaikum*, just checking how you're treating the children here."'

'They wouldn't know you'd been in the army.'

'They'd know, and if they couldn't smell it a mile away, Hamid would tell them. You don't know what's happened to people to bring them here, and whatever their reasons, no-one enjoys having foreign armies on their soil. You also don't know what links Hamid has where he's living. For me to go there questioning their decisions would be insulting.'

This took Gennie aback. She'd never heard Jack express a political opinion before, let alone so vehemently.

'Okay, I'll go on my own then,' she said, folding her arms and looking out of the window. 'What d'you think will happen?'

'I think you'll be invited in, given tea and treated with the utmost politeness. Everyone in the house will come to eavesdrop and stare at you, and you will leave none the wiser.'

He smiled at last.

38

The traffic on the M5 to Birmingham was bad but Gennie had seen worse. She'd also expected worse, given that everyone was stockpiling food and scuttling for cover before they were ordered to stay at home. Surely the worst-kept secret in the history of secrets. A five-hour drive instead of a standard four felt like a lucky escape.

It gave her plenty of time to question the sanity of her trip. She had further pause for thought when she arrived in Edgbaston and forced herself to drive past her old house and stop outside the one next door. Five years they'd lived there, Alice's primary-school years, and they'd been happy, at least Gennie had thought so. Gennie couldn't resist a peek. The four-bedroomed semi looked huge compared to her cottage; she could barely believe they'd lived somewhere so grand, comparatively, with two new cars on the driveway and ornamental shrubs either side of the door, but she and Mikkel had been those people. Now her front door was framed by a muddy boot scraper and abandoned wellies, and she was driving a borrowed car, eight years old and a few scratches here and there, but perfectly serviceable. She edged along the kerb and into the driveway of her friends' house next door, tucking her car behind the yew hedge.

'Are we allowed to hug, still?' said Carrie, grabbing her warmly before embracing Alice. 'Sorry about the mess,' she said, leading them past a line of fitted cupboards and into the extended kitchen, 'but there's not a lot you can do with three kids around.'

To Gennie, attuned to the daily disturbance of twelve teenagers all pulling in different directions, the atmosphere was unusually calm and civilised. She admired the new kitchen, which had been completely remodelled and, with the amount of glass and squishy sofas around low tables, would not have looked out of place in a Malibu beach house. The wine they drank had been imported by Lee after he and Carrie had taken an anniversary wine-tasting tour in Portugal. Gennie ate her perfectly cooked risotto and thought how easy it was to pretend for an evening and slip back into this life. Tomorrow evening it would all be gone again. It was only when Lee recommended she speak to his financial adviser if she was having difficulty with pensions, that Gennie remembered the excuse she'd invented for the trip. Something about getting all the payments sorted out before lockdown. She finished her wine and curled up in her friends' cosy spare room with its cream and teal colour scheme and planned how best to tackle her real assignment. From what she could work out from Google Maps, the house Hamid was living in was in Sparkbrook and about ten minutes away by car. The factory was a little further.

From her watching of TV cop shows, she gathered the best chances of finding anyone at home were in the early morning. That was fine; she could be there and back before Alice had surfaced.

Despite what she'd told Jack, she wasn't that keen on wandering around on her own, looking for evidence of wrongdoing. She'd lived in Birmingham for five years but parts of the city were completely unknown to her, including Sparkbrook, and even from her quick drive through the previous day, she'd seen that there were areas, long promised to be up-and-coming, which hadn't come up much since she'd left. She felt out of the loop; all those months hiding in her country kitchen and she'd lost her urban edge.

There was nothing like having a point to prove to get you out of bed in the morning and Gennie was out of Carrie's silent house just after seven and parked outside Hamid's address well before eight, which must be the earliest that anyone reasonable, i.e. not arresting police officers, would call. As she waited, she looked for signs of life from the two-bedroomed terraced house. There were grubby-looking net curtains at the windows and weeds growing in the cracks in the concrete path. The front garden was empty apart from two black dustbins and it was hard to tell whether the house was occupied or not. There was a bus stop further down the road and she imagined that on a weekday, there would be plenty of passers-by, but this early on a Sunday, the street was empty. She felt conspicuous, especially when she tried to take a sneaky picture of the house on her phone.

At eight, Gennie walked to the front door and rang the bell. She'd dressed carefully in jeans and her smart belted raincoat, and had covered her bright blonde hair with a bobble hat. After a minute, the door cracked open and a man peered out.

'Hi,' said Gennie chirpily through the gap. 'I'm sorry to call so early but I'm looking for Hamid. I'm in Birmingham visiting friends and I thought I'd take the opportunity to call in and see him. He used to live with us, you see, and I don't want to lose touch. Is he in?'

The man closed the door again and called to someone. It wasn't clear if this was a signal to leave or whether he'd gone to fetch the head of the household. She hovered on the doorstep for a minute, wondering whether to ring the bell again or turn tail and leave. She peered through the door's frosted glass panels and saw a shadow approaching. The door opened a little wider this time to reveal a dark-skinned, clean-shaven man in a T-shirt, tracksuit bottoms and flip-flops.

'Yes?'

Gennie smiled again and repeated her speech. The man half-smiled back, nodded and said, 'Hamid? Hamid isn't here.' There were a couple of other people moving about at the end of the hallway and the sound of raised voices.

Gennie was prepared for this. 'Oh, I see. Is he at work? D'you know when he'll be back? Could I leave a message for him?'

'He isn't here. He leave this house.' The man started to close the door.

Gennie put her hand against the panel. 'He left? When did he go? And d'you know where he went?'

'I don't know where he is. You can leave message. I can pass it to him.' Gennie thought this last suggestion was more to do with finding out who she was than a genuine offer of help.

'No, it's okay. Thank you. I'm sorry to have disturbed you.'

Once in the car, she looked back at the house. The curtains moved in one of the upstairs rooms and a third man peered out. She drove away, trying to process what she'd seen. Jack was right. Culturally, she had no benchmarks; she couldn't decipher the dynamics of the situation. The man she had spoken to had been pleasant but closed, no more than mildly curious about her. He was utterly confident in his surroundings while she wasn't even sure which language they were speaking. There was nothing to suggest anything wrong at the house. On the other hand, there were at least three adults in the building and she'd glimpsed the shadows and heard the voices of several more. The house was of the smaller terraced variety with two bedrooms, three if the loft had been converted. The police had told the social workers that Hamid would be renting a room there but the place simply wasn't big enough for him to have his own room, not with all the other people there. From her time working for Marion, she knew that social services wouldn't sanction a child sharing with an adult. In all likelihood, he'd never stayed there at all.

She drove around for a while, then went to take a look at the factory in Small Heath. While she was here, she might as well follow up all her leads before she gave in and accepted Hamid wanted to go his own way.

The address placed the factory on a small industrial estate. There was a security barrier blocking the entrance, but if she pressed the call button, she'd only draw attention to herself, so she reversed and left the car on the road outside before walking back into the estate and counting along the units until she found number 19. It turned out to be a large blue warehouse with a windowed door at the front and a sign indicating 'Reception'. There was another, tiny, sign identifying the building as belonging to Kandahar Foods, but it wasn't necessary; the aroma of spices floating around the perimeter identified it as the right place. It reminded her that she'd not had breakfast yet. Maybe she could pick up some samosas to take back to Cornwall. There was no chance of peering inside the warehouse; other than the door, the factory was windowless. As Gennie wandered up and down, she spotted a Portakabin marked 'Security'. It was manned by a young black security guard in a blue uniform who was reading a newspaper.

'Morning,' she said. 'Can I ask you something?'

'You can try,' said the guard with a smile.

'You see, there was a foster child used to live with us,' said Gennie, making a split-second decision to tell the truth. 'I'm trying to get in touch with him. I know he was working in that factory. I don't want to embarrass him by going in and asking for him but I could pop back and meet him after work. Do you know what time they knock off?'

'That factory runs day and night. The shifts are twelve hours long – like mine. They change over at six o'clock.'

'Thanks. That's really helpful. Maybe I'll wait outside and see if I can see him then.'

'The workers come in by bus so they don't hang around. You could try leaving a message at reception.'

'Do they take a lunch break? I could try and catch him then.'

'Not that I've seen. No-one comes out of that place during the day.'

Gennie thanked him again and wandered back out to her car, taking a discreet picture of the factory on her phone as she passed. She wouldn't go to reception. She couldn't risk her contact with Hamid to be filtered through other people.

'Jack?'

'Uh-huh.'

At least he'd picked up, although to be fair to him, he generally did. 'If for some reason I was going to be late back, could you cover for me?'

'Is everything okay?' Now she had his full attention, which wasn't what she wanted. Her plans would not stand up to detailed examination.

'Yes, of course. I wanted to stay here until this evening, that's all. You know, I haven't seen Carrie for a while and it would be nice to go out for the day while we can.'

'Okay...' he said slowly. 'What d'you need?'

'Supervising the kids' food. It's dead easy, they're doing stir-fry. Just make sure they don't chop their fingers off.'

*

At half past five, after a pleasant day of walking and talking and eating out, she was back on the pavement outside the industrial estate, eyes peeled for any sign of buses or workers moving around the site. Just before six, two white minibuses drove up, their drivers swiped cards against the entry posts, the barriers opened and in they went. Gennie scanned the side of the vehicle closest to her. It seemed to be full but as they passed through the barrier in seconds, there was no time to get a good look at the passengers. She hadn't spotted Hamid but she couldn't really distinguish anybody.

What to do now? Her plan had only run to getting to the factory and seeing if Hamid was there. From where she was, she had a distant view of the factory doors but no crowds of tired workers appeared wandering out towards the road.

Suddenly, the minibuses were back at the barrier and exiting the trading estate. Without thinking, she started the engine and set off to follow them. This wasn't smart; she had no idea where she was going, but she could not return to St Illick empty-handed. She had at least to find out whether she'd been lied to and the passengers were headed for the little house in Sparkbrook. She took some deep breaths to steady her pounding heart. There was no reason to be nervous. She wasn't doing anything illegal or dangerous, just daft. There was considerably more traffic than there'd been earlier and it was a job to keep up with drivers who switched lanes and jumped lights as frequently as these did.

Her heart sank when she tailed the minibuses back to the street she'd visited that morning and rose again when they drove straight past and further into Sparkbrook. They took a left turn, stopped abruptly outside two equally small and neglected terraced houses, and opened the sliding doors. Gennie drove slowly past, committing the name of the street and house numbers to memory. As she passed the first minibus, she looked across and her breath caught in her throat. Hamid was sitting by the window. He must have sensed her staring as he turned his face to her. She pulled her eyes away and back to the road. It was only a split second, but Gennie couldn't miss his stricken look or the way that he grabbed briefly at the window.

There was nowhere to stop here; no parking places and the only way to turn round was to take a side road and execute a couple of awkward manoeuvres. By the time she snaked her way back to the houses, the minibuses had gone and so had all the passengers.

Gennie drove back to Edgbaston, parked on Carrie's drive and sat for a while. It wasn't what she'd hoped to find. There must have been at least twelve people on each of those buses, perhaps even fifteen, and if Hamid and all the other occupants were living in two houses in Sparkbrook, they must be using every room in the house and sleeping three or four to a room. Admittedly, there were no laws preventing it, no laws against people choosing to work long hours for minimum wage and living in squalor. Nor was Hamid banging on the window screaming for help. Until, or unless, he did, Jack was probably right and she had to leave him to get on with it, even if she couldn't understand why he'd give up his dreams like this. It looked like a miserable existence. He must want money very badly.

39

Where was he? Gennie had been sitting in the hospital car park in Truro for almost two hours trying Jack's number every fifteen minutes and the only response was one auto-message: 'Can I call you back later?' There were literally no reasons to be unavailable. The 'stay-at-home' rules didn't allow them to go out other than for food, daily exercise of thirty minutes or medical emergency. It might be Sunday night and his night off but it was gone midnight, and if he was taking his daily exercise now, there were only a couple of things he could be doing and he wasn't walking Roxy as the dog was with Alex at the farm. Jack disappeared a lot in the evening and no-one liked to make an issue of it. The two things which kept him sane, surfing and time with his daughter, were out of bounds, and if he needed to find other outlets to ward off his dark nights, who would blame him? Gennie had far too much to do to wonder where Jack went when he was off duty, except for now. She needed to find him because Marion had been taken off in an ambulance and Jack was her next of kin.

Gennie was still not sure what had happened. This evening had started like any other. Dinner followed by ninety minutes of study for those with exams coming up and then a film or games in the barn – with an adult on hand to keep an eye on things. After Gennie had supervised the cooking and clearing-up of the evening meal and checked on Alice's homework, she and Alice headed over to the barn to join in the fun or break up some fights, whichever was needed.

After an hour, Gennie popped back to the kitchen in search of peppermint tea as the energetic rounds of 'Duck, Duck, Goose' hadn't sat well with her chili con carne. The lights were still on in Marion's office but that was to be expected. She'd asked to be left in peace while she prepared for the grant assessors' meeting in the morning. Ordinarily Gennie would have popped her head round the door to ask if her boss wanted anything, but leave alone meant leave alone. She was about to carry her tea back out to the yard when one of the girls burst into the kitchen from the hallway.

'Gennie, you have to come. Marion's fallen down the stairs!'

She ran back through to find Marion lying awkwardly on her side in the hall. Alex and Sean were sitting on the floor next to her. A few of the young people, who'd come indoors to watch television, hovered in the doorway of the sitting room, their planned viewing of *Spider-man* abruptly interrupted. Gennie ushered them into the room and closed the door.

'So bloody stupid,' winced Marion, apologetically. 'I was rushing downstairs to make some more copies of the accounts and I slid. I can't move my right foot. I couldn't get up because of my knee so I don't know how bad it is.'

'When did this happen? How long have you been here?' said Gennie, running her hands through her hair.

'An hour or so, I think.'

Gennie sat back on her heels, stunned. It seemed impossible that their lockdown operations keeping the children educated and entertained should run like clockwork, with the residents shepherded and supervised from task to task and minute by minute but someone could fall down the stairs and no-one would hear a thing.

'I've called an ambulance,' said Alex, who was holding and stroking Marion's hand. 'Do you know where Jack is?'

'I honestly have no idea,' said Gennie.

Alex raised an eyebrow. 'In which case, can you go with Marion to the hospital? We have to have two staff here because of the young people and Elizabeth's off this evening as well.'

'Yes, of course,' said Gennie, and tried not to wonder how Elizabeth was spending her evenings without leaving the farm.

'And while you're there, I'll try to get hold of Jack,' continued Alex.

'No, darling, no need,' insisted Marion. 'We can manage. Let's call him when we know if I've broken anything.'

The paramedics arrived in gloves, masks and aprons, and refused to enter the building until everyone else had moved aside. They made a quick assessment, loaded Marion into the ambulance and were on the point of closing the doors when Alex and Gennie ran out.

'Can I come too?' said Gennie.

'Not a chance,' said one of the men while the other rushed round to the driver's door. 'Infection control.'

'Is she okay?' asked Alex.

'Not too bad. BP's a bit low but that's not a surprise when she's been lying for so long on a cold floor. She'll need an X-ray on the ankle, but don't worry,' he said, hurrying them out of the way, 'we'll look after her.'

'My folder!' called Marion as the paramedic attempted to shut the door.

'I'll follow you!' shouted Gennie, but the ambulance was already making its way over the gravel, blue lights but no siren.

*

Jack still wasn't answering. The hospital reception had reluctantly accepted Marion's bag with her phone and the apprenticeship folder, but Marion had not been seen yet and it was looking less and less likely she'd be released in time for them to get decent sleep before the morning.

Gennie called Marion from the car. 'Shall we postpone?'

'No,' said Marion, in a tone so forceful it made Gennie jump. 'We'll never get another date. It's fine, I'll talk you through what we need to do.'

'I think you should relax, Marion. You're probably in shock. Maybe you hit your head as well. Aren't you in pain?'

'As long as I don't move, I'm fine. Although I do think I'm struggling to digest the children's chilli. D'you think we can get some peppermint from somewhere? Anyway, think of this time as a bonus. Have you got a pen, darling?'

Gennie rummaged in the glove compartment. There was

bound to be a random letter from school that she could jot notes on.

'You see, tomorrow's meeting is so vital for all of us.' Marion took a breath. Or did she wince? 'Getting the sponsorship would bring so many benefits. We'll be able to expand the programme to more young people. I'm convinced that Jack can deliver this but he needs the backing. He knows his trades – he got all his building qualifications in the sappers – and he's very good at motivating people. You've seen that. Look, we need to get him the money but it's more than that. It's about giving his ideas legitimacy, getting external validation. Jack really needs to find a defined purpose to his work. This will give him direction and the stability will be good for Millie. Otherwise, he might drift again.'

Drift or drink, change one five-letter word to another in as few moves as possible. Drift, grift… Gennie's tired brain was at seven before she gave up. Not so easy then. That had to be a good sign. Did Jack really need so much approval? He wasn't the cheerful optimist he'd been at eighteen, but few people were.

'I thought you made a point of not interfering in Jack's life?'

'This isn't interfering,' said Marion, quite sharply for her. 'This is personal development and encouraging people to make the most of their abilities. You, for example, could be playing a much bigger role in business planning and it would be good for you, get you out of that bloody kitchen. You'll come to the meeting with me, won't you?'

'Well, yes. If you want me to.'

'Hang on a minute, someone's coming.' She rang off.

Fifteen minutes later she was back.

'X-ray?' asked Gennie, with hope that they might soon be able to leave and go home.

'Not yet, but my leg's swollen up so they've cut the seam of my jeans. Shouldn't be long now. Anyway, once we've developed the model, this programme could be reproduced elsewhere. Perhaps it could be franchised...'

Gennie laughed. 'You know what you sound like? A mafia godfather, on his sickbed, trusting his nominated successors with his plans to clean up the family.' That was the trouble with the lockdown; she'd watched an awful lot of movies.

Marion laughed and then groaned. 'Oh, there's a plan, all right. The next stage will be building the accommodation for people with more severe disabilities. The apprentices can work on that, and then Jack can set up his surfing holidays for disabled veterans. That's what he'd really like to do.'

Marion rang off to speak to a nurse and Gennie resorted to sending Jack a text.

'Call me ASAP. Marion at hospital. Don't panic. All fine.' It wasn't quite fine but she was never sure how Jack would react.

Marion was back on the phone within minutes. Gennie didn't know how much more detail she could absorb. At two, a porter arrived to take Marion for X-ray and she hung up again. Gennie's eyelids were drooping but she came to the moment a Land Rover drew up opposite and a familiar figure jumped out. Gennie wound down her window.

'Don't worry,' she said, quickly, 'she's basically okay but she's probably broken her ankle. She's in X-ray now.'

'What happened?' Jack asked, opening the car door and getting in beside her.

'She fell down the stairs. I think her bad knee gave way. She was on her own for hours though. She didn't want to contact you yet, but I thought you'd want to know. Sorry to drag you away from whatever you were doing.'

'No problem,' he said. He touched her shoulder to get a better look at her face. It was the closest they'd been for weeks. 'Are you okay, G?'

'Yeah, fine. Where were you, anyway?'

'Doesn't matter. What you don't know can't harm you, as they say. In any case, I would've been here sooner if you answered your bloody phone!'

'Me?' Gennie was indignant. 'I've been calling you for hours and you didn't pick up!'

'I kept missing your call! And when I called back, your number was busy. Every single time. Six missed calls and no fucking messages!'

Gennie stared at him. 'Oh, yeah, your mum kept calling. She made me take notes.'

'I was getting worried. I thought you were in trouble, got yourself stuck trying to escape through a cat flap or something.'

Gennie pursed her lips. On some level, her presence reassured him. Okay, she'd play along. 'Now who's got the saviour complex? And I'm not sure it's appropriate for you to be making jokes at my expense when I'm not the one in distress right now.'

'Whatever. Got any cigarettes? I've run out.' He fidgeted like someone going cold turkey.

She rummaged in her bag and handed him the packet. Jack opened it to inspect the contents. His hands looked a little shaky. She'd noticed it before, the way he used smoking to control his breathing and that simply putting a cigarette in his mouth calmed him.

'And you haven't been at these in the meantime?' he asked.

He was nothing like as relaxed as he was pretending. Edgy, hypervigilant even.

'Nope.' She leaned back in her seat and rubbed her ribs. 'Can I have one of your mints? Haven't you got indigestion?'

'No.' Jack looked surprised. 'But my digestion's been hardened by your terrible cooking – and obviously the British Army's.' He nudged her with his elbow. She gave him her coolest stare. She'd humour him, for Marion's sake. They sat quietly for a moment.

'Will you be all right if I go now?' said Gennie.

'Course. S'long as you leave me the fags,' he said. 'D'you need one for the morning?' He took a cigarette from the packet and tucked it behind her ear, the gentlest of gestures. 'In case of emergency.'

*

How could it be morning already? Gennie rubbed her face awake and dragged herself out of bed. The show must go on. This was something she was good at – pretending everything was fine when it was all falling apart.

'Marion's doing well,' she told the young ones when they crowded into the kitchen for breakfast. 'She'll be back soon.' She prayed it was the case. 'Yes, I'll tell her you love her.'

Once all the residents were out of the kitchen and into their home tutoring groups, Gennie set about tidying Marion's office. If they were doing the meeting by video, they'd need a decent backdrop and good light. She moved the lamps, tidied the books on the shelves and angled the computer camera to pick up the best view. Flowers! She rushed out to the front to see whether there was anything in bloom she could pick and cram into a jug.

Jack arrived home when Gennie was pressing the black and white dress she'd worn for business meetings – in the days when she'd had meetings to attend. He was on his own.

'They kept her in?' asked Gennie, heart sinking.

'It's a bad break. It'll need pinning.' He flopped into the armchair. 'She's seeing the surgeon later. They're completely overwhelmed. Can't decide whether to sort her out and send her home quickly because of the pandemic, or send her home to wait because of the pandemic.' He pressed his fingers to his forehead. 'She's insisting we do the fucking meeting, though.'

'Who? Alex?'

'No, you and me. She won't let us cancel. Says it's too late. It's like she's possessed. I've been talked to death and she's given me a list of things to do.'

Gennie snatched the piece of paper and compared it with her own scribbled page.

'Where d'you think the papers are?' she said.

'I thought you'd know.'

'Well, I know they're in the folder,' said Gennie, 'and I know where the folder is. I gave it to the hospital to give to Marion.'

'Smart move.'

'Well, I didn't know we'd be doing this.'

'I thought you were Little Miss Organised.'

'I just hide my mistakes better than you do.' It was Gennie's turn to rub her eyes. 'Oh, God, what are we gonna do?'

Jack pushed himself out of the chair. 'It's probably all on her computer. I'll grab a shower and then I'll help you look.'

He reappeared in the doorway of Marion's office in a clean shirt and underwear, clutching a bundle of material. 'My suit,' he said. 'I found it screwed up in the corner.'

Gennie lifted the edge of the fabric and sniffed. 'It doesn't smell too bad.' She sniffed again. 'You probably don't need it, they'll only see you from the waist up.'

'No way, I'm not doing the meeting in my pants.'

'Okay.' Gennie handed him the paperwork she'd printed. 'I'll press your suit while you check these. Do the numbers look right?'

'Fuck knows,' Jack answered. 'We'll just have to wing it.'

*

Gennie sat in front of the screen and adjusted her position so that the camera would pick up both of them, squeezed shoulder to shoulder on two kitchen chairs. She was nervous but Jack could not keep still. He was up and down like a yo-yo.

'Here,' she said, placing a cigarette packet just out of sight of the screen. 'Play with this and be glad they can't smell you.'

Her heart started racing when the three faces appeared on the screen, two men and a woman, each in a different box, but Jack seemed to relax. He was warm and charming when introducing himself and the work at the farm but lost it again when they started to discuss the apprenticeships. His right leg was jiggling so much, it was shaking the table and Gennie. She moved her hand across to grip his knee.

Gennie was used to the effect Jack had on women, especially those of an age approximating his mother, like Shirley, for example, so it was no surprise when his anxiety was met with sympathy from the female panel member. What impressed her more was how quickly Jack won over the others. Once he found his stride and started to describe the profiles of the young people who could benefit from the programme, he was animated and full of a vision that Gennie hadn't seen before. There was none of the casual smiling that characterised most of his interactions. He was sincere and persuasive, and that, in turn, gave her confidence. Neither of them was as well prepared and knowledgeable as Marion, but Gennie could see that their conviction carried weight.

'There are a couple of things that we'd like to review in terms of outcomes,' said the panel chair.

'Of course,' said Gennie, exchanging a glance with Jack. 'We can look at those.' At that moment, she'd amend anything they asked as long as they gave them the money.

'And then there's the building completion date.'

'It's finished,' said Jack. 'Ahead of schedule. Would you like a tour?' He jumped to his feet and grabbing his phone, went outside. Within seconds, he was back in the virtual room, camera turned outwards. Gennie turned herself to mute and watched Jack, in his element, showing off the new accommodation block which he'd completed early as there'd been nothing else to do for six weeks. He even included a quick peek into the first of the greenhouses and Hamid's nascent fruit farm.

The panel confirmed they'd make a recommendation but the final decision didn't rest with them. It would be four weeks until the board met to agree which organisations to support and for how long.

Alex burst in as soon as they left the meeting. He must have been listening outside the door. Gennie was glad she hadn't realised earlier.

'You could not have done better,' he said, offering both Gennie and Jack a high five. 'I'll call Marion.'

'I'm going to sleep,' said Jack, heading for the stairs.

'Guess I'll do lunch then,' said Gennie. To be followed by an afternoon on the farm, leading the young people in the backbreaking and muddy tasks that no-one except Hamid really enjoyed – like planting out the potatoes. How ironic that they'd sold the project to the funders partly on the basis of his ideas.

By the time she went to wake Jack, Gennie was so tired she could barely lift her limbs to climb the stairs. She knocked on his door armed with a mug of tea and a sandwich filled with leftovers from lunch – some chicken, sliced potato, salad and mayonnaise. When he didn't answer, she padded in in her socks and put the plate on the desk before switching on the table lamp. The curtains were drawn but light still filtered through from outside.

'Jack,' she said quietly. 'Wake up or you won't sleep at all later. You need to call the hospital and see how your mum is and if you can take her stuff in. I've packed a bag for her.'

There was a groan from the corner and Jack sat up, rubbing his hands over his head, instantly awake. 'What time is it?'

'It's four. I've brought you some lunch. Or maybe it's breakfast. What time zone are you in?'

'Thanks.' He smiled as he took the tea. 'We did all right today, didn't we?' He was looking very pleased with himself.

'I think so. Hamid may have played a part – even from a distance. I want to try and contact him again, to let him know we're making progress. Will you come with me next time? When we're allowed, of course.'

'Let me think about it.' Jack patted the bed beside him. 'Sit down, talk to me.'

'I'm filthy. I've been on the farm all afternoon.'

'I don't mind,' said Jack.

'I do, though. I do the laundry and I can do without muddy sheets. My jeans are disgusting.'

'Take them off then,' he suggested, and Gennie laughed.

'Come on,' he said, lifting the side of the duvet. 'Dump your clothes and get in. Keep me company for a minute. I've been thinking about you.'

Did he mean it or was he teasing her? If he was, she should call his bluff. He still hadn't told her how he'd spent his Sunday night. She held his eyes for a second before dropping her jeans and socks on the floor and climbing in with him in her T-shirt.

'What have you been thinking?'

'Come here and I'll tell you.' He put his arm around her and pulled her close.

'I smell of manure,' she said as he nuzzled his nose into her neck and smoothed her T-shirt down across her stomach.

'One of my favourites,' he said, brushing his lips across her cheek. 'Tell me again how good we were.'

'Are you looking for reassurance, Jack?' She concentrated on the distant sounds of the teenagers clattering in and out of the kitchen downstairs and ignored her quickening pulse.

'No, that's not what I'm looking for. Are you?' He leaned over to look at her. 'How are you doing, G?'

Why did he keep asking?

'I'm fine,' she said. 'But I've got to...' She pointed in the direction of the increasing noise and started to remove herself.

'Yeah.' He nodded and looked at her again before pressing his lips to hers for a second. 'See you later.'

Gennie trudged back down the stairs. What did that mean?

40

Gennie woke with a start. Her phone was ringing. For a second, she was back in Exeter, heart thumping, where every night-time phone call brought bad news of one sort or another. Then she remembered where she was.

'Jack? What time is it? Has something happened?' She sat up, body shaking with exhaustion.

'You don't feel like walking, do you? I can't sleep.'

Gennie looked at her clock. It was just after one. Being his friend was seriously overrated. 'Where are you?'

'I'm outside your door. D'you want to come with me?'

'No, of course not. I'm asleep. At least I was. But the door's open. I'll come down.' She rolled out of bed and stumbled downstairs in her pyjamas.

Jack and Roxy were already in the hall. Gennie put her finger to her lips. Alice was asleep upstairs.

'Did you see Marion?' she whispered.

'They wouldn't let me in. They only just agreed to take the

bag from me, so it was FaceTime in the car park again. The op's tomorrow but they want to keep her in a couple of days because of her ribs.'

'What?' Gennie pulled him into the sitting room.

'Indigestion, my arse. She's cracked a couple of ribs! That's why she's in such pain. It hurts to breathe. She's usually always on the go but she's barely moving. I've never seen her so still.' He shook his head as if trying to dispel the idea.

Gennie leaned a little closer. 'You haven't been…?'

'No! For fuck's sake! That's why I need to walk. If I stay in the house, I'll start on your cooking sherry.'

'Shush.' Gennie shot an anxious look out of the room and up the stairs. 'There is no cooking sherry. Why would I need cooking sherry? But Jack, I'm so tired.' She sighed. Her whole body ached. 'I want to sleep. And you need to sleep. Maybe you'd better stay here.'

He followed her as she crawled upstairs and into her room.

'Get into my bed,' she said. She wandered into her bathroom and returned with a plastic box of small bottles and cardboard boxes which she dropped onto her duvet. 'Maybe we can find something to knock you out. What would you prefer? Sleeping tablets or tranquillisers?'

Jack sat next to her and rifled through the container. 'How many have you got? You're like some kind of dealer. Does my mum know you've got all this?'

'I've had a lot of stress,' she said, defensively.

Jack chose a box. 'What are these?'

'Sleeping pills. I got them in France. I think they're all right.'

'What's the difference?'

'Dunno. Flavoured with garlic and parsley?' She looked up at him from under her eyelashes.

'Hmm,' he said, pursing his lips. 'I'll do the jokes.' He rummaged some more. 'I have these. Give me a couple of those and some of these.' He opened a bottle of diazepam and helped himself while she handed him the sleeping pills. He swallowed both, tugged off his jeans and got into her bed.

Gennie was reading the packet. 'Are you sure you should have two? I'm only supposed to have one.'

Jack checked the box. 'Oh, maybe. These are a higher dose than mine.' He laughed. 'Oh well, I should sleep then.'

Gennie pulled the duvet over him and fought the impulse to stroke his head and kiss him goodnight. 'Go to sleep,' she said.

She moved to the end of the bed and sat with her back against the wall. What was she doing? She wouldn't let Jack drink but was quite happy to anaesthetise him with prescription medication. How was that acceptable? She closed her eyes for a moment.

'Is this how you treat Alice when she's upset?' he asked, amused.

'Yes, but I don't usually drug her. I need to sleep now.'

'Aren't you cold?' he asked.

'Go to sleep.'

She woke a little later, cramped and chilled, lying on her side. The dog was snoring and the cat was crouched at the end of the bed growling and looking over the edge at the dog. Jack, meanwhile, was sound asleep. She took her clock and Sergio into Alice's room to sleep the remainder of the night in peace. She drifted off before she had come up with an explanation for Jack's presence which her daughter would believe.

*

Gennie was in the main kitchen clearing away the breakfast things when Elizabeth, the other key worker, wandered in. Elizabeth was young, not much older than the teenagers she supported, and with the sort of long dark hair that gave Gennie a pang of recognition.

'Seen Jack?' Elizabeth asked.

'Still asleep, I think,' said Gennie.

'He's not in his room, though.'

Gennie stared at her. Elizabeth shouldn't know this. Key workers were strictly prohibited from going into the family side of the house. Only she and Marion freely accessed all areas. She didn't know Elizabeth well but her skin prickled at the back of her neck each time the girl passed by. This must be how Sergio felt about Roxy.

'Oh, well, he hasn't been through here yet,' said Gennie truthfully as Elizabeth swept out again. She carried on peeling vegetables for the evening's casseroles, pondering the significance of what she'd heard.

Jack sauntered into the kitchen. 'Why didn't you wake me?'

'I tried but failed. I may have over-medicated you.' This wasn't true. She'd looked in on him before she and Alice had left the cottage, but he looked so peaceful they'd left him to sleep. 'Are you hungry?'

'I'll help myself. D'you want coffee if I make some?'

'Please. Did you sleep well?'

'I did, thanks. Your bed's more comfortable than mine. I might come round more often.'

Gennie shook her head gently to warn him off.

'I'm sorry I chucked you out, though. I thought you'd stay with me,' he said, busy opening cupboards, his back to her.

'I needed my rest.' It was more than this. She wanted their encounters to have more value than Jack's momentary neediness. She rested a hand on his arm and leaned close to his ear. 'Also I should tell you that, while, "I've been lying here thinking about you," is a good line, "I'm really worried about my mum," doesn't have the same impact.'

'That's exactly what Marion says. Words make a difference,' he said, shovelling a handful of cereal into his mouth. 'It's why poetry's so popular.'

'For the record, "You sound like my mum," also wouldn't do it,' Gennie said, returning to the sink.

'What about, "You remind me of a girl I fell in love with fifteen years ago"?' he said in an undertone.

That went through her like a hot knife through butter. Her eyes pricked. 'Yes, that would do it.' She put the back of her hand to her eyes. 'Sorry, it's the onions.'

Jack leaned over the sink. 'They look like potatoes to me, G. But you're the expert.'

'There's nothing of that girl left,' Gennie wailed. 'You didn't even recognise me for three months.'

He draped an arm round her shoulder. 'You don't know that for sure. Anyway, right now, all I'd need to say would be, "No, no, you're exactly the same," and you'd be putty in my hands!'

She nudged him away from her. 'Go away you brute. And anyway,' she said, recovering herself, 'you didn't love me!'

'Exactly, I didn't love you then and I don't love you now.'

Gennie turned to offer him a curse or two but saw that Alex had come in and witnessed that last exchange.

'Is everything okay between you two?' He sounded concerned.

'There's nothing between us,' Gennie reassured him as Jack left the kitchen. 'You heard him.'

'Did I smell coffee?' said Alex. 'It's none of my business, but I think he's giving you mixed messages.'

Gennie laughed. 'And he wonders why he has troubled relationships.'

'I've got Elizabeth bending my ear about him, too,' Alex said as he helped himself to the dregs in the cafetiere.

This was interesting and also reminded Gennie that she had forgotten to tell Jack that Elizabeth had been looking for him.

41

Shirley's counter was now sheathed in Perspex, as was Shirley, hidden behind a see-through visor. Gennie stood the required two metres behind the shopper in front and read the notices limiting customers to two of any product. This could only be to encourage people to visit the shop more often as the store was stocked to the rafters and now the toilet-paper crisis was over, there were no shortages.

'Is there any chance I can have more than two packs of cigarettes for Jack?' she asked when she reached the front of the queue.

At the rate Jack was smoking, Gennie would be back by tea-time to pick up more supplies, but his stoicism was impressive. Marion had insisted on quarantining herself for two weeks when she was discharged from hospital, to keep the farm as plague-free as possible. They'd had a meeting and agreed the only place on the farm with true separation was the cottage. Gennie's offer to care for Marion was rejected as she had to keep the kitchen running and Jack, who hadn't offered, was drafted in. He had the least day-to-day contact with anyone else and accepted that he was the most expendable. Alice agreed to de-camp to the farmhouse on condition she didn't have to sleep in Jack's bed nor he in hers so she took Marion's room and Gennie ended up with Jack's sofa-bed.

'You are not to smoke in the bedrooms,' she told Jack as she stocked the cottage kitchen with food. It was the most homely the place had ever looked with a full fridge and freezer, flowers on the table and brand-new toiletries in the bathroom. 'And you'll have to feed Sergio.' She looked at Roxy, who was in her usual place, hovering around Jack's ankles. 'Time to choose,' she said. 'Farmhouse or Jack?'

There was no contest; they both knew who she'd pick, but Jack saved the dog's embarrassment. He lifted her up and tickled her ears. 'I need an ally.'

It was strange sleeping in Jack's bed – without Jack. His presence was still evident in the smell of his cigarettes which still hung somewhere in the air and clung to the sofa cushions. It was comforting rather than unpleasant. She slid a pillow down next to her to imagine how it might feel with the two of them there and then quickly replaced it. She'd steeled herself to resist the temptation to rifle through his stuff but he'd left nothing lying around. He'd done a better job of tidying his room than she had in the cottage.

'So, Gennie,' said Shirley as she slid three packets across the counter before putting through the rest of the shopping, 'you know that little dog, Roxy, whose dog would you say she is now, yours or Jack's?'

Gennie laughed. 'Jack's adopted her, or she's adopted him.'

'That's what I thought.'

'Why d'you ask?'

'Because of the cottage, of course.'

Gennie shook her head to indicate she didn't understand, conscious as ever that their chat was holding up the queue, and that every ear in the line was tuned to their conversation.

'It's Jan's will. Whoever takes in the dog has use of her cottage for as long as the dog needs a home. I was only thinking that they didn't need to bundle you out of your cottage, they could have had that one.'

But Roxy doesn't need the cottage, Gennie thought, she's got a home.

'Does Jack know?' she asked, struggling to find her voice, understanding now what was meant by strangled tones.

'I'd be surprised if Marion hadn't mentioned it,' said Shirley.

'Thanks,' said Gennie, fumbling with the handles of her shopping bag as she made a quick exit.

Why, on earth, had nobody mentioned this to her? She would never have taken up the offer: she had a home and a job and there was no way she was leaving. Jack, though, he needed somewhere. Was this why he'd been so keen on taking care of Roxy? He didn't need to go to those lengths. He only needed to say the word, 'There's a house, G, but I need the dog.'

Maybe Roxy would be happier living in her old cottage and she'd certainly be happier with Jack. Gennie kicked at the gravel as she turned into the drive, feeling like she'd found out her best friend was off to the school prom with the guy she liked. Was that the problem? Her best dog was stealing away the guy she liked? Good God, she was pathetic.

She threw Jack's cigarettes through the door of the cottage. Wait until he found out that the rules were about to be relaxed, and if it weren't for being locked in with his mum, he'd have been able to meet his daughter outside again. He'd probably have to go chop something down to get over it. Gennie prepared herself for the angry sound of the chainsaw.

42

It was Millie, this time, in pyjamas and flip-flops, standing by the bed. Gennie came to with a sharp intake of breath, sat up and checked the time. It wasn't yet seven o'clock on a Sunday morning. Did this family never sleep?

'Excuse me, Gennie, I need the present now. Where is it, please?' Millie said, without any preamble.

'Oh!' Despite the roughness of her awakening, Gennie's heart swelled to see the little girl at the farm. Like old times. The previous two weekends had seen Millie visit for the day, permitted as long as she stayed outside, before she was dragged away with tears and howls of rage by Claire. It had been hell to witness. How to explain to an eight-year-old that, for the good of everyone else, she wasn't allowed to sleep in her own room in the same house as her dad? Who would look after him if she wasn't there? Jack had sweet-talked and reassured her but she wouldn't be bought off. He'd disappeared as soon as she'd gone – off to the far reaches of the farm, or his soul, whichever was most distant. Gennie had felt for him. Alice, the person she loved most, was right in the next room.

Gennie climbed out of bed, opened the wardrobe door and extracted a bubble-wrapped package. 'It's here but it's heavy. Can you manage? Have you got wrapping paper and a card?'

'I've got a card but I haven't got paper. Have you got some?'

Gennie took her down to the kitchen and rummaged in the cupboard. 'I have brown paper or red tissue paper. I only wrap presents for Alice.' She felt she owed an explanation for the limited selection.

Millie, unsurprisingly, chose the red. Before they wrapped it, they opened the bubble wrap. The package contained a framed drawing. It was in pastel, depicting Millie in a pose she'd informed Gennie was an *arabesque par terre*, leg extended behind her, arm raised in front, her form outlined and shaded in multiple jewel colours. The image of a child in movement.

'D'you like it?' asked Gennie. 'It was a rush to get it finished in time for Uncle Max to get it framed. It's a bit rough round the edges.'

'It's lovely,' said Millie, running her fingers over the silver frame. She bounced up and down as Gennie resealed the bubble wrap.

'Look,' she said, and showed Gennie the card she had made. 'To My Daddy', it proclaimed in multicoloured lettering framed by glittery stickers. Gennie's eyes pricked, as they did whenever a child spoke about their father.

'What shall I write?'

'What d'you want to say?'

'To the best daddy in the world. Love you forever. From Millie,' she spelled out, and covered the inside of the card in rows of 'x's and 'o's.

Gennie ran a finger under her eye. 'Don't be surprised if it makes him cry. But in a good way,' she added hastily, remembering the card game.

She helped Millie carry the parcel through to the farmhouse, before going back to shower and change.

By the time Millie and Jack came down to the kitchen, Gennie was already supervising breakfast. Millie skipped up to her, turning pirouettes and grinning.

'Daddy really likes it. It did make him cry – but he said it didn't,' she confided.

Gennie looked at Jack. 'Happy Father's Day.'

He nodded. He might even have been looking a little sheepish.

When all the pans of food were on the table, Gennie turned her attention to Alice, who was sitting before an empty plate, still half asleep. Gennie stroked her hair. Days like this were difficult for her, but it had to be easier at the farm, where almost none of the children had a conventional and functional two-parent family in their backgrounds. Alice had more than they did.

'Happy Father's Day,' said Alice. 'What does that mean, even? Is it the fathers who are happy or just the day?'

Jack, still sitting at the table with Millie, widened his eyes at Gennie and then turned to Alice. 'What are you doing today? D'you want to come out with Millie and me? We're going to the beach. We'll take the boogie boards, maybe do some crabbing and then we'll try find somewhere selling chips. If the ferry's running, we might go across to Padstow.'

Alice looked across at her mother. 'I would, but...'

'I'm dropping her in Bodmin,' said Gennie. 'She's meeting some friends from school. Thank you, though.'

'I haven't seen them in sooo long,' said Alice.

'What about you?' Jack asked Gennie.

'Oh,' she said. It would be lovely to go to the beach, but she'd be intruding on his time with Millie and it didn't feel fair. Not on Father's Day. 'I'll stay here, I think. I need to fetch Alice later, anyway.'

'Up to you,' he said, with a shrug.

He stayed in the kitchen while the girls went to get ready.

'When did you do the drawing of Millie?' he asked, half hanging out of the kitchen door while he smoked.

'Over the last couple of weeks. She saw Max's portrait of Alice and demanded one too, but he hasn't been able to see her yet. Millie suggested I draw her in the meantime. Claire sent me some photos and then Max, somehow or other, got it framed. D'you like it, though?'

'I do like it. Especially the mad colours. It's exactly like her. Thank you.' His smile was gentle, wistful even.

'Not too safe for you?' Gennie taunted him.

'Nope. Not at all. I like it.'

She laughed.

'What's funny?' he asked.

'I gotcha. Usually it's you that makes me cry with your horrible sentimentality, but I got you this time.'

Jack shook his head. 'It doesn't count. You used a child. That's against the rules.'

'What rules? You don't play by any rules,' Gennie scoffed. 'Anyway, I think the child used me. She was very determined.'

43

The landline in the office started ringing as soon as Gennie entered the kitchen in the morning. It was the building inspector looking for Jack.

'Have you tried his mobile?' said Gennie. 'He's usually on site by now.'

As she hung up, she heard the kitchen door crash and the sound of footsteps on the stairs.

'Jack?' She poked her head into the corridor but she'd missed whoever it was.

Back in the kitchen, she consulted her whiteboard and menu plans – Monday again, it came round so quickly – and started pulling things from the fridge. Would they really want hash browns with their scrambled egg?

The door to the corridor opened and Jack appeared, hair wet from the shower but unshaved. He was wearing his fight-or-flight look, his jaw rigid, eyes burning.

'Morning,' Gennie said cheerfully.

'Yeah, morning.'

'Tea?'

'Maybe later.' He had his hand on the kitchen door and was about to go when she remembered the building inspector.

'Hang on. Mike Perrett called. He can't make Thursday anymore and as we can't make Friday, he suggested coming today. Otherwise, it will have to be next week. Can you call him?'

Jack looked relieved, in the sense that his brow was marginally less furrowed. 'Yes, okay. Today would be fine but next week would be better.'

'Good, thanks. Why are you so moody?'

'Just tired,' he said, and left.

After breakfast, she collected the sets of bedlinen she'd washed and ironed the previous afternoon and climbed the stairs. She had her routine, starting with the family end of the house, the ones who'd strip and make their own beds without prompting, before moving to the residents' block next door and the ones that needed chivvying. Marion was still in her room, foot in its surgical boot propped up on a pillow and already at work, phone in one hand, typing on a tablet with the other. Gennie left the clean sheets, collected the breakfast tray and signed that she'd be back later. Out of habit, she knocked on Jack's door before walking straight in to put the linen on the chair. She nearly jumped out of her skin when she spotted someone in the bed.

'Oh, sorry,' Gennie stammered as a girl with dark, messy hair emerged from under the duvet.

'You shouldn't walk straight in,' said Elizabeth, sitting up and stretching.

'I knocked. I'm sorry, I didn't expect anyone to be in here. I saw Jack outside five minutes ago.' Gennie didn't think it would be helpful to mention that technically, Elizabeth shouldn't be on that side of the house at all if Jack wasn't there, and possibly not even if he was.

'What time is it?' asked Elizabeth. 'I'm back on duty at twelve.'

'It's about nine. I'll, erm, get on with...' Gennie muttered backing her way out of the room.

She knocked and entered Millie's room much more carefully, even though it was extremely unlikely to be occupied. Millie's was the only bed, other than Marion's and her own, that she usually made. Her hands shook as she went through the motions of putting the duvet the right way round in the cover and she had to sit down for a moment. What was going on? Yesterday he was inviting her to the beach and today, he was jumping the key workers. Is that what happened when she turned him down?

Alex was waiting for her at the kitchen table, ready for their daily coffee and gossip.

'You okay?' he asked.

She was clearly no poker player.

'I may need a biscuit.'

Gennie sat down while Alex poured her coffee. They were stirring in their milk as Elizabeth clattered down the stairs and into the kitchen.

'Have you got any towels for upstairs, Gennie?'

'They're all in the rooms,' said Gennie, coolly. 'Could you use the key workers' bathroom in the other block, though? The one upstairs is Marion's and she'll be using it any minute.'

Elizabeth glared at Gennie, who held her gaze.

'Yes, please use the other block,' said Alex mildly, continuing to stir his coffee.

Elizabeth scowled and flounced out of the kitchen and back into the corridor. Gennie fetched a packet of chocolate digestives from the cupboard and sat back down, offering one to Alex before taking two for herself.

'I am assuming the obvious explanation is the correct one,' Alex asked, in the same casual tone.

'I can't think of any other,' said Gennie, sucking the melted chocolate from the biscuit she'd dunked, something she told Alice off for doing. 'Although I have to say, I'm a little confused by it.'

She didn't dare pick up her cup; her hands were still shaking from the face-off with Elizabeth. Why was she challenging her in that way?

'I think confusion would be a reasonable response,' said Alex, dunking his own biscuit. 'Do you have any other feelings about it?'

'Are you fishing or counselling?'

'A bit of both,' Alex admitted. 'Off the record, of course.'

'Well, it's the usual thing. When someone says they don't want to get involved in anything or with anyone, they simply mean they don't want to get involved with you,' said Gennie, continuing to look straight ahead. 'So if you'd been having thoughts in that direction, it could make you feel a bit stupid.' This was the closest she'd come to admitting anything to anyone. 'To be honest, I don't understand most of what he does, but this would make sense. Elizabeth carries no baggage. Maybe that's what he needs, what he wants.'

'I don't think you've read that right,' said Alex slowly. 'When you two are in the same room, he's never out of your orbit. Elizabeth gave me the impression she wasn't making much progress. I assumed his attention was elsewhere.'

At least Alex was also confused. Perhaps she hadn't made a total fool of herself.

'So what's this about then? Putting me off by proving he's as unreliable as everyone says?' Gennie sucked on another biscuit.

'Or proving to himself that he doesn't want anything more serious?'

'Could be, I suppose. Actually, I agree with him about that. No-one wants to rush into anything, especially at the moment.'

'And are you upset by it?' Alex probed.

'No, not really. I'm surprised, that's all. To be honest, I'm used to feeling betrayed and let down, so it's familiar territory.'

'Gennie! The fact that you're used to feeling like this doesn't make it right. I'd say it's very unhealthy to accept a situation that you'd otherwise find unacceptable because you're used to feeling like that.' He pronounced the last words like they were in bold and underlined.

'Thank you for your insight, Dr Alex.'

'Can I ask you this, though? Is this something you want? Have you thought about that?'

Gennie sat back in her chair. It really might be. The thought of Elizabeth's hands on Jack made her feel positively ill.

'Maybe not,' she said. 'I mean, I like him a lot and I thought we were good friends, but I don't need more trouble in my life.'

'Well, I expect things will settle down again. In the meantime, someone better might come along.' Alex patted her hand in fatherly fashion. Her poker face must have let her down again because he laughed. 'Don't look so horrified. You can't stop living your life, Gennie. He might never come to his senses.'

Gennie nodded and reached for another biscuit before checking herself. 'My God, how many have I eaten?' she asked, lifting the packet to check if any remained.

The kitchen door to the yard banged open and Jack came in. He muttered a quick greeting before kicking off his boots and diving through the kitchen and up the stairs.

Gennie turned to Alex, teeth gritted. 'I was wrong,' she said. 'Did you see him? He can't even speak to me. I'm not okay with this, I'm livid. How could he do this? He doesn't face up to things. Everyone talks to me about repeating damaging behaviour! What's this then? If he's feeling bad, he should deal with it. Instead, he waits for someone else to kick off about it so he has an excuse to self-destruct. I won't give him the satisfaction,' she hissed.

44

D-day, grant decision day, the last Friday in June.

Until the encounter with Elizabeth, Gennie had been looking forward to it – and the trip to Bristol, where the results would be announced. It would be the first time she'd been further than Bodmin for three months. Now she was desperate to get out of it. Jack had never been keen on going and didn't see why it couldn't be done online. Gennie was half expecting Marion to stand one or both of them down, in case they brought the project into disrepute by having an argument mid-session, but Alex had been as good as his word and kept their secrets.

'Are you sure you wouldn't rather go?' asked Gennie when Marion called her in the evening before to give her a copy of the programme for the day.

Procedures had been changed because of the pandemic. Whereas in the past, all applicants would have been invited to a large event to receive their decisions and a half day's training on reporting and monitoring before an evening reception, now the meetings were staggered. Each group would meet the trustees, receive their decisions and an individual session on monitoring before being paired with two other groups for peer mentoring. This would remain within the rule of six and also provide a supportive working structure for the life of the project.

The organisers were pleased with what they'd devised. Gennie was starting to agree with Jack that Zoom would be fine.

Marion smiled. 'Definitely not. You did the first meeting and it's important that you remain the face of the project. I don't want to be hobbling about in this boot and nor do I want to spend three hours in the Land Rover with Jack, bouncing along country roads. I'll dislodge another rib.'

Gennie wasn't that keen on spending three hours in the Land Rover with Jack either. She'd been avoiding him since Monday and ducked into the laundry or her cottage whenever she saw him striding towards the farmhouse. It was very possible he'd been avoiding her too. She was used to seeing him at the end of every day when he scrubbed his hands at the sink and helped himself to her hand cream and cigarettes, but there were none missing from the packet. Checking whether he'd eaten the leftovers wasn't a reliable sign either as she hadn't been leaving any for him. He was on his own as far as she was concerned.

That went for his hair as well. She was getting quite skilled with the clippers and if they were still friends, she'd have offered Jack a quick trim. Not that longer hair didn't suit him, but if he wanted it cut, he'd have to ask someone else. Elizabeth, for example. Her own hair was looking quite good.

She'd grown out the length, although she'd kept the colour topped up, with the assistance of the girls at the farm, who were only too happy to spend a day dyeing each others' hair, and lend her some straighteners so she could style her hair properly for the occasion rather than just bunching it into a ponytail as she did on most days.

Jack looked long and hard at Gennie when she emerged from the cottage, ready to go. It felt good to be venturing into the world again. Choosing the right outfit had been tough. It hadn't been pleasant to find that most of her tailored clothes, which admittedly she hadn't worn for some time, were now a bit tight. All that pandemic baking! She'd spent one evening trying on everything in her wardrobe for Alice's perusal, less fashion runway, more running the gauntlet of teenage brutality. No-one winced like a fourteen-year-old or got bored so quickly. They agreed on a sleeveless dress, which was a little stretched across the buttons at the front – and a fitted blue blazer to hide the fact. Fortunately, the skirt had a nice flare to it.

'What's wrong?' Gennie asked. 'Does it look dangerously tight?'

'It depends.' Jack shrugged.

'On what?'

'Exactly,' he said, and got in the car.

Thank God she'd brought an audiobook with her. It was going to be a long drive. She put her headphones in and settled down to a dystopian vision of total female rebellion. She'd be the first to sign up.

After an hour or so, Jack requested a cigarette break.

'If I smoke in the Defender, our clothes will stink of smoke,' he said.

Gennie nodded. She raced off to the services for a comfort break and returned with two coffees. Consideration was a two-way street.

Jack was still smoking. Given how long it had taken to queue for coffee, it must be his second.

'So, are you going to stay at the farm?' he said, sipping his coffee. 'You know, if we don't get the money.'

'Yes, of course,' she said. 'I'll stay as long as there's a job for me. I need to stay until Alice finishes school, at least.'

She should ask him the same question. Even though she felt used by him, she dreaded hearing that he'd be leaving soon. That's what you got when you ignored all your own red flags. Once they were on the road again, she waited a while before she put her headphones back in.

'What about you?' she asked. 'Will you stay?'

'I don't know,' he said. 'I dunno whether there'll be anything there for me.'

'Where would you go?' she asked tentatively. She couldn't bring herself to ask whether he was talking about work or something else.

'I need to stay close enough that I can have Millie at weekends.' He smiled for what seemed like the first time that day. 'Which probably rules out Australia and working for my dad. It depends where I can get a job.'

Gennie lifted her earbuds to replace them.

'But listen,' he said, 'whatever happens, I'll go with you to Birmingham to check on Hamid. I heard on the news that we'll be allowed to travel again from next week. We can go then.'

Gennie nodded and turned her face to the window. Whatever happens… Why did it feel like a break-up?

*

The Bristol meeting started at two. There were two women behind the desk – one from the board of trustees and another from the monitoring team.

'We'll put you out of your misery,' they said as soon as their visitors had sat down.

Gennie smiled involuntarily. It would take an entirely new life to do that. She smiled genuinely at the news that Hope House had been given a grant for two years, at ten per cent less than they'd requested, but it was enough to get them started. She hoped Jack was concentrating on all the reporting requirements because she'd absorbed none of the details.

'You got it, Jack. Congratulations,' she whispered as they left the room at the end of the session.

'Thanks.' He looked neither as cheerful nor relieved as she'd expected.

'You can't run now,' she said, and wondered if she'd hit the nail on the head.

They went their separate ways during the break – Gennie called Marion while Jack disappeared outside before heading to the reception hall to meet the teams they'd been partnered with. There was a buffet, which was a relief, as Gennie had been too anxious to eat the sandwich she'd packed for the trip, and now that the pressure was off, she was ravenous. She was less thrilled to see the lines of glasses of wine, but surely Jack wouldn't be tempted, not if he was driving.

Gennie crammed a plate with mini quiches and sausage rolls and made a start on finding out what it was about these four other people that had made the trustees believe they were well matched. It had to be more than that they were all from the south-west. She nursed a single glass of white wine and turned away from Jack to chat to the other project leaders. Her eyes would stray to him if he was nearby and she didn't want him to catch her watching. She couldn't help it. It was like pressing a bruise to see if it still hurt.

When their time was up, Gennie was still deep in conversation with Miles, trustee of a youth drug rehabilitation project and, in his pinstripe suit, vying for the title of best-dressed person in the room, the other candidate being Jack. Miles told her he was a property developer and had got involved in the charity because he had a brother who'd been drug-addicted. As soon as Gennie heard the words investment and buildings, her ears pricked up. Marion would want to hear about this.

'Looks like they're getting ready to clear away,' said Miles. 'It would be good to continue the conversation. Do you have time for a drink? They do takeout down at the Harbour. We could get some food too. I think they do Chinese.'

Gennie looked around for Jack and spotted him at the other side of the room. He waved goodbye and left. She and Miles stared after him.

'Erm,' said Gennie, embarrassed, 'I'm very sorry but I've got to go as, quite bizarrely, my lift seems to be going without me. Can I email you?'

She hurried towards the door without waiting for his answer. Jack was already at the bottom of the stairs and in the lobby, heading for the front door.

'Jack!' She called after him, only now realising how sore her feet were in her heels. It was fine standing still in a carpeted room, but walking was going to be a problem. 'Where are you going?'

'Home,' he said simply. He waited while she hobbled to catch up.

'Without me?'

'You seemed to be getting on fine,' he said. 'I assumed I'd be in the way.'

'What? You can't just leave me! You didn't even check I was all right. What happened to never leaving a man behind? Would you leave your mates behind?' She was raising her voice now.

'Well, yes. If they'd pulled. It would be pretty much compulsory to bail out and leave them to get on with it.'

'But you can't do that with a girl! How did you know I was going to be okay? How was I going to get home? It's bloody miles!' She could not believe what she was hearing. 'And anyway, I hadn't pulled!'

'You've got the car keys in your bag, remember? You said they ruined the line of my suit. And you looked well set up. You were smiling and laughing.'

'Trust me, that doesn't mean anything,' she said drily. They were out in the street now and she could yell if she wanted.

'And he spent the whole time looking down your dress.'

'I asked you if it was too tight and you said it wasn't!'

'I said it depends what you are after,' he said calmly.

'Oh my God.' It was very difficult not to shout at him. 'Is this what this is about? He's a property developer! I was trying to get more money for your damn project! The surfers with disabilities? They'll need somewhere to sleep. Isn't that what you want to do next?' She bent down to take her shoes off and threw them at his feet. He stepped back to avoid them. 'And I'm going to be disabled if I have to wear these bloody things any longer!'

Jack picked up the shoes and handed them back. 'You'll have to put them back on. I'm not carrying you to the car.'

Gennie fumbled in her bag for the car keys and threw those at him instead. He made no attempt to catch them as they fell to the ground.

'Can you get the car and pick me up here, then?'

'You know, Cinderella wouldn't have behaved like this,' he said, scooping the keys up off the floor.

Bad jokes were not the answer.

'She bloody well would have!' Gennie retorted. 'If Cinderella had spent all day transforming dresses and pumpkins and wearing horrendously uncomfortable shoes, at least partly for the benefit of some spoilt and ungrateful man, and then he got up and left halfway through the party, I'm sure she would have found a better use for those glass slippers! And you really need to broaden your reading.'

Her anger spent, Gennie went to sit on a wall outside an office building. She felt utterly drained.

'I can't believe you were going to leave me to take my chances with some random man. Don't you care about me at all?' She dug her nails into her hands to stop herself crying.

'Of course I do, but I wasn't sure you wanted me around. I thought you might want a bit of space.' He came to sit next to her.

'You're such an idiot.' She was almost too tired to explain. 'D'you think this is point-scoring? I've got nothing to prove. And what were you going to do while I was hooking up with a stranger? Get drunk, I suppose, and justify it by saying I'd abandoned you. I'm not playing your stupid games.' She stopped. 'And anyway, how would you have got back?'

'I would have coped,' he said. He touched her hand. 'I'm sorry.'

She wasn't sure which misdemeanour he was apologising for, but his physical closeness soothed her. He was also upset, she realised. If a situation became difficult or competitive, he'd make himself scarce. He couldn't deal with conflict of any kind anymore. He'd take punishment but he wouldn't fight.

'And anyway,' he continued, 'I'm uncomfortable in a room full of suits. I don't fit in there, but you do.'

'Oh, Jack,' she sighed. 'You're not being realistic. If you want the money for what you want to do, you're going to have to put on your best clothes and sell yourself. I saw you do that. You only got uncomfortable when people started drinking. And anyway, you look good in your suit and your beautifully ironed shirt.'

He looked down at his pale grey shirt. 'You ironed this one.'

'Can you actually tell the difference?'

'Well, yes.' He smiled.

'Well, all right then, in your adequately, but not quite beautifully, ironed shirt.' She made an effort to be nice. 'But you look better in a suit than the other people there. They all looked like accountants. I spent most of the time wondering who the handsome man was and remembering it was you.' She smiled sweetly at him.

He winced. 'Are you taking the piss?'

'Look,' she said, slowly, 'you need to decide if you want this. Do you?'

'I think so. Maybe,' he said, looking at her for the first time in days. He stood up. 'I'll go get the car.'

Gennie pulled herself to standing. 'I'll come too. I don't trust you not to leave me here.'

Jack smiled again and offered her his hand. 'Come on, I'll carry you.'

'I'll walk,' she said, gingerly replacing her shoes as she held on to his elbow.

The drive home was shorter but seemed to go on forever. Gennie sat in the front seat, arms folded, watching the weather worsen as the journey progressed. She didn't know what else to say to him. Eventually, he broke the silence.

'What will you do with your summer break?'

'I'll go to France. If it's allowed. My mum messages each time the rules change. She's invited you and Millie too, if you fancy spending time in Provence. She feels a maternal responsibility and that Marion has borne the brunt of caring for us all so she needs to return the favour.'

'That's kind of her. I'd like to go to Australia, though – as soon as it's allowed. I expect you'd be welcome too. Shall I ask?'

He smiled and she laughed, possibly for the first time that day.

It was gone eleven when they reached home and the farm was dark. They parked the car and made a dash through the rain to Gennie's door.

'Can I come in?' he said. 'We need to talk.'

Gennie didn't respond. He picked up her hand and stroked her knuckles. Roxy had evidently recognised Jack's steps and started scratching at the inside of the kitchen door.

'The other woman,' Jack said, with no trace of irony.

Gennie didn't want to know how many other women there were in Jack's life.

'I've got to walk her. Can I come back later?'

She nodded. 'Yes.'

He hadn't asked her to join him on his walk, which was just as well as her feet really hurt. She threw her shoes on the floor of the hall and dragged herself upstairs. The day should have felt like a triumph so why did she feel so deflated? She doubted Jack would come back. He was more likely to put on his 'out of office' face and be very busy on the farm. Even if he did come back, she wasn't sure that she wanted to hear what he had to say or indeed what she'd say to him. She lay in bed in her pyjama shorts and vest and groaned. This was all so predictable. Well, whatever Jack decided for himself, she would not run; she'd stay at the farm. The worst that could happen was that she'd join the list of people yearning after Jack. Max would commiserate.

She fell asleep curled round Sergio. The buzz of her phone woke her. It was earlier than usual, just before one.

'Jack?'

'I'm downstairs. Can I come up?'

'Alice is asleep. Wait there.' What sort of state would he be in? She was in no mood to be wrangling drunks out of the house.

Jack was in the hall, dog under his arm. Both of them were very wet. 'I'm sorry. I lost track of time. Is it still okay for me to be here?'

'I suppose so. You're both soaking, though. Where've you been? That poor dog,' Gennie sighed. 'We'll go next door. You'd better give me your suit.'

Jack attempted to smile. 'Do I need to get out of my wet clothes before I catch my death of cold?'

'No,' she said, putting her wellies on and opening the door.

'That won't happen. You need to get out of your wet clothes because we'll probably need the suit again.'

She led him into the farm kitchen and fetched a coat hanger and two towels from the laundry. She handed a towel to Jack, who bent down and used it to dry the dog. Gennie shrugged and used the second towel – which she'd planned to use on the dog – to dry Jack's hair. She took his jacket from him and put it on the hanger and waited for him to peel off his sodden trousers and socks. When she returned from the airing cupboard, he was sitting at the table, in his damp shirt and shorts, formal despite his state of undress.

'There's a lot I want to say but I don't know where to begin,' he said.

'Start with Elizabeth,' she said, sitting down next to him. She had a surreptitious sniff but couldn't smell alcohol, only damp wool.

'Elizabeth?' He sounded surprised. 'Oh…' His voice fell. 'Okay, so that's another mess.'

'I know you slept with her.'

'Well, yeah.' He glanced sideways. 'But that was ages ago, before…'

He remained completely still, making no sudden movements, treating her as if she was an unexploded bomb. She remembered her promise to Alex. Nothing which would give Jack any excuses.

'All I want is a simple life. Now it's really fucking complicated. You know, she lets herself into my room. Mostly on a Sunday. She'll say stuff like it's not worth her going home because she's on early the next day. I've held out as long as I can. There's only so much spooning a person can do.'

Gennie laughed in spite of herself. 'I suppose you can't really say you're not interested in her, not if you've got history,' she said. 'Your only decent excuse for turning her away would be if you were seeing someone else and I can see why you wouldn't have said that.'

Why was she making excuses for him?

'You think I haven't tried saying I might be at the beginning of something with someone and I wouldn't mind seeing how things went? No points were awarded. I've asked Alex to make sure her shifts aren't like that again but she can just swap them with other staff if she wants. I'm scared to go back to my room at night. Then last Sunday, after I'd dropped Millie home, she did it again. I said I had to walk Roxy and drove straight to Max's. I've spent so many nights there recently, I've become his support bubble.'

'So, you didn't…?'

'No, of course not. I came back on Monday and she was still there. I was so angry, and I didn't know how to get her out of my room without dragging her out of there, but then you told her it was fine.'

'What? No, I didn't.'

'You said you were glad I'd found someone who made me happy. And then, because you'd been so nice, she was embarrassed to ask you for towels so she made me come back and find some for her. I mean, what the fuck? First you do the drawing of Millie and then you give me the brush-off and then you say you're happy I'm with Elizabeth. It made no sense.'

Gennie leaned back in her chair and ran her hands through her hair. 'I didn't say any of that. How could she do that? I'm not happy and I didn't give you the brush-off. It's just… I've got a daughter to think about, that's all.'

'And so have I.'

A thought occurred to her. 'Wait, when Marion broke her ankle, were you with Millie?'

'Busted,' he said, with a grimace. 'That's the other thing. Elizabeth knows I've been breaking lockdown.'

'She only knows that because she was also somewhere she shouldn't have been. And apart from that, we've been very careful here.'

'Even so, you can't tell anyone. Nick's petrified of getting caught. You've got to feel for the guy. We tried FaceTime but Millie was hysterical, crying and pleading. She accused Nick of stopping her seeing me and he cracked.'

'I can imagine her with her hands on her hips, giving him what for,' said Gennie, smiling now.

Jack laughed. 'So can I! So Claire sorted it so I could sneak round the back, have some dinner, read a few stories and sneak back out. It was nice. Nick's all right, it turns out.'

'Yeah?'

'Yeah. I think...' He looked up, lost to her for a second.

'You think Andy...?'

'Yeah.' He nodded.

She made to touch his arm and swiftly withdrew her hand before it made contact.

'And everyone thought you were with Elizabeth.'

'Did they? I didn't know that.'

'And Jack, if we're talking brush-offs...'

He leaned back. 'Can we open the door so I can smoke? Or go upstairs?'

Gennie opened the door and sat on the kitchen step, knees drawn up under her chin. She patted the space beside her. Even though the stone was cold under her pyjamas, she wasn't going upstairs with him. Jack lit up, inhaled and lowered himself next to her. His bare feet rested on the wet gravel. He didn't seem bothered. It had stopped raining at least.

'I know what you're talking about, I won't pretend I don't. What can I say? I panicked, G. People say that all the time but I actually panicked. I mean, what we had was kind of intense and it stirred a lot of things up. And the news was so bad and I thought that if I fucked this up while we're all stuck here in one place, it would be a nightmare for everyone and there'd be no escape.' He shook his head. 'I couldn't risk it.'

Gennie breathed in the smoke from his cigarette, only the second time in all these months she'd been tempted. 'I thought you had an escape. What about Jan's cottage?'

Jack looked confused.

'You know, the keeper of the dog is the keeper of the cottage.'

'Is that even a thing?'

'It's certainly empty. You could always go there.'

'D'you want me to?'

'Well, no, not if you don't want to. And you were right, Jack, it was better not to get involved.' She thumped the step. 'Why do I end up defending you when you don't care what happens to me?'

'That's not true. I couldn't bear to watch you with that guy. I couldn't see that you were doing your job well.' He turned towards her. 'I didn't want to hurt you. I never want to hurt you and yet, I do.'

She thought about this. Did she make it impossible for people?

'Well, you're not going to break my heart, Jack,' she said bitterly. 'Someone got there first. And he did a really good job of it.'

Jack grimaced. 'Is that so? No prospect of recovery?'

Gennie stood up. 'I'm going to bed now.'

'You won't stay with me?' He reached for her hand.

'I'm not comfortable with you being involved with someone else.'

'I'm not involved with anyone else!' he said through gritted teeth.

'Well, even if I'll support your need for casual, opportunistic sex, I'd rather be the only one you're having casual, opportunistic sex with,' she said with an artificially sweet smile.

'It's not… Okay, I can't win here.' He lifted his hands in surrender. 'I never really know what you want.'

She kissed the top of his head. 'Good night.'

45

Gennie let herself back into the cottage and headed for the stairs. She paused on the bottom step, hand on the bannister. She believed him and she also believed he wouldn't fight for her. He was done fighting. And she'd lied when she said he couldn't hurt her, couldn't reach beyond what she'd already endured. He had hurt her. He hadn't meant to but she'd been hurt nonetheless. Not because she was a person full of pain but because she'd opened her heart to him, because she cared for him. But that wasn't the worst thing that could happen. She turned around.

Jack's room was dark but she could make him out sitting propped at the head of his bed. His lighter flared, illuminating his bare chest and the lower part of his face.

'Are you coming in?' he asked, dragging on his cigarette.

She slid into his bed and he put his arm very casually around her shoulders, stubbing out his cigarette with his other hand. She was careful not to lean into him.

'So, what's keeping you awake?' she asked.

'You mustn't think I don't care,' he started. 'I do care… about what you do and who you're with.'

'And is that it?' she asked. It wasn't the most effusive declaration she'd ever received.

'Yes, except I'm glad you're here.'

Gennie curled into him finally, arm around his chest, breathing in the scent of him – the combination of cologne, smoke and the outdoors, fresh and warm, that pervaded all the spaces he inhabited, so familiar from the weeks she'd slept in his bed. He tightened his arm around her shoulder.

'I shouldn't have left you in a room full of suits,' he said. 'I'm sorry. I can see it's a risk area for you. You might have been carried off by an accountant or a lawyer.'

If he was teasing her, he must be feeling better.

'Would that be so bad?' she asked.

'Can't imagine anything worse. Can you?' he said, softly, wrapping his other arm loosely around her.

Gennie turned her head and kissed his shoulder. Jack responded immediately, stroking her cheek and pulling her face towards his. He pressed his lips hard against hers in fierce apology.

Gennie leaned away. 'Actually, Jack, it was worse than that. Miles suggested we got takeout Chinese.'

Jack slapped his forehead. 'Why didn't you tell me?'

'I tried. I took to my heels as soon as he said the words, but you'd already gone.'

'I am so sorry. I promise to check the catering offer before I abandon you again.'

'And also, I'm quite in favour of you being carried off by an accountant. Might be good for you.'

'I see, and do you have any accountants in mind?' He kissed her again, but gently.

'I could put together a shortlist,' Gennie suggested, lifting her arms and folding them around Jack's neck. She closed her eyes. It was a relief to be here, in this room, kissing him again, but if it was so easy why, the rest of the time, did it feel so impossibly complicated?

'Don't put more than one name on your list.' Jack put his face close to her ear and kissed her neck. He paused for a couple of beats. 'Otherwise, I might not pick you.'

'I hate you,' she said, pushing him off her and turning on her side to face him. When she traced his brow with her finger he kissed the inside of her palm. Gennie could feel his cheek muscles under her hand.

'Are you smiling or yawning? What's the time?' she asked.

'It's about three, I think,' he said, biting the ends of her fingers. 'D'you want to sleep then? Now we've kissed and made up.'

'Sleep would be nice,' Gennie admitted, smiling in the darkness and wondering how long Jack's respectful behaviour would last. So far he hadn't made a move she hadn't invited him to make.

'Turn over then,' he said, moving her to face the other way, leaning into her back and wrapping her arms in his.

'I thought you hated this.' Gennie closed her eyes and tried to ignore the signs of his arousal and the loudly snoring dog. Sleep wouldn't be so easy.

'I'll make an exception. Why did you come back, by the way?'

'Because when I thought about it, staking a claim to the

moral high ground was going to be cold and lonely, and also, it wasn't fair that Elizabeth might get what I wanted.'

Jack was awake now and leaning over her. 'What you wanted? Why didn't you say this before?' He stroked her face. 'I'd pick you out of any list, G, however long. Don't go to sleep on me now!' He sounded panicked. His hand slid lower and under her vest. 'Is this opportunistic?'

'I hope so.' She wriggled out of her clothes before he pulled them off her. He must be in no doubt about her intentions. 'I've had enough intense for one day.'

His mouth was on hers, his hand on the back of her thigh as he pressed his hips against her. 'It'll be intense,' he murmured. 'Everything is with you.'

46

Alice was still asleep when Gennie crept back into the cottage wearing a T-shirt and leggings that Jack had borrowed from the laundry. She hadn't meant to fall asleep and hadn't realised she had until Jack woke her with a mug of tea and the news that Marion wanted a meeting at ten.

'How long have you been up?' she asked, grateful for the tea to disguise her morning breath.

'Didn't bother going to sleep,' he said, stretching out next to her. 'Wasn't worthwhile. So I got up and did all my farm jobs. I need to get Millie after the meeting.' He hugged her to him and kissed her cheek. 'You okay?'

'I'm fine,' she said, cautiously. If things followed their previous pattern, he'd be MIA for a few days, although childcare was a better excuse than an urgent need to go to the builders' merchants.

'Hurry up and get washed and I'll make you some breakfast.'

Alex was already making coffee when Gennie made it back to the kitchen. She grabbed a cup and sat at the table, stifling a yawn. A bowl of porridge and blueberries appeared in front of her.

'With coconut milk,' said Jack. 'You won't need honey.'

She'd have opened her eyes wide in surprise if her eyelids weren't too tired to lift beyond halfway.

'Wow. This is a change from your usual five-minutes-in-the-pan-fifty-years-clogging-the-arteries style of cooking. Looks amazing.'

Jack sat down next to her with a bowl for himself.

Alex smiled. 'Well, this is cosy. You two friends again?'

'I think we might be on the verge of considering the possibility of becoming friends.' Gennie smiled at Alex and carried on eating.

Alex nodded with mock solemnity. 'I admire your commitment. I do think it's important to throw yourself wholeheartedly into things.'

'Oh, I agree,' said Gennie with a straight face. Jack had stopped eating. She turned to face him. 'Yes?' she asked, innocently.

'Is this how it's going to be?'

'I'm glad you've sorted it out,' said Alex, sincerely this time. 'Jack was telling me there was a moment last night when he thought he might need surgical help to remove your heel from his head.'

'I'd have aimed lower,' said Gennie, clearing her bowl. Jack's porridge was delicious, lighter and sweeter than she'd have made it. She might add it to the regular menu. 'Did he tell you why, by any chance?'

'He was very discreet,' said Alex, but this was coffee time so he would certainly be after gossip.

'I didn't think you'd want him to know how much you'd drunk,' Jack said, shaking his head theatrically and laughing as Gennie threw her spoon down on the table.

'Mother! How glad I am to see you,' said Jack, leaping to his feet as Marion entered the kitchen, still limping in her surgical boot. 'Let me help you.' He kissed her cheek and pulled out a chair for her.

'What have you done?' She smiled at him, in on the joke.

Marion's project folder had grown even bulkier since Gennie had delivered it to the hospital. She unfolded a spreadsheet. 'I have a schedule of deadlines.' She looked over her glasses at the group around the table and Gennie realised she'd been bumped up the pecking order from bit part to full player. She even had her own column.

'My thought was that Jack would manage the practical aspects of the apprenticeship content, the building, farming and so on, and you, Gennie, will look after the finances, the publicity and business skills. Alex will be in charge of the young people's welfare. You can select the apprentices together. We'd obviously have to discuss the finer contractual points, but what d'you think in principle?'

Suddenly, she empathised with Jack's panic. This was a promotion and she was flattered, but if she agreed now, she was committed, and for at least two years. There was no way of bailing out halfway. If the choice were between working with Jack or being with Jack, which way would she go? And taking Jack out of the equation, because not everything had to be about him, she liked her simple life of menus and ironing. Giving it up for something with risk and challenges might not be the gift Marion believed, not if it involved other sacrifices.

'I understand if you're worried about managing this along with everything else,' said Marion, misreading Gennie for the first time in all the months she'd worked with her. 'But I'm not asking you to do two jobs. If you take this one, we'll hire someone else to help with the cooking and laundry.'

Jack was already on the doorstep with a cigarette. Gennie glanced in his direction but he was studiously examining the brickwork around the door even though it had only recently been repointed. He'd agreed to his part of the deal, but why wouldn't he? It was his project.

'I'll do it,' said Gennie. 'Thank you.'

'Good.' Marion smiled at her. 'But look, you two, you're going to have to work together. Don't get distracted from what you are trying to achieve.'

'We'll be fine,' said Jack, dismissing her worries with a wave of his hand.

'Of course,' agreed Gennie. She'd chosen. Project first, everything else second. 'There are a couple of things, though.'

Marion nodded, pen at the ready.

'I'd like to give Hamid another chance,' she said.

Jack came back into the room.

'You promised,' she told him.

'I did.'

'And also, there's this guy, Miles, who's in our peer group. He has building projects all over the county and I was thinking we could talk to him about other opportunities for our students, find them different sites to work on.'

'Thinking about Miles, eh?' said Jack, head to one side.

'Thinking about you,' said Gennie, firmly, 'and your project, and organising a meeting for you both.'

'It's a good idea,' he said, with a smile that said he believed it.

47

Gennie knocked gently on the glass-panelled front door. She didn't want to wake Carrie's younger children or draw too much of Lee's attention to Jack's mud-splattered Land Rover on his pristine drive. They were late as Jack refused to spare more than a day for her mission, insisting that if they really had to go to Birmingham they would drive up after work, see Hamid in the morning and drive home the following evening. They were even later as Alice had seen an opportunity. If her mum was going away, she would too, and they'd had to divert to drop her with friends in Exeter.

'I don't know why I agreed to this,' said Jack.

'Yes, you do,' said Gennie, 'but however we got to this point, I'm grateful.'

Carrie looked surprisingly pleased to see them. Perhaps any visitor after a three-month lockdown was a treat. 'Have you eaten?'

'Yes, thank you,' said Gennie, hugging her. 'We're only

really after a bed for the night. We'll try not to get in the way.'

'You'll have a drink, though, won't you?' Carrie offered, as she led them through to the kitchen, where Lee was sitting at the table with a bottle of wine.

'I will. In fact, I've brought supplies,' said Gennie, brandishing two bottles of wine. 'But Jack likes to keep a clear head.'

Jack nodded obligingly and shook Lee's hand.

'So, you work with Gennie, then?' asked Lee, as he filled a glass for Gennie.

'Yes,' said Jack. 'Well, we're about to start. I've been hanging out at my mum's place doing a bit of building work but now we've got this new thing on the go.'

He looked at Gennie for help. This was entering nightmare territory for him – a social situation requiring small talk with strangers with no nicotine or alcohol. She needed to move the conversation on to more comfortable ground.

Carrie got there first. 'You used to be in the army, didn't you, Jack?'

Gennie's heart sank. Lee was a local Labour councillor and he'd been known to express very robust views on the British Army in Afghanistan and Iraq. He wasn't averse to expressing strong opinions on a lot of things – migration, the EU (which had been awkward given that Mikkel was Danish and she was French), wind farms and the lack of NHS dentists being a few.

'Yes,' said Jack. 'Royal Engineers.'

'I have to say that I was against us going into Iraq,' said Lee.

'I wasn't totally sold on it at times,' said Jack, unsmiling.

'Carrie went on marches.'

'She might have seen my mum,' said Jack.

'But I think the armed forces have given so much over the past twenty years and we have to support returning servicemen,' said Lee.

Gennie poured herself another glass of wine and listened in amazement as he and Jack proceeded to have a detailed discussion about budgets and military restructuring, before moving on to running and cycling, which Lee had taken up again in the last few months.

Gennie left them to compare their personal bests and went to help Carrie make up the sofa bed in the study.

'When you said a bed for the night, I wasn't sure whether you meant one bed or two,' said Carrie. She was smiling, more like grinning, in fact.

'We're not really...'

'So tell me!' insisted Carrie.

'He's more of an old friend.'

She'd have to make sure she spoke to Alice before news of their sleeping arrangements filtered back via Lucy.

'I like him,' said Carrie, still fishing.

'Everyone does. Look, this will be fine,' Gennie said. 'We've got sleeping bags and mats and one of us can sleep on the floor. Well, that will be Jack, obviously. And we'll be up very early.'

Gennie went to bed at midnight and tucked herself in under one of Carrie's duvets. She'd finished off a lot of wine in a very short time and her head was spinning. She woke to find herself being shoved gently to the side as Jack wormed his way onto the bed, limbs enclosed in a slippery nylon sleeping bag.

'Move up. I don't want to sleep on the floor,' he whispered.

Did he always have to do this in the middle of the night?

'Don't worry. I'll stay in my space. I don't want you breathing alcohol fumes in my face. D'you snore when you're drunk?'

Gennie had no idea whether she snored or not. She'd drunk so little in the last few years and her only regular sleeping companion had been the cat. She sighed.

'D'you always have to wake me up?'

'Sorry,' he said insincerely. He lay on his back, hands folded across his stomach. 'Is this what your house was like then?'

'This one's bigger,' she murmured, not sure if she was articulating the right words in the right order.

'D'you miss it? Is this what you mean when you say Mikkel threw it all away?'

'I suppose so. I don't know if I miss it exactly. It's like it belonged in someone else's life.'

'You had a really nice life,' he told her.

'Thanks,' she said, rolling onto her back.

'And now you've got nothing.'

'Thanks again.' She laughed.

'It reminds me that I've got nothing either.' He sounded serious.

'We have each other.' She reached across to pat his hand.

'Fuck. We're doomed then.'

Now she laughed properly. He didn't.

'Don't you worry, though,' he turned to her, 'that whatever happens in your life now, that it's not going to be good enough, not as good as before?'

Gennie pulled herself up on her elbows. Jack wasn't usually this insecure. 'No, not at all,' she said. 'If anything, it makes me want less, but I want it to be real and solid. I don't want to feel like it's floating away from under me.' She lay back down again. 'Anyway, Jack, you've got everything you need to build your life. And plenty of time. You're at least ten years younger than Lee.'

'Yeah, maybe. He was giving me the benefit of his business wisdom, telling me all the stuff he'd done by the time he was thirty and so on. I started feeling like a total loser. If I slept on the floor, I might as well sleep there forever.'

'It's you, you made him feel inadequate,' said Gennie, unable to stop herself laughing. 'I couldn't believe it when he started on about his sporting achievements. He'll be bragging about wrestling bears next.'

Jack finally cracked. 'He did tell me about the massive fish he'd caught in Ireland.'

Now they both had the giggles and had to muffle their laughter in the bedding.

'Shame you've been drinking,' said Jack.

'I know,' she said. 'Why did I do that? It's something about being here, being with Carrie and Lee. You come in the house and have a glass of wine. That's how it was.'

'See?' said Jack. 'Not that easy.'

*

Gennie regretted the wine even more when her phone alarm rang at five o'clock.

'Five more minutes,' she murmured, without opening her eyes.

'No chance,' said Jack, who was already out of bed and looking for clothes. 'Come on, this is your idea, remember?

Get dressed. You can wash later. Are the binoculars still in the Land Rover?'

'Yes,' said Gennie, crawling out of bed and across the landing to the bathroom. She had to clean her teeth at least. She also needed a couple of glasses of water.

They were outside the industrial estate by twenty to six, the Land Rover, which would be instantly recognisable to Hamid, parked in plain sight on the street. Jack obviously had his own plan but whether it was to make contact with Hamid or prove to Gennie that he didn't want to be found wasn't as clear.

They left the car and walked into the estate to do some quick reconnaissance in the quiet of the early morning. Gennie pointed out the factory and the security guard's hut before she was sent back out to wait in the Land Rover, with instructions to fix her mobile to the hands-free kit and do nothing else until Jack called her.

Just before six, a single white minibus pulled up to the entrance and the driver swiped his card against the reader to open the security barrier. As before, Gennie scanned the tinted windows but had a view of only one side of the vehicle. The light and the angle were so bad she couldn't pick anyone out, let alone identify Hamid. Surely, though, if he were on the bus, he would have spotted the Land Rover even if he couldn't see her clearly. And in any case, if he were there, Jack would see him from the position he'd taken up opposite the factory and out of the sight line of the security guard.

Ten minutes later, Gennie's phone rang.

'I think he's on the bus now,' said Jack. 'One of the group that just left the factory. But I'm really not sure. There's a boy who looks like a thinner, scruffier version of him with a beard and long hair. They were only outside for a few seconds. I thought I knew him well but in a crowd of other Asians I struggled to pick him out. Can you believe that? He definitely wasn't one of the group that's just started their shift. Can you go after the bus and pick me up later? Stay in contact.'

Gennie started the engine as the minibus appeared at the barrier and followed it as it took the familiar route to Sparkbrook. She was more confident tailing the vehicle today, even daring to overtake it at a set of lights, but not brave enough to look at the passengers as she passed them. At that hour, there were few cars on the road and she would have been conspicuous even if she hadn't been in the Defender. The minibus stopped in the same street as before. Gennie couldn't risk stopping but drove straight past. She knew the area now. When she couldn't see Hamid among the passengers on her side of the bus, she raced round the block to see if she could get a better look as the passengers descended onto the pavement. She was wide awake now, adrenaline pumping.

As she passed for the second time, a line of weary-looking men was already entering the house. This time Gennie was almost sure that the young man near the back of the group was Hamid. It was his walk, the slouch-shouldered shuffle. She wanted to hoot the horn and yell to him, but she needed a subtler way to attract his attention so crunched the gears, which was the sort of teeth-clenching metallic screech which made passers-by wince and stare. Several of the men turned but the one she was watching didn't react at all. She thumped the steering wheel in frustration.

Jack was waiting on the corner of the road away from the entrance to the industrial estate.

'They went back to the same house,' said Gennie as she moved across to let him drive. 'I'm ninety-nine per cent sure it's Hamid but I couldn't get him to turn around. I can show you where it is. Shall we go there and knock on the door?'

'No, I think you should calm down and show me the house and then we'll go and get something to eat and think about this.'

Jack would say no more until they were in a coffee shop and waiting for their food order. He hunched over his mug of tea and spoke quietly. 'You're right, G. There's something weird here. I watched the minibus arrive and leave, and the people on it are escorted on and off while the driver stays with the bus. If it was simply a bus to bring people to work, why would you need an escort? You only need an escort if you don't know where you're going or someone is in charge of you – either responsible for you or controlling your movements in some way.'

'Do you think he was abducted?' Gennie asked, caught between fear and satisfaction. She'd been right.

'If he was abducted, he would have told the police,' said Jack. 'Unless he couldn't, I s'pose. Did you get a good look at the workers?'

'No, only a couple turned round. They were all male, and they weren't well dressed – old joggers and jeans – and they weren't all young. One guy looked about forty-five. I couldn't say where they were from.'

'One of them had bruising around his eye,' Jack said. 'I'm going to try and get into the factory. I could say I was delivering something. D'you know if there are any cash-and-carry outlets round here? We need a big box of something.'

Gennie surfed the Internet on her phone. She was out of her depth. She glanced at Jack, working out whether he was feeling reckless or cautious and meticulous, because he was capable of both. She hoped it was the latter.

'There's a cash-and-carry on the other side of Small Heath,' she said. 'It probably doesn't matter what's in the box as if they're not expecting anything they shouldn't accept the delivery. Maybe we can buy something we actually need.'

While she thought about suitable products, Jack drove to the warehouse and, once inside, she directed him towards the ranges of plastic food takeout boxes.

'I can make use of these at the farm as the kids always need picnics and snacks, and it wouldn't be that strange for them to have been wrongly delivered to a place called Kandahar Foods.'

'Not bad,' Jack agreed. 'We won't have delivery paperwork, though, so I'll have to busk that bit.'

Gennie steered the trolley past a towering stack of toilet rolls. 'While we're here, can we get some other stuff as well? It will save me a trip. I need a big bag of rice, ten kgs, and we could get some loo roll too, as I never want to go through rationing again.'

'Fuck's sake.' Jack shook his head. 'Generally people don't do reconnaissance with their weekly shop in the back of their vehicle.'

Gennie ignored him. 'Your Millie needs some felt pens too. They're cheaper here.'

'This is what's known as mission creep.'

'It's what's known as multitasking,' corrected Gennie, lifting a huge plastic-wrapped package into the trolley.

When they drove back to the factory, it was Gennie's turn to wait outside while Jack drove to the entrance barrier and buzzed for access to the estate. He was back after twenty minutes, laughing as he picked her up.

'Well, that was interesting! The guy on reception was very puzzled about my delivery but helpfully pointed out there are two takeouts and a restaurant nearby also called Kandahar and they gave me the addresses. I don't think he's the owner. They do make Indian food, as you thought, and supply it to small supermarkets. They have another factory in Bradford. You can't see into the factory from the reception as there's a door to another hallway and all you can see are the plastic screens beyond that.'

'Did you find out about the workforce?' asked Gennie.

'I didn't ask directly. I commented about them being busy and the guy said business wasn't as good as it had been. I asked if they'd had to furlough people and he said it didn't affect them because an agency supplies all their staff and they get the numbers they need. He didn't act like he had anything to hide.'

'So,' Gennie mused, 'they're using sub-contractors and the workers are supplied as a group to the factory. That's why they're controlled, because someone else will lose money if they don't work.'

'It looks that way, doesn't it?' said Jack. 'But it doesn't explain why Hamid is there. He could work wherever he wanted.'

'Did you get the name of the agency?'

'No, sorry, but it doesn't feel right. The minibus is unmarked, with no logos. What sort of agency doesn't advertise itself?'

'We need to rescue him,' said Gennie.

'I hate to keep pointing this out, G, but he hasn't actually asked to be rescued. What we need is a way to speak to him away from the escorts and find out whether he wants to leave. And we only have two places we know he goes.'

302

'What about if I go to the house and say I'm doing market research or checking on TV licences, and you sneak round the back and see if you can see him?'

'No, we need a sensible plan, not one where I am stuck in someone's back garden, peering through their windows or being arrested for trespassing. We need a plan where we can get out quickly in case he says, "No," and they set the dogs on us and where no-one can follow us in case he says, "Yes," and we all have to make a fast exit.'

'It has to be at the house, then, not the factory,' reasoned Gennie, 'as we can't get the Land Rover in and out of the estate without going through the security barrier and we'd need to be close to the factory to speak to Hamid.'

'Unless,' said Jack, 'we can get the passengers off the minibus outside the estate so they have to walk in.' He looked as if he had an idea.

'What are you going to do? Nip round slashing the minibus's tyres?'

'No, that's the third condition,' Jack answered. 'We can't cause any damage and no-one must get hurt.'

'It's like one of your extreme video games – but you have to get in and out safely avoiding kidnapping, trespass, criminal damage and assault charges.' She counted off the possible offences on her fingers. 'Can we go back to Carrie's now? I need a shower.' And a nap. Her rare hangover had caught up with her, and she was feeling quite rough.

48

Jack was moving about in the room. Gennie stayed under the duvet and pretended to be asleep until he left and then opened one eye to check her watch. Three o'clock, so she'd been asleep for over an hour. She closed her eyes again and when she woke, Jack was back, wrapped in a towel and squatting as he rummaged in his bag.

'You feeling better?' he asked, with his back to her.

'Yes, thanks,' she said, although she wasn't really. Napping in the middle of the day didn't suit her. She felt clammy-skinned and greasy-haired.

'What are you looking at?'

'You,' she admitted, 'although I'm not so much looking at you as trying to focus.'

'Maybe I won't get dressed yet,' he said, and sat down on the edge of the bed.

Gennie traced the water droplets on his arm. 'You're not getting in here, you're still wet. It reminds me, I need a shower.' She jumped out of bed and ran for the bathroom, evading his outstretched hand.

She hoped he'd wait, but when she returned to the study, he was gone. She found him sitting on the steps outside the French windows and smoking.

'So, d'you have a plan then?' she asked, hugging him briefly as she sat down next to him.

'I think so. It has to be done at the factory and we need to disable the security barrier in some way so the workers get out in the street. We'll then get a chance to speak to him while he walks through the estate. There's a snag, though.' He pulled on his cigarette. 'We need another car and another driver.'

'For today? How can we do that?' Gennie couldn't imagine who'd be free or would rush up there to help them.

'We can't. We'll need to stay another night. Will it be okay with Carrie?'

Carrie wasn't the problem. There was Alice to consider. In reality, they could only play at being international rescue on weekdays if the children were in education or otherwise occupied and never on weekends. Gennie took her phone upstairs and into the study.

'Hey, Ali,' she said when her daughter picked up. 'How's it going? Are you having fun?' She waited for her daughter to catch her up on the latest news while she ordered her thoughts.

'Would you like to stay another day there? Would they let you? Thing is we saw Hamid but haven't had a chance to speak to him yet, so we fixed up something for tomorrow.' It was only a small lie and one that would be forgiven and forgotten whatever happened. 'And the other thing is, that Carrie got a bit confused and I didn't like to make a drama of it because she's been so kind but she only made up one room for us.'

'What d'you mean?' asked Alice, also sounding confused.

'So, I'm sharing with Jack.'

'Well, that's better than camping, isn't it? I thought you were worried you'd be in a tent in the garden.'

'Well, yes. And also, do you like Jack?'

'Yeah, of course. Oh,' said Alice, in a tone that was too knowing. She was only fourteen, for heaven's sake. 'Do you like Jack? Is that what you mean?'

'Yes. Is that okay?'

'I guess. Is it official?'

'What? No, no.' Telling her daughter that it was only casual was entirely the wrong message to be giving a teenager but telling her it was official was entirely the wrong message to be giving Jack. How did people navigate these things?

'And, Mum, can I come back here next weekend? Her dad's going to do a barbecue for us.'

*

'I've asked one of my mates to help,' said Jack when she returned. He obviously took it for granted she'd have sorted out their accommodation and childcare issues. 'Dan. He lives near Oxford. He's got a security firm. We'll see if Hamid's there again when the shift changes, and then if we give him the go-ahead, he'll come over later. In the meantime, I need a builder's merchants or an electrical shop. You coming with me?'

'Yes, and I'll get some supplies. We need food for a stake-out.'

There was really no need for all the swearing. He went to a builder's merchants at least as frequently as she went to the supermarket and she wasn't rolling her eyes at him.

*

Exactly twelve hours after their previous visit, they were in the road outside the factory, parked as close to the entrance as they dared. The back of the Land Rover was now a little cluttered, with the box of plastic cartons, packages of toilet rolls, Jack's tool box, and a bag of bits and pieces he'd bought, two bags of food, two hundred cigarettes and twelve bottles of water.

'Concentrate,' said Jack, smoking as Gennie munched her way through a bag of crisps. 'First, we need to see if Hamid is on this bus, and if he is, we must be sure he sees us and that we signal to him in some way that we'll be back. We won't have much time so we need to warn him so that he's ready. It's possible they use more than one factory, and if he isn't brought here, we'll have to start tailing the minibuses again.'

At ten minutes before six, they left the car and took up places against the metal fence, one on either side of the entrance, so they could see both sides of any vehicle which stopped to pass through the barrier. Gennie's heart was pounding. Jack must be nervous too as he kept checking his phone and looking towards the Land Rover.

Five minutes later, two plain white minibuses drew up to the gate. Gennie was momentarily confused. It made no sense for two buses to collect one load of passengers, unless they collected workers from more than one source. Jack could be right and this was a bigger operation than she thought. As the buses passed her, Gennie saw that each one was only half-full, which was handy as she had a better view of the passengers. Even so, she nearly missed Hamid as he was sitting in the back seat of the first bus and she only noticed him when he turned to stare at her out of the rear window. He didn't smile or wave, which she took to mean that she shouldn't make any movements either. Instead she mouthed, 'See you tomorrow', at him as obviously as she could. He didn't react. Neither did any of the other passengers, who looked to be at least half, if not wholly, asleep.

She held her position until the buses were well inside the estate, using the time to note down the registration numbers of the minibuses – although what she'd do with the information she wasn't sure – before running over to Jack. She was almost jumping up and down with the adrenaline release.

'He was on the first bus. Did you see?'

Jack nodded and then frowned. 'Why did they send two fucking minibuses? It won't work if there are two of them.' He walked back to the barrier to measure out the distances again.

'I think we should try it anyway. We can always drive away if there are two minibuses.' She was gabbling; she really had to calm down. 'It would be easier to do this if Hamid was arriving at the factory and we could catch him before he ever went in.'

'Yeah, but as we don't know his shift pattern we could never be sure he would be on the bus. It could take days. At least this way, we know he's definitely here. We'd also need to stay longer and Claire would kill me if I didn't get back for Millie. Especially if it was because I was jackassing around, being the "A-Team" with you and Dan.' Jack threw away his cigarette.

Carrie was quite amenable to them spending another night. It might be the adult company or the fact that Gennie offered to make dinner while she put her younger children to bed. At nine, Jack excused himself as Dan had arrived.

'Is that an arc welder?' asked Lee as he joined Gennie and Carrie at the French windows, watching astonished as the other men compared bits of kit and set about manufacturing other pieces.

Gennie stayed in the kitchen, chatting to Carrie and passing a single glass of wine from hand to hand. As she'd been obliged to embarrass herself in front of her daughter, she'd make sure it had been worthwhile. While Jack and Dan were busy making sparks fly on the patio, she did some online research and downloaded the title documents and plans of the houses in Sparkbrook where the workers were living. There was nothing helpful. The houses were owned by the same person but they hadn't changed hands for eighteen years. Rundown rental properties, that was all.

Eventually, she went outside to introduce herself to Dan. Jack clearly wasn't going to.

'I'm not staying behind tomorrow, if that's what you think,' she said. 'I was the one who saw Hamid and he'll be expecting me.'

'See?' Jack said to Dan. 'I told you.'

He turned to Gennie. 'Listen, Dan and I are used to working together. We know what we're doing and we know when things are going tits up and we need to get out. We don't know who any of these people in the vans are and we have limited time and limited means of finding out. So we can't know what's going to happen, plan for known risks, etcetera, and this isn't how we like to do things.' He slowed, emphasising his words with a prod to her chest. 'So if you come with us, you have to do exactly what we tell you and don't wait for us to say "please". I don't want you questioning our decisions.'

This was somewhat ironic, this demand that she trust his judgement absolutely when his usual refrain was that no-one should rely on him.

'Do I ever do that?' she asked.

'Okay, maybe you don't,' he said more reasonably, 'but you have to stay focused. You can't disappear in the middle to try on a nice pair of shoes you spotted in passing, and for God's sake, resist all special offers on pasta or toilet cleaner.'

'Yeah, yeah.' She patted his cheek none-too-gently. 'So what's the plan then?'

Dan and Jack outlined how they wanted things to happen, and the various scenarios which would lead to the mission being aborted.

'Whatever goes down, whether the target decides to go with you or not, the vehicles will leave the scene separately,' said Dan. 'We'll aim to meet up just before the M5. That's point A. If the other vehicle can't get there within thirty minutes we have another meeting point at B further down the M5 and point C is Exeter. If the worst comes to the worst, we won't meet up until we get back to the farm.'

'You'll need to wear this as well,' said Jack, handing her a plastic bag.

Gennie looked inside. 'Body armour? What d'you think is going to happen? And where on earth did you get this?' Her stomach turned over.

'Better be on the safe side,' said Jack, looking anywhere but at her. 'Like I said, we don't know who they are. It's stab-proof. In case it gets rough – but there's no reason to believe it will,' he said quickly. 'It's Dan's wife's. She was in Iraq with us.'

'On that note, I'd better go,' said Dan, bending down to pick up his bag. 'I'll see you in the morning. Will you need any help with the plates?'

'No, it's good. Thanks, mate,' said Jack, opening the French windows and ushering him back through the house and out of the front door.

What plates? Dan hadn't eaten anything. Gennie was wary of asking any more questions: Jack was rather intimidating when he was with Dan, talking and acting like a soldier.

'Jack,' she said tentatively, clutching her stab proof vest to her chest. 'About point C. Don't forget, we have to stop off there to pick up Alice.'

49

Jack dragged Gennie out of bed at half past four and ran through the exit plans again while he zipped up her body armour and buttoned his shirt over the top. He handed her a phone headset and, while she fixed the clip round her ear, tucked the handset into a pocket on her vest.

'No more kissing until Cornwall,' he said, hugging her tightly as she clamped her jaw shut to disguise her chattering teeth. Her nerves only worsened when Jack strapped a vest under his khaki jacket with the ease of someone utterly comfortable with the practice. He had dealt with this fear every day. It was part of his existence.

They tiptoed out of the house as it grew light. Gennie found out what Dan had been talking about when Jack stopped the Land Rover around the side of some grimy-looking garages and changed its number plates. She was about to protest and demand to know what was going on but remembered her promise.

'Did you get those from Dan?' she asked in the lightest voice she could manage.

'Yep,' said Jack. 'He does security. He has lots of useful stuff.'

Gennie didn't want to know what sort of security Dan provided. It wasn't much of a stretch to imagine him arranging hostage exchanges and delivering ransom money.

'They're from another Land Rover. I'll change them back as soon as possible. You'll be okay with Dan, G. Do exactly what he says.'

He was matter-of-fact and unsmiling this morning. There was no chance at all she'd be questioning him.

They arrived at the factory and put stage one of the plan into action. Jack parked the Land Rover out of sight of the entrance and Gennie went to chat to the security guard to distract his attention from the cameras at the entrance. She was lucky. It was a different man than on her previous visit and he was tired and impatient to go home. She was able to recycle her earlier questions and receive the same advice – that if she wanted to speak to one of the factory workers she needed to go to reception or wait by the doors as the workers left straight after their shifts.

When she had exhausted the limited conversational opportunities, she went back to the entrance where Jack was waiting out of sight of the cameras.

'Did you do it?' she asked.

'Yeah. Let's hope it works.' Still no smile.

'It will,' she said, in case he needed her belief in him.

They moved the Land Rover nearer to the entrance to the estate and settled down to wait. It was so quiet that when Dan phoned to confirm that he was in position around the corner, the buzz of the phone made Gennie jump. Jack lit a cigarette and offered it to her.

'Is it enough of an emergency?'

It was, but she didn't dare take it. Her hand would shake and she'd feel worse.

'I hope it's one bus,' she said instead, more to fill the silence than anything else. 'After we've gone to so much effort.'

After a wait that seemed interminable but must have been only ten minutes, Jack pointed to an approaching vehicle. 'That's them.' He dialled Dan's number to alert him, hanging up before he answered.

Gennie was facing the traffic and so wouldn't be able to see whether there were one or two minibuses until the front vehicle slowed to turn into the entrance.

'Go, go, go,' said Jack quietly into his headset, and Gennie's relief that there was a single bus was swiftly overtaken by fear as the butterflies which had been fluttering round her stomach surged upwards.

As they jumped out of the Land Rover and ran towards the bus, Dan's silver van raced down the road and pulled in behind the minibus, which was now at the barrier and apparently stuck there. The driver tried again and again to swipe his entry card against the car reader, but the plate Jack had stuck there did its job and the barrier stayed firmly shut. Dan drove right up to the minibus's rear in a textbook display of poor driving and started pounding on his horn.

'You need to move your bloody vehicle out of the way, mate,' shouted Jack at the driver, as Dan did his best to hem him in, to increase his stress levels and force the passengers off the bus.

Gennie went back into the estate at a fast walk to wait for Hamid's group to emerge from the factory. The security guards must have changed over as she saw a different young man leave his post to saunter across to the entry barrier to discover the reason for all the racket. She rushed to head him off with yet more questions about the best place to wait to catch the factory workers. Her rehearsed script had done the trick so far so why switch? It was essential that the escort let the passengers off the minibus at the entrance before the security guard worked out what was wrong with the barrier. Just as she was giving up hope, she saw a group of unkempt-looking men walking towards the factory led by a very angry-looking man, shouting as he hustled them along. She kept an eye on the group while continuing to occupy the security guard with pointless enquiries. The escort's raised voice and accented English could be heard over the noise from the entrance. He was dressed similarly to some of the workers in salwar kameez, long tunic and trousers, but with a quilted body warmer and trainers. As he came closer, Gennie registered with shock that the expression on his face was not anger, or impatience, but terror. He wasn't threatening the group but begging them to get moving.

The car horns fell silent suddenly, but the security guard was still intent on checking the state of the barrier.

'Oh, thank God that's stopped,' Gennie said, pleasantly. 'Is that where the reception is, over there, by those double doors?' She attempted to steer the man towards the factory and away from the vehicles at the barrier.

At long last, one of the blue doors opened and the night-shift workers emerged from the factory and started to walk slowly towards the entrance as their escort, the frightened man, chivvied them along. Gennie dialled Jack to alert him and searched the line for Hamid. She found him at the back of the group. She was staring straight at him but he gave no sign that he'd seen her. While she had her phone in her hand, she pretended to take a selfie while snapping a surreptitious photo of the men. The distance from the factory to the barrier was less than two hundred metres, but to give Hamid a chance of escape, she couldn't approach until they were within sight of the still-trapped minibus, and despite all the shouting from their chaperone, they were still moving at a snail's pace. Gennie dropped to a crouch and pretended to do up a shoelace until the group was close enough to speak to, and then she ran towards Hamid, on legs so rigid with nerves, it was as if she was wearing splints.

'Hey,' she said breathlessly as she trotted alongside. 'You okay? D'you want to come back to the farm with us?'

He turned at the sound of her voice and Gennie was shocked at the change in him. He was grey with exhaustion. His hair, which hadn't been cut for a while, was thick with grease and his clothes mismatched and worn.

They were now at the barrier and the escort, who had calmed down a little, was ushering his group towards the exit. The bus driver was still out of his seat, examining the barrier arm. Hamid looked at Gennie briefly and nodded. She indicated the road where the Land Rover was waiting, engine running, Jack at the wheel.

'Go with Jack,' she said. 'Run!'

Hamid hesitated for only a second before taking off towards the car.

The plan then was for Dan to take his time ripping Jack's improvised plate from the card reader and for he and Gennie to jump in his silver van and drive off, giving Jack a five-minute head start, at least. But while Gennie watched to see Hamid safely into the Land Rover, something hit her from behind and spun her round. She was thrown to the floor as the escort barged her out of the way and hared after Hamid. As she fell, she swung her legs round aiming to trip him but missed, managing only to knock him off-balance. There was a heavy clang as he dropped what he was carrying and it bounced off the concrete. A crowbar! Was that how he controlled the workers? Gennie leaned but couldn't stretch far enough and watched in slow horror as the man picked up the iron bar and ran to the Land Rover. He arrived too late and swiped at the door, the scrape of metal on metal confirming he'd reached his target and the smell of burning rubber and screech of tyres that the Defender had got away.

Gennie had no time to breathe as Dan was yelling at her, telling her to get up off the floor. The silver van had started to edge slowly out of the drive. The man with the crowbar ran back towards it, his face a mix of fury and panic. He was screaming, bashing at the side of the van, shouting to Dan to move it out of the way and let the minibus out. Gennie flinched and covered her face with her hands as he smashed the passenger window, the glass shattering and disappearing in tiny fragments.

If she couldn't get into the van, she'd lost her escape route and the alternatives were limited – and grim. Facing down the angry man was not an option so her best bet was to get to the security guard and seek sanctuary in the Portakabin. First, though, she had to get the plate back. She scrambled to her feet and ran between the minibus and the reversing van to reach the barrier, peeled Jack's invention off the card reader and was about to make off across the yard towards the Portakabin when Dan yelled for her again. He was holding the driver's door open with one hand and steering the reversing van out of the estate entrance with the other. She ran towards him with an idea to leap on to the footplate. It's what people did in films. Was it possible for a real person, someone like her, to do it? She jumped. Dan let go of the door and with his free hand grabbed her by the bottom of her stab vest and, with a loud grunt, hauled her into the van and across his lap, winding himself in the process. She lay sprawled across the front seats, face down in a pile of shattered glass. She wriggled further in and finally managed to turn and lift her feet in, only to kick Dan in the head.

'Aargh! Fuck!' he cursed. He heaved the door of the van shut, somehow managing to steer while her body was wedged between his stomach and the wheel. While he drove, Gennie did an imperfect tumble turn into the passenger footwell and scrambled into the seat. She was incapable of speech, gulping for air like a beached fish, worried she might pass out.

Dan lit a cigarette and gave it to her. 'Inhale,' he said, with a grin.

It took both of her shaking hands to find the way to her mouth, and when she did, the nicotine made her head spin.

'Bloody hell,' she said when she finally had enough air in her lungs to speak.

*

Jack called. He was going to stop at point A to sort out the number plates, but Dan decided that he and Gennie, having taken a very circuitous route out of Birmingham to lose any followers, should press on to point B.

They drew into the service station car park and deliberately parked in an adjacent aisle before going into the main building in search of breakfast.

Jack was at the food counter with Hamid.

Gennie rubbed Hamid's shoulder. 'You all right?'

'I need to find my brother,' he said.

Gennie looked at Jack, lifting her eyebrows and shoulders in enquiry. He shrugged, unable to elaborate.

'All okay with you, yeah?' he said casually.

'Yep, fine,' answered Gennie, airily, waving a hand to reassure him. 'You?'

'Yeah, no probs,' he answered. He looked at Dan. 'Maybe I was a bit over-the-top with the vests and the plates.'

'Oh, I don't know,' said Dan, smiling at Gennie. 'I think they served their purpose.'

Gennie inhaled sharply, tormented by the memory of the man with the crowbar, beating the hell out of Dan's van, and imagining what would have happened if he'd reached the Land Rover and Hamid or if he'd turned on her. She squeezed her eyes shut for a moment. When she opened them, Dan was smiling at her.

'She did well, your Gennie. She can come and work for me anytime.'

Gennie managed to laugh. 'Thanks, Dan, but no thanks. No offence.'

Her mouth was still dry and her knee had started to hurt where she had crashed into the tarmac. They'd got what they came for and she was elated for sure, but she was still stunned – by the speed of events and how the margins for success or disaster were so small, seconds either way. Jack and Dan were busy munching their way through an enormous rescuers' breakfast while Gennie was still so shaken up, she had to talk herself through the steps to butter toast. She held her teacup with both hands to get it to her mouth without spilling it. Hamid was not much better. He'd taken one bite of croissant and nothing more.

After, they went outside to the Land Rover to hand back the number plates and the body armour. It wasn't until they drove past Dan on their way out of the car park that Jack caught sight of the van.

'What the fuck happened to that?' he asked, eyes wide. 'Thought you said it went well. Are you all right?' He put a hand on her shoulder, turning her towards him.

'I'm fine.' Back in the Land Rover, with three cups of tea inside her, she felt better. 'I wasn't in it at the time. I don't think they'd read your rules, Jack.'

50

Marion and Alex came out to the yard to meet them. Alex took one look at Hamid and ushered him inside.

'Bath and a hot meal, I think.'

Marion looked enquiringly at Jack, who was busying himself unloading the back of the Defender. 'Care to fill me in?' she asked eventually.

'Later,' said Jack. 'He can stay, can't he?'

Gennie glanced at Marion. It had never occurred to her that there wouldn't be a place for Hamid at the farm. It was his home.

'But where? Where's he going to sleep?' asked Marion.

'He can have my bed,' said Gennie, quickly. 'I'll sleep on the sofa. That's okay, isn't it, Alice?' She gave Alice the nod, willing her to agree.

'I guess,' said Alice, but she looked worried, tearful even.

Her excitement at seeing Hamid asleep in the back of the Land Rover had turned swiftly into distress at the state he was in.

'He smells, Mum,' she'd whispered, leaning on the back of her mum's seat.

Gennie made pacifying comments but Alice was right. Hamid's clothes and his hair all smelt dirty, as if they hadn't been washed in a long time. She didn't want to think about how awful the last few months had been. Clearly no-one had been caring for him at all.

'He can have my room,' said Jack. 'I'll sleep on Gennie's sofa. Unless Jan's cottage is a possibility?'

'I can find out,' said Marion. 'But if Gennie's happy for you to squat at the cottage for a couple of days, it would give me time to sort something out.'

*

Gennie woke at two in the morning. The bedside lamp was still burning, the only sound the wind in the trees. She'd excused herself the moment dinner was cleared away. She needed a bath and time alone to process what she'd seen. She crept downstairs to check on Jack. His bag was there, along with the pile of bedding she'd left for him, but there was no sign of the man himself or his faithful dog. Should she make up a bed for him? If he didn't come back, she'd only have to clear it all up again in the morning. He could look after himself.

When she woke again it was seven and time to start her working day. She poked her head into the sitting room on her way out. The bedding was still in a tidy pile but was it at the other end of the sofa? Or was she imagining it? And now she thought about it, Jack's bag hadn't been open earlier.

Hamid didn't come down to the kitchen until lunchtime, moving so slowly he might have been sleepwalking.

'Hey,' said Gennie. 'Are you hungry? How about pancakes?'

Hamid sat at the table and stared blankly at the window. Gennie put a mug of tea and a couple of scotch pancakes in front of him. He ate mechanically as if he had no interest in what it was or if it was even edible. Gennie took in his hair, which now it was clean, was fine and had a curl to it.

'Shall we go into town?' she asked. 'You could get a haircut. The shops are open again.'

This time, he looked at her. He shook his head, eyes dark with fear.

'Okay, not that then. Let's go outside, see how the farm is doing.'

Jack was over by the greenhouses, trying to marshal a couple of the young residents into putting canes in the tomato plants.

'Thought Hamid would like to check on the watermelons,' Gennie said brightly.

'Yeah, sure,' said Jack, making an effort to smile. Did he really only have two expressions? At least when he was frowning, she had a better idea of what he was thinking. 'Come with me.'

They followed Jack into the second of the glasshouses.

'Did you sleep at all?' Gennie asked him.

'Not much,' he said, 'but on the plus side, my step count's right up there.'

*

Jack brought Hamid back to the farmhouse for dinner.

'Did he say anything?' Gennie asked him, grabbing his arm. He didn't flinch exactly but he didn't lean into her either.

323

'He's still on about his brother. He wants Marion to contact the Red Cross and see if they can find him.'

'Is that it?'

'Oh yeah, and he's scared we've been followed. I've told him there's no way we can be traced back here. Even if they took down the number plates, they'll only lead to an address in Newcastle.'

'Oh God, Jack.' She cringed and had a quick look round to make sure they weren't overheard. 'Also, you know you don't have to sleep on the sofa. Alice is in the picture.'

'Oh, right, thanks,' he said, but the frown was back.

If he slept in the cottage that night, he was there so briefly, she didn't notice. He clearly wasn't ready for official, then. She could do with his help reconnecting with Hamid, but instead they were behaving like separated parents, each spending contact time with their child, she in the kitchen, he on the farm, always one without the other.

*

Gennie didn't know how Jack had explained Hamid's lack of luggage to Marion but Gennie had so far dodged the question by saying he hadn't wanted to bring anything. He'd never had a lot of stuff but now he had only one set of clothes and any spares Gennie could find in the laundry. They hadn't checked if he had his wallet with him. They should have done because the loss of his identity card was going to be a problem. It would need to be reported to the police at some point. His lack of underwear could be easily solved by a quick trip to the shops – if he'd only agree to leave the farm.

'You've got a bank account,' Gennie said, 'you could order some things online.'

They were in their familiar places, Gennie bustling around the kitchen, Hamid sitting in the corner armchair, leaning over his knees, eyes glued to the door to the yard.

'I haven't got any money.'

This couldn't be right. Hamid always had money. His pocket money was paid into his bank account and he didn't waste it.

'What happened to the money you earned?'

'I gave it to my uncle,' he said.

'Your uncle? The one who disappeared. Have you found him then?' Gennie stopped moving around and started to pay more attention. If his uncle had turned up, that would explain a lot.

'No, not that uncle. I don't know what it's called in English. It's the cousin of my mother's friend. We call it my uncle.'

'Why did you give your money to him?'

'To find my brother,' Hamid said simply.

Gennie sat down opposite him. 'And has he? Found your brother, I mean?'

'No, but my uncle said that he knows where he is, and that he could bring him to me, but he need the money to pay for the agent.'

Slowly and horribly, things started to make sense.

'Where did you meet this uncle?' Gennie asked softly.

'My friend give me his number. He told me he helps people to find their relatives. I told him about my brother and he said his cousin knew my parents. But I didn't have enough money to give him so he said he can find me a job and then I can earn the money to pay for Ibrahim to come.'

'So you went to Birmingham?'

'Yes. They told me I need to pay £10,000 to bring Ibrahim. I gave them the money from the bank which was £2,000. They said they will pay me £5 per hour and I think if I work every day for six months I will have enough money. But they never pay me.'

'What? Never?'

'No, they say I need to pay £1,000 because they find me this job, then I need to pay £40 a day for the house and food. Then there is tax. And then they say I need to pay petrol for the minibus. They write it in this book. It don't matter how much you work, it always end up you owe them money.'

Gennie sat back in her chair. It was so cruel. She'd suspected he'd been exploited but not to this degree. 'Did you complain?' she asked.

'Yes, when I say they haven't found my brother and what did I give them the money for, they say I have to stay because they paid money for my job and they have to pay someone to go look for Ibrahim. They say be patient and when I've paid what I owe them, they will bring him. Then when I see they lied to me and I want to leave, they won't give me my travel document back as they said they need it for Ibrahim.'

'Hamid, you need to go to the police,' said Gennie. 'They can help you get your documents back – and your money.'

'No, no.' Hamid jumped out of the chair and ran for the door. 'They said if I go to the police, they will kill me and kill my brother.' His panic was absolute, his face white, his hand gripping the door handle. 'It's better they think I'm dead.'

Gennie rose from the table, put a hand on Hamid's arm and steered him gently down the corridor. It was time to tell Marion.

'What d'you think will happen to the man who was with you on the bus? The man who brought you to the factory?'

'They'll kill him.'

Gennie exhaled. She believed him. The man's screaming face was etched on her memory like a ghoul in a horror film. He'd lost a business asset. He thought he was dead already.

She left Hamid with Marion and returned to the refuge of her kitchen. It was possible, just, that these people ran a sophisticated smuggling business and had the capacity to deliver Hamid's brother to him, but it was much more likely that they'd found a way to take advantage of the naïve and powerless. They probably laughed about it, the ease with which they separated anxious relatives from their money under false pretences. They traded in fear, each link in the chain under pressure to deliver someone somewhere for profit. Her stomach churned and she felt sick, transported back to that moment, swirling to the ground while voices yelled around her and metal clanged against metal.

*

There was someone moving around in her cottage. The tap was running in the kitchen. Gennie slipped out of bed and padded down the stairs.

'Jack?'

He was in shorts and a T-shirt, leaning over the sink, taking deep shuddering breaths in through his nose, followed by a short sigh out. His entire body was shaking.

She turned off the tap and put an arm around him. It wasn't the first time she'd been woken in the middle of the night to manage a medical situation. She could hear Alex's voice in her head chiding her that it didn't make it desirable because it was familiar. For better or worse, this was her normal.

Jack's back was clammy through the thin cotton. The glass he'd been attempting to fill sat empty in his hand.

Gennie touched his forehead. 'You're not hot. Chest pain?'

He shook his head.

'Nausea?'

Another shake of the head.

'Right, so I'm guessing panic, not pandemic. You may have strayed into my specialist area. What d'you need? Have you got something you can take, or will it pass?'

'It'll pass,' he managed through a clenched jaw.

'Paper bags... I must have some.' She rummaged in the cupboard among the saved carrier bags and brown paper. 'Or maybe a couple of balloons.' She took out her box of birthday cake candles, gift tags and streamers, and hunted through the contents. Where were all her useful bits and pieces? 'Hang on. Where's your wash bag?' She dived into the sitting room and had a look around.

'Here,' she said, returning to the kitchen with two foil-wrapped condoms. She ripped the top of one packet, unrolled the sticky latex and handed it to him. 'Come on, I'll do it with you.'

She stood next to him, limp condom pinched between finger and thumb. She brought it to her lips. 'Breathing in, two, three, and hold, two, three, and breathing out, two, three, four, five, extra slow, Jack. Inflate the balloon. And again.' She took a deep breath to prepare.

'You're insane,' he said, letting some of the air out of the condom with a squeal and inhaling to start again.

After a couple more breaths, Gennie had inflated the

condom to an impressive dimension. She tied the end and batted the cloudy white balloon towards Jack, who headed it back. He continued inflating and deflating, his breathing growing more regular with every moment.

'You were right about Hamid,' he said abruptly. 'I should've listened to you, we could have gone to get him sooner.'

Gennie nodded. She'd been thinking about this too. 'He didn't realise he was in trouble straightaway. He believed what they were telling him. If we'd gone there sooner, he might not have come with us and then we would never have gone back.'

'I dunno.'

'Don't blame yourself,' she said, aware that this was exactly what Jack had said to her three months earlier. 'Marion told us to stay out of it and the police said they'd dealt with it. We didn't let him down.' She turned to look at him. 'You certainly haven't. D'you know what he told me? He said the only reason he and his brother were able to go to school in Kabul was because the soldiers rebuilt it for them. The British soldiers. Did you know that?'

Jack shook his head.

'If you're okay now, can we go to bed?'

'Together? Alice is here.'

'She isn't bothered.'

'I am. I can't look her in the eye. I nearly got her mother killed. You didn't tell me the guy went for you. I had to hear it from Dan.'

'I'm fine, Jack. Look, all in one piece.' She performed a twirl in her pyjamas. 'I've got one small bruise on my knee, that's all.'

'It's not a joke, Gennie.'

'No.' Now it was Stella's voice she could hear; she didn't have to hide how she was feeling. 'I'm sorry I didn't tell you. I couldn't get the words out. Truth is I couldn't think about it. Suppose he'd hit someone? With that thing?'

He nodded this time. 'I know what you mean. At the time, you get on with it. Things get scarier afterwards. I had the shakes all yesterday. I can't do it anymore, my nerves have gone. Did Marion haul you in for a chat?'

'Yes, and a reminder about concentrating on the project. I think she's secretly glad we went. She might even be proud of us.'

'I'm guessing you didn't tell her about the crowbar and the stab vests, then.'

'No need to trouble her with trivialities,' said Gennie. 'You were right, though. I had no idea what we were taking on.'

'That's what scares me. After that first day, I had an inkling of what it was about, but I carried on regardless. My judgement's all off.'

'Why d'you say that?' she said. 'Don't. It was perfect. Now I'm going to sleep. What about you?'

'I won't sleep.' He was still playing with the condom, wrapping it round his finger and unrolling it again. Gennie held out her hand.

'Waste not, want not,' he said.

'You're disgusting.' She took it from him and threw it in the dustbin. 'Go to bed. I'll see you in the morning.' She put her hands to his cheeks and kissed him briefly.

'Thanks, G.'

'No problem.'

51

Monday morning dawned sunny. Gennie put aside her jean shorts in favour of a summer dress, one with a flippy skirt and no sleeves, nothing too fancy but an expression of optimism nonetheless. Summer was here, the world was opening up again and she couldn't wait for normal life to return.

Miles phoned after breakfast. Gennie's plan could work both ways. He was going to suggest to his project that they partnered up with Jack and identified candidates on their programme who might benefit from his apprenticeship.

'By the way,' he said, 'we're looking for a financial controller at the moment. Don't suppose you know anyone, do you?'

''Fraid not,' said Gennie.

'And you wouldn't be interested?' Miles asked casually.

'Not at all. I'm happy here.'

'Thought so, but worth asking. Anyway, we should meet up. You and Jack got any time next week?'

'I'll check, suggest some dates.'

Jack wasn't picking up so Gennie pushed her feet into her wellies and traipsed across the farm to find him. The sun was now hidden by huge black clouds but she ought to be able to outrun them. She'd not long left the kitchen when it started spitting, and a minute later, the heavens opened, drenching her within seconds. Jack was standing outside the new block, sensibly dressed in his Driza-Bone coat and leather hat.

'You look like a shampoo advert,' he said as she approached. 'You know, the ones with a waterfall and a girl in a flowery dress.'

'Am I the "before" or "after"?' she asked.

'During, I think,' he said. 'You're soaked.' He steered her towards the barn. 'You need a better raincoat. I'll get you one when I go to Australia. If I ever get to go.' He spread his coat across the bales of hay and they sat, gazing at the pouring rain through the open door. 'Is this a social call?'

'Not during working hours,' she said primly. 'Eyes on the prize, remember? I want to fix a time to meet Miles in Truro. Can we do Thursday?'

'Sure.' He lit a cigarette. 'Claire's pregnant,' he said when he exhaled. 'The baby's due at the end of December.'

'Ah.' Gennie's heart sank. That would be why he hadn't answered his phone. 'You all right with that?'

'Yeah. At least, I am at the moment. It will be good for us. It makes a proper break and it will be easier for Claire as there'll be no competition. Nick will have his baby and I'll have mine. I think we can make it work as a real family.'

Gennie stared at him. A real family. That didn't sound like Jack. Unless that was what he'd been after all along.

He shrugged. 'You can't tell anybody. She's not three months' gone yet and she hasn't told Millie. They told me first.'

She'd been about to admonish him for smoking in the barn but the rain was blowing in against her legs and everything was sodden so she let it go.

'Did you ever want another baby?' he asked.

'I did, but by the time Mikkel agreed, he was quite ill and it didn't seem like a good idea. But the other thing was,' she confided, 'by the last year of his life, he was often either drunk and incapable, or when he wasn't drunk, just incapable. It was never really going to happen.'

'Ah, that explains it,' said Jack, oblivious to another cautionary tale. 'I suspected you were only using me for my body, but then I thought, no, you wouldn't buy me Sugar Puffs if you didn't love me.'

'I buy them for everyone.' She was admitting nothing where he was concerned. 'But you eat them before anyone else gets a look in.'

'And also, I couldn't be bought like that.'

'I'm not sure that's true, Jack. A handful of non-branded puffed wheat and you'd be off with anyone.'

'Talking of which,' said Jack, with a smile and a confidential nudge, 'I have news. You can have your sofa back.'

'Oh! Has Jan's cottage come good?' Each time the topic was raised, she felt a twinge of something. Fear? Possessiveness?

'I've no idea, but listen to this. Elizabeth's been fired – or her contract hasn't been renewed, not sure which – so if they can sort out a Covid test for Hamid, he can go into the accommodation block and I can have my room back. Marion thinks her behaviour was inappropriate and potentially dangerous.'

'Her behaviour?'

'Yes.' Jack looked very smug. 'She'd seen Elizabeth letting herself into my room. At first she'd believed her when she said I'd asked her to wait for me but soon worked out it couldn't be the case. And she'd seen how Elizabeth would come to find me when she knew I was a bit shaky or would throw herself on me, looking for sympathy, and always put me in a difficult situation. Marion said it was too much like grooming. There's a risk she'd behave like that with the young people and that's a concern because of what happened to Hamid. Honestly, I didn't say anything. She called me in and I thought I'd get a real talking to about boundaries but instead I found I was the bloody victim!'

Gennie was astonished as well as impressed. Marion really didn't miss much. She had a sudden thought. 'You didn't tell her about my medicine box, did you?'

He shook his head, laughing.

Gennie looked out at the rain which had returned to a light drizzle. 'I'd better go. I'm late for coffee with Alex.' They'd need at least two cups and a full plate of biscuits with all this going on. 'I've been so long everyone will think we've been rolling in the hay. I'll put some bits of straw in my hair so I don't ruin your reputation.'

'Yeah, and tuck the back of your dress in your knickers.'

She tutted and set off across the yard. Ten metres out, she tucked the hem of her dress up and wiggled her hips suggestively as she strutted through the mud.

'Genevieve!' He ran after her. 'Behave yourself.' He tugged her dress back down. 'Working hours, remember?' The way he rubbed her lower back as he kissed her cheek sent an entirely different message.

52

Gennie drove Alice to Exeter.

'You know what I'm going to say,' she said, stopping outside Alice's friend's house.

'It's a barbecue!' said Alice. 'Her parents will be there.'

'Yeah, but still, someone will smuggle in a bottle of something or pop it over the back fence.'

'Mum! I know this. You're exactly like Granddad. "Be good and if you can't be good, be careful." Alice pulled a prim face, worthy of her mother. 'But actually, I could say the same to you.'

Gennie raised her eyebrows and assumed the same expression. 'Well, now, that's just rude.'

When Alice laughed, she did too, unable to hold it together any longer.

'Yes, I'll be good. And careful. Promise you will, too.' She hugged her daughter. 'Have fun, Ali.'

'Love you,' said her daughter, hugging her before grabbing her bag and diving out of the car.

'You too,' called Gennie.

Now she was on her own, feeling the same wrench she'd felt since Alice's first day at school, when she'd walked across the playground with only the briefest backward glance.

Gennie dropped in on Stella on the way back. She hadn't seen her in person since March. Counselling by video was fine in its way but allowed for no contemplative silences as she gazed out of the window.

'It's so nice to see you,' she began, dropping into the armchair by the window. 'Wow, those trees have grown.' She pulled some boxes of fudge from her bag and offered them across awkwardly. 'In case your clients need a snack. You can re-gift it.'

'Thank you. So, how've you been?' asked Stella, in their usual introduction.

'Fine. Oh, you know.' Gennie leaned back, raked her hands through her hair, rubbed her scalp and leaned forward again. 'I really need to talk about Jack.' It was a little theatrical, but all their interactions were characterised by drama. 'So, we went to meet a business contact yesterday. He's called Miles and he could be really helpful to us but all Jack can see is a man in an expensive suit and cufflinks. Honestly, it would be ridiculous to pass up a chance like this solely because Jack thinks Miles is too smooth and successful. But add to that the fact that Miles and I hit it off and Jack starts sulking. He's not interested in why we get on, which is because we're talking numbers and Miles knows a good deal when he sees one.'

*

Jack had been closed and quiet for most of the journey back.

'We don't have to work with him if you don't like him,' said Gennie, when they reached home. She sat for a moment, hand resting on the handle of the car door. 'We'll find someone else.'

'I don't dislike him. Why would you think that? I just don't understand why he has to touch you every time he makes a point.'

'Maybe he's like that. Anyway, he was only touching my arm,' Gennie replied, mildly. 'And only while he was directing us around the site.'

'And your shoulder, and your back.'

'But there was nothing that made me uncomfortable,' she said to reassure him, although if she'd been on her own, it might have been a different story. She felt safe because she wasn't on her own.

'That's because you were all over him, too.'

'I was not! But this isn't about concern for my safety, is it? What's going on? I can't believe you feel threatened by him. Are you actually jealous?' She tried to decipher his expression.

'I dunno. Maybe. You don't touch me when you talk to me.' Jack looked across at her.

Gennie shook her head again. 'You're unbelievable. These are your rules. And the project's rules, remember?' She leaned across to stroke his cheek, running the tip of her finger down his jawline and tickling him under the chin. 'You want me to touch you? You only have to say. I'll touch you whenever and wherever you like.'

He smiled now, the proper Jack Aspinall amused grin. 'Okay, okay, I'm sorry! You flirt with who you like.'

'I'm trying,' she said, unclenching her teeth.

*

'I mean, I understand,' said Gennie. 'He's scared of messing things up and doesn't want distractions. But he complains I keep my distance when I'm practically sitting on my hands to avoid touching his arms and stroking his back. I want to hug him every time I see him, which is all day at the moment. It's ridiculous.'

'And if you tell him all this?' asked Stella.

'I don't know. I'd need to find the right moment,' said Gennie, remembering how Jack had moved out when he thought Elizabeth was waiting for him. 'He's like a wounded animal. He'll meet you halfway, but if you get too close, he runs off again.'

'Just because he won't acknowledge his feelings, it doesn't mean you shouldn't. You might feel less conflicted.'

'How did you know?' Gennie asked. 'The more I think about Jack during the day, the more I dream about Mikkel.'

Gennie drove home with the sun in her eyes, chasing it on its journey west. With luck she'd make it back for sunset. She'd suggest they went out and go to one of the little bays, the most deserted they could find. They could sit on the rocks, maybe go for a swim, and when the sea had worked its magic, she'd tell him.

Jack was in the sitting room of the cottage, hunched over his laptop. They'd moved the project office there, the bonus for Jack being that Gennie permitted smoking if the windows were all open while it was banned in the farm kitchen.

'Y'all right, my lover?' she said in her best West Country accent.

He didn't respond.

338

'Are you working?'

Jack didn't look up from the screen. 'Miles phoned. He wants soft copies of the documents we gave him yesterday. I've found most of them.'

'I'll do it if you like,' said Gennie, moving to sit on the arm of the sofa to unlace her trainers.

'No, it's okay. I've got it. Need to make sure I can manage without you.' Jack finally looked at her, although it was more of a stony-faced glare. 'When were you going to tell me that he'd offered you a job?'

'Never. Because he didn't,' answered Gennie, her heart bouncing between her boots and her mouth. She stood to face him. 'He asked me if I was interested in a job with him and I wasn't.'

'So why do I have to hear about this from Miles?' he said coldly.

'Because we've been busy and I haven't had a chance, because it's irrelevant as I'm not interested, because I didn't think it was serious, and frankly, Jack, because I didn't think you'd take the news as well as you obviously have,' she snapped back. How had her romantic evening derailed quite so fast?

'But this is what I hate the most – when people don't tell me stuff because they think I'll overreact. Don't you trust me?' He was quiet, reining in his fury, no expletives.

He stood up, snatched the cigarettes from the table, strode out of the front door and slammed his way into the farm kitchen. She scrambled after him in her trainer socks and bumped into him as he left again, carrying his khaki jacket and car keys.

'Jack, where are you going?'

She stuffed her feet in her wellies which were parked inside the kitchen door, checked the pockets of her hoodie for her own phone and keys, and ran outside to find Jack, who was locking the door of the Land Rover and putting something in the pocket of his coat.

'Where are you going?' she repeated, more insistently.

'For a walk,' he said, striding off, ignoring Roxy dancing at his heels.

Oh, Jesus. 'Wait for me,' Gennie said as she ran after him, holding on to his jacket sleeve. 'I'll walk with you.'

He didn't shrug her off but he continued to walk down the darkening lane at a punishing pace.

'Jack, slow down!' she insisted, tugging on his arm. He took a moment to light a cigarette and allowed her to catch her breath.

'Look, I'm sorry I didn't tell you,' she said as she stood before him, studying his face, the scowl that was the flip side to the Aspinall smile. You didn't always know which way the coin would fall. 'I'm surprised Miles mentioned it to you at all. I said I wasn't interested. Please, just tell me why this makes any difference. Nothing's changed – professionally or personally.'

Jack stared at her, his expression a mixture of hurt and astonishment, and carried on walking at a more manageable pace. 'How can you say that? Why d'you think you couldn't have discussed this with me? Am I not allowed to feel some emotion, get angry, upset, whatever, if what you tell me is upsetting? And even if I do, it doesn't mean I'm not capable of rational thought. D'you think I'm really not capable of considering your best interests? Maybe it's a good opportunity for you. Would you only have told me when you'd agreed to take the job?'

Gennie grabbed his arm again, forcing him to look at her as they continued towards the village. 'Jack. Listen to me. If it was something that had interested me at all, I would have talked to you about it. And as far as my best interests are concerned, I think if you'd known, you would have looked for reasons why I should go, told me not to stay on your account.'

Jack started to protest. Gennie ignored him.

'How could you believe I'd want to go?' She was confused rather than upset. 'Especially now, when I've worked hard getting this project ready. I feel like we're at the beginning of something good and new. I've got so much scope here. Why would I want to go and work for someone else? And then there's Alice. She's really happy at the farm.' She paused. 'It's not always about you, Jack.'

'I don't expect it to be, but I expect you to give me a bit of consideration,' he said, and managed to sound bitter rather than petulant.

'I did. That's why I didn't tell you.'

Gennie was still holding on to Jack's arm and suddenly realised that the solid object she kept bumping against was a bottle.

'Ha!' she said as she brandished the half litre of whisky before his face. 'What's this? Where did you get it?'

'Security blanket,' he replied. 'I keep it in the Defender for emergencies. You know how that is. You do the same. I won't necessarily drink it. Give it back.'

Gennie felt her pulse soar. 'Well, this is what I hate,' she said. 'You create a situation and then use it as an excuse to drink. Well, you have no excuse. There is no problem here.'

She threw the bottle over the hedgerow into the field behind and instantly regretted it.

'Oh, Jack. I'm sorry.' She covered her mouth with her hands. It wasn't her job to police him. 'I'll buy you another one.'

'You won't. You'll have to get that one back. You can't go round throwing bottles in fields in the countryside,' said Jack. He peered over the hedge, trying to locate the nearest gate.

'Can't we tie something to the hedge to mark the place and come back in the morning when it's light?'

'What do you suggest?' Jack waited, frowning still.

Gennie looked down at her jean shorts and wellies and rummaged in the pockets of her sweatshirt. She had no scarf, ribbon, or handkerchief. There was no cord in the hood. Jack probably had lots of useful things in his pockets, like string, for example, but she wasn't inclined to ask him. Knowing him, he'd suggest she tied her underwear to the hedge.

'Okay,' she conceded. 'How do we get into this field and how do we find the bottle?'

'Count how many paces you are to the gate and then count back the other side,' said Jack. They climbed over the gate in the darkness and sank down into the mud in the field on the other side. Jack started to walk along the inside of the hedge while Gennie persuaded Roxy through the gaps in the bars of the gate. The little dog planted her feet carefully and would go no further. Gennie picked her up and counted back to where she thought the bottle would have landed, sinking ankle-deep in the muck with each step. She fumbled in her pocket for her phone and turned on the torch.

'What sort of field is this? There aren't any cows, are there?'

'Any cows will be inside now, which is good because you

342

would have brained one with that bottle.' Jack squelched past, sweeping his own torch beam across the rutted ground. 'Was it not at all about me?' he asked, with his back to her.

'Of course it's about you, you dope. I like working with you. You're important to me. You're practically my best friend, God help me.' She paused. Should she say more? She wasn't ready yet. 'But it's also about me. I'm happy here.'

'That's good.'

'Aren't you?'

'Well, yeah, that's… I'm in too deep, G,' he said.

'I'm stuck too,' said Gennie. She could feel herself sinking further. It wasn't going to be easy extricating herself. She bent down, grasping the fidgety dog firmly with one arm, trying not to overbalance while she yanked on each boot.

'I didn't mean that,' said Jack. 'I meant… I fucking hate feeling like this – you know, angry and possessive.'

And scared of being left alone, thought Gennie. 'So don't be. You don't have to be.' She slithered carefully across the mud to join him.

'It's not that easy. I don't mix work and relationships well. When I was in the army and I was at work, it was work and that was that. And when I was on leave, I had time for the other stuff. I don't know how to deal with this.'

'I see. What's that in front of you?' She pointed to a big lump of something. Jack walked closer and shone his phone beam over it.

'It's a holdall of some sort. Someone must have thrown it over. We're miles from any farm buildings.' He bent down to see if it had any labels on it. 'What d'you think's in it?'

'I don't know,' said Gennie, 'but it's not our business. Don't touch it.'

'Aren't you curious? Shall we open it and have a look?' He squatted beside the bag.

'No,' she said, tugging on his jacket. 'Don't go looking for trouble. It might be a bomb.'

'In a swamp in Cornwall? Anyway, there are no wires.'

'It could be a dismembered body. Or a severed head. Come on, let's go.'

'Like I say, this is Cornwall, not Norfolk. I'm going in.'

Gennie groaned as he opened the zip and started digging. 'It's full of tools. Proper tools, carpentry and masonry. Somebody must have had their van broken into and the bastards have just dumped the bag. I can't see a name on it. I'd be really pissed off if it happened to me.'

'Well, we should tell the police, then. Come on, Jack, let's go. I'm getting creeped out now.' She stepped back away from the light and her boot clunked against something. She bent down, wary of body parts and munitions, and tentatively felt the ground by her foot. Her fingers closed round the heel of a bottle. She picked it up, hoping it was the right one, and sneaked it into her kangaroo pocket. After a few more minutes' searching, Jack admitted defeat and they retraced their steps to the lane.

'It must be stuck in the hedge somewhere.'

'What d'you want to do?' asked Gennie as she put the dog back down and wiped her muddy hands on the back of her shorts.

'I think we should slow things down a bit, if that's okay. You know, take some time over the summer. Make sure everything works out in the autumn.'

'Oh, right,' said Gennie. 'If that's what you want.' She'd missed her chance but right now, the mood he was in, it felt like a lucky escape. Just who didn't trust who? 'I didn't mean that, though. I meant, do you want to carry on walking or d'you want to go home?'

'Oh. D'you want to go for a drink?' he asked, looking down the lane into the village.

'May as well,' answered Gennie. As her evening plans were now in tatters, she didn't need to stay sober. When they got to the pub, Jack turned on the outside tap and helped her rinse the worst of the mud off her boots.

'They probably won't let me in,' said Gennie, looking down at her filthy shorts and sweatshirt.

'Perfect attire for a farmers' Friday night.'

They found a bench in a corner of the pub facing the bar and Jack acceded to her request and ordered her a large glass of wine. The bar staff brought it over along with a large fizzy red drink.

'What's that?' Gennie asked.

'Cranberry juice and some other stuff. It's the ingredients of a cocktail without the vodka.' Once Jack was settled with his drink, Gennie took a trip to the Ladies to wash the mud off the whisky bottle. She dropped it down inside her shirt, tucked her shirt into her shorts to keep it in place and put her hoodie back over the top, even though it was really too warm to wear it indoors.

When she returned, Jack was chatting to the group at the next table. A man at the bar turned to watch as she made her way towards her own table, following the route mapped out in yellow tape on the floor. It wasn't clear whether it was the length of her shorts or the mud attracting his attention. Jack beamed at her, which was puzzling, but she wouldn't complain. The man at the bar came over, ignoring the notices to observe social distancing and sit at the tables.

'Evenin'. Don't often see you in here, Jack.'

Jack grimaced.

'How's your mum's leg?' he continued.

'On the mend, thanks. You still with the Five-O, Dave?' asked Jack, unnecessarily in Gennie's view as only a police officer would have that combination of swagger and nosiness.

'Yes, though I'm on leave for a few days. What's up?'

'You could save us a phone call. Gennie and I were looking for something in that field, the one before the lane turns into the village. It's part of Trevelyan's, I think. There's a bag in there full of decent tools. It must belong to someone. Might have been nicked from a van. D'you know whether anyone local has lost anything?'

'I don't,' said Dave, 'but I'll find out. What were you doing in that field?'

Gennie noticed that he didn't look at Jack as he spoke but directed his attention towards her bare legs. She crossed them defensively. Jack must have seen it as well because he placed his hand on her knee. It was gentle, though, protective rather than proprietary.

'We had a bit of an argument and Gennie threw my phone over the hedge so we went in to get it.'

Gennie looked at him.

'Lover's tiff, eh?' asked Dave.

'Well, she gets a bit jealous,' Jack said, ignoring Gennie's raised eyebrows.

'Of your friendship with Mrs Bell, I suppose?' she said.

'Precisely,' said Jack, removing his hand from her knee and putting it round her shoulders.

'Well, thanks. I'll pass on the information,' said Dave, draining his glass and moving to leave it at the bar.

'And what was that about?' muttered Gennie after he'd left. 'I'm the jealous one now, am I?'

'I'm only looking out for you,' Jack said, all innocence. 'He's a bastard. He did me for drink-driving when I was asleep in my car so I wasn't going to tell him about the bottle.'

'I see. But you've just informed the Devon and Cornwall constabulary that we're a couple, and a minute ago, you wanted to cool things down,' she said. It was difficult to control her voice.

'Yeah, well, starting tomorrow.'

Gennie shook her head. 'You make it up as you go along.' She downed the rest of her drink. 'I want to go home.' Jack's glass was still half full. 'Are you finishing that?'

'Be my guest,' Jack said, and handed her the glass.

'Yeuch!' she winced after two mouthfuls. 'You can see why they need to add the vodka.' She handed the glass back to Jack, who replaced it, unfinished, on the table.

'It's cured my cough, though.'

Gennie picked up the dog and started up the lane without him. He lit a cigarette and trotted after to catch up. When he tried to put his arm around her, she wriggled free. He was going to have to work a bit harder to get her back on side, and also, if he brushed against her ribs, he'd come up against the bottle, still wedged inside her shirt, and that needed to stay hidden for a while longer.

'Are you trying to chase me away?' she said. 'Do you want me to go and work for Miles?'

'No, not at all. I just want you to be sure about your decisions.'

'I am,' she said. She moved to his other side and took his hand. He interlaced his fingers in hers, automatically, as if he hadn't thought about the message.

'D'you remember the first time you kissed me?' he asked suddenly.

'Well, yes, of course. It's not that long ago.'

'No, I mean in Austria. When you waved a stick at me and told me it was mistletoe and I said you didn't need an excuse because it was New Year, and after you kissed me, I grabbed you and kissed you properly. I really wanted to kiss you and thought I'd never get another chance.'

Gennie laughed at the memory. 'I don't remember you grabbing me. I do remember Mikkel pretty much hauling me away by my hair.'

'And the next day, I couldn't believe my luck when you kissed me again.'

'Well, you'd made an impression on me.'

'And when Andy interrupted us, I accepted it because I just couldn't get that lucky. And I'm kind of feeling like that again now.'

He'd done it again, stunned her with his vulnerability and lifted the protective covering she'd placed over her heart. They didn't speak about his relationship with Claire but it still cast a shadow. He wasn't coming second to anyone again or fighting a losing battle. Miles was, at least, a rival to be measured against, and not a shifting shape.

She wrapped her arm around his back as they walked up the last slope to meet the lights of the farm. He put his arm round her shoulders.

'Don't say that,' she said, when the knot in her throat had subsided. 'We are lucky. We get a second chance. Don't worry about anyone else.'

He stopped outside her door and kissed her, pushing the hair from her face with his free hand, holding her so close, it felt like a statement. Or perhaps a question.

'Can I stay at yours tonight?' she asked.

'Of course.' He smiled. 'Go get your toothbrush. And when can I have my bottle back?'

'Not 'til tomorrow.' Damn. 'How did you know?'

'Because the girl at the next table asked me why my girlfriend was in the toilet trying to hide a bottle of whisky inside her shirt,' he answered.

She should have thought of that. It was the only realistic explanation for why his mood had improved during her absence.

53

They sat curled together in the armchair in Jack's room. It was past midnight and the window was open but it wasn't cold. Gennie leant against Jack's bare shoulder while he lightly stroked her thigh. At some point she'd need to sleep but that was the only reason she could think of to leave this spot and peel her limbs from his.

She eyed the drooping garment hanging from a hook on the back of the door, trousers hanging by a belt loop.

'You and that suit,' she said. 'You're like Sergio with his collar, dragging it through gorse hedges trying to get rid of it, as if it's a symbol of oppression.'

'Well, there you are. Something to lay at my parents' door. I was raised to distrust the trappings of the rat race,' he murmured, wrapping his arms around her waist. 'It wouldn't be a problem if you didn't have such a thing about men in suits.'

'I have not,' she whispered, with no force behind the words. 'And it isn't a problem. Not compared to all the other stuff.

There are so many elephants in this room. What about the incompatible dog and cat, the children, the unborn children, the ghosts, the ex-wives, the drinking, the taking a break over the summer, to name a few?' She had her arm round the back of his neck and tugged gently at his hair. It hadn't been cut for months but it suited him, the slight dishevelment.

'Minor details,' Jack said dismissively, his nose tucked in the nape of her neck. 'I'm looking at insurmountable obstacles. Are you sure this isn't a deal-breaker for you? Ever since I've known you, you've gravitated towards the guys in ties with the company expense accounts.'

Gennie sat up. Did she? Had she really done that, or did it only look like that because she'd followed Mikkel on his chosen path?

'That was one guy, Jack, and I was young, I knew no better. I wasn't raised like that either. My dad was a businessman but he ran a pub. What's this about? Are you searching for a way out? You'll need to do better than that. Anyway, you used to wear a uniform. Uniforms and suits are pretty much the same thing.'

'Not at all. The idea is that the clothes are unimportant, everyone looks the same. Suits are different; they reinforce the differences and a patriarchal hierarchy. All the symbols of wealth and prestige which are only visible to people in the same club.'

Gennie didn't buy it. 'What about all those regimental ties? Have you got any pictures? Maybe you could convert me.'

Jack leaned behind to the bookcase and took down a lidded box. Gennie forced herself from his lap and the darkness of the corner to sit on the end of his bed, cross-legged in her pyjama shorts and vest. She switched on the table lamp and angled it towards her as she leafed through the photographs in the box, examining each picture.

'You look so young in these.' She stopped to think. 'I do remember you like that. You were practically a child. And all of a sudden, here you are, all grown up. I feel like I missed out not knowing you then. When were these taken?' She held a couple out to Jack, who was still in the chair, smoking, watching.

He took a quick look. 'That's Germany in about 2009.'

'In these you look more like you.' She handed him pictures of a smiling young man in desert combat dress, sleeves rolled up, squinting in the sun, canvas city in the background.

'That's Iraq. Must be 2008.'

'You look happy, though.'

'I was. It only got horrible later.'

Gennie nodded, both wanting and not wanting to know the details. 'What did Marion's friends do when you went to war? Did they disown you?'

'No, of course not. I can't help the fact I'm male and therefore fatally flawed. They wrote me little cards and sent me shedloads of sweets.'

Gennie looked through a few more photographs. 'There are girls in these as well.'

He held out his hand for the pictures, smiling as he flicked through them.

She didn't share the pictures of Andy, and there were plenty of those – in uniform and civvies, on and off duty.

'When you're all lined up and on parade, it's spectacular, isn't it? But I'm not sure whether...' She rummaged through the box some more until she found another of Jack, in full uniform, tie loosened, jacket unbuttoned. He was with two others, drinks in hand, evidently celebrating.

'Oh my. I like this one, Jack. Is this your corporal's uniform? Who were you smiling at like that? I wish I knew. Bet it wasn't your commanding officer.'

He glanced at it. 'I don't even remember where that was. Must be after some event somewhere. Looks like Cyprus. And quite late on. 2012?'

Gennie put the picture to one side. The box was full of photographs – young soldiers bent over plastic bowls and buckets, hanging T-shirts to dry on barbed wire washing lines, pictures of ramshackle showers, soldiers assembling their kit, eating, sleeping and playing sport, pictures of destruction and reconstruction, pictures of devastation. None of the pictures were labelled and there was no order to them. Jack was still watching her.

'Do you mind me looking at these?'

'What? No, it's fine,' he answered. 'I was thinking about something else. It's the light on your face. The shadows are so strong, it would be a great composition. Can I take a picture of you? Can you see my phone anywhere?'

Gennie passed him his phone and sat still while he snapped a couple of pictures.

'I didn't think you drew from photos. Does Max know? What will you give me not to tell him?'

'I do, sometimes,' he said. 'If I can't sleep, and you haven't left any ironing.' He blew smoke out of the window. 'I've done a couple of you dozing in your armchair.'

'What do you mean, dozing?' she whispered indignantly. 'I've only dozed a couple of times, and anyway, you weren't there.'

'I've often seen you having a little snooze, pretending to read a book.'

Jack hesitated and then fetched his sketchbook from beside the bed. He flicked through pen-and-ink sketches of his daughter and tree-filled landscapes and found a picture of Gennie sleeping in the armchair under her down anorak. He passed the book to her. His shyness touched her.

She studied the drawing for a moment and slowly turned the page to find another portrait of herself, this one from a photo from Claire's wedding. She sat at a table, gazing into the distance, waiting for Jack. The lump in her throat was back.

'You should draw more,' she said, when she could trust herself to speak. She didn't dare look at him for fear the tears pricking her eyes would stream down her cheeks. 'I really like what you do. And you don't need to work from photos. I'll sit for you if you like.' She reached for his hand.

Jack came to join her. Gennie kept hold of his hand while he put the sketchbook on the table.

'So which is it, suits or uniforms?' he asked lightly, kissing her shoulder. She handed him the photo she had put aside.

'I like you in this one. A few buttons undone.'

It was no good pretending. At this moment, she'd do anything for this man, but if she told him this or how much she loved him, she had no idea what he'd do. He was still quiet; he'd disclosed so much of himself this evening. She couldn't risk it.

'Undone?' He raised an eyebrow, offering instant reassurance about his mood.

'Yes.' She smiled again and stroked his cheek before pointing at another couple of photos, these ones more recent. 'Are those the guys you keep in touch with?'

'Mainly. I see some of the others as well.'

'And are they, erm, are they okay?'

'No, not all. But things got bloodier again after I left.' He took the box and placed it on the table.

'Time to put the lid back on?' she said softly.

He nodded.

Gennie knelt up, put her arms around his shoulders and hugged him tightly to her. She'd love him, compromise for him, forgive him if she had to. There was no going back. He held her just as tightly in return.

54

The art school annual show, usually held in May but cancelled because of the pandemic, was finally allowed to go ahead at Bodmin Town Hall in July, provided social-distancing measures were in place.

Max was back in business. The show was his main sales opportunity of the year and also his chance to showcase his school and encourage more takers – if he could squeeze anyone else in. He'd badgered his painters to submit pieces for sale, particularly if they were abstracts or still lifes. He felt obliged, he said, to offset the large number of life studies which had been entered and restore some balance, if only to deter the wrong sort of visitor. When there was still space available, he demanded his friends enter pieces for exhibition only. The walls must be filled.

Jack refused to get involved but Gennie gave in and submitted a set of three pastel and chalk drawings of Roxy, which Max placed in sweet white floating frames for her.

She also lent him his portrait of Alice, because much as Max disapproved of painting life from photographs, he was prepared to diversify, particularly if lockdowns were going to be a thing. He had to make a living somehow.

Gennie was looking forward to the show. It was months since she'd seen anyone and she was dying to catch up properly with Clement and Eleanor. The art she could take or leave. Max had set strict rules about numbers of individual entries, size of works and type of medium, but no-one paid attention. It was rumoured that the hanging committee, which was presided over by Clement and invited contributions, ostensibly towards the refreshments, could be swayed by a particularly generous donation. The opening night, the first night of the week-long show, was the closest thing to a party anyone had seen since March.

Jack would have stayed at home if his daughter hadn't demanded to go. Gennie had baked mini cupcakes and that was enough to persuade Millie that this was an event that needed her attendance.

Max was in the entrance as they arrived at the town hall. He was clad in a dark navy suit and sunglasses, looking like the private secretary to a billionaire waiting impatiently outside a jewellery store for his employer to finish browsing. His lilac face mask matched the colour of his shirt. He raised his eyebrows when he saw Millie.

'Don't say I didn't warn you,' he muttered as he stuffed a photocopied catalogue in each of their hands.

There was a table with filled glasses just inside the door, presided over by a black-clad young woman.

'D'you want anything?' Gennie asked Max as she, Jack and Millie helped themselves to fruit juice.

Max shuddered.

'Good night, then?' asked Jack, smirking. 'The clubs are still shut,' he told Gennie as they followed the arrows to the first room. 'So Max is on the dating apps. He's having to do meet-ups outside, round fire pits. I had to lend him a fleece. Imagine his shame.'

There were three rooms of artwork, the walls filled floor to ceiling with paintings, drawings and prints. The first room had a queue outside waiting for people to complete their two-metre-distanced circumnavigation, so Jack and Gennie moved swiftly into the second, while Millie devoted her attention to a bowl of crisps at the buffet table.

Gennie glanced around at the walls and burst out laughing. Almost all of the pictures were life studies and the majority of those were of Jack – Jack in oil, ink, pastel and charcoal.

'Fuck's sake,' said Jack behind her before he also started to laugh.

Gennie checked that Millie was still occupied elsewhere, although whether she'd even recognise her father as he was depicted was questionable, and moved to take a better look at the offerings.

'Some of these are good,' she said to Jack, who looked stunned by the impact of so many images. 'You'll probably have to buy one.'

'I really don't think so,' he said, striding off to find Max, who was hovering in the corridor. 'Give me those,' he said, and lifted the sunglasses from his friend's face.

Gennie was admiring a pen-and-ink drawing signed "Lucille".

'This one is great,' she said, when Jack returned, his face mask pulled up high to meet the sunglasses. In his khaki jacket, it was only the mask's floral pattern that stopped him looking like a security risk. 'Maybe we should get it for your mum. It looks just like you – captures that coiled spring, fight-or-flight look you always have. Half hunter, half hunted.'

'Haunted?' Jack asked.

'No, hunted.'

'You know, G, half the time I don't know what you mean.'

'Does it matter?'

'Not to me. But I suspect it does to you. Fucking hell, what is that?' he gasped.

Jack's attention had been drawn by a lurid oil painting further down the room, which, as she drew closer, Gennie realised was an enormous close-up of male genitalia, almost a metre wide. The effect was exaggerated, inflated and grotesque. Jack lifted his shades, transfixed.

'That's not me. No way,' he choked.

'Not even in your wildest dreams?' asked Gennie.

'Not even in my worst nightmares,' he replied, horror-struck. 'It's like science fiction.'

'Let's hope someone buys it, just to get it off the wall.' Gennie consulted her guide. 'Oh my, this is Janet's! You know the older lady who always sits in the corner in the purple hat? And it's sold.'

Jack carried on staring.

Gennie continued, 'I don't think it can be you, though.' She hesitated, turning her head to the side to get a better look. 'I mean, I haven't exactly studied you from that angle but it doesn't look like you.'

'It doesn't look like Clement either,' said Jack.

'No, no mole,' said Gennie, thoughtfully.

Jack laughed now. 'She can't have painted it from life. Maybe it's from a book, unless she sat in class taking pictures on her phone.'

They exchanged horrified glances. Jack lowered his glasses again and looked anxiously around.

'Jesus, where's Millie? She cannot see this!'

His daughter's attention had, however, been caught by Alice's portrait, which was close to the door of the room. Gennie went to divert her.

'It's Alice,' Millie reminded her unnecessarily. 'I haven't got mine yet and Uncle Max promised.'

'Come with me,' said Gennie, and led her back to Max. 'Dissatisfied customer,' she said.

She left them to it and went to talk to Eleanor and the others from their class and compliment them on their work. She caught up with Jack a little later in the third room looking at her pastels of Roxy.

'I know I told you these were a bit safe,' he said, 'but now they're a blessed relief. From now on, I'm going to hide in the landscape class and paint flowers. This is like a horror film. Surrounded by hundreds of distorted images of yourself.'

'But this must have happened before, surely?' asked Gennie. 'I mean, you've sat for Max for years.'

'I never go to his shows! I'm only here because you and Millie wanted to come.'

'Are you going to suffer permanent damage? Should I hide the cooking sherry?'

'Have you bought some then? I am definitely traumatised, no question. Stop looking at me like that. You're doing it again, looking at me sideways when you think I've entered a high-risk situation. I'm fine!'

Gennie left Jack to feel sorry for himself and went to take another look at Lucille's drawing.

It was typical of Max to have set the event up in this way to create maximum sensation and boost revenue. Jack's discomfort was entertaining but it was also typical of him that he hadn't cared to think about the implications of his actions. In his work he was careful and organised, so aware of his responsibilities, almost too painstaking, but in the rest of his life, he lived entirely in the moment, controlling the things he had an obligation to control and letting go of everything else. A conscious detachment. As a survival strategy, it had merit – as long as things went well – but when things became challenging, the only way he knew how to let go was self-destruction.

'Still mad about the boy?' asked Clement, sliding in beside her.

Gennie blew him a kiss, as hugging was banned still. 'I never know if I'm mad about him or mad at him.'

'A common problem. Come and talk to me about your pictures of the dog,' he said, drawing her away. 'Do me a few more like that and I'll flog them to the tourists in the shop.'

Max was still negotiating with Millie.

'Millie, my love, I can't paint you unless you sit for me. Jack will know the difference and my reputation will be in tatters. Let me speak to your mum.'

'Good idea,' said Gennie. 'But, meanwhile, Uncle Max, can you lend me some money or let me have a picture on credit? Lucille wants £80 for that drawing and they don't take cards. Who doesn't take cards nowadays? I'm £50 short. I thought I'd get it for Marion.'

'For Marion or you?' he asked, pulling out his wallet. 'I've got £40. See if she'll negotiate.'

55

It was six o'clock on a Sunday evening but the volume of vehicles navigating the lanes hadn't lessened in the hours Gennie had been away. Was the holiday traffic always like this or had she become too used to the lockdown silence? Alice wasn't bothered; she was fast asleep in the passenger seat, head resting against the window. It could be tactical, a way to avoid too many questions about her weekend.

The crowd outside the kitchen door was visible as soon as Gennie rounded the final slope into the yard. Alex trotted over, but before he reached her, Hamid wrenched open the driver's side door.

'The police have taken Jack,' he blurted, face pinched with anguish.

Alice came to with a start and looked dazedly in Hamid's direction.

'What?' said Gennie in disbelief, head snapping back to Alex for confirmation. 'Why?'

'Come inside. We need to discuss this away from the children.'

Alex appeared as annoyed as he looked anxious and Gennie racked her brains to think of what Jack could have done to have led to this. She'd last seen him at lunchtime heading to the chicken coop with Millie. Was it something to do with Millie? Things had been going so well with Claire, but could something have happened when Jack took his daughter home?

'Where's Millie?'

She rushed into the kitchen, relief flooding her when she saw the little girl at the table eating an ice cream. 'Oh, thank God.'

'Daddy's been arrested,' she said as if it was the most normal thing in the world.

'Can I have an ice cream?' asked Alice, following on her mother's heels.

'Yes.' Ice cream for tea was not the worst that could happen this evening. Sweet snacks were recommended for shock, weren't they? Perhaps she'd break out the cones for everyone else. 'As long as you put the kettle on too.'

Marion was on the telephone in the downstairs office. Gennie joined Alex outside the doorway.

'What happened?' Gennie whispered. 'Has there been an accident? Is everybody all right?'

'They've taken Jack in for questioning,' said Alex quietly.

If it wasn't about Millie, it could only be about Hamid. Gennie glanced back to the kitchen, where Alice was busily filling bowls with ice cream, and her heart constricted. Alice must have sensed her looking and glanced back at her. They were thinking the same thing. If Jack had been arrested by the police, Gennie would be next. She couldn't leave Alice. Alice was everything. What had she been thinking of with her ridiculous rescue missions? She had way too much to lose.

'It's about a burglary,' he added.

Gennie stared at him. Could stealing a person ever be considered a burglary? They'd been so careful to cause no damage. Jack hadn't even gone into the factory estate on the second day. Unless this was about breaking lockdown, but who would have called the police on him? The only people who knew he'd been at Claire's when he shouldn't were Claire and Nick themselves, and they'd never have said anything, and the only person who knew he'd been at Max's was Elizabeth. Elizabeth was manipulative and untrustworthy, but she'd never have done this. She'd never do anything to harm a child, and the person most affected by this was Millie.

Marion finished her call.

'Is this about Birmingham?' Gennie asked. All she could see were images of crowbars.

'Why would it be about Birmingham?' asked Alex. 'What happened?'

'All they'll tell me is that they have a fingerprint match for Jack,' said Marion. She was frowning, which, in anyone else, would signal only that she was concentrating, but in Marion it was a sign of extreme unease. 'I'm trying to get him a solicitor but there's nowhere open. Anyway, look, the police want to speak to you, Gennie. DC Paul Shepherd.' She handed Gennie a Post-it note with a mobile number on it.

Fingerprints. The only place where Jack's fingerprints would be was the barrier where they'd placed the plate over the card reader, and that was the only place where her fingerprints would be too.

Gennie dialled the officer's number but it went straight to voicemail. She left a message. 'What do we do now?'

'We get on with dinner,' said Marion, attempting a none-too-convincing smile. 'It must be a misunderstanding so we have to hope it's sorted quickly before the news spreads.'

The noise from the kitchen brought Gennie to her senses. The kids needed to eat, whatever else was going on. Thai curry it was, then. Marion and Alex sat down to eat with the others, fixed smiles in place. Gennie pushed her food round her plate and kept checking her phone for signal. Hamid sat opposite her. He too was eating without enthusiasm, struggling on each mouthful. The panic was back in his eyes and it broke her heart to see it.

'I can't go home,' Millie said. 'I told Daddy I'd take care of Roxy.'

'Millie could stay with us,' offered Alice. 'Roxy, too.'

Gennie and Marion exchanged a glance. Gennie didn't like to mention that if she too was kept in by police, there would be another child to mind.

'Mummy wants you back, darling,' said Marion, firmly. 'You can stay longer when Daddy's home. Roxy can come along for the ride.'

Once the table was cleared, Gennie went out to the kitchen doorstep, Jack's spot, and tried again to reach DC Shepherd. She left a message with the switchboard.

'I have to go to the police,' said Hamid, making Gennie jump. 'Jack is been arrested because of me. I have to tell them about the factory. Jack helped me so I have to help him. He's like my brother. I'm going to the police to explain.'

'It's not your fault,' said Gennie, putting her hand on his arm. If it was anyone's fault, it was hers. She was the one who'd insisted Jack help her find Hamid. 'They'll soon see they've made a mistake.'

She persuaded Hamid back indoors to watch television with the others and was working so hard on controlling her anxiety that when her phone finally rang, she almost jumped out of her seat.

'Hi, Mrs Beck? It's DC Shepherd. I got your messages. I'll need to speak to you about where you were on Friday and Saturday. As you know, we're looking into a burglary. Could you come into the station tomorrow morning?'

'Friday and Saturday? We were in Birmingham on Tuesday and Wednesday,' said Gennie, before she thought better of it.

'In Birmingham? I'm asking about Bodmin,' said DC Shepherd, impatiently. 'Can you come in tomorrow? Nine o'clock okay?'

After she hung up, Alex ushered her out of the sitting room and away from the teenage listeners. Hamid followed.

'I have to go and see them tomorrow.' She frowned, searching Alex's face as if the mystery would be resolved there. 'It's to do with something at Bodmin but the only time I've been there recently was the art show.' Jack, too, as far as she knew. She thought of him wandering the exhibition in face mask, dark glasses and with his hood up, a plausible outfit for a housebreaker. Could he have been mistaken for someone else?

'I'm come with you,' insisted Hamid.

*

Gennie lay next to Alice and chewed at her nails. If she could only speak to Jack before she spoke to the police. She didn't know

366

how much to say, or whether to say anything at all. It would also be better if the police spoke to Hamid first. She'd spent an hour before bed assembling a dossier of all the information they had about the work gangs. It had only served to indicate how well the group had covered its tracks – the temporary accommodation addresses, unmarked minibuses, heavily controlled and multinational workforce. She printed copies of the photographs she'd taken and made Hamid write down every telephone number, name and address he could remember.

She hugged Alice again and kissed the back of her head and her smooth apple-scented hair. Her daughter lay curled round Sergio, watching something on her phone.

If the police kept her in or, worse, charged her, she'd need to make plans for Alice. When Marion had given her a job, she doubted she'd bargained on having to take on the childcare. There was only one option. She'd have to call her mum. She'd be so disappointed that things had turned sour again but she'd rush to her daughter's aid, nonetheless. The thought brought tears to Gennie's eyes.

Then there were the apprenticeships. If Jack was charged, the funders would vanish, the project would die and he'd never be cleared for working with young people again. Miles might still give her a job, though.

Gennie sat bolt upright, sending Sergio diving under the bed. How could she have been so daft?

'Mum,' complained Alice at the disturbance.

Gennie hugged her again and smiled as the images of number plates were replaced in her mind by pictures of mud and whisky bottles. She didn't need to worry about Jack. A night behind bars might even do him some good, teach him to be more careful.

'It's going to be fine, Ali.'

'Sure?'

'Hundred per cent. It's nothing to do with Hamid. No-one will be going to jail.'

56

Hamid would not be persuaded. He'd made a commitment and was determined to stand up for Jack, come what may. He was waiting by Gennie's car when she exited the cottage. She was wearing a red summer dress with matching lipstick, her feet crammed into high-heeled sandals rather than her usual flip-flops. If she was cast as the jealous girlfriend, she'd do her best to live up to the role.

The police called her through to an interview room shortly after nine. Hamid had to wait in the street. She hadn't sat down before she started talking, ignoring the voice in her head yelling that she should keep quiet until she knew exactly what they were after.

'Is this about those tools? D'you think Jack took them? He couldn't have as I was with him when he found them and he couldn't have known they were there.'

'You were in the house?' asked DC Shepherd, opening his notepad.

'What house?' She was confused now.

'The house which was burgled.'

'No, we found the tools in a field. You think Jack burgled a house? The tools weren't in a house.'

'I see. You found the tools in a field, did you? Which field?' asked the police officer, with enough suspicion to indicate he was becoming irritated by the disruption to the smooth running of his interview.

'I told him not to touch them!' Gennie raised her eyes and hands heavenwards. 'We found a bag of tools in a field on Friday and we told a police officer about it straightaway. He's called Dave. I don't know his surname. Jack will know.'

'Yeah, well, if we could return to the purpose of this interview? If it wouldn't be too much trouble. Mrs Beck, would you mind telling me where you were on Saturday between the hours of twelve and two?' DC Shepherd sat back in his chair, eyebrows raised.

'Twelve and two?' she repeated. This wasn't what she'd been expecting. She had no idea where Jack was at that time. He'd gone out with Millie before lunch and the next time she'd seen him had been at Max's show. He could easily have been in Bodmin all afternoon. 'I was in the kitchen icing cupcakes.'

'And do you usually ice cupcakes in the middle of the night?'

'What? No, of course not. Hang on, d'you mean between twelve midnight and two?'

'Yes,' said the officer, tetchy once more.

Gennie paused again. How could this be? She couldn't work it out at all.

'I understand if this is a bit awkward, Mrs Beck,' said DC Shepherd, more sympathetically.

'It's fine.' Gennie waved a hand. 'I don't understand. How could the burglary have happened after we found the tools? Surely they were stolen before?'

'Exactly. The tools were stolen and used in the burglary.'

'But not by Jack. We left them where we found them. In the field.'

'I see. In the field. And you didn't remove them from the field?'

'No. But if you didn't get the tools from the field, how do you know that Jack's fingerprints are on them?'

DC Shepherd hesitated. 'Because the tools were found at the scene,' he said finally. 'At the house.'

'Oh,' said Gennie. It was beginning to make sense. 'So the tools were taken from the field and used in the burglary. And it's midnight until two you are interested in? Well, that's easy. I was with Jack from just after eight on Friday evening until about seven on Saturday morning. Apart from trips to the bathroom, he was never out of my sight.'

'Can you be sure he didn't go anywhere else between the hours of twelve and two? Perhaps you fell asleep.'

Gennie smiled. That evening would stay with her forever. 'No, I didn't fall asleep and I'm sure he didn't leave. We were in his room, talking and, erm, doing what people do, and then we went to sleep sometime after two. He also took some photos. Not those sorts of photos,' she added hastily at the police officer's raised eyebrows. 'They'll be on his phone. How much information do you need?'

While DC Shepherd typed the statement, Gennie stared at the wall, trying to figure out what could have happened. Had persons unknown dropped the tools off in the field for the real burglars to collect later, and had she and Jack bumbled in like the comedy duo in a heist movie? Or had someone overheard them in the pub and taken advantage of the situation? Or, the most sinister alternative, Jack could have been set up by Dave the policeman, who knew his fingerprints and DNA were on file because he'd arrested him previously. Given the trouble Jack seemed to attract, the bumbling duo scenario was by far the most likely.

Once she'd checked and signed her statement, DC Shepherd thanked her and showed her through to the exit.

'I'm interested, though, as to why both you and Mr Aspinall thought the police would be interested in something which happened in Birmingham.'

'Ah,' said Gennie. 'One of our former foster children at the farm was tricked into handing over all his savings and going to work at a factory in Birmingham. We went to get him back. He's here now and wants to speak to you about it. He won't be put off. Have you got a minute?'

*

Gennie was back outside by twelve thirty, leaning on a wall as she waited for Jack. Hamid was visible at the desk inside, providing details of his complaint to pass on to West Midlands Police. Whatever happened next, it was a relief that he'd opened up enough to tell people what had happened to him.

Jack suddenly appeared in the foyer, escorted by the officer who had interviewed her. Gennie jumped to her feet. To her surprise, the security doors opened and she walked on through.

'Hey,' said Jack, leaning in to kiss her cheek. 'You look

nice. Where are you going?' His eyes were telling her to be careful.

She put her arms round his neck and hugged him, staying in character as femme fatale.

'Well, you know. Got to look pretty for the man I love.' She looked for his reaction, saw the thought reach his eyes and quickly put her hand to his mouth. 'What were you going to say? "What's he in for?"'

He smiled. 'I was going to say, "Shame, I hoped it was for my benefit."'

'Isn't it always? Anyway, how have they treated you? I hope it was brutal.'

'Medieval.' Jack went to the desk to sign for his belongings. 'Cracking bugs between my fingernails and licking condensation off the walls.' He caught the eye of DC Shepherd, still standing alongside. 'Erm, maybe we should go.'

'I'll show you out, Mr Aspinall,' said the deadpan DC Shepherd, indicating the exit.

'You do look pretty, though,' Jack said, lighting a cigarette the second he reached the outside.

'Thanks.' She smiled at the rare compliment. 'Thought I'd better make an effort, you know, given that the last time I met the police I looked like I'd been mud-wrestling. Which is kind of how you look.' She pointed at Jack's filthy clothes. He didn't smell too good either.

'I know. Sorry. I feel disgusting. Hamid and I were building Millie's vegetable patch, shovelling soil and compost, and you know how hot it was. They wouldn't let me change before they brought me in. They removed my shoelaces but I made them keep the boots too as they smelt so bad.'

'Look, I need to get back, but what are you going to do? I brought you clean clothes, in case you had to go to court.'

'Thanks,' he said sarcastically. 'I'll stay here. I need to see Millie, make it up to her. How was she, G?'

'Cool as a cucumber.'

Jack smiled but his eyes were damp. 'You know what she did when the police arrived? I told Hamid to take her back to the farmhouse, but he froze, like he couldn't hear or understand a word I was saying. I've seen it before in combat but I couldn't yell at him like I would with anyone else so I said to Millie to keep hold of Roxy while I sorted something else out. She picked up the dog, who was wriggling like crazy, took Hamid's hand, told him not to worry, she'd look after him, and started walking.' He shook his head in disbelief. 'Exactly like her mother. Thank God for her. Could you drop me at Max's?'

'Sure,' she said, dropping her gaze to hide the tears welling in her own eyes. 'But, Jack, I told them about the bottle. They asked a lot of questions about the field and I thought it was better to tell it as it was.'

'That's good because I did the same.'

'What d'you think this is all about?'

'Wrong place at the wrong time? We might never find out. But what did you think when they told you the robbery happened between twelve and two?'

'I thought you were lucky – that it was easy to prove where you were then. Why?'

'Because that was my first thought, but when I was still locked up twelve hours later, I got worried that I'd pushed you too far and you weren't coming. Because I knew exactly where we were at that time,' he said slowly, lowering his voice and leaning in so his mouth was close to her ear. 'I was taking pictures of you on my phone at 12.25. And at 12.55, I was kissing the inside of your thigh. I know that because I caught sight of my watch.'

Gennie's head snapped round. 'Did you tell the police that?'

'No, of course not. And at 1.30...' he continued.

'I remember,' Gennie said, pressing her fingers to his mouth once again. She didn't need reminding. The spark igniting her core was memory enough.

'Yes, but I had all night to think about it. And all the things you said.'

'And?' prompted Gennie.

'And it was a long, long night. I really missed you. What can I say?' He half shrugged.

Well, a lot more than that. 'And the slowing things down over the summer?'

'I may have had a rethink,' he admitted.

Gennie took a step back as Hamid emerged through the automatic doors.

'The police are going to send someone to talk to me,' he said. 'And they want to speak to you as well.'

Gennie studied his expression. He didn't look happy exactly but he did look considerably less troubled than he had earlier.

*

Max was out when they reached his house, and when they called him, he told Jack off for leaving his key at home.

'It's fine,' said Jack. 'I know how to get in around the back.

Do you want to wait at the front while I climb in through the window?'

'Not really. I'm not watching you break into someone's house when I've just given you an alibi for a burglary. I'm going. Will you be all right on the bus?'

'Yes, of course, if you leave me the fags and some money.'

Jack walked back to the boot and took out the bag Gennie had packed for him.

'Will you be good this afternoon?' she asked. 'No fare-dodging, jaywalking or dropping litter?'

'And will you go straight home? No talking to strangers?' he retaliated, pulling her towards him, his arms wrapped around her back, to kiss her.

Hamid was watching but Jack didn't seem bothered, despite his aversion to daytime displays of affection. She'd better tell Alice about Jack's alibi – before she heard it from anyone else.

'Did you mean it, G?' he asked, leaning away to look at her properly.

She smiled, knowing exactly what he was talking about. 'Yes.'

He kissed her again. 'Drive carefully.'

57

Gennie stretched out on a towel, luxuriating in the heat of the sun on her stomach and thighs. She wriggled her toes into the sand. It seemed years since they'd been free like this, although it was only a few months. It was certainly the only time she could remember when the whole household, bar Marion, had decamped to the beach. When Sean suggested it, Marion had shovelled them all off the farm with indecent haste.

Every windbreak, umbrella and beach tent they owned had been pressed into service to construct a multicoloured fortress of canvas and nylon. It was needed as although the weather was warm and sunny, the wind at the beach had a bite to it. Every time Gennie lifted her head above the windbreak to check on Alice and her boogie board, her skin was whipped by flying sand. She was quite happy ducking down behind the barricades listening to a podcast and minding basecamp until it was time to swap with Sean and take a turn patrolling the water's edge.

Jack returned, dropped his surfboard outside the enclosure and peeled off his wetsuit. He flopped down beside her, shedding drops of water like a happy dog.

Gennie winced as the cold splashes hit her hot skin. 'How's the surfing?'

'It's great. The kids are doing great.'

Now another adult had arrived, Gennie could go for a swim if she could only rouse herself to move. Her limbs were too warm and heavy to bother. She pulled a book from her bag and turned on her side to read, but her eyes kept straying to Jack. He lay on his stomach dozing, nervous energy evaporated. She'd never seen him relaxed like this, certainly never during daylight.

'Are you actually asleep?' she asked.

'Nearly,' he mumbled. 'What is it?'

'Nothing.' She went back to her book, scanned a few lines but couldn't concentrate. She was mesmerised by the sight of Jack at peace with himself. Something had changed. All the tension was gone from his neck and shoulders. It couldn't only be the sea; that energised him. Maybe it was his recent brush with the law or because they'd finished work for the summer and could look forward to a break. The only sign of life from him was when she drank from a water bottle and he prodded her arm to take a swig himself before drifting off again.

Gennie sat up to stretch and check all was well with the others and received a wave and a thumbs-up in reply. She smeared a bit more sunscreen onto her shoulders and arms and took another look at Jack. She nudged him. 'Shall I put cream on your back? You need to be careful with your scars.'

He murmured agreement and turned his head to go back to sleep. Gennie glanced at his legs, rarely exposed in public, and put a towel over the grafted skin to protect it from the sun. She took the bottle of suncream and squeezed it over his back, automatically drawing the large heart shape she did for Alice before checking herself and groaning. She surveyed it for a moment before leaning over him, dipping her fingers in the cream and painting smaller heart shapes around the larger one. She could amuse herself while no-one else was around to watch. If Alice had wasted this much sun lotion, she'd have told her off. When her design was finished, she sat up to admire her artistry and smoothed the cream in around the edges covering Jack's shoulders, sides and arms. Only the larger heart remained unfilled. His voice made her jump.

'What are you doing?'

She'd almost forgotten he was there.

'Drawing rude shapes on your back.'

'You're wasting your time. I can't do anything to shock people round here. They all think I'm a sexual deviant after Max's show.' He turned his head towards her and closed his eyes again.

'Okay. Go back to sleep.' She dotted his nose with the cream before squeezing a drop more onto her finger. She started to write inside the heart:

I want to tell you take your time, don't worry,
it will turn out fine. But
it might not be true and
I can't hide what
I feel for
you...

When she'd finished, she smoothed it all away, erasing the evidence. There was cream everywhere. She tried to wipe away the excess, smearing it over his neck and the backs of his ears and then over her own arms and thighs.

'What are you doing now?' said Jack, eyes still closed.

'Writing spells.' She knelt back on her heels.

'Love, death or transformation?' He'd been reading to Millie again.

'Transformation,' she said. 'D'you think if you were kissed enough you'd turn into a prince?'

'No. Never. There's no harm trying, I suppose.' He smiled. 'D'you think you could make me invisible? Then I could disappear now and again.'

Gennie rubbed away another trace of cream on his shoulder. 'That sounds so sad, Jack.'

'Don't you want to do that sometimes?' he continued. 'Disappear for a while, take a break.'

'No, mostly I want the opposite. I want the world to disappear so I can catch my breath. Don't disappear for too long, though.' She'd miss him if he vanished. As it was, she wondered how she'd manage when she and Alice went to France and she couldn't see him every day.

Alex entered the den with a newspaper and a bag full of drinks, which he dumped in the cold box. 'I hope they don't want ice cream,' he said. 'The queue's worse than at a theme park. It'll be hours before we see them again.'

Gennie stood up. 'If you're okay here for a minute, I need to cool off.' She grabbed a rash vest from where it was draped over a windbreak and headed for the sea.

Jack caught up with her when she'd been standing in the shallows for a couple of minutes trying to accept the temperature of the water and wishing she'd taken the time to zip herself into her wetsuit.

'Hey. When can we get some time on our own?' he said, brushing his fingers against hers. 'Could we get Alice to take the dog for a very long walk?'

Gennie inched further in, wincing each time a wave hit her legs.

'Here's an idea,' she said, turning to him. 'We could ask Alice to stay in and mind the dog while we go out? Don't you think it would be nice to go out, once, when it's not the middle of the night and when we're not working, exhausted, soaking wet or covered in mud?' She couldn't explain why she felt so irritated. 'Or better still, we bring Alice along, because she's also part of this.'

He looked momentarily surprised. 'Ah yeah, sure. I can't tonight, though,' he said gently, watching her carefully. 'I already have plans. Max needs a wingman. It seems one of the app hookups deserves a second date. You're welcome to come too.'

'I've got Alice,' she said simply.

'Well, if you change your mind, let me know.' He paused. 'Sorry, G.'

'It's fine,' she said, but it was enough to impel her into the sea. She dived in, gasped at the shock of the cold water and managed a few strokes while she regained her breath. She then swam some more while she restored some reason to her thoughts. It was perfectly natural that Jack would want to go out if he was free. They'd all been cooped up for so long. The reason they spent so many evenings together with the children was a function of the pandemic as well as the family life of the farm. She might want to be more than how Jack spent a lazy afternoon or a child-free night, but if he wasn't ready for that, she had to accept it and admit the arrangement suited her too. Or let him go.

When they got back to the farm, Gennie went straight to the kitchen, still wearing her damp bikini under her shorts and T-shirt to rustle up a large and fast meal of pasta. The sooner her new kitchen assistant started, the better. By the time they all sat down to eat, Gennie was the only one in her beach clothes. Everyone else was dressed to go out and Gennie discovered that Sean's end-of-year treat also extended to a trip to the drive-in cinema. As soon as Alice volunteered to help her mother clear the table, Gennie knew what she was after.

'Yes, okay,' she said before Alice had a chance to speak. 'How much money do you need?'

'Thanks, Mum,' said Alice, hugging her and rushing off. Gennie finished loading the dishwasher, kicked the door shut and wiped down the table. She took a cup of tea out to the kitchen doorstep and listened to the youth of the house shrieking, slamming doors and running up and down the stairs as they made their way out for the evening.

She heard the Land Rover fire up and drive off and made a decision. She reached for her phone and called Jack. If he couldn't hear the ringtone over his music, that would be that. She'd have tried.

'Hey,' he answered.

'Alice has stood me up. Can I come with you, after all?'

'Course. I'll come back and get you.'

'I'll be a few minutes, though. I need a shower.'

'Sure. I can help you with that too,' he said, and rang off.

He met her as she was going into her cottage.

'You smell nice,' she said. He looked nice too. It was a while since she'd seen him in his Saturday-night uniform of black jeans and black shirt.

'You will, too. Come on, let's get you washed.' He smiled. His relaxed sunniness only increased her grouchiness.

She led him into the hallway.

'Maybe... wait for me down here,' she said. 'I won't be long.'

He stopped and leaned against the wall at the bottom of the stairs.

'I see,' he said, very slowly. 'Actually, I don't see. What's wrong? Yesterday, you loved me.'

She raked her hands through her salt-sticky hair. 'And today too, and certainly tomorrow. But I don't want to feel like an idiot, not where you're concerned, and at the moment, I do.'

'Why?'

'Well, if you don't love me.'

'Come here,' he said, and hugged her tightly, kissing the side of her head before turning her face to kiss her lips. 'You're not an idiot, you're very patient.' He kissed her again. 'And you know I love you.'

Gennie leaned away. 'No, I don't. You never say so. You only say you don't love me.'

'Same thing,' he said, pulling her close again. 'Didn't 10cc sort that out years ago?'

'Jack,' she pleaded.

'Well, I do, okay? I wasn't sure you felt the same way and it's so good that you do. I don't need to live here to see Millie. I'm here for you, despite your attempts to shove me down the road to Jan's cottage.'

'I didn't… I haven't…'

'Sshh.' He hugged her again. 'You must know how I feel. I sit up at night doing your ironing and drawing pictures of you so I don't come scratching at your door begging to be let in. But I can't make you any promises, not now, so I didn't want to say anything. I didn't think it would help.'

'It will help me,' she said simply.

'How?'

'It will help me validate my feelings for you and deal with my low self-esteem,' she quoted, maintaining a poker face.

'Oh, Jesus!' he groaned, and pulled her into the cottage kitchen, where he rummaged on the table among her drawing materials until he found the whiteboard pens.

'Here,' he said as he took her hand, wrote '*I love you*' on her palm in red ink and kissed it. 'Consider yourself validated.' He wrote it again on her forearm and started to lift her T-shirt up before changing his mind, turning her around and lifting her shirt to write on her back. 'Where else do you need validating?'

'Stop it,' she said, laughing now. She put her arms round him, interlacing her fingers at the back of his neck. 'And you don't have to beg or scratch. The door's open for you.'

'Thank you. And Alice?'

'She'll be fine. If it's official.'

'But G…' He was serious now. 'Listen. I can't do any of this without you, but you… you…'

'No, no…' She shook her head.

'Don't pin all your hopes on me, that's all. I'm not good with that.'

'What about this? I won't pin any expectations but I might pin a hope or two on you.'

'I can live with that.' He wrapped his arms around her, lifting her off her feet. 'If you can.'

'We are going out, aren't we?'

'Yes, of course, let me call Max.' Jack put her back on the floor. 'Hey,' he said when his call was picked up. 'I'm going to be late. Gennie's coming too, but she needs to wash her hair. Won't be long.' He laughed and rang off.

'What did he say?' Gennie asked, starting up the stairs.

'He said, "Don't get shampoo in her eyes." Come on, hurry up. Can you find something too short and tight to wear?' he said, hands on her hips and propelling her on to the next step. 'And tell me what you wrote all over me this afternoon.'

'More or less the same as you,' she admitted.

'That was a lot more than three little words.'

'Well, of course. What did you expect?' She took a couple more steps. 'I'll want conditioner too.'

'Of course. I expected that.'

She stopped, turned slowly and raised her eyebrows at him. He raised his eyebrows back and nudged her up the stairs.

'Come on, hurry up!'

58

'You know, you can make some noise if you like. There's no-one else here.'

'Is that what you like?'

'Not necessarily... but usually, we're all "sshh, sshh" and we don't have to be.'

Not anymore.

'Are we in love then, Jack?'

'Seems so... Maybe you could do better, though.'

'Better than you? Better than this? Are you sure?' She moved his hand to her breast. Couldn't he tell how she was feeling?

'No... Ah... Maybe not... Yeah...'

59

'I think he's abandoned us,' said Gennie as they lounged on a bench in the corner of the pub. Max and his new friend Lloyd had headed out into the garden for some air half an hour earlier and hadn't returned.

'I'm dying for a smoke,' said Jack, getting to his feet to look round the room. 'Can you see them anywhere?'

Gennie scanned the room before shaking her head. 'Must be still outside.' Jack sat down again and Gennie leaned against his shoulder, moving his arm around her.

'So what d'you think of him?' asked Gennie.

'Who? Lloyd? He seems all right,' said Jack, not committing himself. 'He was kind of quiet when we were eating. Nice food, though. Max doesn't usually cook like that. He never usually has any food in.'

Gennie laughed, recalling how nervous Max had been when he introduced them all. She'd been shy too, entering the cottage holding on to Jack's hand, presented to Lloyd as his partner, while Max muttered that it was about time. She'd already eaten so had an excuse to pick at her food but she hadn't been alone. The only one who'd wolfed down everything placed before him was Jack.

'So, will you come to France with us?'

'If you want me to and if your family will have me,' he replied softly, mouth brushing her ear. 'I want to meet your mum. See what you might turn into. Anyway, I don't want to stay here by myself, drumming my fingers waiting for you,' he continued, sounding more like himself, 'so either I come with you or I go to Iran with Sean and Hamid to look for Hamid's brother. And you'll let me bring the dog.'

She patted his leg. His diffidence wasn't convincing.

'Maybe we should go find them?'

Jack stood, pulling her up after him. He handed her a couple of the glasses on the table and took the other two himself.

Gennie spotted Max by a table in the garden. His hand was resting loosely on Lloyd's shoulder as he spoke directly into his ear. Lloyd laughed and turned towards Max, standing close enough that they might have been dancing. The scene was so intimate, she felt like a trespasser.

She touched Max's arm to attract his attention.

'Oh, hi,' he said, looking at them blankly, as if struggling to remember who they were.

'Your drinks,' said Jack, placing two glasses on the table.

'Oh yeah, thanks. Sorry, forgot about those. A table came free, so we...'

'We should go,' murmured Gennie, pulling on Jack's shirt. 'Leave him to it. Unless you want another drink?'

'Nah, let's get out of here.' He fist-bumped Max and shook

Lloyd's hand before weaving his way through the tables to the exit, tugging Gennie behind him.

Jack lit up as soon as they were outside and inhaled like a drowning man. He offered the packet to Gennie but she shook her head.

'No emergencies here.'

'So, d'you think you can sneak me past Alice into the cottage tonight?'

'You not ready for "official" then?'

'I'm ready,' he said, wrapping both arms round her shoulders. 'Question is, are you?'

'You aren't going to be jealous, are you? About Max with a boyfriend?' she asked as they walked to the car.

'No, of course not.' Jack was surprised. 'They don't tend to last long.' He thought for a second. 'He doesn't usually introduce me, though. D'you think this one's different then?'

'Yes, I do. This time it's different.'

60

September 2020

Gennie opened the kitchen door and dropped the car keys on the counter. It was gone seven o'clock and her neck and shoulders were sore. She'd forgotten how exhausting Sunday evenings could be – the hours of driving and hauling Alice's bags up and down stairs and in and out of the car.

The kitchen was empty but for Jack sitting in the armchair, vaping and flicking through a farming catalogue.

'Hey,' she said to him, dropping her bag on the floor and unzipping her fleece and throwing it on one of the kitchen chairs. 'I could really do with a gin and tonic.'

'I can help with the tonic,' he said, 'but alcohol is rarely the answer. There are much better ways to relax.'

'Really? What d'you suggest?'

'I hear camomile tea and honey is very beneficial,' he said, all innocence.

'Good idea. Shall I make one for you too?' Gennie answered, filling the kettle.

'Hell, no! That would be cruel. I expect there's a Geneva Convention about it. Come here.'

He handed her his e-cigarette and she sat between his legs, her back to him while he set to work on her shoulders.

'How do you avoid setting off the smoke alarms?' she asked, groaning as his thumbs worked the knots either side of her neck.

'Long practice. You need to blow the smoke downwards. How's Alice?'

'A bit wistful, I think, but happy to be back with her friends. She had a great summer.'

'That's good. And how are you?' he asked politely.

Gennie giggled. 'What are you up to? I'm very well, thank you. You?'

'Good, thank you. Shall I do your feet now?'

Gennie looked at her feet in their thick socks and work boots, a little incongruous teamed with her summer dress, and shuddered. 'You'd need your face mask and latex gloves. Perhaps some other time?'

'Don't say I didn't offer,' he said as he pulled her on to his lap and stroked her bare leg, his hand sliding up her thigh. 'So what'll it be? Early night or out for dinner?'

'By "out for dinner", you mean chips on the beach?'

Jack sucked in his breath. 'Could stretch to pizza if you want something fancy.'

When his smile was in his eyes like that, he was irresistible. She stroked his cheek and kissed him. 'I don't need fancy.'

They paused at the sound of footsteps hobbling along the corridor.

'Jack, darling, you really mustn't smoke in the kitchen. It'll set the alarms off and gives the young people the wrong idea,' said Marion mildly, ignoring everything else going on.

'It was Gennie,' Jack said, pointing at her hand with a grin. She was the one still holding the evidence.

'Careful, darling, he'll lead you astray,' Marion responded.

'Too late,' Gennie said, shaking her head.

'Come on.' Jack lifted Gennie to her feet and ushered her towards the kitchen door. He whistled for the dog, who appeared from somewhere under his chair. 'See you tomorrow,' he said to his mother, 'and do not under any circumstances knock on that door.'

Author's note

This is fiction and all of the characters are fictional. The opinions expressed by the characters are theirs alone. The background to the story is real, however. This is a story about the consequences of war, rather than its politics, both for the soldiers who fight and the refugees it creates, groups inextricably linked by their experiences.

The Refugee Council (www.refugeecouncil.org.uk) estimates that 4,896 children claimed asylum in the UK in the year up to June 2022, and the Children's Society (www.childrenssociety.org.uk) that nine thousand unaccompanied children have applied for asylum since 2016. Most arrive without documents to prove age or identity. Very many originate from Afghanistan, travelling overland and arriving in the backs of lorries. They are almost exclusively boys, desperate to escape involvement in the decades-long conflict. Their prospects depend on their age on arrival – or their age as assessed – and the care and legal advice they receive. If they are sixteen, they will not receive mainstream education. The Refugee Council is one of the organisations that assist children to navigate the asylum process, obtain legal representation and make contact with the Red Cross. The Refugee Council Children's Section also relies on public donations. Both they and the Children's Society also assist child victims of trafficking for labour exploitation.

It is clear from the actions of charities set up in the wake of the Taliban takeover in August 2021, that those who served in Afghanistan have not forgotten its people or their experiences and still feel compelled to assist. This is not to ignore the physical or mental impact on those who fought in the war.

Jack and Andy's military service in Afghanistan is based on real events, although liberties have been taken with the chronology. Whilst ordnance disposal teams and Royal Engineers regiments were in Afghanistan in 2010, they may not have been at the same place at the same time. No disrespect is intended by this, rather the opposite.

Alcohol misuse among serving soldiers and veterans is recognised to be as great or a greater problem than post-traumatic stress (see a 2010 survey for the Ministry of Defence by Professor Nicola Fear and Professor Sir Simon Wessely of the King's Centre of Military Health Research, King's College London). There are charities working with serving soldiers and veterans (Combat Stress www.combatstress.org.uk, Walking with the Wounded www.walkingwiththewounded. org.uk, Help for Heroes www.helpforheroes.org.uk) who would welcome your support.

Cruse Bereavement Care (www.cruse.org.uk) provides free support, including counselling, to those dealing with bereavement.

There is plenty of artistic licence in my depiction of the life drawing classes. They aren't really like this, but if you want to learn to draw, drawing from life is one of the best ways.

Lastly, apologies to the people of Livø. I have never been there but have no doubt that it is lovely.

Acknowledgements

I want to thank the women of my family – Sasha, Penny and Wanda – for their patient reading of early drafts and sensible suggestions; and the men of my family – Trevor, Henry and Joe – for their support and for humouring me in this project. My friends and colleagues have been amazingly encouraging. Surinder, Alan and Doo provided detailed comments, and Rachiel and my book club (Jane, Sarah, Jackie, Louise and Liz) braved the unedited version. All of your views were valued and virtually all your suggestions have been incorporated. Ed and Kim found me contacts to check my military facts and if I have things wrong, it is no fault of Major Tom Meldrum (Rtd) or Chris, who kindly provided answers to all my questions.

Thanks too to all the young Afghan refugees who lent elements of their stories and personalities to Hamid.

Two things gave me courage to persevere: Alan's scholarly approach to the manuscript, commenting that he wasn't sure it was possible to write that number of words in suncream on his (incredibly slim) wife's back but hadn't yet had a chance to check, implying that he thought the rest of it was at least credible; and Sasha, the first person to read any of the material and the one who has ploughed through more drafts than anyone else, whose early comment that it, 'Actually isn't that bad,' encouraged me to continue.

About the Author

Sofia Due lives and works in London but spends much of her time in North Cornwall, which inspired the setting for this book. She works as a lawyer, specialising in asylum and human rights claims and often acts for victims of modern slavery. Her debut novel, *Ed & Lily*, was published in 2021. *Finding Jack* is her second novel.